Passionate
PROMISES

Passionate PROMISES

ABBY
GREEN

DANI
COLLINS

AMANDA
CINELLI

MILLS & BOON

PASSIONATE PROMISES © 2023 by Harlequin Books S.A.

The publisher acknowledges the copyright holders of the individual works as follows:

THE GREEK'S UNKNOWN BRIDE
© 2020 by Abby Green
Philippine Copyright 2020
Australian Copyright 2020
New Zealand Copyright 2020

First Published 2020
Second Australian Paperback Edition 2023
ISBN 978 1 867 29827 4

THE MAID'S SPANISH SECRET
© 2019 by Dani Collins
Philippine Copyright 2019
Australian Copyright 2019
New Zealand Copyright 2019

First Published 2019
Second Australian Paperback Edition 2023
ISBN 978 1 867 29827 4

THE VOWS HE MUST KEEP
© 2020 by Amanda Cinelli
Philippine Copyright 2020
Australian Copyright 2020
New Zealand Copyright 2020

First Published 2020
Second Australian Paperback Edition 2023
ISBN 978 1 867 29827 4

MIX
Paper | Supporting
responsible forestry
FSC® C001695

Published by
Harlequin Mills & Boon
An imprint of Harlequin Enterprises (Australia) Pty Limited
(ABN 47 001 180 918), a subsidiary of HarperCollins
Publishers Australia Pty Limited
(ABN 36 009 913 517)
Level 19, 201 Elizabeth Street
SYDNEY NSW 2000 AUSTRALIA

Printed and bound in Australia by McPherson's Printing Group

CONTENTS

The Greek's Unknown Bride
Abby Green

DEDICATION

This is for Orwell, my fluffy little shadow who enriches my life and provides vital moral support when I'm banging my head off the keyboard. Even if he is on his back, paws in the air, snoring softly.

CHAPTER ONE

APOLLO VASILIS STARED out of the window at the ornamental lake set in lush grounds. Athens lay under a hazy smog in the distance, and the sea was a barely perceptible line on the horizon. But he noticed none of that. His arms were folded tightly across his chest and tension wound like a vice inside his body. A tension he'd been feeling for months now. Three months, to be precise.

There was a faint rhythmic *beep-beep* coming from behind him and suddenly it changed. Skipped a beat, and became slightly faster. Heart rate increasing. *She was waking up.* Finally.

He turned around. A woman lay on a raised bed. She was as pale as the sheets underneath her. Rose-gold hair spread around her head. There was a gauze dressing on her forehead, over her right eye.

There were bandages around one arm. A scratch down her left cheek. All in all, minor cuts and bruises. A miracle, considering the car that she'd been driving was at the bottom of a narrow ravine about one hundred metres deep, a charred mass of black twisted metal.

He moved closer to the bed. Her almost blonde lashes were so long they cast faint shadows on her cheeks. Her brows were darker, finely etched. He frowned. Her face looked…thinner. The bones of her cheeks were standing out more prominently than he seemed to remember.

But then…looking at this woman in any kind of forensic detail was not something he'd done lately.

Not since he'd looked at her as if he'd never seen a woman before. Four months ago, when they'd first met. When her naked body had filled his vision and made his blood roar so loudly it had deafened him.

He could still see her body now as if the image had been burned onto his brain. The small but perfectly formed breasts. Flat belly, gently curved hips. The cluster of tight reddish curls at the apex of her legs. Slender limbs. She'd looked so delicate and yet when he'd joined his body to hers, he'd felt the innate steely strength of her and it had been the most erotic experience of his life.

To Apollo's surprise and consternation, a heat he hadn't felt in months flooded his veins. He rejected it utterly. This woman had deceived him in the worst way possible.

He despised her.

At that same moment that her eyelids fluttered, the door opened and the doctor and a couple of nurses entered. The female doctor looked at Apollo. 'I need to remind you not to expect too much at first. The extent of the injury to her head can only really be ascertained once she regains consciousness.'

Apollo nodded curtly, and watched as they tended to the machines around the bed. The doctor sat down beside the woman and took her hand. 'My dear, can you hear me? Can you open your eyes for me?'

Apollo could see movement behind the delicate eyelids. For a second he found himself holding his breath as her eyelids fluttered again. As if, for a moment, he'd forgotten, and a small part of him actually *cared* if his wife woke up or not.

She could hear the voice coming from far away. It was like a buzzing bee, distracting her, tugging her away from the lovely cloak of darkness surrounding her in blissful silence and peace.

A pressure, on her hand. The voice. Louder now. She couldn't make out words, just intonation. *Mmm. Mmm!*

She tried to swat away the pressure but it only got stronger. A brightness was pricking at her eyes, pushing away the darkness. Her head felt so thick…fuzzy. Heavy.

And then, as if a curtain had been pulled back, very clearly she heard a sharp voice. 'Mrs Vasilis, it's time to wake up.'

For a second she lamented leaving the peaceful darkness behind but she knew she had no choice but to follow the voice. She understood the words but they didn't make much sense to her… *Mrs…?*

She opened her eyes and light exploded onto her retinas, making her shut them tightly again. She became aware that she was lying in a bed. She could sense the flurry of activity around her. And also, disturbingly, the fact that in that split second she'd noticed a tall dark shape looming at the end of the bed.

A shape that was familiar and made her heart pound for no reason she could understand.

'Mrs Vasilis, can you try opening your eyes again? We've lowered the blinds to make it easier.'

Experimentally, she cracked her eyes open again and this time it didn't hurt so much. The face of a woman she didn't know came into focus. There were a couple of other women, also strangers. They all had dark hair and dark eyes. There was a humming noise and rhythmic beeping of machines. White everywhere. Antiseptic smell.

A word popped into her mind: *hospital.*

There was movement in her peripheral vision and she looked towards the end of the bed. The tall dark shape was a man. She knew him. 'A-A…' Her voice cracked like rust. She tried again. 'Apollo?'

'That's good.'

She barely noticed the relief evident in the doctor's voice as she took in the man at the end of the bed. He wore a dark long-sleeved top. Round neck. Soft material. Broad shoulders and chest. Powerful. But not overly muscular. Lean.

Short dark hair. Strong masculine features. Deep-set eyes. *Green eyes.* She knew this, even though she couldn't see their colour properly from here. Strong jaw. Stubble. Firm mouth. *Hot, on hers.* A shiver went through her. She'd been kissed by this man.

She felt her hand being pressed. The doctor's voice. 'You know who this man is?'

It was hard for her to tear her gaze away from him, as if she was afraid he might disappear. She nodded. 'Yes…we just met, the other night. At a function.' He frowned slightly, but she barely noticed as heat crept into her cheeks, remembering seeing him for the first time. How he'd stopped her in her tracks with his breath-taking beauty and charisma, wearing a tuxedo that had been moulded to his powerful body like a second skin.

He'd looked bored. People had hovered around him but at a distance as if too intimidated to get close.

And then their eyes had met and... *Bam!* Her heart had somersaulted in her chest and she'd never been the same since...

Slowly it was sinking in that she was in a hospital. But what was she doing here? With a man she barely knew?

But you do know him. Intimately.

She felt it in her bones, like a deep knowing. But *how* did she know this if she'd only just met him? She tried to latch onto the question to find the answer but it skittered out of her grasp.

Confusion clouded her brain and for the first time she had a sense that something was very wrong. A tendril of fear...or panic...coiled in her belly. She looked at the doctor. 'What's happening? Why am I here?'

As she said the word *I*, she stopped. *I*. Nothing. Blank. A void. The fear grew. 'Wait... I don't know... who I am... Who am I?'

Then something popped into her head. The doctor had called her... 'You said Mrs Vasilis...'

The doctor looked at her with an expression that was hard to decipher. 'Because you are Mrs Vasilis. Sasha Vasilis.'

Sasha. It felt wrong. Not her. 'I don't think that's my name.'

'What is your name?'

Blank. Nothing. Frustration.

The doctor spoke again. Soothingly. 'Sasha. Your

name is Sasha and you are married to this man, Apollo Vasilis.'

She looked at the man again. He was definitely frowning now and he didn't look particularly happy to be married to her. She shook her head briefly but it caused a sharp pain over her eye. She stopped. 'But that can't be possible, we just met.'

So, if you just met, how can you know him intimately? How can you be married?

A headache was forming, right between her eyes. A dull throb. As if sensing this, the doctor said briskly, 'That's enough for now, she needs to rest. We can come back later.'

A nurse stepped forward and did something to a drip beside the bed. Soon that comforting blackness was enveloping her in its warm embrace again and she eagerly shut out the growing panic and fear, and disturbing questions. And *him*, the most disturbing thing of all, and she wasn't even sure why.

Two days later

'We think your memory loss came from the traumatic experience of the crash. There's no perceptible or obvious injury to your brain that we can see after the scans we did, but you can only remember meeting your husband for the first time and nothing else. Nothing from before or after. Sometimes the brain does this as a form of protection when an event occurs. We've no reason not to believe that in time your memory will return. It could come in small pieces, like a jigsaw coming together, or it could happen all at once.'

Or it might not happen at all?

She was too scared to voice that out loud.

'Which is why...' here the doctor looked expressively at Apollo Vasilis, who was a forbidding presence as he stood by the window with his arms folded '...you need to be monitored closely while you recuperate.'

The doctor looked back at Sasha, who still didn't feel like a *Sasha*. 'Don't worry too much about trying to make your memory come back. You need to focus on recovering from your injuries. I'm sure everything will return to full functionality.'

Sasha wondered what her brain was protecting her from.

The doctor stood up. 'You can go home now. We'll keep in touch to monitor your progress and let us know as soon as you start to remember anything.'

That felt like a very dim and distant possibility. Her brain still felt as if it was just a dense mass of grey fog. Impossible to penetrate. And where was *home*? The doctor had told her she was English, so presumably she'd been born and brought up there.

When she'd enquired about family, her husband had told her that her parents were dead and she had no siblings. Just like that. Stark and unvarnished. She'd felt an ache in her chest near her heart but when she couldn't put names or faces to her parents it was hard to feel profound grief.

The doctor left now and Sasha looked at Apollo Vasilis. Her husband. He looked as grim as he had when she'd regained consciousness. Wasn't he pleased she'd survived the accident? He wore a three-piece suit today, steel grey, with a tie. He oozed urbane sophistication but Sasha sensed the tightly wound energy in his body. As if he was ready to cast off the trappings of civility to reveal a much more elemental man underneath.

Ironically, the one memory she did have, of the night they'd met, she remembered him smiling. Laughing even. His face transformed from breath-taking to devastatingly gorgeous. She remembered his voice. Deep and accented.

Except she'd been told that that night had been four months ago. And since then they'd been married. And she'd apparently moved to Greece from England. It was all too huge to absorb and Sasha found herself avoiding thinking about it too much.

'Are you ready? The car is waiting outside.'

Was she ready? To leave here with a man who was little more than a stranger to her? In a foreign land she had no memory of coming to? But she nodded once, briefly, and stood up, her limbs still feeling a little weak.

Apollo picked up a bag. He'd brought her clothes to change into and they only compounded her sense of disorientation because she couldn't imagine choosing clothes like this. Flared cream-coloured silk trousers with slits up each side, a matching silk singlet top and a cropped blazer jacket. Spindly high-heel sandals that made her feel even more wobbly.

He opened the door and stood back. Sasha locked her limbs and walked out of the room with as much grace as she could muster.

Apollo walked down the corridor beside his wife. She was walking slowly, as if she'd never worn high heels before, with all the grace of a spindly-legged foal.

Which was bizarre because the only time he could re-call ever seeing her in flat shoes had been when they'd met that first night.

She stumbled a little and he took her elbow to steady her. She glanced up at him, her cheeks a little pink. 'Thank you.'

Her hair was down around her shoulders in soft nat-ural waves that he knew she usually preferred to be straightened.

'It's nothing.' He gritted his jaw at his body's reac-tion to the feel of her arm under his hand, her slender body brushing against his ever so slightly. She wasn't wearing the scent she usually did. He'd watched her take it out of the bag earlier and she'd tested it on her wrist, immediately scrunching up her nose. She'd looked at him. 'This is my perfume?'

He'd nodded. Privately he'd always had the same reaction when he'd smelled it. To recoil. It was too overpowering. Sickly sweet. She'd put it back without spraying any.

But now all he could smell was *her*. Soap and some-thing uniquely and mysteriously feminine. Her scent reminded him uncomfortably *again* of meeting her for the first time when he'd been blown away by her fresh-faced beauty. Her impact on him had been like a punch to his solar plexus, driving the breath out of his lungs.

And to this day he couldn't figure it out. He'd seen plenty of women who were more beautiful than Sasha. Slept with them too. But something about her, from the moment he'd laid eyes on her, had got to him. Captivat-ing him. As much as he hated to admit it.

She'd seduced him with her wide-eyed act of innocence, and had then trapped him with the oldest trick in the book. The burn of that transgression and the burn of his momentary weakness for her was like permanent bile in his gut.

His desire for her had dissipated as quickly as it had blown up, and he'd welcomed it, in light of her betrayal, but now it was back, as if to mock him for ever believing he'd had it under his control.

She was playing him all over again but this time he wouldn't stand for it.

Sasha winced as Apollo's fingers tightened almost painfully on her arm. She tried to pull away and he looked at her. 'I'm okay now, you can let go.'

Instantly his expression blanked and he took his hand away, saying smoothly, 'My car is here, just outside the door.'

Sasha saw a sleek silver SUV waiting for them, with a driver holding the open back door. It reinforced her sense of being in an alternate dimension where nothing made much sense.

She stepped out of the hospital and gulped in fresh air, hoping that might make her feel more grounded. The Greek sun was warm but the early summer air wasn't too humid yet.

Sasha climbed into the car. Her shoes were pinching painfully after only walking a few feet. She couldn't believe that she wore this kind of shoe on a regular basis.

Or... She slid a look at Apollo, as he got into the back of the car on the other side, *maybe Apollo liked them and she wore them to please him?*

That thought sent another shiver through her. The thought of pleasing him. Except, if the frosty vibes were anything to go by, he wasn't pleased and she had no idea why.

The car pulled away from the hospital and Apollo exchanged a few words in Greek with the driver, who then put up the privacy partition. Sasha was so aware of him it was as if an outer layer of skin had been removed.

A hand rested on one thigh. Square, masculine. Long fingers. Blunt nails. His suit looked as if it had been made specifically to hug his muscles and emphasise his powerful physique. He looked at her and she didn't have time to pretend she wasn't ogling him.

'Okay?'

She nodded. It was a civil question but the tension was palpable. Instead of asking a question she wasn't sure she wanted the answer to, she asked, 'Where are we going now?'

'The villa. It's not far from here.'

'Have I lived there long?'

'For the past three months, since we married.'

'Where did we marry?' It suddenly struck Sasha at that moment that, if not for the fact that this man had turned up to claim her after the accident, when apparently she'd been found wandering by the road in a disorientated state a day and night after being reported missing, he could be anyone.

He looked at her for such a long and assessing moment that she could feel heat creeping back into her cheeks but then he plucked a small sleek phone out of his pocket and tapped the screen and handed it to her. 'We married in Athens in a civil ceremony.'

She looked at the screen of the phone. On it was a link to an official press release announcing their marriage with an accompanying picture. Sasha enlarged it. It was her. But it didn't feel like her. She wore a knee-length floaty silk sleeveless dress, cut on the bias and slashed almost to the navel. Eye-wateringly high heels. Her hair was teased into big curls and she seemed to be wearing a lot of make-up. Gold jewellery. An enormous-looking diamond ring. She felt a rush of exposure and embarrassment when she looked at the picture. And then she looked down at her bare fingers. 'Did I have rings?'

'Yes. The doctors said you must have lost them in the accident.'

She looked at Apollo. 'I hope they weren't too valuable.'

He gave her a funny look. 'Don't worry, they were insured.'

Sasha looked back at the picture on the phone. She was clutching Apollo's arm and beaming; however, her new husband looked anything but happy in the picture. The memory she had of him smiling had to be a figment of her imagination. A conjured-up image.

She skimmed the press release.

Apollo Vasilis, Greek construction tycoon, weds his English girlfriend Sasha Miller in a private civil ceremony.

The bare minimum of information. Sasha handed the phone back, feeling even more disorientated. A million questions buzzed in her head but she could feel a headache starting and the doctor had told her not to overdo things.

She looked out the window and saw glimpses of huge houses set in verdant grounds behind tall wrought-iron gates or massive walls. Clearly this was a wealthy area.

Before long the car turned in towards a massive pair of wrought-iron gates. They opened mechanically and a man in little security hut outside waved them in after a few words with the driver.

Sasha stared out the window in awe as lush grounds opened up around them. The driveway led up to a massive courtyard and a two-storey villa-style house with steps leading up to the front door where a woman in a uniform was waiting.

Apollo got out when the car had stopped at the bottom of the steps and before Sasha could figure out where the handle was, the door was being opened and she saw his large hand extending towards her.

She had no choice but to put her hand in his and her skin prickled with a kind of foreboding, as if her body knew it would react in a certain way and she had no idea what to expect.

Yes, you do.

Her hand touched his and an electric jolt went right through her. Reflexively her fingers curled around his. Face flaming at her reaction, she let him help her from the car and as soon as she could, she snatched her hand back.

Her reaction to him on top of the fog in her brain was too much. She resolved not to touch him again if she could help it and then that little voice reminded her that they were married.

She stopped at the bottom of the steps at the thought that they must be sharing a room. *A bed.* Her heart seemed to triple its rate. Apollo was almost at the top of the steps. He turned around and she saw a look of something almost like impatience cross his face.

'Sasha?'

She thought furiously as she climbed the steps, taking care in the impractical shoes. Maybe she could suggest they sleep separately until her memory returned? Surely he wouldn't expect her to share his bed when she felt as if she hardly knew him? No matter what her body might be telling her.

At the top of the steps was the older woman in the uniform. She was a stranger to Sasha. And she didn't look welcoming. Dark hair pulled back and a matronly bosom. She seemed to be eyeing Sasha warily, as if waiting for her to do something unexpected.

Sasha stepped forward and held out a hand. 'Hello.' The woman flinched minutely and then she glanced at Apollo and seemed to get some kind of sign because she looked back at Sasha and took her hand, saying in heavily accented Greek, 'Welcome home, Kyria Vasilis.'

Sasha felt a light touch on her back that distracted her from the woman's odd reaction. 'You don't remember Rhea?'

She shook her head, 'I'm so sorry, but no.'

The women let her hand go, eyes widening. Apollo said, 'I'll show my wife around the villa. We'll eat something light in a couple of hours, Rhea. On the smaller terrace.'

The woman nodded and disappeared into the villa. Sasha looked into the massive circular reception area. She felt absolutely sure, at that moment, that she'd never seen these marble floors or set foot in this place before.

Which was wrong. She'd been living here. She obviously couldn't trust her own instincts.

She stepped over the threshold warily, and followed
Apollo as he led her into the first of a dizzying array
of rooms leading off the circular hall. There was a formal reception room, informal reception room. Formal
dining room, informal dining room.

The rooms were all furnished with sumptuous but
elegant furniture. Muted colours in varying but com-
plementary shades in each room. It was modern but felt
classic. Huge canvases adorned the walls and antiques
nestled among more modern artefacts.

Each room had huge French doors that led out to a
terrace that ran the length of the house, overlooking the
impressive garden. Even more impressive was the view
of Athens in the distance.

Sasha walked out of the formal dining room onto the
terrace. They were far above the teeming ancient city,
the air heavy with the scent of the flowers that climbed
the wall of the terrace in colourful profusion. She tried
desperately to conjure up a memory of having looked at
this view from here before, but her mind stayed blank.
Apollo came and stood beside her on the terrace and
her skin prickled. Sasha asked, 'Is this an old house?'

'No, I built it on this site.'

Sasha looked at him. '*You* built it?'

His jaw tightened. 'Not me personally. My construction company.'

Sasha turned to face him. 'So…you own a construction company?'

He looked at her and nodded. 'Vasilis Construction.'

Sasha frowned. 'Is it a family business—do you have family?'

An expression flashed across his face so fast she couldn't decipher it but it had looked for a second like pain. 'My family are dead. A long time ago. My father was in construction but he worked for someone else so, no, it's not a family business.'

'I'm sorry to hear your family are gone.' Both their families were dead. 'What happened?'

For a long moment she thought he wouldn't answer and then he said, 'A series of unfortunate events.'

He stepped back. 'Let me show you the rest of the villa.'

Sasha pushed aside her curiosity about *a series of unfortunate events* and followed the broad shoulders of her husband as he led her back into the hall and up a majestic flight of stairs. *Villa* seemed like an ineffectual word for what was, clearly, a luxurious mansion.

She wondered what it must have been like to come here with her new husband for the first time. A small voice pointed out that she was getting to relive that experience right now. Except, she wondered, had he been any warmer the first time round?

The villa retained that modern but classic feel throughout. Little touches of period features to give it a sense of timelessness.

In the basement there was a state-of-the-art gym and media room, which could convert into a home cinema. On the same level there was a lap pool and steam and sauna room. Not to mention the extra rooms for massage and treatments that opened out onto a lower-level garden with a couple of sun loungers and a hammock hung between two trees.

Apollo waved a hand towards the gardens, 'There's also an outdoor pool and changing area.'

He showed her his study on the first floor. A very masculine room with walls lined with shelves and books. Across the hall he opened another door and said, 'This is your office.'

She couldn't contain her surprise. 'I had an office?'

He put out a hand and she went in, not sure why she suddenly felt reluctant. The room was pretty but over-done. A plush white carpet and a white desk were the simplest things in the room. There was an expensive-looking computer on the desk.

The walls were covered with flowery chintzy wall-paper and there were framed prints of the covers of glossy magazines on the wall. Lots of shelves that were mainly empty. A handful of books.

A pink velvet chair and matching footstool. It looked as if it hadn't been touched.

'What did I use this for?'

Apollo was leaning against the doorframe, arms folded across his chest, a look of almost disdain on his face. 'You said you wanted to set up a PR business.'

Sasha looked at him. 'Is that what I did? PR?'

He shrugged. 'When we met you were serving drinks at a reception. I don't think your knowledge of PR ex-tended beyond the service end of the industry.'

There was a tone to his voice that Sasha chose to try and figure out later. She followed him up to the second level where the bedrooms were situated. He led her past several guest rooms to the end of the corridor, opening a door. 'This is your room.'

She went in and stopped, turning around. '*My* room?'

'Your room.'

Apollo filled the doorway easily. Sasha's mouth felt dry. She was aware of her feet hurting from the high sandals. And a dull ache at the front of her head.

'We weren't sharing a room?'

Slowly he shook his head. 'No.'

Sasha desperately wanted to know why and he looked as if he expected her to ask that question but for reasons she couldn't understand she didn't want to know. Just yet.

Because this would also, surely, explain his cool and aloof manner. Why the housekeeper had looked at her so warily.

She had a very tenuous grip on reality as it was, and she didn't know if she was prepared to hear more revelations about herself.

So she said nothing and walked into the room. It was luxurious, as she'd come to expect in a very short space of time. Carpet so plush her heels sank right into it. Instinctively, she slipped off the sandals, relishing the relief and the sensation of the soft covering underfoot.

She was aware of the massive bed dressed in cool and pristine-looking linens to her left-hand side but ignored it, not liking the way she was so aware of it.

She carried the sandals in her hand over to where French doors opened out onto a balcony that was big enough to hold a sun lounger and table and chairs. From here she could see that the villa had another wing, one storey high, with a smaller terrace covered over with trellis. The outdoor pool was just beyond this area, surrounded by bougainvillea. There were loungers and a changing area.

The grounds sloped away from here, down the hill, leaving the vista open to Athens and the sea beyond.

The full extent of this sheer luxury sank in. It was overwhelming.

She turned back into the room, blinded for a moment by the sun. When her eyes adjusted again she realised that Apollo was a lot closer than she'd expected.

Immediately her pulse quickened and her skin seemed to get tight and hot all over. The bed loomed large behind him. He looked at her with a strange expression, as if fixated, for a moment. She noticed that he had undone his tie and it hung loose now. His top button was open, revealing the strong column of his throat.

He blinked, and the moment was gone. He stepped back and went to a door in the wall, opening it. 'This is your walk-in closet and the bathroom.'

Sasha followed him, feeling light-headed and a little jittery. But those disturbing sensations and the way he'd just looked at her fled her mind when the space revealed itself and she looked upon more clothes than she could have ever possibly seen in her life. And shoes. And jewellery, in a special glass cabinet.

The clothes—dresses, skirts, trousers, shirts, jeans, leisure-wear—were stacked, hanging and folded in a room the size of a small boutique. There was every colour of the rainbow.

Without even realising she'd moved, Sasha found herself reaching out and touching a glittering lamé dress in dark blue. It slid between her fingers. It looked hardly capable of staying on a body.

She dropped it and looked around, half-horrified as much as fascinated. 'These are all…mine?'

Apollo was still trying to get his body back under control. For a moment when Sasha had turned from the balcony back into the bedroom, she'd been backlit by the sun, turning her hair into a blazing strawberry-blonde halo around her head.

Her flimsy silk top had clung lovingly to her breasts, the lace of her bra just visible under the delicate material. And he'd had an almost uncontrollable urge to stride forward and take her by the arms and demand to know what she was playing at with this wide-eyed act of innocence. She'd played that card before.

But that urge had fled, to be replaced by a far more dangerous one when she'd looked at him as if he was a wolf about to gobble her up. Instead, all he'd wanted to do was crush that temptingly lush mouth under his and punish her for reawakening this desire, which had lain mercifully dormant for the past three months, in spite of her best efforts to seduce him.

But not any more. It was awake and ravenous. And she was playing him with this little game. After all, feigning amnesia would be child's play to a woman who had feigned a lot worse.

He'd had enough of the charade. His anger burned bright and hot and he told himself it was *that*, and not desire that he was feeling.

He said in a low voice that barely contained his anger, 'You know damn well these are all your clothes because you spent many vacuous hours shopping for them with my credit card. You might have fooled the doctors and nurses at the hospital but there's no one here but you and me now, so who are you trying to fool with this act, Sasha? What the hell are you up to?'

CHAPTER TWO

'*WHAT THE HELL are you up to?*'

Sasha looked at Apollo and it took a few seconds for his words to sink in, they were so unexpected. But then there was almost a strange sense of relief to have the tension bubble over into words so that she could find out why he'd been acting so coolly with her.

She felt his anger but it didn't scare her. It perplexed her.

'What are you talking about?'

He waved a hand, bristling all over. 'This…farce. Pretending to have lost your memory.'

Sasha felt confused. 'But I'm not. Don't you think I want to know who I am, or what's going on?'

She shook her head. 'Why would I do such a thing?' But just then a pain lanced through the building dull ache in her head. She winced and put a hand to her forehead, feeling light-headed all of a sudden.

Apollo's voice was sharp. 'What is it?'

Sasha was about to shake her head again but she stopped for fear of making it worse. 'It's just a headache, the doctor said that they might be frequent for a few days. If I do too much.'

The recent outburst hung between them, the atmosphere charged, but after a few moments Apollo stepped back and said tightly, 'You should rest for a bit. I can have Rhea bring some food up in a couple of hours.'

Sasha remembered the way the woman had flinched earlier. 'No, I'll come down. I'm sure I'll be feeling better.'

Apollo walked out of the closet space, leaving Sasha with the throbbing pain in her head and feeling utterly bewildered. *He thought she was lying?*

She heard a noise in the main bedroom and went back out to see a young girl she hadn't met placing her hospital bag on the bed. The girl looked at her but didn't smile. She backed away, staring at Sasha as if she might jump at her, and said in halting English, 'Your bag, Kyria Vasilis.'

She left and Sasha stared after her for a long moment. After Apollo's outburst just now, it was patently evident that their marriage was not a harmonious one, and that people didn't seem to like her very much.

Her head throbbed even more, and Sasha went over to the bag that had just been delivered and pulled out the box of painkillers she'd been prescribed. She saw a tray on a table with water and glasses, and took two of the tablets.

She explored further, into the bathroom, which was almost as big as the bedroom. A massive bath and walk-in shower. Two sinks. Cream tiles and gold fittings that looked classy, not tacky.

She caught sight of her reflection in the mirror and sucked in a breath. She was deathly pale. No wonder Apollo had asked if she was okay. She looked a wreck.

Shadows under her eyes. The scratch on her cheek. The yellowing of the bruise on her forehead where she'd bumped her head.

She felt disconnected from herself, which she supposed was only to be expected. But she felt as though didn't belong here, in this hushed rarefied place. Where people looked at her as if she'd done something to them. Where her husband accused her of lying.

Why would he think she'd do such a thing?

She pushed that to one side for the moment, it was too much to absorb and think about.

'Sasha...' She said the word out loud. It still didn't feel right. 'Hello, my name is Sasha Vasilis.' Nothing but a faint echo.

She didn't need to have bruises and scrapes to know that she was very far out of this man's league. But a memory flashed into her head at that moment of feeling effervescent. Of him, smiling at her indulgently.

She'd been so happy.

If anything, that memory only made her feel more disorientated. She spied the bath behind her and suddenly wanted to wash away this confusing chain of events. If such a thing was possible.

She ran the bath and stripped off, stepping into the luxuriously scented silky water a few minutes later. It soothed her bruised and injured body, but it couldn't soothe the turmoil in her belly or clear the pervasive fog in her head.

Apollo stood looking at the woman on the bed. She was in a towelling robe that dwarfed her body, her hair spread around her like a rose-gold halo. One arm was on her chest, the other flung above her head.

One slim pale leg was visible through the gap in the robe and Apollo could see the smattering of freckles across her knee. And it made his blood run hot.

Damn her.

Damn her to hell and back.

He'd met her four months ago and he hadn't had a full night's sleep since then. First of all because he'd been unable to get her out of his head and then because she had shown him who she really was. A manipulative, conniving, mercenary—

She moved on the bed and made a small sound.

Those pale eyelids flickered open and he was looking down into two bright pools of blue. So blue that the first time he'd seen her huge eyes he'd been instantly reminded of the skies of his childhood, before things had grown much darker.

She blinked and Apollo came out of his trance, suddenly feeling exposed. He took a step back. 'I knocked on the door but there was no answer.'

Sasha sat up. He caught a scent of something like crushed roses. And clean skin. He gritted his jaw before saying, 'Dinner is ready. I can have the food delivered to your room.'

She shook her head and that bright hair slipped over one shoulder. He was rewarded with a memory of wrapping it around his hand as he'd tugged her head back so that he could press kisses down along the column of her throat, and then lower to the pouting provocation of her tight pink nipples.

'No, it's fine. I'll come down. My headache is much better.'

Sasha was still somewhere between waking and sleeping. She hadn't expected to conk out like that when she'd lain down for a short nap after her bath, but now she could see the dusky sky outside. It had also taken a minute to realise she wasn't dreaming when she'd opened her eyes to see Apollo standing by the bed. It had been the fierce expression on his face that had woken her properly.

It reminded her of his angry words. *'What the hell are you up to?'*

He'd changed into dark trousers and a dark shirt, open at the neck. Sleeves rolled up as if he'd been working at his desk. In this position, looking up at him, it felt intimate. An echo of a previous moment teased at her memory, as if she'd sat in this very position looking up at him like this, but in a very different situation.

'I'll just change and come down,' she said quickly.

Apollo took another step back and Sasha could breathe a little easier. He said, 'Very well. I'll send Kara to show you down in a few minutes.'

Sasha had the distinct impression that he would have preferred it if she'd said she'd eat alone in her room and in a way it would have been easier for her too. But she also had a strong instinct to try and do her utmost to regain her memory and if that meant interacting with her antagonistic husband then so be it.

'Just through here, Kyria Vasilis.'

Sasha smiled at the same young woman who had brought up her bag earlier. Kara. The girl didn't smile back.

After Apollo had left, Sasha had washed her face and gone into the walk-in closet to find some clothes. She'd finally pulled out the plainest and most modest clothes she could find. A pair of slim-fitting Capri pants and a cropped sleeveless shirt. The shirt was white but the trousers were yellow. Apparently she didn't really do muted colours.

And, thankfully, she'd found some flattish shoes. Wedge espadrilles. Unworn, still in the box.

She walked through a less formal lounge on the ground floor that she hadn't seen earlier and through open French doors to another smaller terrace. The one she'd seen from her balcony earlier, covered by a trellis and surrounded by a profusion of flowers. The view here was of the gently sloping grounds down to the outdoor pool.

The scent of the flowers permeated the air when she stepped outside. The air was warm and still. Peaceful. It soothed her fraying edges and foggy mind a little. Apollo looked up from where he'd been staring broodily into the distance, long fingers around the stem of a glass of wine.

He stood up immediately and something about that small automatic gesture gave her a tiny spurt of reassurance. He pulled out a chair and she sat down, his scent easily eclipsing the sweeter scent of the flowers to infuse the air with something far more potent.

She felt the tension between them. Not surprising after his words earlier but there was also another kind of tension, deep in the core of her body. A hungry kind of tension, as if she knew what it felt like to have that tension released.

He sat down opposite her and picked up a bottle of Greek white wine. 'Would you like a glass?'

Sasha wasn't sure. Did she like wine? Might it help take the edge off the unbearable tension she was feeling? She nodded. 'Just a little, please.'

When he'd poured the wine, she lifted her glass and took a sip, finding it light and sharp. She did like it. The housekeeper Rhea appeared then with appetiser plates of dips and flatbreads. Apollo must have noticed her looking at the food because he pushed a bowl towards her. 'This is tzatziki with mint, and the other one is hummus.'

She dipped some bread in each, savouring the tart taste of the tzatziki and the creamier hummus.

Apollo seemed to have directed his brooding stare onto her and to try and deflect his attention she said, 'Your home is lovely.' It didn't feel like her home, even if she had been living here for a few months. 'You must be very successful.'

Apollo took a sip of wine. She thought she saw a quirk of his mouth but it was gone when he lowered his glass. 'You could say that.'

She had the feeling he was laughing at her. Before she could respond, Rhea appeared again to clear the starters and then Kara brought the main courses. Chicken breasts with salad and baby potatoes. Sasha blushed when her stomach rumbled loudly. She took a bite and almost groaned at the lemon-zesty flavour of the chicken. She felt as if it had been an age since she'd eaten anything so flavoursome.

When her plate was clean she looked up to find

Apollo putting down his own fork and knife and staring at her.

'What?' She wiped her mouth with her napkin, suddenly aware that she'd fallen on the food like a starving person.

'Apparently you've discovered an appetite,' was Apollo's dry response.

Rhea appeared again and gathered up the plates. Sasha said automatically, 'That was lovely, thank you.'

Rhea stopped and looked at her as if she had two heads before just nodding abruptly and leaving. Not wanting to ask but feeling as if she had no choice, Sasha said, 'What do you mean about the food, and why does she look at me like that? And Kara too…as if they're scared of me.'

'Because they probably are. You didn't exactly treat them with much respect. And before, you treated any food you were served as if it was an enemy to be feared.'

Sasha could feel the onset of that faint throbbing, signalling a headache again as she absorbed his answer. 'You really don't believe that I have amnesia?'

Apollo was expressionless. 'Let's just say that your past behaviour wouldn't give me confidence in your ability to tell the truth.'

What happened?

The words trembled on Sasha's lips but like a coward she swerved away from inviting an answer she wasn't ready to hear yet. Especially if what he'd just told her was true. Apollo was looking at her with that disdainful expression that was fast becoming far too familiar, and painful.

'I'm not lying. I promise. I wish I could make the fog

in my brain clear but I can't. Believe me, there's nothing more frightening that not knowing anything about yourself, your past, your future. All I have to trust is that you *are* my husband and that I do live here with you, when it feels like I've never been here before.'

She added, 'I don't know what I did but if your attitude and Rhea's and Kara's are anything to go by it wasn't good. But how can I apologise for something I can't even remember doing?'

Shocked at the surge of emotion catching her unawares and making her chest tight, Sasha stood up and went to the edge of the terrace, arms folded tight across her breasts. To her horror, tears pricked at her eyes and she blinked furiously to keep them at bay.

Apollo's whole body was so rigid with tension he had to force himself to breathe in and relax. He looked at Sasha's tense body. The curve of her naked waist was visible where the cropped shirt rode above the waistline of her trousers. Her skin was pale. Her hair glinted more red in the light of the setting sun, like a flame against the white of her shirt.

She seemed genuinely upset. Agitated. Apollo didn't trust her for an instant but for whatever reason—maybe she was buying time to figure out a way to convince him to stay married—she was insisting on this charade.

For the past three months she'd been playing every trick in the book to try and entice him into her bed, but not wanting her had made it easy to resist. Now, though…he couldn't be sure he would be able to resist and if she knew that…

He stood up and noticed how she tensed even more. He went over and stood beside her. She didn't look at him. Her jaw was tight. Mouth pursed. He was about to look away but did a double-take when he saw the glistening drop of moisture on the lower lashes of her eye. *She'd been crying?* To his shock and consternation, instead of feeling disgust, Apollo felt his conscience prick.

In all her machinations up to now she hadn't ever manufactured actual tears. She'd looked close to tears when she'd turned up at his London office three months ago but she hadn't cried.

Maybe she's telling the truth.

He'd be a fool to trust her after everything that had happened, but he knew who she was now, so she couldn't surprise him again. 'Look,' he said, turning to face her. 'You've been through an ordeal and you need to recuperate. We can talk about whether I believe you or not when you're stronger.'

For the week following Apollo's pronouncement Sasha existed in a kind of numb fog. She was still bruised and battered enough not to fuss when Kara or Rhea insisted on bringing food to her room, or when they appeared as she sat on the terrace to put a light rug over her legs in the early evening, in spite of the Greek heat.

Sasha noticed that as the days dawned and faded into dusk, the women grew less wary around her. Although she still caught them looking at her suspiciously and whispering in corners when they thought she wasn't looking.

Of Apollo, there was no sign. He seemed to go to work as dawn broke—she usually woke when she heard the powerful throttle of an engine as it disappeared down the drive—and she was asleep before she heard it return.

In fact, she realised now, if it wasn't for hearing the engine each morning, she couldn't even be sure that he came home at all. A man with a house like this would surely have other properties. An apartment in Athens?

A mistress?

That thought caught at her gut as she sat in the dusk on Friday evening on the smaller terrace. The end of the working week. The start of the weekend. If they weren't sharing a bedroom then obviously this marriage was not a functioning one. And yet the thought of Apollo with another woman made her feel…nauseous.

She barely knew the man beyond some very hazy memories. And yet…she felt a sense of possessiveness now that shocked her because it was so strong. And also a sense of injury, as if something had been done to her.

'Good evening.'

Sasha nearly jumped out of her skin. She looked around to see the object of her circling thoughts standing just a few feet away. A jolt of electric awareness zinged into her belly. Disconcerting, but also familiar.

He wore dark trousers and the top button of his shirt was open. His hair was slightly dishevelled, as if he'd run a hand through it. His jaw was stubbled.

'I didn't hear you come back, I never do.' She blushed when she said that, aware of how it must sound. 'I mean, I usually hear your car in the mornings, not in the evenings. I wasn't sure if you were staying somewhere else. Do you have a property in the city?' Aware she was babbling now, she clamped her mouth shut.

He walked in sat down on a seat at a right angle to

hers. His shirt pulled taut across his chest and she had to drag her eyes away. What was wrong with her? All week she'd been existing in this numbness but now she felt alive, fizzing.

'I can't account for why you don't hear the car in the evening, as I've been returning to the villa every night. But, yes, I do have an apartment in Athens. It's the penthouse at the top of my office building.'

'You have a building.' Not just an office. A whole building.

He nodded. 'And another one in London. And offices in New York, Paris and Rome. I'm finalising plans to open an office in Tokyo next year.'

Sasha couldn't help but be impressed. 'That's a lot of offices. You must have worked very hard.'

He looked utterly relaxed but she could sense the tension in his form. He said, 'For as long as I can re-member.'

'Did you study for it?'

He nodded. 'Yes, but I worked on sites at the same time, so I got my diploma while I was working my way up the ranks. I didn't want to waste any time going to college full time.'

Apollo went still. He hadn't come here to *chat* with his treacherous wife who may or may not be feigning amnesia, but if she was faking it then he had to hand it to her for stamina. She hadn't let her mask slip all week.

Rhea and Kara had told him that she'd been as civil and polite as much as she'd been selfish and rude in the recent past. There seemed to be no glimmer of that earlier incarnation of his wife this evening. Just those huge blue eyes looking at him guilelessly.

He wanted to get up and walk away. So he did get up. But instead of walking away he went over to the low terrace wall and sat on that.

She'd turned in the seat to look at him. She was wearing a white shirt-dress with a gold belt. The dress was buttoned up to a modest height.

Previously, Sasha would have had a dress like this buttoned so low that her underwear would have been visible. Then it had aroused nothing more than irritation. Now, though, all he could see were those little buttons and think about how easy it would be to undo them, baring her breasts to his gaze.

He could see her pale legs. Long and slender. Together and slanted to the side, ladylike.

He would have laughed if he'd been able to muster up a sense of humour. Not too long ago she'd been involved in activities very unbecoming to a lady.

He diverted his mind away from her dress, her legs. Abruptly he found himself saying, 'My father used to be a foreman for one of Greece's biggest construction companies. He got injured on the job, and became paralysed from the waist down.'

Sasha put a hand to her mouth, visibly shocked.

A familiar sense of rage that hadn't been dulled by time settled in Apollo's belly. 'He never really recovered. All he knew was how to manage a construction site. He could have done that in an office, in a wheelchair but everyone turned him down. His own employer refused to give him any compensation. His pride was in tatters. He couldn't support his wife and two sons.'

She frowned, 'You have a brother?'

Apollo ignored that. He felt ruthless as he told her

the rest, watching her reaction carefully. 'My father killed himself when I was eleven and my brother was thirteen. My mother got cancer not long afterwards and died within a couple of years. My brother and I were sent to into foster care. My brother got involved with a drugs and gang crime. He was stabbed to death when he was sixteen.'

Apollo's eyes were glowing with intensity. Like dark green jewels. Sasha felt pinned to the spot by them. By his words. She couldn't speak. Anything she thought of saying felt too trite. Ineffectual.

Apollo continued. 'I made it my life's mission to go after the man who had employed my father and cast him aside like a piece of unwanted trash. And I succeeded. It didn't take much to dismantle his business because he was corrupt to the core. As soon as he went down, hundreds of disgruntled ex-employees came out of the woodwork looking for compensation and that's what ruined him in the end.'

He was looking at her now as if he expected her to be shocked. And she was. 'I'm sorry,' she said huskily. 'I can't imagine what it must have been like to lose so many when you were so young. I don't know about my family…when my parents died.'

Apollo was reeling that he'd let all of that tumble from his mouth. A bare handful of people knew about his past, and yet he'd just told Sasha everything. The one person in the world that he should trust the least. He waited for the mask to slip, for her to take advantage of sharing his sad story. But it didn't.

She'd gone pale. And her eyes were huge. And she

was frowning now. 'You said my parents are dead, and I've no siblings?'

He nodded. 'You told me that your mother was a single parent. Your father left when you were small. You looked for him but found out that he'd died some years ago and then your mother died a couple of years ago.'

'Oh…it's so strange not to be able to remember my mother. Or looking for my father.'

She seemed to be genuinely tortured. Biting her lip. Apollo had a sudden flashback to kissing her for the first time, feeling the cushiony softness of her mouth opening under his, allowing him to delve deeper…all the way… His hands curled tight around the lip of the wall in a bid to douse the growing inferno in his blood.

He stood up. 'I have some work calls to make. Goodnight, Sasha.'

She looked distracted. 'Goodnight.'

He was walking out but he couldn't get those huge bruised-looking eyes out of his head. He stopped at the door and looked back. She cut a curiously vulnerable figure on the large couch.

'I'm sorry about your parents.'

She turned around and some of that vivid gold and red hair slipped over her shoulder. 'Thank you.'

Desire squeezed Apollo like a vice. He wanted to go back over there and pull apart that flimsy dress material and spread it wide so he could see her pale beauty. He wanted to force her to admit that she was just acting. Messing with his head again. He wouldn't make love to her. He'd have her begging for it and then he'd leave her there, panting and admitting who she really was.

'Goodnight, Sasha.'

Apollo walked out before he followed his base instincts and did something stupid because that way lay madness. The same madness that had made him want her with a primal need he'd never felt before, the first time he'd looked at her.

He got to his study and poured himself a drink and sat down, unable to excise the image of those huge blue eyes out of his brain. Or the impact they'd had on him the first time he'd seen her.

That night, in that anonymous function room in London, had been the first time that anyone had managed to slip past Apollo's defences so skilfully, and without even trying. By just looking at him. Something wild and untamed had crackled to life inside him and he'd realised that he'd never truly felt desire before. He'd taken many lovers but had never allowed them to get close. Satisfying his physical urges only.

After his experiences—seeing his father humiliated and belittled and ultimately destroyed; after seeing his mother wither and fade from their lives, a sad broken woman; and after watching his brother self-destruct— Apollo had vowed never to let anyone close enough to make him care when they would inevitably leave. He'd been left behind too many times.

But for the first time, with Sasha, satisfying his physical urges had taken on a whole new level of need. He'd had to have her. And so he'd followed his base instincts and indulged.

He'd lost himself in her before he'd come back to his senses. And remembered who he was. And what he was. And what he was was empty inside.

Revenge had filled that space for a long time. He'd

only been coming to terms with the fact that it hadn't felt more cathartic to have achieved his goals when he'd met Sasha. He'd put her effect on him down to that curious space he'd been in. Anticlimactic. Restless. Dissatisfied, when he should have been satisfied. At peace.

There was a knock on his door and he tensed. 'Come in.'

Sasha took a deep breath outside Apollo's study door. She knew he'd said he was taking or making calls but she hadn't heard his voice when she'd diverted to his office en route to her bedroom, so she'd acted on impulse.

She opened the door and he was sitting behind his desk, a brooding expression on his face. He frowned. 'Is everything okay?'

She nodded, but immediately regretted her decision when that awareness of him coiled tight, down low in her belly. 'Fine. I just...' She stopped. She shouldn't have come here now. The way he made her feel just by looking at her was so...disturbing. She wanted to run but also stay rooted to the spot.

He frowned. 'Sasha—'

She spoke in a rush. 'I know you're busy, but I want to know why our marriage is...like this. Separate bedrooms. Tense. You don't like me very much.'

At all, whispered a little voice.

Apollo put down the glass in his hand. He stood up and came around to sit on the edge of his desk. Arms folded across his chest, which only drew attention to his muscles. Heat washed up through her body and she couldn't stop it.

Had she always been so aware of men?

Maybe it's just him, whispered a voice.

Somehow, she couldn't deny that it was entirely possible she only reacted like this to him.

Apollo saw the twin flags of colour in Sasha's cheeks. He was almost disappointed that she was showing her true colours again so soon. She'd nearly had him convinced. But coming here like this now…she must have seen his desire for her. And now she was taking advantage of it.

He was tempted to just confront her right now, but something in him counselled against acting too hastily. 'Our marriage had some…issues, but I don't think now is the time to go into them.'

He watched her carefully, which only made him more aware of her. Aware that he wanted her.

Witch.

She looked at him. 'I don't know why but I feel I need to apologise, as if I've done something wrong and that's why you hate me and Rhea and Kara look at me as if I'm about to do something unexpected.'

Apollo fought the pull to believe her. To trust in this image of innocence she was putting forward. She'd done it before. He straightened up from the desk. He told himself he was moving closer to test her, just to see if she would show her true colours. Not because he wanted to.

Her eyes got big and round and the pink in her cheeks deepened as she looked up at him as if he were a big bad wolf. Something snapped inside Apollo, some control he'd been exerting since she'd woken in the hospital bed and looked at him with those blue eyes, re-igniting his desire.

He reached out and caught a lock of her hair, winding

it around his finger. It felt like silk. It reminded him of how it had felt when her hair had trailed over his naked chest the night they'd made love.

'I prefer it like this, loose and wild. You preferred it straightened.'

'I did?' Sasha's chest constricted. Why couldn't she seem to breathe? The air was thick and full of something that felt alive. The awareness she felt turned into a pulse in her blood. Heavy and persistent.

Almost as if he was talking to himself, Apollo said, 'It was like this the night we met.'

'I don't... I don't remember. I mean, I remember bits of that night but not details...'

Apollo stood in front of her, eyes roving her face. 'Are you sure, Sasha? Really? Or is this just an elaborate stunt to gain my trust? To get back into my bed?'

His words acted like cold water in her blood. She pulled back, dislodging his hand from her hair. '*No.* I wouldn't do that.'

He moved closer again and put his hand under her chin, tipping her face up. So much for his words dousing the heat. It sizzled back at his touch, just as potent.

'Wouldn't you? It's no less than you've already done, but I have to admit, if you are acting, your skills are exemplary.'

For the first time since she'd woken up in the hospital something more than confusion and bewilderment rushed through her, distracting her. Sasha took his hand to pull it down. 'Maybe that's because I'm not acting.'

But instead of pushing his hand away to break all contact with him and his cynical words, she couldn't seem to let go. Electricity hummed through her, mixing with the high emotion to create a volatile mix.

For a crazy second she almost thought he was going to kiss her. But then he broke contact and stepped back. His eyes were so dark in the dim light they looked black. Sasha felt a little dizzy, as if they *had* kissed.

He said curtly, 'You should go to bed, Sasha. It's late.' He went to the door and held it open.

Sasha couldn't understand what had just come over her. The depth of the need to have him kiss her still left her shaken.

Dear God, had she actually asked...?

She all but ran out of his office before she could read the disgust on his face or, worse, let him see the awful surge of humiliation climbing up from her gut.

Apollo waited until Sasha had disappeared before closing his door. He went back to his desk and downed his drink in one, as if that might burn away how close he'd come to taking what she was offering, lifting that lush mouth towards him, begging with those huge eyes to kiss her.

One minute he'd been wondering how she'd managed to sneak under his guard again, and the next he'd been on the verge of hauling her closer to relive that night they'd shared—which was exactly what she'd been angling for since they'd married.

His hand tightened around the crystal glass so much he had to relax for fear of breaking it.

Sexual frustration bit sharply into his gut. He'd spent the last three months without so much as a flicker of arousal when he'd looked at his wife. And now it wasn't a flicker. It was an inferno.

He couldn't understand what was happening. But he knew that, no matter how intense it got, he would not be weak. He'd been weak for her once before and she'd upended his life. It wouldn't happen again.

CHAPTER THREE

SASHA WENT UPSTAIRS to her bedroom, feeling dazed. She stood in the middle of the room and put her fingers to her mouth, almost as if to test that they hadn't kissed, it had felt so real, so inevitable. But, no, her mouth was the same. Not swollen. Throbbing with sensation.

Because she knew what that felt like.

It hit her then, like a sledgehammer. She'd wanted it so badly because she knew what it felt like to be kissed by him. That's why her body had literally ached...from the memory of knowing his touch. Wanting it again.

She sat down on the end of her bed, going cold inside. Thank God he'd pulled back before she'd have been able to articulate her need any more than she already had, silently. She cringed to think of how he'd put his hands on her arms, literally pushing her away.

She realised something else. Maybe she'd craved it so badly because it had felt familiar to her body to be kissed by him. And since everything else around her was so unfamiliar she'd gravitated towards that. A natural response of her body to seek anything familiar?

And exciting, whispered a little voice.

It didn't give her much relief to put it into this context. A flimsy justification for what had nearly happened.

And with a man who resented her presence and had told her to her face that he didn't trust her. What kind of a masochist was she?

When Sasha made her way down to breakfast the next morning she felt ragged. She'd woken at dawn, sweaty, tangled in her sheets. Dissatisfied. She'd slept fitfully and her dreams had been full of X-rated images. Images that she couldn't be sure now *were* just from her dreams. They'd felt like memories...

When she walked onto the small terrace where she'd eaten breakfast alone all week, she wasn't prepared to see Apollo. She hadn't heard his car that morning but she'd still been hoping she might have missed it. But then she realised it was a Saturday so he must be off work.

He looked up at her as he lifted a coffee cup to his mouth, but immediately put it down again and stood up. There was no discernible expression on his face.

She avoided his eye, hating the way her body prickled all over with the same heat she'd felt last night. She almost resented his presence, which was ridiculous when it was his house.

Their house.

But it didn't feel like her house. 'Good morning.'

'Kalimera.'

Sasha sat down and Rhea appeared with coffee, which she poured into a cup for Sasha.

Sasha smiled tentatively at her and said carefully, *'Efharisto.'*

Rhea nodded her head and smiled. When she was gone Apollo said, 'You've been learning Greek?'

Sasha picked up a pastry, anything to avoid looking at Apollo and reliving that moment last night when she'd all but begged him to kiss her. 'Just a few everyday words. Kara helps me.'

'You didn't seem inclined to want to pick it up before.'

Sasha's knife stilled. She looked at Apollo. 'Can we agree that perhaps things might be different now? You keep telling me things I did, or the way I was, and I can't remember any of it. Can we just…go forward from here?'

He looked at her for a long moment. So long that she felt her face get hot. Eventually he inclined his head. 'Very well. That's fair.'

Sasha breathed out.

'How are you feeling now? Physically?'

She took a gulp of coffee, composing herself. 'I'm fine…much better. Physically.' She made a face. 'Mentally…the fogginess has gone but now it's just a great big blank.'

And the way you make me feel like I'm plugged into some hot electrical force.

She clamped her mouth shut in case the words fell out.

Apollo wiped his mouth with a napkin. 'I've arranged for the doctor to come this morning to check you over.'

Sasha's gut clenched. Was he trying to get rid of her? What would happen once she was well enough? Why did she feel sick at the prospect when he obviously resented her presence? Impulsively she asked, 'Was it ever good? Between us?'

Apollo put his hand on the table, face unreadable. 'Briefly.'

The thought of him wanting her as much as she'd wanted him last night was too overwhelming to contemplate for a moment. She struggled to understand. 'But…then why—?'

'Didn't it work?' His voice was harsh.

Sasha nodded. Just at that moment Rhea appeared and Sasha cursed the interruption.

Rhea said, 'The doctor is here to see Kyria Vasilis.'

Apollo looked at Rhea and smiled. A proper smile. The first smile Sasha had seen on his face. Her heart flip-flopped. It transformed him from merely gorgeous to devastating.

But then he looked back at her and it faded. Sasha felt a chill breeze up her spine. He really hated her. For whatever she had done. And a moment ago she'd been ready to hear it but now she was glad of the interruption.

'Physically you've made a remarkable recovery, Mrs Vasilis. Emotionally, how are you doing?'

Sasha tucked her shirt back into her trousers. The doctor had seen her in her bedroom. The same kind female doctor who had attended to her in the hospital after the accident.

She sat down on a chair by the writing desk, aware of the doctor's keen dark eyes on her. 'I'm… I guess I'm okay. Getting used to my life.'

And the husband who doesn't want me here.

The doctor nodded. 'I can imagine it'll take some adjustment. And your memory…anything coming back yet?'

Sasha shook her head. 'Not really. It's just all blank. But I had dreams last night.' She stopped, blushing.

The doctor said, 'Go on, my dear.'

Embarrassed to have mentioned this, Sasha said, 'It's just that they felt like memories more than a dream. Of me and my husband.'

The doctor nodded. 'That could very well be the case. I'd advise you to keep a notebook by the bed, write down your dreams and that could help jog something. But don't put too much pressure on yourself, our minds work in mysterious ways.'

The doctor stood up and Sasha stood too. 'There was something else.'

'Oh?' The doctor was putting things back into her bag. She stopped.

'I just… My husband tells me that I'm behaving differently from how I was before. Would that be normal?'

The doctor considered this and then said slowly, 'It has been known…for head trauma injuries to cause some kind of personality change but we saw no indication of such trauma in your brain scan. You just got a very hard knock to the head. It's just going to take time to readjust to your life, Mrs Vasilis. Don't worry, and let me know as soon as there are any developments with your memory.'

By the time Sasha had waved the doctor off, it was late morning. She turned around to see Kara adjusting a vase of exotic blooms on the table in the middle

of the hall. Sasha walked over, 'Have you seen Apo—
my husband?'

Kara nodded, 'He left a little while ago for the office.
He said to tell you he'd be home later this afternoon.'

'Oh.' Silly to feel so disappointed. She wasn't even
sure what she would have done if he had been here.

Feeling her way, she said, 'He seems to work a lot.'

Kara looked at her and rolled her eyes. 'Always he
is working. Morning, noon and night, except before we
thought it was because—'

Suddenly she stopped and Sasha felt a burn of humiliation rise up inside her.

To get away from her?

She swallowed it down. 'Thank you, Kara. The truth
is I'm not sure what to do with myself. What did I normally do?'

Kara avoided her eye, clearly embarrassed. 'You
liked shopping, a lot.' Sasha's heart sank at the thought
of shopping. What could she possibly need?

'Was there anything else?'

The young girl's face brightened. 'You could go and
lie by the pool, you like that.'

'I do?'

Apollo walked into the gardens towards the pool, where
he'd been told Sasha had been all afternoon. Maybe
she'd finally cracked and was showing her true colours
again. He'd found her by the pool countless times before, surrounded by the detritus of afternoon snacks
and sugary drinks. Dog-eared magazines.

Once he'd questioned whether it was good for her, but
that had been before he'd found out about— He came

to an abrupt standstill as he rounded the bush that artfully hid the pool from prying eyes.

Apollo lifted his sunglasses onto his head. Sasha lay on a sun bed under an umbrella. At first he thought she was naked and his blood rushed straight to his groin. It wouldn't be the first time. She'd habitually sunbathed topless, scandalising Rhea. Trying to tempt him. Not that it had worked.

But, no, he realised she wasn't naked. She wasn't far from it though, in a flesh-coloured one-piece, which was low-cut enough to reveal the plump pale flesh of her breasts. He could already imagine what it might look like if she stepped out of the pool, her red hair slicked back like a wet flame down her back. The clingy material would leave nothing to the imagination. The way her nipples would have gone hard in the water, pressing against the—

Christos.

Disgusted at his lack of control, Apollo tore his gaze off his wife's body. There was no detritus around her. Just a book. And a glass of water.

He could still recall how close he'd come to hauling her against his body last night, crushing that rosebud mouth under his. He could try to convince himself that he'd just been testing her, but he knew his motivations went much deeper and darker than that.

He wanted her again.

When his assistant in London had told him that she was waiting to see him three months ago, a month had passed since their night together. She'd been on his mind constantly, especially at night, when he'd got used to waking from erotic dreams, aching with frustration.

He'd taken more cold showers in that period than he'd ever taken in his whole life.

And he hadn't been able to stem the tide of something that had felt a lot like…relief. That she'd been the one to make the move. To expose herself for wanting more.

But then as soon as she'd walked into his office that day, he'd felt…nothing. Less than nothing. Not a blip of response. Even though she'd looked exactly the same. Fresh face. Hair loose around her shoulders. Innocent. Tremulous.

He hated to admit it now but relief his desire for her had waned hadn't been the overriding sentiment. It had been a sense of disappointment. Because it was proof that she wasn't different from any other woman he'd slept with. And that what they'd shared that night couldn't have possibly been as amazing as he'd remembered it. Amazing enough to make him regret telling her—

Suddenly her body jerked on the bed and a sound came out of her mouth, like a cry. Indistinct words. Something like, *'No, please don't stop!'*

Before Apollo knew what he was doing he'd come down beside the bed, two hands on Sasha's bare arms. They felt impossibly slender. Her body was tense all over, he could see a slight sheen of perspiration on her skin. His insides clenched with an emotion he didn't want to name.

'Sasha…wake up.'

Apollo's hands were on her skin. Burning. She ached all over with a hunger she'd felt only once before. It was

so clear now. She needed him to assuage that hunger...
to make her come alive—

'Sasha!'

Sasha opened her eyes and all she could see were the deepest pools of green. A kind of green that made her think of mysterious oceans. Vast. Impenetrable.

'You were dreaming.'

Apollo's voice. Hard. Unyielding. Suddenly Sasha's consciousness snapped back. She was on the lounger. She'd fallen asleep. But Apollo still had his hands on her. She could smell his scent. See the stubble on his jaw. She wanted to reach out and see how it felt. She imagined it would prickle against her skin.

She remembered how that felt.

Dreams and the present moment were meshing disturbingly and she felt disorientated.

She sat up abruptly, dislodging his hands. He stood up. She reached for the robe, pulling it on awkwardly, very conscious of the revealing swimsuit. It had been the only one-piece she could find in a sea of brightly coloured string bikinis.

'Apollo, I didn't hear you. What time is it?'

Sasha looked deliciously tousled, cheeks flushed, eyes sleepy. Apollo gritted his jaw as his eyes tracked her movements, her small breasts high and firm under the stretchy material. She was so pale her skin was almost translucent. He frowned. She'd been more tanned before. But, of course, it must have been fake. A welcome reminder of who he was dealing with. Memory loss or no memory loss.

The lingering tendrils of concern for her distress

made his voice harsh. 'You should watch yourself in the sun,' he said. 'You can burn even in the shade.'

Sasha flinched inwardly at his abrupt tone, belting the robe tightly around her. The robe chafed against her tingling skin. She could still feel the imprint of his hands on her arms. Defensively she said, 'I found sun block in the bathroom, of course I put some on. I may have lost my memory but I'm not clueless about the dangers of the sun.'

She risked looking up at Apollo now that she was covered up again, diverting her mind from the vividly disturbing dream. He was wearing a short-sleeved polo shirt and cargo shorts. Unexpectedly casual and effortlessly sexy.

He said, 'I just came to tell you that I'm going out this evening.'

'Oh.' It was strange but for the first time she was aware she hadn't left the confines of this estate since her return from the hospital. She had a sense of claustrophobia. 'Where are you going?'

'It's a charity ball, in aid of research into cancer.'

For some reason that struck a chord with Sasha and for a moment something hovered on the edge of her mind but then it was gone.

She stood up. 'Should I come with you?'

He shook his head. 'No need. I'm just letting you know I won't be here for dinner.'

It wasn't as if they'd been having cosy dinners all week but Apollo was the only constant familiar thing in her world right now and she was determined to try and improve relations. What else could she do? She couldn't continue to exist in this limbo where they circled each other like suspicious foes.

She still didn't know exactly what had happened between them and she wasn't even sure if she wanted to know what she'd done to lead to this impasse, but she could work with what she had. She wanted to at least try to mend bridges.

'Didn't I go to events with you? As your wife?'

Apollo searched for any hint of a crack in her facade but she looked utterly guileless. Did she really not remember saying to him, 'Why not use me? Surely it's better for you to be seen with a wife than not? It'll help your business to be seen as more settled.'

When they'd married, he hadn't had any intention of involving her in his life more than he'd had to, but he'd had to admit that on some level she was right. And so he'd taken her to a couple of events.

Sasha was looking at him now. 'What is it? Why are you looking at me like that?'

'You don't remember?'

She went pale. 'No. What did I do?'

'Let's just say that you ruffled some feathers.'

'How?'

'You were rude to staff and visibly bored when you realised that the social and corporate events I attend aren't generally designed for entertainment purposes.'

Sasha felt queasy. Was there anything she had done right? 'I can't keep apologising for things I can't remember. But maybe this is an opportunity to make it up to you. No matter what I did, won't your friends and colleagues be wondering where your wife is?'

He didn't refute her question so she asked, 'What

time do you have to leave? It won't take me long to
get ready.'

He arched a brow. 'I'll believe that when I see it.' He
put his sunglasses back over his eyes and without that
laser-like gaze stripping her bare she breathed easier.

'I have to leave in an hour. If you're coming, be
downstairs waiting for me, or I go alone. I won't wait,
Sasha.'

Less than an hour later, Sasha waited nervously downstairs in the main hall for Apollo. After his ultimatum
she'd panicked. She had no idea how on earth to get
ready for such an event. She'd found Kara in the kitchen
and had begged the young woman to come with her
to help her. Initially she had been reluctant but then
she'd relented, telling Sasha that Apollo had asked for
his tuxedo to be ready for him so at least they knew it
was black-tie.

They'd managed to find a dress that was suitable and
not too revealing, and Kara had helped with her hair and
make-up. And now Sasha stood here, wondering what
on earth she'd been doing, saying she'd go along to an
event—she had no idea if she would be able to handle
herself in such a milieu. She'd been serving drinks when
she'd met him, not drinking them!

She would make a fool of herself and any hope she
had of redeeming herself in Apollo's eyes would be
gone. And what deeper impulse was whispering to her
to look for redemption? Then what? Did she want him
to like her again?

Want her again?

Panic gripped her. She couldn't do this. She turned

to flee back to her room before Apollo saw her—he'd obviously not expected her to be ready anyway. But it was too late. He was at the top of the stairs and staring at her as if she were a total stranger. Her own eyes widened and her chest constricted as the air rushed out.

He was wearing a classic black tuxedo. White shirt, black bow-tie. She was not prepared for his impact on her. And yet she'd seen him like this before, the first night they'd met. A vivid flashback assailed her before she knew what was happening—Apollo had been helping her with her heavy tray of drinks and she'd been laughing and getting hot with embarrassment. 'Honestly, I'm fine. If my boss sees you helping me, I'll get into trouble.'

He'd kept hold of the tray, 'I'm not letting go unless you agree to come for a drink with me afterwards.'

She'd seen her boss then, across the room, clocking her. Terrified she'd lose the job, she'd said, 'Okay, fine! Now, please…let me go.'

That memory faded but, as easily as if it had been there all the time, just hiding behind a curtain, she now remembered that evening, and fragmented images from another evening, a date…going for dinner with him in a beautiful restaurant in a tall glittering building with London laid out before them, a sea of twinkling lights… She'd been so excited. Nervous. Incredulous.

Happy…

Apollo couldn't believe what he was seeing. Sasha, waiting for him. Ready. And looking presentable. More than presentable.

Beautiful.

She was wearing a black silk one-shouldered dress, with ornate silk flowers trailing over one shoulder. Cut on the bias, the dress fell in soft billowing folds to the floor.

A braid framed one side of her face and her hair was pulled back into a low bun. It was all at once pretty and youthful but also elegant. Discreet diamonds shone in her ears. Her hands and throat were bare. Her make-up was minimal.

The starkness of the black dress only served to highlight her delicate fair colouring. Those vivid blue eyes. It was a far cry from her usual style, which was showing as much skin as possible, with lots of make-up, jewellery and big hair.

Desire pulled taut like a drum inside him. He had to force himself to move down the stairs. When he got close, her eyes were huge, on him, as if she'd never seen him before. She looked pale and he could see that her fingers were holding her clutch bag so tight her knuckles were white.

'What is it? Are you okay?'

She swallowed and nodded jerkily. She sounded a bit breathless. 'I just… I just remembered London. More about that night we met. And another night?'

He nodded slowly. 'I took you out the following evening for dinner.'

'We were in a building…it looked like a piece of broken glass.'

'The Shard?'

She nodded. 'Yes. I still don't remember much else beyond that building, the view…but it's a start.'

Something uneasy moved through Apollo. If she *was*

acting then she'd gone beyond a point that most people could keep up a pretence. He said carefully, 'That's good.'

A little colour came back into her cheeks and now she looked nervous. She gestured to the dress. 'Is this okay? I wasn't sure... Kara helped me.'

'Kara?'

She nodded and then looked worried. 'Is that a problem? Shouldn't I have asked her?'

Apollo, for the first time, had to bite back a smile. 'On the contrary, she tried to help you before but you insisted on getting in a professional stylist.'

Sasha looked tortured. 'I had no idea. I should apologise.' She made to go towards the kitchen but Apollo caught her hand, aware of how small it felt in his.

'It's not that big a deal, you can tell her another time.' But he couldn't seem to let her hand go. His gaze swept up and down, taking in the way the swells of her breasts pushed against the thin fabric of the dress. He wondered if she was wearing a bra—imagined cupping one firm weight in his hand, feeling the stab of her nipple— He shut down his rogue imagination and let her hand go. 'We should leave, or we'll be late.'

He took her by the arm and led her out of the villa and into the passenger seat of his car.

Sasha took in the view of Athens as they came down from the hills and entered the ancient city. The view was helping to distract her from the proximity of Apollo's all too masculine presence beside her.

The city was bustling, full of young people out on the streets, enjoying the weekend, laughing and enjoying life. She could see the Acropolis standing majestically over the city, like a sentinel. 'Have I been to the Acropolis?' she asked, as the thought occurred to her.

Apollo glanced at her, slowing to a stop at a set of lights. 'No, you didn't express an interest in seeing it.'

Sasha frowned. It was so disconcerting that some-one else knew more about her than she did. Before long, they were driving into a wide leafy street with tall ex-clusive townhouses, and then through huge wrought-iron gates manned by serious-looking security men. They pulled up outside what could only be described as a neo-classical mansion.

Lots of people were milling around outside, then slowly making their way inside. Women dressed in long glittering dresses, men dressed like Apollo, in tuxedoes.

Nerves erupted like butterflies in her belly. Again, she regretted ever saying anything about coming. But the car had stopped and Apollo was uncoiling his tall body out of the car and handing the keys to a young man.

Then he was opening her door and holding out a hand. She took a deep breath and let him help her out. Not even her awareness of him was able to eclipse her nerves. Her palms were clammy. She didn't belong in a place like this and she didn't need to regain her mem-ory to know that.

CHAPTER FOUR

APOLLO'S HAND WAS on Sasha's elbow, guiding her through the throng. He noticed the looks from his peers. The widening eyes as they registered his wife by his side. He gritted his jaw. He'd never asked for this—to be married—but he'd been surprised at what a difference it had made. Much as he hated to admit it, Sasha had been right in her estimation of the worth of having a wife by your side.

It made his married colleagues less nervous. It kept predatory women at bay. And it had lent a more stable veneer to his business. A couple of business associates he'd been trying to meet with for years had finally agreed to meetings and Apollo had realised that it had been because they were family men and they hadn't totally trusted him when he'd been a bachelor. He'd been seen as a rogue operator.

He looked down at Sasha to check how she was reacting and saw her expression. Genuinely awed, as if she'd never been in this kind of environment before. Certainly not how she'd reacted the first time he'd brought her to an event. Then she'd looked as entitled as everyone else here. Or, at least, she'd tried to.

Now she wore the kind of expression that one would never see in a place like this because everyone was too used to this level of luxury, or wouldn't be caught dead admitting to being impressed. Or too cynical.

To his surprise, her reaction reminded him of how he'd felt when he'd first started being invited along to high society events: out of his depth and as if he didn't belong.

He quickly quashed the sense of empathy. Sasha had led him a merry dance for months now, and she owed him. She seemed determined to act the part of his wife again and he'd be an idiot not to take advantage of that. After all, they wouldn't be married for much longer— as soon as she had fully recuperated—

She interrupted his thoughts, asking, 'What *is* this place?'

'It's the French Ambassador's residence. He's hosting this evening. His wife died of cancer some years ago and now he and his family host this ball every year.'

'Oh, that's sad.'

Apollo looked at her suspiciously. But she seemed genuinely concerned. A little frown between her eyes. Mouth turned down.

Sasha was unaware of the speculative look from her husband. She was too consumed and awed by her surroundings. She'd never seen such glittering opulence. The ceilings had elaborate frescoes and the walls seemed to be made out of gold.

Hundreds of candles and sparkling chandeliers imbued everything with a golden glow. It truly was another world. She was sure she'd never seen so many beautiful people in one place. Or maybe she had, if she'd been serving them drinks. But not like this…not as one of them.

Frustration bit at her insides. She hated this…*not knowing*. Being at the mercy of her mind choosing to reveal memories totally at random. When *it* chose to. Like when she'd seen Apollo in the tuxedo.

To distract herself, Sasha tried to tune into the conversation Apollo was having with some men, but she gave up as it was in Greek, or other languages she didn't understand.

Waiters came around offering champagne and canapés. Sasha was too afraid to eat in case she ruined her dress. Then they were led into another large and impressive room with round tables set around a small stage. They sat down and a charity auction took place. The items up for auction included cars, date nights with famous celebrities and even a small island off the coast of Ireland.

Sasha gasped when that lot was announced. 'That's outrageous!'

Apollo looked at her and his mouth twisted slightly. 'That's the super-rich.'

Then a lot came up for a luxury yacht. To her shock and surprise, Apollo started bidding on it. Within a few short minutes people were clapping him on the back and cheering. He'd paid an extortionate amount of money for it.

Sasha was in shock. 'You just bought a yacht.'

He looked at her. 'Well, I already have an island and an island isn't much use without a yacht.'

He said that without any discernible sense of awe

that he owned such fantastical things. In fact, he almost sounded…bored.

'You don't seem very excited to own such things.'

Apollo felt something hitch in his chest at Sasha's comment and the way her blue eyes seemed to be looking right inside him, to the place where a sense of novelty had become something else. Something *less* novel. When had that happened?

He shrugged nonchalantly when he felt tight inside, not relaxed, 'Like I said, an island needs a yacht.'

'But will you use it?'

Apollo was surprised at the hollow feeling that seemed to spread outwards from his centre. He hadn't even consciously bought the yacht with a view to using it. More as a reflex to do what was expected of him. But now he couldn't help imagining the vessel bobbing in azure waters under a clear sky, and this woman laid out in all her slender, pale glory…red hair spread around her head—

The crowd seemed to stand en masse as the auction came to an end and Apollo seized the opportunity to divert Sasha's attention. Since when had his wife had the ability to probe so insightfully and deeply with just a casual question?

He stood up and reached for her hand. 'It's time to move on.'

Sasha had a very keen sense that Apollo hadn't appreciated her innocent questions. Clearly she'd hit on a nerve and maybe she was being spectacularly naive: in this world, islands and yachts were mere luxury trinkets to be added to a portfolio of even more luxury items.

There was just something about his lack of enthusiasm that struck at the heart of her, making her feel a little…sad.

The crowd was moving into yet another glorious room, even bigger. A ballroom. There was an orchestra and a singer singing sultry jazz songs. The lighting was dim and intimate. French doors were open, leading out to a terrace lined with flaming lanterns. Dusk was falling and the sky was a deep lavender colour. It was like a scene from a fairy-tale or a movie.

Her hand was still in Apollo's and she was very conscious of his long fingers wrapped around hers, so much so that she didn't even notice that he was leading her onto the dance floor. When she realised where they were, it was too late. He was drawing her in front of him and wrapping one arm across her back.

She went rigid in his arms from the impact of his body against hers as much because of where they were; in the middle of a dance floor. Around them, couples were moving sinuously to the music. Graceful and elegant. At ease.

Apollo started to move, taking Sasha with him, and she hissed, 'I don't even know if I can dance.'

'Just follow my lead.'

After a few robotic moments, Apollo pulled her even closer to his body. Sasha couldn't fight the force it took to remain rigid and so she softened against him.

She was surrounded by him, his steely strength. They were so close she could smell the sharp tang of his aftershave. Her heels put her even closer to his jaw and mouth. She wanted to press her lips there, taste his skin. Immediately she tensed again and he lowered his head, saying in her ear, 'Relax. Just let me lead.'

After a few torturous seconds she allowed herself to soften again. She realised they were moving around the floor with relative grace. She looked up, avoiding looking at his jaw and the faint line of stubble.

'Where did you learn to dance?'

She felt the tension come into his body. 'My mother. She loved to dance, she used to dance with my father all the time.'

'That's romantic.'

He looked down at her, his expression anything but romantic. 'It was, until he had the accident and couldn't dance any more.'

Sasha thought of what he'd told her about getting revenge for his father's death. She shivered slightly, thinking of how ruthless he must have been. Single-minded. But she remembered him being like that with her—until she'd agreed to go for a drink with him.

She wondered how on earth she'd caught his eye in London when they'd been surrounded by women as beautiful as the ones here tonight, in their peacock dresses and glittering jewels. Even though she was dressed like them now, she felt dowdy and colourless in comparison.

She noticed one dark brunette pass by in the arms of her partner, her voluptuous body poured into a silver sheath dress. She also noticed how she looked at Apollo, and then at Sasha, dismissing her with a flick of her hair. No competition.

The song came to an end and Sasha seized the opportunity to escape for a moment, hating this feeling of insecurity. Especially when she thought of how close she'd come last night to showing Apollo how much he affected her. When he clearly felt nothing similar. She pulled back from Apollo's arms. 'Excuse me, I just need to go to the bathroom.'

Apollo watched Sasha hurry from the dance floor. Her face had been the colour of milk. He couldn't stop the spike of concern. Was she feeling ill? Was it her memory? Was she remembering more?

He cursed and made his way over to the bar. Concern for his wife was a novel and unwelcome sentiment. Also unwelcome was the raging arousal still lingering in his blood after that dance. Holding her so close, smelling her scent. The thin fabric of her dress doing little to hide how her slender curves had felt against his body… no other woman had ever had such an effect on him.

He took women he desired to bed. He told them up front that he wasn't looking for anything permanent. Except *her*. Everything about his experience with her had been so novel, and that's why he'd let his guard down momentarily. A moment she'd exploited when she'd come to him in London a month after their night together with her shock announcement.

But all of that was in danger of being forgotten with the rush of hot desire in his blood. Clouding his judgement. Blunting his control. Changing things. He should never have agreed to let her join him tonight. They weren't a couple.

They never would have married if it hadn't been for—

Apollo saw Sasha return to the room. Her head was turning left and right, clearly searching for him.

She looked vulnerable. Out of place. He saw more than one man look at her twice, caught by her fresh-faced beauty. She stood out in a crowd of rich and jaded cynics. And that's why she'd appealed to him that very first night.

But it had all been a mirage. Her memory loss might very well be real, but underneath it lay the true Sasha Miller. A liar and a mercenary bitch. It wouldn't be long before she showed her true colours again. At that moment, as if hearing his thoughts, she saw him and their eyes locked across the room. Apollo vowed not to forget who she really was.

The journey winding back up the hills to Apollo's villa was taken in silence. Sasha was engrossed in her own thoughts. The questions buzzing in her brain were growing increasingly loud and hard to ignore. Especially after tonight when she'd gone out in public, pretending to the world that she was this man's wife. When reality couldn't be further from that truth.

Apollo parked the car at the foot of the steps leading up to the front door of the villa. Sasha turned to him in the gloom of the car. 'Why did you let me come with you tonight?'

Apollo put his hands on the wheel. 'Primarily because I didn't expect you to be ready on time. You never were before.'

'So that would have been your excuse for leaving me behind.'

He looked at her and shrugged minutely, unapologetic.

Sasha shook her head. 'What happened, Apollo? Why are we like this? You liked me in London. You pursued me…asked me for a drink. Took me for dinner.'

Took me to bed?

She couldn't remember those details but she sensed *yes*, because her body was attuned to his on a level that she couldn't deny. And would a man like Apollo have married her without sleeping with her? He didn't strike her as the traditional type.

Was she? Had she been a virgin?

'You really want to get into this now?'

Once again she wasn't sure. Did she want to know everything? But she heard herself say, 'Yes.'

'Are you sure you're ready?'

Sasha swallowed the rising fear. 'I need to know. I feel like I'm the only one left out of a secret.'

'Very well. But not here—inside.'

A feeling of panic eclipsed the fear as Sasha followed Apollo inside the villa. Was she really ready for this? *No.* But she knew she couldn't continue not knowing either.

It was quiet. The staff had gone home or were in bed. He led the way into one of the less formal drawing rooms, flicking on low lights.

He went over to a drinks cabinet, tugging at the bowtie around his neck. He looked back at her, 'Would you like a drink?'

'Will I need one?' Sasha joked, but it felt hollow.

He arched a brow and she said, 'A small brandy, please.' She wasn't even sure if she'd ever had brandy before but felt like it might be necessary.

Apollo poured a drink for himself and brought her over a small tumbler. She took a sniff and wrinkled her nose at the strong smell. She took a tentative sip and the liquid slid down her throat and into her stomach, leaving a trail of fire and a lingering afterglow of heat. It wasn't unpleasant.

Apollo shrugged off his jacket and Sasha wished he hadn't because now she could see the play of muscles under the thin material of his shirt. He faced her. 'What do you want to know?

Everything.

She swallowed. Where to start? 'Did we sleep together?'

'Yes. We spent one night together.'

An instant flush of heat landed in Sasha's belly that had nothing to do with the alcohol. Her instinct had been right. She'd slept with this man.

That was why her body remembered.

But she didn't.

She swallowed. 'The night we had dinner in… The Shard?'

He nodded. 'Yes, then you came back to my apartment.'

Ridiculously she almost felt like apologising for not being able to remember. Instinctively she felt that it had been memorable, and that a man like Apollo wasn't easily forgotten.

Her hand gripped the glass. 'Was I…? Was it my first time?'

His jaw clenched. 'I believed it was, yes. But since then…let's just say that I can't be sure you didn't make it seem that way.'

Sasha felt something like shame creep up inside her. 'Why would I lie about being a virgin?'

He looked at her and she couldn't escape that green gaze or the clear admonishment. 'To make yourself appear more innocent than you were. Because you thought it would appeal to me, a jaded cynic? Who knows?'

'I didn't tell you beforehand?'

He shook his head. 'You said you were afraid that if I'd known how inexperienced you were, I wouldn't want you.'

Sasha sat down on a seat behind her, her legs feeling distinctly wobbly.

'What happened then?'

Apollo drank the contents of his glass and put it down carefully. He faced her and folded his arms across his chest. He looked like a warrior, preparing for battle. All sinew and muscle. Not an inch of softness.

'After that night we went our separate ways.'

Sasha absorbed that. Had it been a mutual decision? She shied away from asking that question now. It was enough to absorb that he'd been her first lover.

Or had he?

She felt an instinctive need to reject his claim that she might not have been innocent. But how could she defend herself when she didn't know for sure?

She took another sip of the fiery drink, her hand not quite steady. 'If we went our separate ways…then how… did we end up here, married?'

For a second her heart palpitated. Maybe he'd come after her? Maybe one night hadn't been enough?

He paused for a moment and then he said, 'Because a month after that night, you came to my offices in London and you told me that you were pregnant with my child.'

Sasha stood up slowly, there was a roaring sound in

her ears and she had to shake her head to clear it. 'I'm sorry... I what?'

He spoke slowly. 'You told me that you were pregnant with my child.'

CHAPTER FIVE

THE WORD SANK into Sasha's head but didn't make sense. *Pregnant.* She put a hand to her belly but it was flat. Something occurred to her and she felt her blood drain south. The glass fell out of nerveless fingers but she barely noticed Apollo stride forward to pick it up and take her arm, pushing her gently back into the chair.

She looked up at him. 'Did I lose it?'

How could she not know if she'd lost her own baby? Was that why Apollo hated her? For losing their baby?

Both hands were on her belly now as if that could help her to remember something so huge…so cataclysmic.

But Apollo was shaking his head. 'No. You didn't lose it, because you were never pregnant in the first place. You deliberately lied about being pregnant to get me to marry you, Sasha.'

She hadn't been pregnant.

In the midst of the relief that she hadn't forgotten such a seismic event, Apollo's words sank in.

'You deliberately lied. To get me to marry you.'

Sasha's first reaction was denial. Rejection. She

shook her head. 'No… I wouldn't have said that. I couldn't have done something like that…'

'But you did,' Apollo countered curtly.

She was glad she was sitting down because she was pretty sure she would have collapsed otherwise. 'I… I told you I was pregnant. But I wasn't?'

He nodded. His face was impossibly grim.

She tried to make sense of it all, and also the gut-wrenching knowledge that he *hadn't* come after her, because she'd been the one to go to him in the end. 'But why would I do such a thing?'

His mouth went thin. 'You really have to ask that question? We slept together and you saw an opportunity.'

He indicated with a hand. 'Look around you. You hungered for a better life and you were going to use me to get it.'

A moment ago Sasha had felt as if her legs wouldn't support her but now she stood again, too agitated to keep sitting. She paced back and forth. 'But that's…' She stopped. 'That's an awful thing to do.'

'Yes, it is,' he agreed.

She struggled to recall any hint of what might have led her to do such a drastic thing but her mind stayed annoyingly blank.

'Maybe I believed I was pregnant? Did we…use protection?'

His whole body bristled. 'Of course. I would never be so lax. But I will admit that I didn't check afterwards. There's always a possibility of failure and you capitalised on that, sowing the seed of doubt in my mind.'

'But how were you so sure I'd lied about the pregnancy?'

'I had my suspicions when you showed no signs of pregnancy and then after an…incident you admitted it was a lie.'

'An incident…?'

He nodded and paced away from her, turned back. 'I was in London on business and came back after a panicked call from Rhea. You were hosting a party with some new-found friends.'

The way Apollo's lip curled on *friends* told her what he'd thought of them. 'I found you snorting cocaine and drinking. When you'd sobered up you admitted it had been a lie to trap me.'

Sasha went back to the chair and sat down again. Reeling. She felt cold and wrapped her arms around herself.

She forced herself to look at Apollo. She felt deep in her bones that she wouldn't have done such heinous things—lying about being pregnant, taking drugs—*couldn't* have. And yet why would he lie? This explained his antipathy and also the way Rhea and Kara had looked at her like an unexploded bomb on her return from the hospital.

She went even colder as she absorbed the full extent of everything he'd told her. 'You didn't want to marry me.'

His jaw tightened. 'No.' Just that. *No.*

Why not? trembled on her lips but she didn't have to ask that question. He hadn't been interested in her after their night together in London. Her innocence must have been a huge turn-off.

Desperately trying to salvage something positive, she said, 'But in London you took me for dinner...to your apartment... You liked me then?' She hated how insecure she sounded.

A sense of exposure hit Apollo again. His voice was taut with self-recrimination. 'You captivated me. Briefly. You were different.'

'Different from what?'

Sasha looked so guileless. Pale. Eyes huge.

Was she really faking this amnesia? Was it too convenient that she was remembering snippets but not everything? Was she laughing at him? Forcing him to articulate why he'd wanted her?

But something uneasy in his gut told him that she couldn't be faking it. She looked too tortured.

He said, 'Different from everyone else. Other women.'

Twin flags of pink made her cheeks flush and for a moment Apollo was rewarded with a flashback to watching her face flush with pleasure as she'd moved under him, around him.

She said tightly, 'You mean I wasn't as sophisticated.'

Apollo had to use every atom of his control to counter the rush of desire. Damn her. 'You caught my eye. You were refreshingly unaffected. Open. Friendly. But it was all a lie.'

Sasha remembered feeling invisible that night. Until he'd looked directly at her, and the flash of pure heat that had gone through her body. Her tray of drinks had wobbled precariously and he'd stepped forward and steadied it. His lazy, charming smile.

'Promise to meet me for a drink and I'll give the tray back.'

She couldn't remember sleeping with him or the aftermath, but she could imagine all too easily how he would have laid it out. Telling her not to expect more. A man like this would have been used to such scenarios with women. Had she been so desperate that she'd begged for more? She felt ashamed for herself.

In a way now Sasha was glad she couldn't remember exactly what had happened. This was humiliating enough without recalling in excruciating detail how banal the experience must have been for a man of the world like him. To sleep with a virgin. She'd obviously been a novelty for a jaded billionaire and her appeal hadn't lasted long.

Her head was starting to throb faintly. 'What happens now?'

'Nothing. Until you've recovered fully. Then we can discuss the future.'

The future.

Sasha felt slightly hysterical. She couldn't recall much of the past, never mind the future.

She stood up. 'I'm getting a headache. I think I'll go to bed.'

Apollo watched as she turned and walked out. She was the colour of pale parchment. Maybe it had been too soon to tell her the unvarnished truth? No matter how much she'd insisted she wanted to know.

He felt an impulse to go after her and make sure she was okay but he told himself he was being ridiculous. The woman who had engineered a fake pregnancy to trap him into marriage was no delicate soul. Accident or no accident.

He poured himself another shot of whisky and downed it in one. It burned his throat. But he couldn't get her pale face and huge shocked eyes out of his mind. He had to admit that he was finding it hard to continue suspecting that she was faking the amnesia. Sasha would never have been able to play this far more innocent incarnation for so long without cracking.

Which meant…this news was as shocking to her now as it had been to him when he'd first heard it.

Apollo cursed and put down the glass. He went upstairs and stood outside Sasha's bedroom door for a long moment. He heard no sounds.

He knocked lightly but again there was no sound. He opened the door and went in. His eyes took a moment to adjust to the dim light. He could see no shape in the bed. And then he saw her, standing outside on the balcony.

She must have heard him because she turned around. She'd changed. She was wearing a diaphanous robe over what looked like a short negligée. From where he stood, Apollo could see the outline of her body. All slender curves and pale skin.

His blood surged, and he realised in that moment that he shouldn't have come up here. Sasha stepped into the room. 'Is something wrong?'

But instead of leaving, Apollo moved towards her as if drawn by a magnet. The moon was behind her, low in the sky. A perfect crescent. The milky glow made her look ethereal, adding a silver tinge to her rose-gold hair. It was down again, falling in soft waves over her shoulders.

He had an urge to touch her to make sure she was, in fact, real. He stopped a couple of feet away. Her scent reached him—lemon, underlain with something more tantalisingly exotic. But soft, not overpowering.

Different.

'You said you had a headache.'

She touched her head. 'It's okay now, thank you. I think it was just taking in all that information...'

Sasha wasn't sure that she wasn't hallucinating right now. Was Apollo really standing in her room, looking at her as if he'd never seen her before?

But then, at that moment, he said, 'I just wanted to check you were okay,' and then turned around as if to leave.

Sasha acted on an impulse, reaching out with her hand. 'Wait.'

He stopped. Turned around. Sasha wasn't even sure what she wanted to say. And then she did. She dropped her outstretched hand. 'I don't remember anything of what you said... It doesn't feel like something I would do but then how do I know?'

She bit her lip. 'Did you even care about the baby?'

Apollo had to school his expression in case she saw something he didn't want to reveal. The pain of losing his entire family over a period of a few years had been so acute that he'd always vowed to avoid such pain again by not having a family of his own.

But, to his surprise, after the initial shock and anger at Sasha's pregnancy news had abated, he'd found that the thought of a baby he could protect and nurture had softened something inside him. And had restored a broken sense of hope, optimism.

But then, the fact that she'd lied about it and roused those feelings had made a cruel mockery of the defences he'd built up over the years. They hadn't been strong after all. Now, though, they were ironclad. Not that he would ever reveal to her what she'd done to him. She'd revealed a weakness, and reopened a wound and he would never forgive her for that.

'I had never intended on having a relationship or becoming a father. Not after losing my entire family. But of course I would have cared for any child of mine. I'm not a monster.'

Sasha's eyes were huge. Full of emotion. Exposure prickled over his skin just as she said huskily, 'I'm sorry…for what happened. I don't know why I pretended to be pregnant but I'd like to think I had good reasons.'

He fought against the image she was projecting of someone compassionate, who *cared*. He should move back, out of her dangerous orbit, but instead he found himself moving closer. All he could see was her. Looking impossibly innocent. Impossibly because she hadn't been innocent at all. Or had she? Physically perhaps, at least.

He had an intensely erotic memory of how it had felt to thrust deep into that silken embrace. Her muscles had clamped so tightly around him he'd seen stars.

Angry at his lack of control, he asked curtly, 'Are you really sorry, though? Or is this just an elaborate showcase of your acting skills to entice me back into your bed so you can try to get pregnant for real?'

Horror at his relentless cynicism made Sasha take a step back. '*No*. How can you say such a thing?'

Apollo's mouth was a thin line. 'Very easily, because you did it before, countless times, including the memorable occasion when I came home to find you naked in my bed.'

Shock and disbelief made Sasha take another step back. She shook her head. 'No, there is no way I would have ever done such a thing.'

Apollo just arched a brow. 'Why would I lie? You have to agree it made sense. After all, you weren't pregnant so you needed to get pregnant. Fast.'

Sasha swallowed. Had that really been her? So desperate? Conniving? She struggled to defend herself when she felt as if everything inside her was crumbling. 'But it's obvious you don't want me—why would I have humiliated myself like that?'

Apollo was looking at her so intensely she could scarcely breathe.

He said something under his breath then, a word she didn't understand, and then said, almost as if to himself, 'I thought I didn't want you any more, but now it's all I can think about. What kind of sorcery is this?'

Sasha's heart slammed to a stop, and then started again in an erratic rhythm. She suddenly became very aware of her flimsy garments. The silky thigh-skimming negligée and floaty dressing gown. Garments she didn't feel particularly comfortable in, but apparently she hadn't favoured comfort over style.

She tried to speak. 'I don't… There's no sorcery.'

His gaze raked her up and down and she trembled under its force. Her breasts felt heavy, their tips tightening into hard points, pressing against the silky material. Her body remembered this man. His touch. But she didn't. Frustration coursed through her. She couldn't take her eyes off his mouth, the firm sculpted lines.

Apollo barely heard Sasha's denial. He knew this was madness. That he shouldn't have come to her bedroom. But rational thought was fast dissolving in a haze of lust. He reached out and caught a loose tendril of silky hair, winding it around his finger, tugging her gently towards him.

When he looked down he could see her breasts rising and falling with her rapid breath, pale swells framed enticingly by lace, inviting him to touch, explore. Electricity hummed between them, thick and urgent.

He tipped her chin up with his forefinger and thumb. Her eyes were huge pools of blue. He had a flashback to the first time he'd kissed her, sitting in a discreet booth of the exclusive hotel bar where he'd taken her for a drink when she'd finished work on that first night.

It had been a rare novelty, waiting for her to emerge from a staff entrance of the hotel. He could remember the sensation of something loosening inside him. He'd been so focused for so long and suddenly he'd been diverted from that single-mindedness.

She'd been endearingly self-conscious in her black skirt, white shirt and black jacket. Flat shoes. Sheer tights.

He'd wanted her then and he wanted her now. He lowered his head, anticipation prickling across his skin. He'd thought he'd never kiss her again.

Hadn't wanted to.

But he was being punished for that complacency now, because here he was, as consumed with lust as he had been the first time.

* * *

Tension was a tight coil inside Sasha as she waited for Apollo's mouth to touch hers and she told herself desperately that he'd kissed her before—more than kissed her, so it shouldn't come as a shock—but when his mouth touched hers, it was more than a shock. It was an earthquake, erupting from her solar plexus and spreading out to every nerve-ending, bringing with it thousands of volts of electricity.

She wasn't even aware of her hands going to his shirt and clinging on for dear life. His hands were in her hair, angling her head, and their mouths were on fire. She tasted the whisky he'd been drinking and she felt molten and solid all at the same time. It was intoxicating, and nothing could have prepared her for this.

His chest was a steel wall against her breasts. She arched instinctively closer, seeking closer contact. One of his hands moved down, skimming over her arm, around to her back, pressing her even closer.

His arousal pressed against her lower belly and the flood of damp heat between her legs was almost embarrassing. She pressed her thighs together in a bid to stem the rising tide of desire but it was impossible.

But at that very moment Apollo pulled back. It was so sudden that Sasha went with him and he had to steady her, putting his hands on her arms. She opened her eyes, feeling dizzy. Stunned.

She was breathing as if she'd run a race. Her heart was hammering, and a hunger that was new and yet familiar at the same time pounded through her blood, demanding to be satisfied. She felt greedy. *Needy*.

It took a second for Apollo's face to come back into

focus and when she registered his harsh expression she pulled free of his hands, even though her legs still felt jittery.

He said, 'That shouldn't have happened. It was never part of this marriage deal. Go to bed, Sasha, it's late.'

He turned and left the room and Sasha stared after the empty space for a long minute. She felt too shell-shocked to even be irritated that he'd spoken to her like a child, as if she'd walked into *his* room and kissed *him*.

Her skin felt seared alive, her heart was still racing and her whole body was crying out for a fulfilment it knew but couldn't remember. Her breasts ached and she throbbed between her legs, and that was after just a kiss.

She moved on autopilot, closing the doors to the balcony, slipping out of the robe and under the covers of the bed. She eventually fell into a fitful sleep, with thoughts and dreams full of disjointed, disturbing images.

Apollo stood under the punishing spray of a cold shower for longer than he could almost bear. Eventually he got out and hitched a towel around his waist, catching his reflection in the mirror above the sink.

He looked pained. And he knew it wasn't from the cold shower. What the hell had he been thinking—going to Sasha's room? Kissing her? He hadn't been thinking. That was the problem.

It had taken every ounce of his restraint to pull back and not rip apart those flimsy garments, spreading her back on the bed so he could relive the night they'd shared in London. So that he could consummate this marriage.

This marriage was not about consummation or sleeping together. And while he hadn't wanted her it had been all too easy to forget he had ever wanted her.

You never forgot.

He scowled at his reflection.

But now the floodgates were open. He'd tasted Sasha again and she was as potent as she had been the first time.

He wanted his wife.

But she was the last thing he should want. Especially not when she had the ability to reopen old wounds with just a look from those huge eyes. What he needed was to excise Sasha from his life once and for all.

And for that to happen she needed to regain her memory. The sooner that happened and she reverted to her duplicitous nature, the sooner Apollo could get on with his life and forget she'd ever existed.

What he needed to do now was provide every opportunity to nudge her memory in the right direction.

Sasha was trying to avoid looking at Apollo across the breakfast table on the outdoor terrace. She was still raw after that kiss and gritty-eyed after a mostly sleepless night, broken by disturbing dreams she was afraid to analyse.

The impulse to look, though, was too strong and she glanced his way to see him lifting a small coffee cup to his mouth, his gaze on the paper in his hand. To her intense irritation he looked as if nothing had happened last night. He was as cool and fresh as if he'd enjoyed the sleep of a baby.

He was clean-shaven and the memory of his stubble against her jaw made heat rise up through her body. For a breathless panicky moment she wondered if she'd, in fact, dreamt that kiss, but then he put his paper down and looked at her and the jolt of electricity that went straight to her solar plexus told her that kiss at least hadn't been a dream. It was of little comfort.

'We're going to go to Krisakis for a few days.'

She forced her brain to function. 'Kris— Where?'

'It's the island I own. It's part of the Cyclades chain of islands. Santorini, Naxos, Paros...'

She'd forgotten that he owned an island.

'I'm constructing an eco-resort and I need to check progress and meet with some of the designers.'

'Have I been there before?'

He nodded. 'I took you there when we first came to Greece.'

Sasha tried to conjure up an image of what the island might be like but her mind stubbornly refused to provide anything.

Right at that moment, after the dreams she'd had last night, she relished the thought of a change of scenery. 'When do we leave?'

Apollo looked at his watch. 'In an hour. I've instructed Kara to pack some things for you.'

She felt prickly. 'I can pack my own bag.'

Apollo shrugged. 'As you wish. I need to make some calls before we go.' He got up and walked out of the room and Sasha's breath got stuck in her throat as she watched him go. He was wearing a polo shirt and faded jeans that lovingly hugged his buttocks and thighs.

Rhea bustled into the room and Sasha looked away quickly, mortified to have been caught ogling her husband, but also when she recalled what Apollo had told her about the party she'd hosted.

Taking drugs.

Her conscience wouldn't let her say nothing, though, and she caught Rhea's hand before she could clear the plates. The woman looked at her warily. Sasha said, 'I'm so sorry, Rhea…for what happened. For disrespecting you and this house.'

The older woman's expression softened. She patted Sasha's hand awkwardly. 'Is okay, Kyria Vasilis. Don't worry.'

She cleared the plates efficiently and left the room. Sasha still felt humiliated but a little lighter.

She stood up to leave the table and on an impulse walked down through the gardens. In spite of the sun, tentacles of those disturbing dreams from last night lingered, making her shiver a little.

The dreams had been shockingly erotic. She'd been on a bed, making love to Apollo. Their naked bodies entwined in the most intimate way possible. He'd held one of her hands over her head, capturing it, and his head had moved down, over her body, his mouth fastening over one nipple, feasting on her tender flesh. She could still feel it now, the delicious pulling, dragging sensation that had gone all the way down to between her legs where he'd pushed them apart with his thigh, opening her up to his body…

But then, abruptly, Sasha had realised that she was no longer in the body on the bed; she was standing apart, looking at him making love to another woman. Not her. But then the woman's face had been revealed and she'd smiled mockingly at Sasha and Sasha had realised that it *was* her. But it wasn't her.

She'd been separated from them by a glass wall. Able to see everything but not feel it. The woman on the bed was an imposter, pretending to be her. And Apollo didn't realise. She'd watched helplessly as he'd moved his powerful body between the woman's legs, how she'd opened up for him, and then the moment when he'd thrust deep inside.

The woman's legs were wrapped around Apollo's waist and the whole time she'd looked at Sasha and then her mocking smile had turned to nightmarish laughter and that's when Sasha had woken, sweating and trembling from the force of it, filled with a feeling of doom and betrayal so acrid that she'd felt nauseous.

Sasha shook her head to try and dislodge the images and that horrible feeling of betrayal. But it had felt so real. And it couldn't be, obviously.

She went back inside, but on her way to the bedroom she passed by her office. She could hear the deep tones of Apollo's voice through his own office door.

On an impulse she went into the white and fluffy room, still a bit bemused at the thought that she'd insisted on having an office. There was a computer on the desk and she sat down and tapped a key experimentally. It opened automatically in an internet browser.

Wondering how it hadn't occurred to her before, she put Apollo's name into the search engine. The first items to pop up were recent deals and headlines like *Vasilis and His Midas Touch Strike Again!*

Sasha skimmed a recent profile article done for a prominent British financial newspaper where it talked about Apollo's myriad achievements and rapid rise to stratospheric success. He was also one of the first construction titans to commit to working ethically. Every worker on one of his sites had proper healthcare and insurance and if accidents occurred, workers were rehabilitated and then redeployed either back to where they'd been or to a new area more suited to them.

Consequently, his workers were among the happiest in a normally fickle industry and by holding himself to a higher standard, he was forcing the industry to change around him. He was a trailblazer.

At the end of the article it said:

When asked about his recent marriage to Sasha Miller, Vasilis was curt, saying, 'My private life is off-limits.'

Sasha felt sick. Unsurprisingly he hadn't wanted to divulge the details of his marriage of inconvenience to an interviewer.

It only made Sasha want to know more about her own past—what had happened to her to make her behave like that? To trap a man into marriage? She went back into the history of the computer and saw some social media account tabs and clicked on them. But they'd all been logged out and she couldn't remember the passwords.

For one of the main social accounts she could see a small picture of herself, smiling widely against a glamorous-looking backdrop of a marina. She was wearing more make-up. Her skin was tanned…which must have been fake because she was naturally the colour of a milk bottle. She was holding up a glass of sparkling wine. It sparkled almost as much as the massive diamond on her ring finger. It eclipsed the much plainer gold wedding band. The rings that had gone missing in the accident.

She rubbed her finger absently, imagining them being torn off somehow, but there was no mark on her finger or bruising to indicate what had happened. Something about that niggled at the edges of her memory. A sense that she had seen them somewhere…but not on her hand. But the memory refused to be pinned down. Again.

Sasha touched the picture of her face with a finger, as if that could unlock the secrets of her past.

Nothing.

Nothing except a tiny shiver down her spine. Looking at her face like this reminded her of that dream, because it was like looking at another person.

She turned off the computer, eager to put that image of her face, and the dream, behind her. She saw a drawer in the desk and opened it, vaguely wondering if she might find some other clues to her past.

There was a thick manila envelope inside and she pulled it out. It had her name on it. For some reason, she felt superstitious about looking at the contents but the envelope was open and it was addressed to her.

She pulled out a thick sheaf of papers and read the words at the top of the first page: 'Application For Mutual Consent Divorce Proceedings Between Apollo Vasilis and Sasha Miller'.

It was dated a few days before the accident.

Sasha started to look through the pages, which weren't signed yet. They outlined the grounds for divorce. Irreconcilable differences. And non-consummation of the marriage.

They hadn't slept together.

So he really hadn't wanted her. But last night…he had. And he hadn't welcomed it.

'What are you doing?'

Sasha looked up to see Apollo standing in the doorway. She was too shocked to be embarrassed or feel like he'd caught her doing something illicit.

She held up the document. 'We were going to divorce?'

'We were always going to divorce.'

Sasha dropped the document back on the desk. 'But what about at first…when the baby…?' She trailed off, realising what she was saying.

He arched a brow, 'The baby that never existed?'

She flushed guiltily.

'When I believed you were pregnant we agreed to marry for a year, enough time to have the baby and then reassess the situation.'

Sasha frowned. 'What does that mean?'

'Custody.'

She struggled to understand. 'But presumably as the mother I would have had custody.'

Apollo shook his head. 'In the pre-nuptial agreement you signed away your right to full custody. You agreed to an arrangement where I would have full custody and I would set you up somewhere close enough for you to see the child on a regular basis.'

Sasha stood up. She shook her head. 'I can't believe I would have signed away full rights to my own baby.'

Apollo's lip curled. 'Don't forget there *was* no baby.

I should have guessed something was amiss when you agreed so quickly to that, and when you were more interested in the alimony you would receive in the event of a divorce.'

Sasha remembered what he'd told her last night about how she'd tried to seduce him. To try and get pregnant. She felt sick. And even sicker when she thought of how he'd found her in such a debauched state. Taking drugs.

She forced herself to look at him. 'That's when you initiated the divorce, after the party, when you knew I wasn't pregnant.'

He nodded.

'Why didn't you just throw me out, once you knew?' She would have thrown her out. She felt angry at *herself.*

'I considered it. I wanted to. I never wanted to see you again. You disgusted me.'

Sasha felt every word like a little sharp knife to her heart. 'So why didn't you?'

'Because we are married. I couldn't trust you. I didn't know what you would do. You could have gone to the papers with some sob story and I have a reputation to maintain. The last thing I needed was adverse press attention.'

'And then I had the accident.'

He nodded. 'A few days later, you took one of the cars and disappeared for hours. When you hadn't returned by dinner-time, Rhea called me and a search was started. You eventually appeared by the side of a road not far from here, further up into the hills.'

Sasha felt cold. 'This marriage never had a chance.'

Apollo faltered for a moment when he thought of that first night he'd met Sasha. How easily she'd caught him with her fresh-faced beauty. How novel it had been to meet someone unjaded. Open. Joyful. But it hadn't been real. He forced the memory out. 'No.'

Sasha looked bewildered. 'Why did you agree to marry me at all? Why did you believe me?'

Feeling almost defensive now, he said, 'You had a note from a doctor confirming the pregnancy. And I consulted my legal team. We came to the conclusion that once you agreed to sign a pre-nuptial agreement, marrying you would offer me the best chance of custody and securing my child's future. There was a clause to say that if anything happened to the pregnancy or if the baby proved not to be mine after a DNA test, you would get nothing. Obviously you'd decided that the risk of marriage was worth it, even though you weren't pregnant. Hence your attempts to try and seduce me once we were married. Attempts that didn't work.'

Sasha winced at that. 'Why did you bring me back here after the accident? Why not just kick me out of your life for good now that you can?'

Why not indeed? mocked a little voice in Apollo's head. He could have done exactly that. He could have taken advantage of her amnesia to get her to sign the divorce papers and set her up in an apartment in Athens with a small allowance and a nurse to attend to her needs until the divorce was through.

But no matter how much he'd hated her for what she'd done, the way she'd looked after the accident—so pale and defenceless on that hospital bed—it had caught at him. And then she'd woken up and looked at him and it had been as if the previous months had fallen away and all he could remember was that night they'd met.

Her memory loss had only complicated things further. Changing her. Reminding him of that first impression she'd made. Re-igniting his desire.

He said now, 'I'm not letting you go anywhere until we sign the divorce papers. I don't trust that you won't do something to exploit the power you have as my wife.'

He went on, 'I don't know why you took the car on the day you disappeared or where you went to…and until you regain your memory and you can tell me, you won't be going anywhere. For all I know, you took your wedding rings off because you have a lover, perhaps someone you were hoping to turn to because I hadn't fallen under your spell.'

A memory of that kiss last night blasted into Apollo's head, mocking him. He was under her spell again whether he liked it or not.

Sasha held up the sheaf of papers. She was pale. They were trembling lightly in her hand and that evidence of her emotions caught at him, making him feel an urge to protect her. He rejected it.

She said, 'So why don't we just sign the papers now and be done with it?'

To his disgust, his immediate emotion wasn't one of relief that she was showing a willingness to put all this behind them and get out of his life. It was something much more ambiguous and disturbing. Reluctance to let her go.

He said, 'It's the weekend, my offices won't be open. And next Monday is a national holiday. In any case I've made plans to go and inspect the site on Krisakis. We will stick to this arrangement and sign the papers when we return to Athens in a week. We'll be out of each other's lives within a month. And perhaps Krisakis will help jog your memory.'

Sasha felt winded. 'Once we sign the papers, it can happen that quickly?' The thought of never seeing Apollo again made her feel panicky. She told herself it was because he was the only familiar thing in her life, not because he'd come to mean anything to her. Clearly there had been little love lost between them.

Apollo's mouth firmed. 'Yes, it can happen that quickly. But obviously if your memory still hasn't returned by then, I'll make sure you're set up in a situation and place that feels secure and safe for you.'

Sasha wanted to curl inwards. The thought of Apollo pitying her enough to have to keep an eye on her after their marriage was over was a whole new level of humiliation.

'I'm sure that won't be necessary, but thank you.'

CHAPTER SIX

A COUPLE OF hours later, Apollo's words still reverberated in Sasha's head.

'I'll make sure you're set up in a situation and place that feels secure and safe for you.'

The perks of a rich man. Able to dissolve marriages and set up inconvenient ex-wives with a minimum of fuss.

The fact that the imminent dissolution of a marriage she'd apparently engineered into being through lies and deceit wasn't filling her with a sense of relief, only brought about more confusion.

She could remember being stunned by Apollo's interest in her when they'd first met. Intimidated but excited too. How had she gone from that to wanting to deceive him so heinously?

With a sigh, she let the landscape beneath her distract her from circling thoughts that were going nowhere and not helping.

They were in a helicopter, flying over the Aegean, and she looked down in awe at boats and islands that looked like toys beneath them.

When she'd seen the sleek black machine at the private airfield, she'd balked. Apollo had looked at her. 'You flew in this when I took you to the island the first time. You loved it.'

'Did I? Sasha had asked doubtfully. For the whole journey, in spite of her tortured thoughts and the beauty below them, her heart had been in her throat. And even more now as they started descending over an island and the helicopter tipped perilously to the left.

This must be Krisakis. Sasha forced down the fluttering panic and took in the rocky coastline where pockets of brightly coloured flowers flourished along the cliffs. The sea lapped against rocks and then they rounded a headland and an empty white sand beach appeared, like something on a postcard.

Sasha could see steps cut into the rocks, leading up to lush grounds and then up further to a white modern building—a series of buildings laid out like interconnecting cubes. Sunlight glinted off acres of glass. An infinity pool with sun loungers had never looked so inviting.

Apollo was saying into her headset, 'This is the villa, the first thing I built here. The island was hit by an earthquake about half a century ago, leaving only a small population behind. With the development I'm building on the other side of the island, it's becoming a thriving community again. People who were born here but who had to leave have returned to live out their last days, bringing their sons and daughters with them to make new lives.'

Sasha couldn't help thinking it was ironic for a man who'd professed little interest in having a family to be invested in bringing them together like this.

The helicopter was landing now on a helipad a little distance from the villa. When the pilot had touched down, Apollo got out. He opened Sasha's door and helped her out. Her legs felt like rubber and Apollo's hand tightened on hers. 'Okay?'

She locked her knees to stop them wobbling. 'Yes, fine.' She took her hand back.

Apollo stepped aside to talk to the pilot for a moment and then once the bags were unloaded he led her over to a safe spot while the helicopter lifted back up into the air before tilting to the right and heading off into the azure-blue sky.

Sasha put the sun hat she'd carried on her head, glad of Kara's thoughtfulness. Which was even more thoughtful now considering what she'd put them through. Sasha heard a faint sound and turned around to see what looked like a golf cart bouncing across the grounds towards them.

Apollo waved at the person driving who waved back enthusiastically. He said, 'That's Spiro—he's the son of my housekeeper here, helping out before he goes back to college.'

The young man jumped out when he'd come to a stop beside him, a big grin directed at Apollo as he took the bags, stowing them in the back.

Sasha couldn't help smiling at his cheerful effervescence but when he looked at her his smile faltered. Sasha's insides plummeted. Not again. Had she been rude to him too? The young man's eyes grew round and he said something to Apollo, who said something sharp back.

He held out his hand. 'Kyria Vasilis, nice to meet you again.'

Sasha forced a smile and took his hand, mentally apologising for whatever she'd done.

By the time they reached the stunning villa, she was preparing herself for the same reaction as she'd got from Kara and Rhea when she'd returned to the villa in Athens. Sure enough, Spiro's mother, Olympia, looked wary but kindly. Maybe Sasha hadn't behaved too badly on the island. After all, it didn't seem as if there was much in the way of distraction.

Apollo said something to his housekeeper and then turned to Sasha. 'Olympia will show you around, and take you to your room. I'll join you after I've made a couple of calls.'

Sasha took in the bright white spaces and minimalist furnishings as she followed the matronly woman through the villa. It oozed modernity and serenity. A contrast to the more traditional villa in Athens. Sasha liked it. She liked the starkness. The lack of fussiness. Its simplicity soothed some of her ragged edges.

Olympia led her down a long corridor and opened a door, standing back. She smiled. 'Your room, Kyria Vasilis.'

Sasha tried not to be self-conscious about the fact that she obviously had a separate room here too. She forced a polite smile, which promptly slid off her face as she walked into the vast room. Actually, it was a suite of rooms. They flowed into each other, no doors between them.

There was a vast bed with a four-poster frame and muslin drapes pulled back. The bathroom had two types of shower, one outdoor and one indoor, and a bath that was more like a private lap pool.

There was a dressing room and then a lounge, with its own soft comfy couch and media centre, with TV and a sound system. Perhaps, Sasha thought with an edge of hysteria, he was going to lock her in here, and keep her prisoner.

But then Olympia was signalling for her attention and Sasha followed her to the huge windows that were actually sliding doors leading outside to a private terrace, with sunbed and umbrella.

Olympia said in halting English, 'We will unpack your things while you take tea on the terrace. Follow me, please.'

Sasha smiled, silently trying to communicate her apologies for however she'd behaved before. Olympia led her back through the villa to the main living area again and out to a shaded terrace where a table was laid out with fruit and small cakes and pastries. Tea and coffee were in two pots, or there was sparkling water.

Everything was hushed and very exclusive. Sasha poured herself some tea and could feel herself loosening in spite of herself, as if she couldn't *not*, against this breath-taking backdrop. All she could see in the distance was the blue of the sparkling Aegean and the hazy outline of other islands on the horizon.

She didn't think she'd ever been anywhere so deeply peaceful. But apparently she had been here before, so why wasn't there even a tiny piece of recognition? Sasha fought off the feeling of frustration. She had to trust that her memory would come back to her sooner or later. It had to. And yet…with that assertion came a little shiver of foreboding.

Apollo stood in the shadows for a moment, watching Sasha where she sat on the terrace. She was wearing pale blue culottes and the white sleeveless shirt tied at the waist. She consistently seemed to choose the very opposite of what she would have gone for before.

He'd never imagined a woman in this place. There was something about the peace and tranquillity of this island that had always soothed a raw part of him and it had felt too personal to share, apart from with the islanders, of course.

He'd never brought a lover here, and he hadn't counted Sasha as a lover when he'd brought her here nearly three months ago. It had been a strategic decision.

But much as he hated to admit it, this time was very different from that first visit. She looked good here now. As if she belonged. In spite of that pale colouring. Her hair was down and it blew gently in the breeze, the rose-gold strands wavy and untamed. He could almost see her freckles from here. Freckles she'd always seemed obsessed with covering up, apart from that first couple of nights they'd met. He could still remember being fascinated by them on her naked body, the little clusters in secret spots. She'd been embarrassed…until he'd distracted her.

Heat gathered in his groin, making his muscles tight. Hard. He cursed. It was as if she'd had a personality change. He'd seen a film once about a man who had been ruthless and uncaring and who'd lost his memory

in a shooting, and how, afterwards, his whole personality had changed.

Could it be something like that? Sasha looked trou-
bled now, as if she was thinking the same thing as he
was. He couldn't imagine what it must be like to know...
nothing of yourself. A curious small ache formed in
Apollo's chest. For a moment, he felt a sense of...pity?
Concern?

She looked at him then, as if sensing him, and Apollo
shoved down the fleeting moment of whatever it was. It
wasn't welcome. He came out onto the terrace, shades
hiding his eyes from the sun. And her.

'How do you like the villa?' he asked, sitting down.

Sasha sat up. 'It's beautiful, stunning. I feel like I've
never seen anything like it, but apparently I have. And
this island...it's so...'

Apollo took a sip of coffee, 'Boring?' he supplied.

She shook her head, looking away. 'No, not at all,
it's so peaceful.' Apollo went still, looking at her suspiciously. Her voice was husky, as if she was genuinely moved.

She glanced at him then, her mouth taut. 'Don't tell
me, I didn't like it the first time around?'

He shook his head, almost feeling slightly guilty
now. 'No. You looked around and asked when we were
leaving. You stayed one night.'

'Why did you bring me here the first time?'

Apollo's conscience pricked. He ignored it. 'I thought
it would be somewhere you'd enjoy relaxing.'

'You mean, somewhere you could hide me away?
Your inconvenient wife?'

Sasha stood up suddenly, shocked at how incensed

she was. 'What about now? Is this where you're planning on hiding me away until the divorce comes
through?'

She went to walk off the terrace, her sense of peace
shattered, but Apollo stood up and caught her hand.
Electricity sizzled up her arm, and she bit her lip against
the sensation.

'*No.*' And then, grudgingly, 'Maybe, the first time.
I wasn't really thinking. I was still in shock that you
were pregnant and how that was going to affect my life.'

Sasha looked at him, forgetting for a moment that she
hadn't been pregnant. 'What about my life?'

She flushed and pulled her hand free, walking a few
feet away. This was all so messed up.

Out of the corner of her eye she could see Apollo run
a hand through his hair. 'Look,' he said, 'we're here for
a few days. I've got some business to attend to with the
resort they're building and I've been invited to an opening of another resort on Santorini, not far from here,
later this week. You're still recuperating, so take this
time to rest and it might help your memory.'

Sasha looked at Apollo. She couldn't see his eyes
behind his shades. Just the hard line of his jaw. That
decadent mouth. The width of his shoulders and the
breadth of his chest. Her heart beat faster. 'You're not
leaving me here, then?'

Apollo's jaw clenched as if her words had affected
him. 'I'm not a gaoler, Sasha. When we leave here,
we'll sign divorce papers and we'll be able to move on
with our lives.'

'*Move on with our lives.*'

Whether her memory was back or not. Suddenly

the thought of going back into a world she couldn't remember was beyond intimidating. At that moment she'd never felt so alone.

Sasha looked vulnerable to Apollo, with a tiny frown between her eyes. Pale face. Very slight and slender. Yet he could remember the innate strength of her body as she'd taken him in so deeply he'd seen stars. The press of her breasts against his chest, nipples like bullets.

He took a deep breath, fought for control. He heard himself saying the words before he'd really articulated them to himself. 'I told you, Sasha, I'll make sure you're in a safe and secure environment. You won't be expected to navigate a world you don't remember if your memory hasn't yet returned.'

Something flashed in her eyes, an emotion Apollo couldn't decipher. 'Thank you. I appreciate that…after everything…'

She looked away from Apollo and gestured with a hand. 'This is paradise. Thank you for bringing me here.'

Her expression had turned indecipherable. Her voice and tone as if she were a guest. For a moment Apollo had to battle the urge to take her arms and force her to look at him, force her to reveal the emotion she'd just hidden from him.

Disgust at himself made him say something curt about checking work emails and he strode off the terrace, every cell in his body crying out for another taste of the woman who had torn his life asunder.

During the days following their arrival on Krisakis, Sasha found that with the peace and tranquillity she was finally feeling totally recuperated. And also it gave her mind time to settle too, and absorb all the revelations. The fake pregnancy, the divorce. Her behaviour.

Questions kept niggling at her—what had happened between them when she'd met Apollo and had then pretended to be pregnant? Why would she have done such a thing?

She still couldn't remember sleeping with Apollo. But she suspected she was remembering in her dreams, which were becoming more and more vivid and erotic. Last night she'd dreamt of him again.

They'd both been naked and he'd been kneeling between her legs, pushing them apart. She'd felt gauche, self-conscious, but all of that had dissolved in a pool of electric heat when he'd lowered his head and pressed kisses up the inside of one thigh.

She'd been shaking, trembling with need. Body dewed with a fine sheen of perspiration. And then he'd hooked her legs over his shoulders and he'd put his mouth to her *right there*, at the centre of her being. His tongue and mouth had done such things to her—she blushed in the late afternoon heat just thinking about how his tongue had felt, thrusting inside her.

She'd woken up, her nightshirt clinging to her damp body, heart racing, inner muscles clamping around a phantom erection. Mortified, she'd dived into the shower in a bid to bring herself back to reality.

She took a deep shuddering breath and forced her mind away from disturbing dreams. She didn't know what was worse—inhabiting her body in the dream or watching herself making love to Apollo from a distance. Both were equally disturbing.

She liked this time of the day best, late in the afternoon, when the intense heat of the sun had died down and it was more bearable. She'd found books on the well-stocked shelves of the informal living room and was reading a very unchallenging thriller. What did they call them? A cosy mystery? It was perfect for her exhausted and frayed brain.

She woke late most days, and wondered if she'd always had a habit of sleeping in. She was too scared to ask Apollo when he appeared every evening for their dinners on the terrace for fear of what he'd say.

He'd been gone every day from early, much like he had in Athens—presumably tending to business on the other side of the island.

They were both careful to stick to neutral topics at dinner, but Sasha couldn't ignore the growing pull she felt towards him. The throbbing undercurrent of electricity that sprang to life as soon as he came near her.

As if on cue, the small hairs stood up on the back of her neck and she heard a movement and looked around to see Apollo walking out to where she sat on a sun lounger near the pool, under an umbrella.

She was glad of the light covering of a kaftan over her swimsuit—the only one she seemed to own—as her body reacted to seeing him. And the memory of that dream. His clothes didn't help to calm her pulse. He was wearing board shorts and a polo shirt that showcased the bulging biceps of his arms and the hard pectorals of his chest. She saw dark hair curling just above the top open button.

As he came closer she said quickly, 'I'm wearing sunscreen. Factor fifty.'

Was that the slightest twitch at the corner of his mouth? He sat down on the lounger beside her and Olympia appeared with a tray holding two tall glasses of homemade iced lemonade.

He smiled at Olympia. *'Efharisto.'*

The woman smiled back, looking ridiculously pleased with herself. Sasha couldn't blame her.

Sasha watched as his Adam's apple moved up and down as he took a gulp of the drink. Even that movement was sexy. She took such a quick gulp of her own drink to calm her ragged nerves that she coughed and spluttered. Immediately he was beside her, a hand on her back. 'Are you okay?'

Eyes watering, Sasha could only gasp and try to breathe but all she was aware of was his hand on her back and the tight musculature of his dark naked thigh near hers.

When she could, she got out, 'I'm fine…fine.'

Thankfully he moved back to his lounger. He'd pushed his glasses up on his head and Sasha spotted something in his hair. Feeling shy, she pointed to his head. He ruffled his hair, dislodging fine dust. He grimaced. 'I need to take a shower, it's dust from the site.'

'Are you actually working on the site, too?'

'Just a little here and there. I like to be hands on.'

That only made Sasha think of how it had felt to have his hands on her thighs, pushing them apart, in the dream. Without even thinking about what she was saying, she asked, 'Could I come and see it?'

He lifted his brows in surprise. 'You want to see a construction site?'

She felt self-conscious now. 'If it's not too much trouble?'

His expression was bemused. 'Sure, if you want. I can take you with me over the next couple of days.'

Sasha smiled tentatively. 'I'd like to, as long as I won't be in your way.'

For a second something shimmered between them, a lightness. Then Apollo stood up. 'I'm going to go for a swim. Cool off.'

He downed the rest of his drink and put his glass down. Before he left he said, 'I'll see you at dinner? Unless you want to join me for a swim. I'm going to go down to the sea.'

The thought of swimming in the sea was immediately appealing but then something occurred to Sasha. 'I don't even know if I *can* swim.'

'Have you been in the water yet?

She shook her head. It had looked inviting but something had held her back. A wariness.

Apollo waited a beat and then he said, 'Okay, wait here, I'll be back in a minute.'

Sasha wasn't sure what he meant by that but it was apparent when he returned in a few minutes, carrying a towel and wearing nothing but short swim shorts. She stopped breathing. They were moulded to his hips and thighs. Their black colour only made his skin seem even darker. He was six feet plus of hard, honed male, not an ounce of spare flesh. He threw the towel down on the lounger and held out a hand.

Sasha averted her gaze from acres of honed olive-skinned flesh and looked at his hand suspiciously. 'What's going on?'

'We're going to see if you can swim.'

Suddenly reluctant, she said, 'I don't know if I want to know.'

'We'll go into the pool at the shallow end. You won't drown, I promise.'

Reluctantly, she stood up and lifted up the kaftan, very aware of the flesh-coloured swimsuit underneath. She avoided Apollo's eye, self-conscious and more nervous than she liked to admit.

He was still holding out his hand and after a moment's hesitation she took it, feeling his long fingers close around hers. His touch immediately soothed the nerves that had sprung from nowhere.

She followed him over to the steps that led down into the infinity pool. He tugged her along gently and she stepped in, the water a cold shock against her sun-heated skin.

He led her down until the water reached the tops of her thighs.

'Take my hands, keep coming.'

Sasha looked at Apollo. She took a breath and put her hands in his. He kept pulling her in until the water lapped up around her chest. She sucked in a breath.

'Now, come onto your front and just let me pull you along.'

Sasha shook her head, suddenly scared. 'I'll sink.'

'You won't. I'll be holding you. Your body is buoyant in the water. Trust me.'

Something about his voice was so…reassuring. So implacable. Sasha literally had no choice but to do as he said. She leant forward, putting her chest in the water, and suddenly her feet were off the bottom and she was floating and being pulled along, on the surface of the water, by Apollo.

When she realised she was no longer touching the bottom she panicked, her fingers tightening around his. 'Don't let me go.'

'I won't. Just keep looking at me and kick your legs.'

She kept her eyes on his, and did as he asked, tentatively kicking her legs. She could feel herself being propelled forward. Apollo leant back. 'Keep going, that's it.'

They went around and around the pool while Sasha got used to the sensation of being in the water, kicking her legs. It moved like silk along her body. No longer cold. Pleasantly warm.

After a while, Apollo stopped in the middle of the pool. He said, 'I'm going to let your hands go now. But I'll be right here. Just keep kicking your legs and use your hands and arms like this to move through the water.'

He mimed doing the doggy paddle.

Before she could protest, or say anything, Apollo was letting go and moving backwards, away from her. Sheer instinct kicked in and Sasha's arms moved of their own volition in a sloppy kind of movement, along with her legs. It was several seconds before she realised that she was following Apollo as he trod water on his back, moving away from her all the time.

She stopped and promptly started to sink once she'd stopped using her arms and legs. She couldn't touch the bottom here and her head went under the water. Immediately she felt strong hands under her arms, hauling her up before she could start panicking. She broke the surface, spluttering and coughing. 'You tricked me!'

He held her securely as her heart beat frantically. 'You were swimming, Sasha, and you didn't even notice.'

Her legs were scissoring back and forth as she took that in. Impulsively she said, 'Let me go again, I want to check something.'

'Are you sure?'

She nodded. He let her go and she moved her arms and legs frantically. Euphoria gripped her. 'I'm not sinking!' She had to be making the most graceless fool of herself but she was elated with this tiny success.

Then Apollo smiled. And suddenly Sasha's body stopped functioning and she slipped beneath the surface again.

When Apollo pulled her up this time she was choking with embarrassment, not water. The effect of his smile had almost drowned her. He was frowning now. 'Okay?'

She nodded, just then realising that his hands were under her arms, brushing the sides of her breasts. The corded muscles of his arms were like steel under her palms.

They were very close. So close that Sasha could see the darker flecks of green in Apollo's eyes. The start of fresh stubble on his jaw. Droplets of water clung to his skin. The dark curling hair lightly dusted his chest.

The air between them became charged. And she watched as his gaze seemed to fixate on her mouth and then drop, colour flaring across his cheeks. He muttered one word: *'Theos.'*

Sasha looked down too, and saw what he was looking at. The swimsuit had turned translucent in the water and she could see the pink buds of her nipples and the pebbled areolae as clearly as if she were naked.

Her entire body flooded with heat and she became all too aware of Apollo's naked flesh. All she'd have to do was bend her head forward and press her mouth to his chest. She wanted to taste his skin.

He muttered something else in Greek and started to tug Sasha back towards the steps. Her body felt like jelly. She wasn't sure if she could ever stand again. Apollo still had his hands under her arms and he moved her so that she was sitting on the steps leading down into the water.

He loomed over her, hands either side of her body. She was half in, half out of the water.

'What are you doing to me, witch? All I can think about is having you again.'

Sasha struggled to make her brain work but it wouldn't form coherent thoughts. All she could see was him and that sculpted mouth. She wanted it on hers. She was jealous of her body because *it* knew how it had felt to make love to him. But she didn't.

'Please, Apollo.'

'What is it, little flame? What do you want?'

Little flame.

It echoed in her head. He'd called her that before. He'd been lying beside her on a bed and her hair had been in his hand and he'd said, 'It's like a living flame…'

She forced her mouth to work. 'You… I want you.'

He brought a hand to her shoulder and with excruci-

ating slowness pulled the strap of her swimsuit down.
Anticipation prickled across her skin in goosebumps.

He dragged down the top of the swimsuit, baring her
breast. He looked at it for a long moment before cupping it in his hand, a thumb rubbing her nipple, making her gasp.

And then he bent his head and his mouth surrounded
her nipple in hot, wet heat. The same kind of heat she
could feel between her legs. She tried to push them together to stem the tide, but Apollo was between them,
his mouth on her breast and his hand moving down to
cup her bottom, hitching her against him.

Apollo had gone past the point of restraint. Past the
point of his last shred of control. He rolled the taut
bud of Sasha's nipple in his mouth, feeling it swell and
harden even more against his tongue. He nipped at her
flesh gently with his teeth and then laved her with his
tongue again.

Her body was quivering against him, like a taut bow-
string. He dragged the rest of her swimsuit down and
lavished attention on her other breast. When he pulled
back both peaks were pink and wet. She was lying back,
panting, her hair spreading in long skeins of red-gold
in the water. She was like a sea nymph. *A siren.* Lur-
ing him to his downfall. But right now he didn't care
about any of that.

He was throbbing with need—seeking a fulfilment
he'd thought couldn't possibly be as earth-shattering as
he remembered. But tasting her skin, feeling her shudder against him in response, he knew it hadn't been a
one-off.

He looked down into unfocused blue eyes. Dark with

desire. Bee-stung lips. A distant sane part of his mind couldn't believe he was capitulating like this but he was only human and he couldn't resist...

'I want you, Sasha.'

Sasha looked up at Apollo. He eclipsed the sun and the sky. She'd never felt so attuned to someone else. The words he spoke resonated through her entire body.

'I want you too...'

His gaze dropped down over her body and he pulled her swimsuit up over her breasts, the wet material chafing against her sensitive breasts. She shivered slightly and he looked at her. 'Okay?'

She nodded, hands gripping his arms. 'Please... Apollo.' She wasn't even sure what she was asking for, just knew that she needed to be with this man in the most elemental way. Now.

He muttered something in Greek and gathered her into his arms, standing up from the water. But just as he was about to walk towards the villa he stopped.

Sasha was about to ask, *What is it?* when she heard the noise. The distinct *thwack-thwack* of a helicopter's blades. Apollo tensed. He cursed. Then Sasha saw it— the black spider shape of the machine, coming closer to the island.

Apollo walked over to the loungers, carrying her as easily as if she weighed no more than a bag of sugar. He put her down on her feet and she had to lock her knees to keep upright. He handed her the kaftan and said, 'Put this on.'

The sensual desperation that had been so urgent between them only moments ago now seemed like a mirage. Apollo looked grim. Sasha pulled on the kaftan, feeling the need to hide herself a little. Especially when she thought of how needy she'd just felt.

Still felt.

'What is it?'

Apollo looked at her and ran a hand through his hair. 'I forgot. The party in Santorini tonight. I arranged with the pilot to transport us to the party and back later.'

'Us?'

'Yes.' There was a burning intensity in his dark green gaze that made Sasha shiver all over again. He reached out and tipped up her chin with a finger, just as the whining roar of the helicopter's blades died down in the distance.

'You're coming with me. I know what you did and I can never forgive you for that, but, God help me, I want you, *agapi mou*. We will finish what we just started.'

Sasha jerked her chin free, his arrogant words setting something alight inside her. 'Maybe I don't want to finish what we started. Why would I allow someone who doesn't even like me to make love to me?'

She realised she was feeling hurt. And that was humiliating.

Apollo was shaking his head. 'This goes way beyond *like*. This is pure chemistry and I don't think either one of us is strong enough to resist it.'

Sasha felt conflicted. Torn between wanting to throw caution to the wind and acquiesce to his arrogant assertion that they would finish this, and wanting to pull back and defend herself against his mistrust.

There was a sound and Sasha tore her gaze from his to see Olympia appear. The woman said something in

Greek to Apollo. He answered and then said to Sasha, 'Go with Olympia, she will help you to get ready.'

After a moment when she felt ridiculously like a petulant teenager wanting to stamp her foot, Sasha followed the woman back into the villa. Who was she kidding? Apollo was right. There was a force of nature between them powerful enough to make her feel awed.

She felt an awful sense of futility because she knew that even in spite of Apollo's mistrust and all that had happened, if he so much as touched her again, she wouldn't have the strength or will to deny him. *Or herself.*

CHAPTER SEVEN

APOLLO WAS WAITING for Sasha outside the villa, by the golf buggy. She wasn't late but his skin prickled all over. He'd gone beyond the point of no return earlier, and there was no way now that he could, or would, deny himself where Sasha was concerned.

However inconvenient it was, he wanted her and he would have her until she was burnt out of his system once and for all.

He heard a noise behind him and turned around but nothing could have prepared him for the vision searing itself onto his retinas.

It was a deceptively simple dress. Off-white, sleeveless, it dipped in a V between her breasts, with narrow gold straps criss-crossing across her bodice, highlighting her high firm breasts and narrow torso.

It fell from her waist in soft billowing folds to the floor. Her hair was caught up in a bun, a plain gold band holding it back from her face.

She looked like a Greek goddess. Albeit with red hair, and pale skin and freckles. She made him think of the myth of Helen of Troy. Achilles, his brother, had used to love that story.

She indicated the dress. 'Kara packed it, is it okay?'

Apollo looked at her suspiciously. She was genuinely uncertain. Did she really have no idea how stunning she was?

'You look beautiful.'

Her face went pink. 'I... Thank you.'

Apollo desperately wanted to resist this act of innocence. It *had* to be an act. But his gut told him it wasn't. No one could keep up an act like this without slipping.

He couldn't stop imagining peeling that dress off her later, revealing her breasts to his gaze. Pulling up the layers of chiffon to find the centre of her body where she would be hot and— *Enough*.

The sooner he'd had his fill of her, the better. As soon as this crazy heat dissipated between them he'd move her into an apartment in Athens for the duration of the time it took for the divorce to be finalised. He would be done with her.

They reached the resort just as the sun was dropping in the sky. The was a palpable air of anticipation among the crowd assembled, the women tanned and lithe and beautiful, and the men in their suits.

She still hadn't fully regained her breath from the view as they'd descended over Santorini with its distinctive white and blue buildings perched precariously on cliffs over the caldera—an underwater crater—which had been formed in a volcanic eruption.

Not to mention the sheer magnificence of Apollo in a dark bespoke suit and white shirt. It was open at the neck, and he oozed casual masculine elegance and a raw sex appeal that reminded her of how needy she'd felt earlier, at the pool.

A hostess greeted them and handed them glasses of champagne. 'Welcome, you're just in time to view the stunning sunset. Please, make yourselves comfortable.'

The delicate layers of chiffon in her dress whispered around Sasha's legs. She'd never felt like a princess before, but she felt like one now. Kara had somehow unearthed this dress from all the more revealing ones in Sasha's wardrobe in Athens and for once she felt as if she was in something she might have chosen for herself.

Which was a weird thought to have...who else could have chosen her clothes?

Apollo took her elbow at that moment and led her over to where a terrace jutted out over the cliff edge, nothing but a stone wall between them and certain death. Sasha took a sip of champagne to try and alleviate the nerves jumping in her belly.

She pointed to a nearby town. 'That's Oia?

'Yes. That's where everyone goes to watch the sunset...give it a few minutes, you'll see why.'

They stood in companionable silence as more and more of the guests started to join them along the terrace wall. The sun was dipping lower now, casting out an orange and pink glow into the vast sky.

Sasha could see how the sun was bathing Oia in a warm golden glow, making the white buildings look even whiter. And then the sun touched the horizon and the world was bathed in pink and orange and apricot. It seemed to fill the entire sky and Sasha could see thousands of flashes coming from cameras and phones in Oia.

'It's stunning,' she breathed, deeply touched by the

natural phenomenon. And then just as quickly the sun was gone, leaving behind the faintest of pink trails and a bluish gloaming. Lights started to come on in Oia, like fairy lights in a string.

Reluctantly Sasha left the view behind to follow Apollo as they were led around the resort on a private tour. It was beautiful. Idyllic. A place for romance and decadence.

When they were seated at a series of long trestle tables, beautifully laid out with silverware and wildflower centrepieces, Apollo asked her, 'So, what do you think?'

Sasha swallowed a piece of delicious herb-infused fish. 'You want my opinion? But I don't know anything about this kind of thing.'

He shrugged. 'Still…indulge me.'

She took a drink of water and wiped her mouth with a napkin, hiding how pleased she was that Apollo cared for her opinion. 'I think this is beautiful, luxurious. I know I haven't seen your resort yet but I don't have to, to know that it'll be far quieter than here. Krisakis isn't overrun with tourists. How long would it take to get to there from here by boat?'

Apollo shrugged again. 'About two hours.'

'Krisakis could become a very exclusive day trip or couple of days' trip from here when it gets too frenetic. From what I've seen, you might not have the stunning geology of the caldera but you have peace and solitude and that counts for a lot.'

Apollo tipped his head to one side and regarded her. 'Not a bad assessment and you're right about Santorini being overrun.'

Again, Sasha was embarrassed by how Apollo's regard for her opinion made her feel. Was she so starved for praise?

When the dinner was over, the guests were led down to another level where a DJ was playing salsa music. The happy compelling beat resonated in Sasha's body. It was infectious.

Apollo pulled out a chair for her at a small table near where couples were already dancing, moving sinuously to the beat. He got her a glass of champagne. 'Excuse me for a second? There's someone I see that I need to speak to.'

Sasha feigned a nonchalance she wasn't feeling to be left on her own. 'Sure.'

She watched him walk away through the crowd, lithe and graceful, and saw how everyone he passed turn to look. Women especially. Her insides tightened low down when she thought of what he'd said. *We will finish what we just started.* He couldn't possibly want her that much. Could he?

A sense of insecurity assailed her. This party was peopled by some of the most stunning-looking women Sasha had ever seen. Women that Apollo couldn't fail to notice. What had happened earlier had been an anomaly. A heated moment.

She looked away from his departing figure and took a sip of her drink in a bid to try and pretend she was part of the wealthy crowd around her. The bubbles fizzed down her throat. That sensation, together with the uplifting music, the warm air, the scents, the vast starry sky, all conspired to make her forget her insecurity, and feel lighter than she'd done in days. Weeks.

Her toe tapped to the music.

'Come on! You look like you want to dance.'

Sasha looked up to see a young man holding out a hand. He was with another couple, and they were dancing energetically to the music. She immediately drew back, smiling, 'No, no, I'm just a spectator.'

'Don't be silly!' Before Sasha could object the man had taken her hand and was pulling her up from her seat. She spluttered a surprised laugh and put down her glass, with no choice but to give in to his exuberant invitation.

Apollo frowned as he looked over the heads of the people he was talking to. Sasha wasn't sitting at the table. Then a flash of billowing white caught his peripheral vision and his breath stopped in his throat.

Sasha was dancing—inexpertly, it had to be admitted—but all the more compelling for that because she was clearly enjoying her efforts, head back, laughing.

She was dancing with a young man who was swinging her round with more enthusiasm than skill. She stood out effortlessly and he could see people stop to look, smiling in spite of themselves at her sheer happiness.

A sense of possessiveness he'd never experienced before rose up before he could deny it.

He was jealous.

And then another emotion, less identifiable, made Apollo's chest go tight. He remembered she'd smiled like this when they'd first met. She'd captivated him like she was now captivating everyone here. And that's how she'd sneaked under his guard, by defusing a set of defences he hadn't even been aware of. A need to be controlled and on guard at all times for fear that the world would pull the rug out from under his feet at the next moment, like it had each time he'd lost a family member.

He'd believed his defences were impenetrable, vowing not to allow anyone to get too close, and certainly never entertaining thoughts of family—until she'd appeared and wreaked havoc.

You let her wreak havoc.

She'd exposed a weakness in him, a need for something he'd denied himself…and she was doing it again.

Yet even now, with this knowledge, he knew he wouldn't be able to resist her. A spurt of rebelliousness rose up from his gut. Why should he? She owed him…

Even before her dancing companion had noticed him and stopped and turned pale, Sasha was aware of Apollo's presence a nanosecond beforehand.

He snaked an arm around her waist and in the lull between one song and the next he said, '*Agapi mou*, the next dance is mine.'

Sasha might have laughed at how quickly her dance companion handed her back to Apollo, if her insides weren't coiling tight with awareness and something much sharper.

Apollo swung her expertly into his arms just as the music slowed to a more sultry beat. He was all around her and she could barely breathe because of her proximity to his tall, whipcord body.

To her relief, he didn't speak. Didn't say anything about the man she'd been dancing with, even though she hadn't missed the tightness of his jaw when he'd

appeared to interrupt them. She didn't think it was for
any other reason, though, than because here in public,
no matter what had happened between them, she was
his wife.

He pulled her close and after a moment of trying
and failing to resist sinking against him, Sasha gave in,
allowing her body to cleave to his. He held one hand
up, and brought it in close between them. Her breasts
were pressed against his chest. She stumbled for a moment when she felt the evidence of his arousal against
her belly. She looked up and met that dark green gaze.

'You look surprised.'

Sasha swallowed, her previous sense of insecurity
burning away in the face of this evidence. 'I thought…
There are so many beautiful women here…' She
stopped, feeling inarticulate.

'You thought I wouldn't want you?'

She couldn't speak or nod or move, and he stopped
moving too so now people danced around them. He
said, 'I won't stop wanting you till I have you again.'

He let her hand go and cupped her jaw and time was
suspended as she waited for his mouth to touch hers.
When it did she clutched at his jacket to stay standing. The kiss was all-consuming, and Sasha had no
defence for it.

After long drugged moments Apollo broke the contact and pulled back. Sasha opened her eyes with effort, everything blurry for a moment. He was looking
at her with a harsh expression on his face. 'What do
you do to me?'

She had no answer because she could ask him the
same question. A sense of urgency seemed to infuse the

air around them. Apollo took her by the hand to lead her off the dance floor.

He stopped next to a couple of people and exchanged a few words and then they were sitting into the back of a car and being driven back to the helipad where the helicopter was waiting.

The short journey back to Krisakis felt like a dream and Sasha purposely kept her mind blank as if that could help to not think about what was to happen, because she was in no doubt where this evening would end. In the reality of Apollo's arms and bed. Not a dream of a hazy memory.

All was still and quiet at the villa when they returned. The air was heavy with the scent of night-blooming flowers. Sasha took off her three-inch-heeled sandals and relished the feel of the cool marble floor under her aching feet.

Apollo took off his jacket and draped it over a chair. He walked to the sliding door that led out to the back of the villa. His back was to her and Sasha took a moment to let her eyes linger on his tall, broad form.

He was so beautiful. Her heart gave a funny little skip.

Had she fallen for him after sleeping with him that first time?

Was that why she'd engineered a fake pregnancy? Because she'd been so desperate to cling to him by any means?

Was she in love with him now? Her heart thumped. She knew he consumed her on every level. And she wanted him with a fierce desire she didn't even really understand. The thought of him casting her out of his life made her feel breathless with pain. Not fear. So it had nothing to do with the memory loss.

Dear God, she loved him. Was that why she'd lied to him?

He wasn't moving but standing very still. For heart-stopping seconds Sasha thought he might have changed his mind. But then he turned around.

'Come here.'

It was a command. A command that Sasha could not ignore or disobey, even if she'd wanted to. The relief that he wanted her made her feel weak. She walked towards him and came to a stop in front of him. His eyes were so dark they looked black. His jaw was already darkening again with stubble.

'Take down your hair.'

Sasha complied, lifting her hands to where pins held the bun in place. She took them out and her hair fell to her shoulders. Apollo reached out and caught a strand. 'It's like golden fire...little flame.'

Sasha's nerves were tingling. Her breath came in short choppy bursts. She closed one hand around the pins and they dug into her palm. As if sensing she was hurting herself, Apollo took her hand and opened it, taking the pins and putting them on a nearby surface.

Then he caught her face in his two hands and moved closer. All she could smell was him. The scents of the island clung to him. Citrus, sea. And something infinitely more masculine and human.

She didn't need his hands to raise her face to his as she was already doing it, every cell straining to get closer, for his touch. When his mouth covered hers, she wound her arms up and around his neck, telling him with her body that she wanted him.

Sasha could have happily stood there all night just kissing Apollo, but he drew back and took her by the hand, leading her through the softly lit villa to his room. Her dress whispered around her legs, heightening her sensitivity.

His room was at the opposite end of the villa from hers, with its own suite of rooms like hers, except much grander. She hadn't been shown this part of the villa and felt a little pang of hurt now to think of how divided they'd been.

But all her thoughts fled when they entered the room. It was palatial but minimalist enough to be a monk's cell. Albeit a billionaire monk. The sky was dark outside, cocooning them.

The massive bed was the focal point in the room. It didn't have four posters like Sasha's. It had no adornment apart from pillows and sheets. Stark. Like the expression on Apollo's face now as he turned to her. Sasha locked her knees in a bid to stop her legs trembling.

She'd never been more aware of the disparity in their sizes. Everywhere he was broad she was narrow, slender. He was tall, she was short. He was hard, she was soft.

His hands were on her shoulders. He tugged her gently but inexorably towards him. He tipped up her chin and bent his head, hovering mere centimetres from her mouth for a second. Then he said, 'Do you want this, Sasha?'

There was a tiny flicker of something in her brain at the way he said her name. Like something not fitting quite right. Like when she'd had that curious sense earlier that she hadn't actually chosen her own clothes. But it was too elusive to try and analyse or pin down.

Apollo was asking her permission to make love to her, when he didn't even have to. She'd answered him in the pool earlier that day. Her answer was in every cell of her body, in the rush of blood and liquid heat between her legs.

She nodded jerkily. 'Yes, I want this.' She put her hands on his chest, the heat of his skin nearly burning her hands through the thin material of his shirt,

His mouth touched hers and Sasha melted. One arm wrapped around her back and his other hand speared through her hair, cupping her head and holding it as he plundered and demolished any last coherent thought with his mouth and tongue.

He swept inside and explored with devastating precision. It was all Sasha could do to accept him and mimic his movements. He'd told her he wouldn't let her drown earlier in the pool, but she was drowning now, her arms and hands climbing around his neck, arching her body against his in a bid to get even closer.

This felt familiar.

New, but familiar.

She was barely aware of him undoing the zip at the back of the dress, and then peeling the straps of her dress down over her arms. The top of the dress fell down to her waist. He pulled back and looked at her and she could feel her nipples tighten under his gaze. The design of the dress had precluded her wearing a bra. She brought her arms up and crossed them over her chest, suddenly feeling embarrassed.

He stepped forward and pulled them apart. 'No, *agapi mou*, let me see you.'

There was a husky tone in his voice that made her feel less self-conscious. Feeling shy now, more than embarrassed, she said, 'I want to see you too.'

Apollo put down his hands and looked at her. Presenting himself. She reached for his buttons, undoing them one by one, little by little revealing that broad impressive chest with its smattering of dark curly hair.

When it was open he shrugged his shirt off and it fell to the floor. With efficient movements, he undid his belt, opened his trousers and pulled them down and off, taking his underwear with them.

He stood before her, naked. Sasha's eyes widened as she took in the sight of him. How could she have forgotten this? He was erect, long and thick. The head was glistening with moisture.

'If you keep looking at me like that, this will be over before we've even started.'

Sasha looked up, mortified. There was an echo of a memory now, feeling the same way, gauche. Inexperienced. Out of her depth. But before she could focus on it, Apollo was taking her by the hand again and leading her to the bed.

He sat down on the edge and pulled her in front of him. He slowly pulled the dress down over her hips, leaving her standing before him in just skimpy lace underwear.

He spanned her waist with his hands and tugged her forward, pressing kisses against her exposed skin, mouth and tongue finding a nipple and sucking it into his mouth. Sasha gasped and clutched his head, losing all sense of reason and sanity at that delicious tugging sensation.

Her legs finally gave way and he caught her, placing her back on the bed, coming over her on two hands. His eyes were glittering.

He claimed her mouth again in a kiss that felt almost desperate. It resonated inside Sasha and she matched him, stroke for stroke, reaching for him.

Apollo's hands were on her breasts, cupping them, thumbs stroking her sensitive nipples. Tension pulled tight low inside her. She felt empty, hollow. She needed him to obliterate those disturbing dreams. To replace them with reality. To finish what they'd started earlier, exactly as he'd promised.

Ever since she'd woken in the hospital with nothing but blankness in her brain, she'd felt rudderless. Here in Apollo's arms, his mouth fused with hers, she felt anchored again.

Safe.

He pulled back and Sasha realised how fast her heart was beating.

His mouth trailed across her jaw and down to her neck. She was panting. And her breaths got even faster when his hands expertly dispensed with her underwear.

His torso lay against her belly. Her thighs were spread wide to accommodate his body. His mouth lingered on her breast, teasing. She let out a little moan of distress and he looked up at her. 'Patience, little flame, patience...'

He dipped down lower, spreading her legs even further apart and he just looked at her there. A moment ago she'd been breathing like she'd run a marathon and now she couldn't breathe at all.

When Apollo put his mouth on the centre of her body she nearly wept.

She knew this. It hadn't been a dream.

Apollo was so drunk on the taste and feel of Sasha's body under his mouth, and his hands, that he almost forgot.

Almost.

At the last second, he reached for protection in his bedside drawer, ripping it open with all the finesse of a horny teenage boy and rolling it onto his penis.

He looked down for a moment after donning protection and almost came there and then. Her breasts were rising and falling with her breath, pink after his ministrations. Her entire body was flushed with arousal.

Her lips were swollen. Her eyes were huge and blue enough to make his breath catch, as if he'd never seen them before.

Making love with women had always been a short-lived thing—he'd gone through the motions dictated by society in order to find fleeting physical satisfaction—the chase, the seduction and the consummation. Invariably the seduction and the consummation never lived up to the promise. And Apollo had always chosen women who were experienced. The kind of women who understood not to ask for more. The kind of women who were not expecting anything beyond physical fulfilment.

But with Sasha there had been none of that. They'd met and combusted. There had been very little logical thought involved.

And right now all of his logical faculties were melting in a haze of lust. He notched his erection against the centre of her body, where she was so hot, and wet.

Ready for him.

He hadn't even entered her yet but his mind was already blasting back to that night in London and the way her body had clamped so tightly around his, sending him into orbit.

Something desperate caught in his gut. It couldn't possibly have been as amazing as that—and in a bid to try and prove to himself that he'd misremembered how amazing it had been before, Apollo thrust into Sasha's body, seating himself deep.

He saw her eyes widen even more, colour race across her cheeks. Her hands went to his arms, fingers curling around his biceps.

For a second he couldn't move, because in that moment he knew that the last time hadn't been as amazing as he remembered. It had been *more*. And that this was going to eclipse everything.

Sasha's hips moved tentatively and he nearly exploded. 'Please, Apollo...make love to me.'

A thousand horses couldn't have stopped him from obeying her entreaty. He pulled out slowly, feeling her tight muscles massage his length, and then...back in.

Sasha's body was moving with his in ways that were totally instinctive. She had no control. She was his. Body and soul. It was as if they'd been made to fit exactly.

Apollo came down over her body, twining his fingers with hers and lifting one hand over her head. His other arm was around her back, lifting her into him, deepening his thrusts even more.

A tight coil of need was building inside Sasha, a need for this tension to end, to explode. Apollo's rhythm was remorseless. He had the precision of a master magician or a torturer. Bringing her to the edge, keeping her there, stoking the fire but never letting it burn itself out...

Sasha cried out brokenly, her body dewed with sweat, her mind incoherent with need. 'Please... I...'

'Look at me, Sasha, look at me.'

Something inside Sasha went very still. She forced her eyes to focus on Apollo's face. That flicker was there again, but more than a flicker... Her name. It was *wrong*.

Apollo was saying, 'What do you need, little flame?' He moved and sent fresh tremors through her body.

Her thoughts scattered, flickers forgotten. She couldn't think, she could only feel. 'You...' she said brokenly. Apollo's powerful body moved over her, into her. Stealing her breath and her sanity.

She remembered this.

Being with him like this.

The next moment Apollo touched Sasha so deep and hard that she cried out as ecstasy tore her apart. Seconds later, Apollo convulsed with pleasure and his broken cry of 'Sasha...' echoed around the room.

She went very still deep inside, even as the powerful waves of ecstasy held her in their grip. Something cataclysmic had just happened. Shockwaves slowly obliterated the effects of the intense orgasm as the knowledge sank in.

At that moment of peak union, every cell in her body had rejected his calling her by another woman's name.

Because she wasn't Sasha at all. She was someone else entirely.

She remembered now.

She remembered everything.

Apollo was barely conscious when he felt Sasha wriggle out from underneath him, every touch of her body against his sending fresh flutters of need into his blood. Again. *Theos.*

He flipped onto his back just as he saw a sliver of pale curve of skin disappear into the bathroom and out of sight.

He was stupefied in the aftermath of one of the most erotic encounters of his life. The fact that the other most erotic encounter had been with the same woman made an uneasiness prickle over his skin.

But then his whole body went still when he heard the sounds of retching coming from the bathroom. He sprang out of bed and went to the doorway. The toilet was discreetly tucked away behind a wall and something held him back from intruding. 'Sasha? Are you okay?'

Nothing. Then a weak-sounding 'I'm okay, I'll be out in a minute.'

Apollo's mind raced. Had he been so consumed with his own insatiable need that he'd assumed Sasha had been with him all the way? He went cold—had he? But no. He could remember her nails digging into his hands as she'd begged him to keep going.

'Don't stop.'

He pulled a pair of sweats out of a drawer and put them on. He went back over to the bathroom door. Now he could hear the shower running—also hidden from view by a glazed glass wall. He paced back and forth for what seemed like ages, and then the water finally stopped.

He gave her a few minutes to get out, dry herself. He heard nothing. Impatience and something that felt like a tendril of fear made him say, 'Sasha? Are you sure you're—?'

But then suddenly she appeared, enveloped in a white towelling robe, and Apollo sucked in a breath. She looked like a ghost. Ashen.

Her hair hung in wet tendrils over her shoulders and the red looked dark against the white robe covering her body. He stepped back so she could come into the bedroom. She scooted past him, her eyes huge. Haunted.

Apollo's hands fell to his sides. 'What is going on, Sasha?'

She'd backed away into a corner, looking at him but not really seeing him. It was eerie. And then her gaze focused on him and her saw her throat move. She said in a broken-sounding voice, 'That's just it. I'm not Sasha.'

Apollo shook his head as if that might help him understand what she was saying. 'I'm sorry, what are you talking about?'

He noticed that she was trembling violently now. He cursed and went towards her, catching her hands. They were icy. Her teeth were chattering.

He drew her down to sit in a chair and knelt before her. Concern punched him in the gut. 'Should I get a doctor?'

She shook her head. 'N-no. I don't… I think it's just sh-shock. I can remember ev-everything. My memory. It's back.'

Apollo went very still. He'd actually forgotten for a moment. A cold finger traced down his spine. He'd become so used to *this* Sasha. He forced himself to focus. 'Are you in pain? Is your head hurting?'

She shook her head, more hair slipping over her shoulder. She looked very young. She looked scared.

He stood up. 'If I leave you for a minute, will you be okay?'

She nodded jerkily. 'I think so.'

She watched Apollo leave the room. She felt numb. She didn't even feel herself trembling but she could hear her teeth. She clamped her mouth shut and tried to wrap her head around what had just happened.

It had been the way Apollo had said, *'Sasha, look at me.'*

At that moment in her head, a very clear voice had said, *But I'm not Sasha.*

And then, when he'd said *Sasha* again, everything in her had rejected it, even as a powerful climax had torn her apart.

As if she'd known all along but had just blocked it out—she now knew everything. All the pieces of the puzzle were sliding back into horrific place.

She heard a noise and looked up to see Apollo return. He was holding a bottle and two glasses.

He said, 'Brandy.' He poured her a shot and handed her a glass. When her hand shook too much he put his hand around hers and lifted it to her mouth. She drank and winced as the fiery liquid burnt down her throat into her stomach. It worked almost instantly, sending out comforting tendrils. Creating a warmth between her and the numbness that had taken hold.

The shudders started to subside slowly.

Apollo poured himself some brandy and slugged it back. He held up the bottle. 'More?'

'A tiny bit.' She didn't want to become insensible, not when her mind was actually functioning again. She took another small sip and the warmth extended from her stomach out, creating a calming effect.

Apollo sat on the edge of the bed. After a minute he said, 'So, do you want to tell me what's come back exactly? How much of your memory?'

She forced herself to look at him. What they'd just shared… She knew that would be the last time he'd ever allow intimacy between them once she had finished telling him what she had to.

'All of it. Everything.'

'Why are you saying you're not Sasha?'

She took a deep breath. 'Because I'm not. I'm Sophy. Sophy Jones. Sasha is…*was*…my twin sister.'

CHAPTER EIGHT

Sᴏᴘʜʏ ᴄᴏᴜʟᴅ sᴇᴇ Apollo try to absorb this. Eventually he said, 'Twins.'

She nodded. She felt sick. Again.

He stood up. 'What the hell is this…some kind of joke? Now you're trying to convince me you're some-one else? Did you ever have amnesia?'

Sophy stood up, even though her legs felt like jelly. 'The accident…happened. It was real. Sasha was driv-ing, she'd picked me up from the airport.'

'Well, if you're a twin, and she was driving, where is she now?'

She was driving manically up a winding road, speaking so fast that Sophy couldn't understand half of what she was saying. And then she turned to Sophy.

'You have to seduce him, Soph,' she said. 'He wants you, not me. Isn't that ironic? He wouldn't sleep with me—he knows the baby doesn't exist now. But if you sleep with him you can get pregnant. Then there will be a baby.'

Sophy looked at her sister, her insides caught in a

vice of anxiety and confusion. 'Sash, what are you on about?'

And that was when Sasha took a bend too fast.

Sophy could see that they were too close to the unprotected edge and she called out. Sasha slammed on the brakes but it was too late.

They stopped right on the edge, the front of the car tipping over. Sophy felt nothing but blood-draining terror as the ravine appeared below them, narrow, deep and dark.

She said, 'Sasha, don't move.'

She pushed through the gut-churning terror to open her door carefully and undid her seat belt. If she could inch out of the car then the weight would be redistributed...

Sasha was crying. 'Soph, I'm so sorry... I should never have done this to you. I've ruined everything.'

Sophy looked over and saw blood trickling down Sasha's forehead. She must have hit her head on the wheel.

She said, in as calm a voice as she could muster, 'Sash, don't think about that now. Just look at me, and keep looking at me—not down. I'll get you out.'

Sophy put her leg out of the car and felt for the ground. Then she eased her body so that she was perching on the seat, her feet on the edge of the cliff.

She looked back at her sister. 'Keep looking at me, Sash.'

Sophy kept her eyes on Sasha while she reached out to try and get hold of something that might anchor her if she jumped free of the car.

But at that moment a strange expression crossed

her sister's face and Sasha said, 'I'm sorry, Soph, but I won't take you down with me.'

And then, before Sophy could stop her, Sasha was reaching across and pushing Sophy out of the car.

Sophy fell into space, her breath strangled in her throat, and then she landed on a hard surface, the breath knocked out of her body.

The only thing she heard before blackness consumed her was the faint sound of metal crashing far below her...

Sophy looked at Apollo.

Sasha was gone.

She tried to answer Apollo's question but her voice sounded very far away.

'She's in the car... I couldn't get her out. She's dead.'

And then, like when she'd landed on that ledge, far above the bottom of the ravine, darkness came over her again like a comforting cloak.

The next few hours passed in a blur. Sophy was aware of coming round and a concerned doctor asking her some questions. Olympia had helped her to dress and then they'd been flying over the sea with Apollo's voice in her ear.

'Are you okay? We're nearly there.'

When they reached the bright hospital in Athens where a team of doctors and nurses was waiting for them, Sophy knew that, as much as she wanted to, she couldn't hide from the painful reality waiting to be unearthed from the depths of her newly returned memory.

* * *

'It would appear that the trauma of the crash, of seeing the car disappear with her sister in it, along with the bump to her head, caused a classic case of trauma-induced amnesia. And, because her sister was in the accident, she blocked out everything about her sister, which was her whole life. Effectively.'

Apollo was silent. Taking this in. He was standing outside the private suite at the hospital with the same doctor who had treated Sasha—*Sophy*—after the accident.

Theos. Even now it was hard to get his head around it. No wonder he'd always thought of her as so pale. She'd been a different woman. He realised now that all those little anomalies he'd noticed since the accident hadn't been anomalies.

He didn't think he'd ever be able to excise the image from his mind of Sophy crumpling before him like a ragdoll and the terror he'd felt as he'd waited for the island doctor to arrive.

She'd come round at the villa but she'd retreated to some numb place Apollo couldn't reach. Even if the doctor hadn't recommended it, Apollo would have returned to Athens as soon as possible to seek further treatment.

Through the window he could see a detective talking to Sophy now. She was still deathly pale. Any lingering doubt he might have had about whether or not she'd been lying about the amnesia was well and truly gone.

It was too huge to absorb and try and figure how he felt about this, and the fact that Sasha—his wife, however inconvenient she'd been—was now dead.

The detective stood up and came out. He stopped in front of Apollo. 'I'll have a team sent to look for the crashed car immediately. And your wife's body. We should find Ms Jones's documents in the car if they haven't been destroyed. That will help clear things up.'

'Thank you.'

When the detective had disappeared the doctor said, 'We'll keep Sophy in for the rest of the night as a precaution, but she should be okay to go home tomorrow. It's going to take her some time to adjust to having her memory back. Be gentle with her.'

Apollo's mind was instantly filled with vivid images of making love to her with a desperation that hadn't exactly been gentle. His conscience smarted. Had sex precipitated her memory's return?

The doctor was waiting for his response. He said, 'Of course.'

She walked away and Apollo went into the suite.

Sophy knew when Apollo walked in. A volt of electricity went through her blood. Steeling herself, she turned her head to look at him. She quailed inwardly. His expression was stony. She had a sense of déjà vu from when she'd regained consciousness after the accident to find him with a similar expression.

'How are you feeling?' he asked.

'Okay, I think. My head feels full again.' She put a hand to it briefly.

Apollo looked at her for a long moment. 'Can you tell me one thing?'

She nodded, tensing inwardly. There was so much she had to explain but she needed to make sense of it herself first.

He asked. 'Was it you that night? The night we met?'

Something inside her relaxed a little. That was an easy question. 'Yes, it was me.'

An expression crossed his face fleetingly. Too quick for her to decipher. She tensed again. What would he make of that information?

He took a step back from the bed. 'I'll leave you now. The doctor said you need to rest. I'll come back in the morning.'

Sophy watched as he turned to leave. She only noticed now that he was wearing sweat pants and a long-sleeved top. Hair mussed. Not his usual pristine self. The thought that he hadn't showered since they'd made love made her skin prickle with awareness. She wondered how on earth she could be feeling so carnal after what had just happened.

After what she and her sister had put him through. He was almost at the door and on an impulse she called out, 'Wait… Apollo?'

He stopped and turned around. A muscle clenched in his jaw. 'Yes?'

Her fingers plucked at the sheet nervously. 'I just wanted to say… I'm so sorry. For everything.'

Apollo nodded tersely. 'We'll talk about it when you're ready. Get some rest.'

He walked out, closing the door behind him. That was the problem. Sophy didn't think she'd ever be ready to talk about it. She sagged back against the pillows. She felt more fatigued than she'd ever felt in her life.

There was little relief in remembering everything, even though she was grateful to have her memory back. To have *herself* back.

Sasha was dead.

She knew it instinctively, if not factually yet. There was no way she could have survived that crash. Sophy was still too numb with shock to fully absorb the death of her sister who she had loved more than life itself for so long. But who had also caused her more heartache than anyone else.

To say they'd had a complicated relationship was an understatement, but Sophy would never have guessed that Sasha would go as far as she had to engineer a good life for herself.

She'd also never forget that awful last haunting image of Sasha, pushing her free of the doomed car and saying, *'I won't take you with me.'*

For all of her faults and frailties, her sister had saved her twice in her life…

Oh, Sash…what did you do?

Tears filled Sophy's eyes and she turned her head to the wall, unable to stem the rising tide of emotion that engulfed her. She realised she wasn't just crying for her sister, she was also crying because she now remembered everything that had happened the night she'd slept with Apollo.

She remembered why he hadn't pursued her after their night together.

Because he hadn't wanted to see her again. Because she'd been inexperienced, a virgin.

And now she knew why. Because he'd told her he didn't *do* relationships after losing his entire family.

So not only had she lost her sister and realised she'd been betrayed by her too, she'd also remembered that she'd fallen for Apollo all those months ago, when they'd first met.

And they'd never had a chance.

Two days later

Sophy's nerves were wound tight. She'd had a reprieve of sorts from facing Apollo and the inevitable discussion since returning to the villa because he'd had an emergency meeting to attend in London.

He'd left her in the capable hands of Kara and Rhea and the doctor had come to check on her that morning. Apollo must have explained everything to his staff because at one point Sophy had attempted to start to tell Rhea but she'd just patted her hand and shaken her head, saying, 'You don't need to tell us. We knew something was different. We're sorry for your sister.'

Sophy had been inordinately touched, especially after everything Sasha had put them through. She knew how difficult her sister could be. She'd endured a lifetime of it and had never been quite able to break away completely.

They'd been living together in London and that was how Sophy had ended up covering for Sasha that night at the function where she'd met Apollo and where she'd had to call herself Sasha. It had been a classic Sasha request: *'Cover for me, Soph, please! This other thing has cropped up—I'll lose my job!'*

She'd done it, of course. Just as she'd said yes to most of Sasha's requests. After all, she'd owed Sasha so much... If it hadn't been for her sister, Sophy might not even be—

There was a sound behind Sophy on the terrace and she looked around. It was Kara. 'Kyrie Vasilis is in his study—he'd like to see you.'

Sophy's heart thudded against her breastbone. She'd known Apollo was due back but hadn't heard him return.

She'd dug through all of Sasha's clothes to find something vaguely suitable to face him and she'd found an unworn shirt dress, blue stripes, with a black belt. Wedge sandals. It was strange, looking at Sasha's choice of clothes now and realising why they'd never felt like *her*. Because she and her sister had always had diametrically opposed taste, in everything.

Sasha had been flamboyant, into fashion and pop culture. Always ambitious for a life more glamorous than the one they'd experienced growing up in a small market town outside London.

Sophy had been bookish and studious. Into clothes that made her fade into the background. She'd been happy to let Sasha shine but for the first time in her life she found herself wondering uneasily why it had been so easy for her to let Sasha claim the limelight.

She was outside Apollo's study now and had to collect herself. She knocked on the door and there was an abrupt, 'Come in.'

She took a deep breath and steeled herself but seeing Apollo after a couple of days' absence hit her straight in the chest like a sledgehammer. He was wearing a dark grey three-piece suit. And he'd never looked more gorgeous. His physicality was overwhelming, as if she was seeing him all over again with new eyes.

He was also a million miles away from the man who had been uncharacteristically dishevelled at the hospital.

Her heart skipped a beat and she sounded breathless when she said, 'Kara told me you wanted to see me.'

Had his gaze always been so dark green and unnervingly direct? He pulled at his tie and opened the top button of his shirt. 'How are you feeling?'

Dizzy.

But Sophy knew that had nothing to do with regaining her memory and everything to do with him.

'Fine. Much better. Thank you.'

He went over to the drinks cabinet and asked if she wanted anything. She shook her head. He poured himself a shot of golden spirits.

Something inside her ached. A few days ago she'd lain in this man's arms, their bodies entwined. Her soul had sung. Now there was a gaping chasm between them. And how could she blame him?

Apollo downed the shot he'd just poured. It did little to calm his thundering heart or douse the heat in his blood. He'd hoped that a couple of days' distance from Sophy and time to absorb all the revelations would somehow miraculously defuse this intense need he had for her…but as soon as she'd walked into the room his blood had boiled over.

He'd never expected to see her again after that night in his apartment in London. He'd told himself he didn't want to see her again but the relief he'd felt when she'd turned up in his office in London had made a mockery of that.

Dealing with Sasha had been easy because she hadn't been Sophy. Now he had to deal with Sophy.

He poured himself another shot and turned around.

Sophy hoped her emotions weren't as nakedly obvious as she feared. She'd never been as adept at hiding them as her sister. She had no idea what would happen now. What to expect. What she wanted.

You still want Apollo, whispered a voice.

She pushed it down.

Apollo came over and stood with the window at his back. It cast him into shadow slightly, making him look even bigger.

'I need to tell you something.'

She swallowed. 'Okay.'

'The detective contacted me. They found the car. And they found a body… They've identified your sister by her dental records and the DNA sample you provided.'

Sophy sat down on the chair behind her, the wind knocked out of her, even though this wasn't a surprise.

'Are you sure you don't want a drink?'

She shook her head. 'No, it's okay.' She looked at him. 'Did they find anything else?'

He nodded. 'Your bag, with your passport and personal items. There was luggage in the boot but it was ruined. Your things will be returned to you once they've been catalogued. They've ruled her death as accidental.'

Sophy sucked in a sharp breath. 'Was…was there any suggestion it wasn't?'

Apollo's face was expressionless. 'They have to look at everything. You'd just arrived on a flight from London that morning. Sasha picked you up from the airport?'

Sophy nodded.

'Yes.' Her voice sounded raw.

Apollo said, 'We can do this later, or tomorrow.'

She shook her head again. 'No, I know you have questions and you deserve answers.'

She steeled herself but wasn't prepared when Apollo said, 'I'm sorry for your loss, Sophy. I know what it's like to lose a sibling. I might not have liked Sasha very much but she was your sister and you must have loved her.'

Sophy couldn't stop the tears that sprang into her eyes. She stood up and fished a handkerchief out of the pocket of the dress. She went over to the other window and gathered herself.

Apollo said from behind her, 'We really don't have to do this now.'

Sophy swallowed down her emotion and turned around when she felt more composed. 'No. It's okay. Really.'

She said, 'I know Sasha was…a difficult person. More than anyone. But I did love her. I owed her a lot…'

Apollo frowned. 'What are you talking about?'

She looked at him. 'When I was eight, I contracted leukaemia. I needed a bone-marrow transplant. Because we were identical twins, Sasha's bone marrow matched mine so she was asked to donate her marrow.'

Apollo said nothing so she went on, 'She had no choice really, and she never forgave me for having to go through the painful donor procedure without the benefit of actually being sick and getting the attention. I think, unconsciously, I spent my life making it up to her.'

Sophy had never really analysed that before now but something clicked into place inside her as if finally she was acknowledging the role she'd given her sister out of a misplaced sense of guilt.

Apollo said, 'That must have been traumatic. The illness.'

Sophy made a face. 'A lot of it has faded with time. In a way, Sasha's constant demand for attention helped to distract from the memories...

'She was never content with what she had. She lied about our parents to people, friends in school. They were too boring for her. Our father was a postman and our mother was a part-time secretary for the local doctor's office. We had a perfectly happy home life, albeit modest. The worst thing that happened was that they both died within a year of each other, when we'd just left school. My father had a heart attack and then my mother contracted breast cancer.

'After they died, Sasha wanted to move up to London to make her mark. She'd never been happy in our little town. I went with her because the truth is I felt lost without her. She'd been the dominant one for so long.'

Sophy looked away from Apollo as she admitted that. She'd *let* Sasha dominate her, a dynamic they'd played out since they were children, exacerbated by her illness.

Apollo asked, 'Why is your name different from hers if you're sisters? Her name is Miller on her passport and papers.'

Sophy forced herself to look at him again. He was frowning. 'Sasha took our mother's maiden name, changed it legally—she thought it sounded more interesting than Jones. She did it when she was going through a phase of wanting to be an actress.'

Apollo paced away and back, and then stood at the

window for a moment with his back to Sophy. It all made sense in a sick kind of way. He'd met Sasha. He could attest to her ruthless deviousness. If anything, he suspected that Sophy hadn't really acknowledged half of what her sister had been capable of. The woman had tried to seduce him so she could try and get pregnant for real.

Her childhood illness… It tugged on him deep inside. Imagining a small girl with huge blue eyes and light red hair losing that hair because of chemotherapy. Being subjected to all manner of invasive procedures.

To counteract the sense of sympathy he felt, Apollo turned around again. Sophy's chin was tipped up, as if she was mentally preparing for the next onslaught. He pushed down the surge of something more than sympathy. He needed to know.

'That night in London. Why did you pretend to be your sister?'

Sophy's insides clenched with guilt. 'Because I wasn't meant to be there. I work—worked—as a receptionist in a solicitor's office. Sasha asked me to cover for her. She was double-jobbing at another event. It wasn't unheard of for me to cover for her like that. I didn't tell you my real name afterwards because I was afraid she'd get into trouble and lose her job with the event company.'

He frowned. 'Why didn't you tell me the following night when I took you for dinner? When we slept together?'

How could she explain how overwhelming it had been for a man like Apollo to show interest in her? Mousy Sophy. She lifted a hand and let it drop. 'I should have told you…but I couldn't believe that you wanted *me*. Sasha was the one who was confident. Glamorous. Not me.'

She shrugged minutely. 'Somehow it felt more appropriate to be her…not me.'

She winced inwardly, knowing how ridiculous that sounded. Apollo shook his head. 'I wanted you, not your sister. I think we've established that pretty comprehensively.'

A wave of heat, uncontrollable, moved up inside Sophy's body. She clamped down on her response, terrified he'd see the effect of his words. His gaze was too direct, too incisive. She felt as if she was being sliced open and all her vulnerabilities and frailties being laid bare for inspection.

She put her arms around herself and walked over to the window again, staring out unseeingly. Maybe if she didn't look at him as she tried to explain, it would be easier?

'The truth is that I felt out of my depth with you. Really out of my depth. You were suave and cultured. Way out of my league. Sasha was more experienced than me—'

Apollo cut in, 'You mean she wasn't a virgin? Unlike you.'

Sophy's face burned at that reminder. Her arms were so tight around herself now she was in danger of cutting off her air supply. 'I thought you wouldn't notice.'

'Well, I did.'

Yes, he had.

And Sophy could now remember his reaction in full glorious Technicolor. She remembered being so caught up in the moment that when he'd thrust into her and it had hurt, she'd tensed all over.

He'd looked down at her. 'Sasha? Are you—?'

Terrified he'd stop, she'd put her hands on his buttocks and said, 'Please, don't stop.'

For a torturous moment he hadn't moved. She'd felt impaled, stunned at the feeling of being so invaded, but then he'd started to move and the pressure and pain had eased.

What had followed had been nothing short of life-changing. Earth-shattering. She'd still been lying in a sated stupor when she'd felt him leave the bed and heard the shower come on in his bathroom.

A few minutes later, he'd emerged with a towel around his lean hips, his face rigid with anger.

'What the *hell*? You were a virgin.'

Sophy had reached for the sheet to cover herself, suddenly feeling very small and exposed. 'I thought you wouldn't notice.'

He'd emitted a curt, unamused laugh. 'Notice? How could I not? Why didn't you tell me?'

He'd spoken before she could formulate a response. 'I seduced you because I thought you were experienced... that you knew.'

'Knew what?'

He'd run a hand through his damp hair, muscles rippling, making Sophy's tender inner muscles clench again in reaction.

'Knew how these things go. Knew not to expect anything more.'

'More than what?' She'd known she'd sounded like a parrot but had been unable to stop herself.

'More than one night.' He'd folded his arms. 'I don't sleep with virgins, Sasha. If I'd known, I wouldn't have touched you.'

The thought that she might not have made love with this man had been a physical pain. 'But…why?'

A scarily blank expression had come over his face. He was like a statue. 'Because virgins are innocent and have expectations. The kind of expectations I can't, and don't want to, meet.'

'What do you mean?'

He'd emitted something that had sounded like a curse and his green eyes had narrowed on her face. 'Can you deny that you'd thought this was something more? That this wasn't just about sex?'

Mortified heat had flooded up her body and into her face. She *had* thought there was something between them. Romantic. Unique.

He'd seen it instantly. 'That's what I'm talking about. An expectation of something *more*. I don't do relationships, Sasha. I have no desire for a girlfriend. I have short-term relationships with women who know better than to attach emotion to the proceedings. This is just sex for me.'

She'd winced at that.

He'd said icily, 'This ends here now. Take a shower and get dressed. When you're ready I'll have my driver take you home.'

Sophy's focus came back to the present. It wasn't much comfort that she had more context now for why Apollo would have found seducing a virgin so unappealing. He was averse to relationships after losing his family. And she knew what that loss felt like. Ironic that they had so much in common.

She turned to face him, steeling herself not to show him how the memory of that night flayed her.

Apollo tried to resist the image of intense vulnerability Sophy displayed when she faced him again. Arms wrapped around herself. Her cheeks had two bright pink spots but the rest of her face was pale.

It didn't help that images of that first night they'd spent together kept intruding on his thoughts. The way her hair had spread out around her head like a halo of fire.

Little flame.

He gritted his jaw and bit out, 'We really don't have to continue this now if you're not up to it.'

She looked at him. 'No, I want to do this now. Maybe I will have a small drink, though.'

Apollo went over and poured her a measure of brandy. He brought it over and said gruffly, 'Sit down, before you fall down.'

She sat down again in the chair and he handed her the drink. He let her take a sip, and sat back on the edge of his desk. 'Were you and your sister in on the act together? Was she sent to me a month later because you didn't have the nerve?'

Sophy sat up straighter, a look of shock and horror crossing her face. 'That's… *No*, it wasn't like that. I had no idea.'

Apollo forced himself to resist trusting his first impression of her innocence. 'You weren't working together?'

'Not at all. How can you think that?'

'How did she end up in my office then? Telling me she was pregnant, if you weren't working together? How did she know if you hadn't told her?'

He saw the slim pale column of her throat work as she swallowed. She avoided his eye, as if ashamed. 'Sasha and I lived together. She knew something had happened...she eventually got me to confide in her. I told her your name. I know Sasha had her faults, but I never in a million years thought that she would use that private information. She looked you up, kept going on about how I should contact you, try to go out with you again...but I wouldn't.'

She looked at him again. 'After all, you'd left me in no doubt as to how you felt about seeing me again.'

His conscience smarted. Yes, he'd told her that but he also hadn't been able to get her out of his mind in the following days, weeks. Making a total mockery of his words to her.

Sophy continued, 'It was around the time of our birthday and Sasha said she was concerned about me, so she bought me a return flight to one of the Canary Islands for a holiday. I didn't want to go but she insisted.'

Apollo said. 'Go on.'

'By the time I got back she was gone. She'd left a note saying something about securing our future. Then I saw it in the papers. Your marriage.'

Apollo remembered the feeling of claustrophobia that day. 'If you weren't working together, when you heard about the marriage, why didn't you contact me to tell me who she was, who *you* were? That she was tricking me?'

Sophy looked sheepish. 'I didn't know about the

pregnancy. It wasn't inconceivable to me that you'd met Sasha and had been more attracted to her. That you'd wanted something *more* with her.'

Apollo felt a surge of anger mixed with frustration rise up inside him. Before he could say anything Sophy cut in, 'I know it sounds pathetic. But in a weird way it made sense. I'd been innocent and you hadn't wanted to see me again. Sasha was experienced...the experienced version of me. I felt like you'd seen something in her that I hadn't been able to give you, and that had made you fall for her. I know how convincing Sasha could be.'

Apollo grimaced at that. The fact that he'd fallen for her act negated his anger a little. Sasha had managed to dupe them both.

He stood up again, paced back and forth. 'Why did you come to Athens?'

Sophy fought not to squirm under that exacting gaze. 'Sasha rang me, she was hysterical. Incoherent. It must have been when you found out she wasn't pregnant. When you'd shown her the divorce papers. She begged me to come as soon as I could... I arrived the next morning.'

She went on. 'I couldn't even understand half of what she was saying when she picked me up at the airport. She was gabbling about you not wanting her, and that I needed to go and pretend to be her so I could seduce you...'

Apollo went very still. 'She was hoping that if you switched places, I'd suddenly want you and in spite of everything sleep with you and get you pregnant?'

Sophy avoided his eye. 'Something like that, I think.'

Apollo cursed. And then he said, 'The truth is that

she wasn't that far off the mark. As soon as I saw you again I wanted you.'

Sophy's face got hot again. She risked a glance at Apollo, who looked grim. He might be admitting he hadn't stopped wanting her but it didn't feel like a compliment. More an accusation.

'And if this crazy plan of hers had worked and you'd managed to seduce me and get pregnant, then what?'

Sophy felt sick. 'I don't know. I don't think she'd thought it through… I certainly had no idea what she'd planned. It sounded like gibberish to me.'

Apollo hated to admit that *if* Sophy had returned to the villa in Athens in the place of Sasha, and he'd wanted her as much as he wanted her now, she could very well have seduced him.

It was a bitter pill to swallow. He wanted her now. He was acutely aware of the buttons on the shirt-dress— how easily they would come undone, baring her to his eyes and touch.

No make-up. No adornment but her exceptional natural beauty. How could she have ever thought she was less attractive than her sister? The minute Sasha had turned up in his office in London he'd had an adverse reaction to her. Much to his relief.

At first you were disappointed.

He ignored that unwelcome reminder.

Sophy looked at him and he noticed the shadows under her eyes. He felt wrung out. He could only imagine how she felt.

'What happens now? I expect you want me to leave as soon as possible.'

Apollo couldn't stem the visceral rejection he had to

that suggestion. He told himself it was incredulity that she could think she could walk away so easily, not the pulsing ever-present desire in his blood.

He shook his head. 'I'm afraid that's not possible.'

Sophy hated the little jump in her pulse when he said that. He must despise her after everything. She wasn't even sure if he believed her. 'Why?'

'For one thing, we have a situation on our hands. Obviously we won't need to divorce now. But I've been seen out in public with a woman who is not my wife. A wife who has been deceased for some weeks.'

'We'll have to announce the accident and her death and the press attention will be intense. You'll be hounded when they find out she had a twin sister and that you were also in the car, but we can try to delay that until her death has been announced and the press moves on to the next story.'

Sophy frowned. 'How can you do that?'

'By taking you back to the island for a couple of weeks when the news is announced tomorrow. It'll keep you insulated from the press and it'll take about that long to process the repatriation of your sister's body. By then, the press should have moved on. Also, it'll give the authorities time to return your personal items.'

CHAPTER NINE

AND THEN WHAT? That was the question that had been reverberating around Sophy's head for the past twenty-four hours since they'd landed back on Krisakis. Olympia had shown her back into her bedroom, separate from Apollo's. Sophy chastised herself. What had she expected? For them to blithely continue where they'd left off before her memory had returned?

Yes.

Her conscience stung. How could she be so selfish when her sister was dead?

Because it was your sister who was selfish in the first place, betraying your trust, going behind your back to try and seduce Apollo to further her own ends. Lying to trap him.

Sophy sighed deeply and hugged her knees tighter to her body. Yes, she could blame Sasha for so much, but also it had been *her* who had set this chain of events in motion by not revealing her true self because it had been easier to hide behind her sister, rather than believe that someone like Apollo could possibly be interested in her.

The waves lapped up gently onto the shore near her feet. It was soothing. It was also very quiet here on the beach in the late afternoon. The heat was less intense now.

Since they'd arrived on the island, Apollo had been busy, either in his study in the villa or when he went to visit the construction site. They hadn't talked about anything since that last conversation.

Sophy knew she should be feeling some sort of cathartic weight lift off her shoulders, with her memory returned and full knowledge of what had happened, no matter how painful it was to face.

But she felt more tangled up than ever. Aware that her feelings for Apollo ran far deeper than she liked to admit. And she hated the sense that she was now a burden for him to deal with until the press attention died down.

Because surely he was just waiting for the earliest opportunity to let her go? Get on with his life? Say good riddance to her, and Sasha.

He couldn't want her any more. Surely his desire was well and truly eclipsed by disgust for what her sister, and she, however unwittingly, had done to him?

Sophy shut down her circling thoughts. Torturing herself like this was getting her nowhere. Apollo was keeping her here to protect himself as much as her from the adverse press attention.

The water was lapping at her feet now, refreshingly cool. She was about to move back but she was too slow as another wave on the incoming tide rushed in faster, soaking her bottom. She jumped up with a little squeal.

She was about to step back out of the way but another wave broke over her bare feet. Suddenly she was filled with a sense of longing to feel the water on her body. Even though the thought of walking into the sea terrified her. She remembered now why she couldn't swim and with a kind of sickening predictability it came back to Sasha.

They'd been very little and she and Sasha had been playing in a pool while on holiday. When their parents had been momentarily diverted, Sasha had taken the opportunity to dunk Sophy's head under the water, holding it there until Sophy had panicked and taken in a lungful of water, nearly drowning.

She'd been too terrified to swim after that, refusing to take lessons. Until Apollo had taken her into the pool that day.

Something defiant rose up inside Sophy. Anger and an impotent sense of rage at her sister—for all that she had done, for all that Sophy had allowed her to do, and for dying, before Sophy had got to tell her that she loved her one more time.

Tears were sliding down Sophy's cheeks before she could stop them, emotions overflowing. Obeying an urge she couldn't ignore, she stripped down to her underwear, pulling the sundress she was wearing over her head.

She wanted to feel a wave breaking over her head, as much to prove to herself that she wasn't scared as to cleanse something inside herself. Something she couldn't even really articulate.

At the last moment she looked around. The beach was entirely empty and private. Not another soul.

She could almost hear her sister's voice in her head. *'Go on, Soph, don't be such a scaredy-cat.'* It spurred her on.

She stripped off her knickers and bra and threw all her clothes to a safe distance from the incoming tide and took a step into the water.

It felt glorious—the cool water on her sun-warmed skin. She took another step and the waves crashed around her knees. Another step. She gasped as the water reached her hips and lower belly.

Another wave was approaching, bigger, and taking a deep breath, heart pounding, she ducked down, letting it break over her head. Instantly she sprang back up, sucking in deep breaths, skin tingling all over from the cold and exhilaration, and the decadence of being naked in the water.

Another wave was coming, and she ducked down for that one too, spluttering a little as she came back up, but suddenly she realised she was in deeper water that came almost up to her breasts and another wave was coming, breaking over her head. When she emerged again there was another wave almost immediately and suddenly she couldn't get her breath.

Before panic could set in, a strong pair of hands was under her arms, lifting her out of the oncoming wave. She blinked and spluttered, hands going out and landing on a wall of muscle.

'What do you think you're doing, you little fool? You don't know how to swim, you're not ready for the sea yet. You could drown out here.'

Apollo.

Waves were breaking around them now. Apollo's hair was slicked back from the sea. His face stark. He looked down and she saw his cheeks flush. 'You're naked.'

Sophy was gasping. 'I…didn't bring a swimsuit… I

wasn't going to get into the water…but I just…wanted to feel it against my skin.'

Her teeth started chattering, as much in reaction to Apollo as because the water was cold.

Apollo was grim. 'There's a storm coming, this tide is coming in fast.'

He swung her effortlessly into his arms and carried her out of the water. It was only then she realised how far in she'd wandered. Her arms were around Apollo's neck, her bare breasts pressing against his chest.

She burned with mortification but also something stronger.

When they reached the shallows she said, 'You can put me down, I'm okay now.'

He ignored her, long legs striding back up the beach. She could see a towel on the ground, near her discarded clothes. Apollo put her down and picked up the towel, wrapping it around her shoulders. He caught the ends and pulled her towards him.

She was very aware that he was naked too, apart from swimming shorts that hugged his body, leaving little to the imagination.

'What were you thinking? You could have drowned.'

Sophy blinked up at him. 'I wasn't thinking… I didn't expect it to get rough so quickly.'

She didn't even realise she was still trembling until Apollo cursed and started rubbing her skin with the towel. She wanted to say she wasn't cold—it was his effect on her. His eyes dropped and his hands stopped moving. She didn't have to follow his gaze to feel its effect on her breasts, nipples tight and sensitive after brushing against his chest.

She wanted him with a desperation she'd never experienced before. That recklessness that had sent her into the water rose up again and for a heady moment Sophy wondered if this was the real essence of herself that she'd repressed for so long, while she'd hidden in Sasha's shadow?

She dislodged his hands and the towel fell off her shoulders. There was something very elemental about being naked in front of him like this. Apollo's eyes flared bright green. His jaw clenched. 'What are you doing?'

Sophy also realised in that moment that she desperately needed Apollo to make love to *her*. To Sophy. To know who he was making love to this time. To call out *her* name. Exorcise Sasha from their past.

She opened her mouth but then she went cold inside. She'd just imagined seeing his reaction to her. He didn't want her any more. How could he after everything that had transpired? All her bravado leached away and she crossed her arms over her chest, looked for the towel. 'I'm sorry... I know you can't still want—' She spied the towel and bent down to retrieve it but when she straightened up Apollo took it out of her hands and pulled them apart, baring her to his gaze again.

'I can't still want *what*?'

'Me.'

'*Theos.* If only I didn't want you, my life would be infinitely simpler.'

He tugged her towards him and she stumbled slightly, landing against him, a sense of relief rising inside her. He took his hands off hers and cupped her face, tilting it up to his. Then he bent his head and covered her mouth with his in a kiss that was so explicit and carnal that Sophy lost all sense of time and place.

When he pulled back she felt dizzy, plastered against his body. She could feel the bulge of his arousal through the thin material of his shorts and put her hand down there, exploring tentatively.

He put his hand on hers. His voice was rough. 'Stop, unless you want to make love right here, right now.'

She must have communicated her desperation silently because Apollo muttered something unintelligible and let her go briefly to pull down his own shorts and spread the towel on the sand.

He pulled her down alongside him on the towel, shielding her from the rough sand with his body. His hands stroked along every curve of her body, sending her into a frenzy of need. Big hands cupped her buttocks, squeezing, kneading. Her hands moved over the wide muscled plane of his chest, mouth seeking and finding the blunt nub of his nipple, hearing his sucked-in breath when she explored with her tongue and teeth.

He put a hand in her hair, tugging her head back gently. Her vision was blurry.

'Sophy... I want you, now.'

Hearing her name on his lips made her feel absurdly emotional. She ducked her head into his neck. 'I want you too...'

He moved her over his body so that her legs were astride his hips. The centre of her body was embarrassingly hot and damp, but before she could dwell on that her entire being suffused with pleasure when she felt the head of Apollo's erection nudge against where she was so hot and needy.

He looked at her. 'Okay?'

She nodded. He notched the head inside her and she sucked in a breath. He put his hands on her hips. His expression was strained. 'Move up, and back.'

She bit her lip, every part of her being focused on doing as he asked. She came up and felt him under her, power barely leashed…and sank down, taking him inside her. It was the most exquisite agony she'd ever experienced as she felt herself stretch to accommodate his hard length.

She moved experimentally, up and down. Apollo's hands were on her hips, but not controlling her movements, letting her take the lead. It was heady.

A rhythm slowly built and built until Sophy couldn't control it any more. Apollo held her hips then, showing her how much restraint he'd exercised as he pumped powerfully up and into her body. She couldn't stay upright as she convulsed with pleasure, curving over him as he followed her over the edge and into an ocean of total and utter sated bliss.

As the after-shocks pulsed through their entwined limbs, neither one of them was aware of the incoming water lapping around their heated bodies.

Apollo hadn't intended to make love to Sophy. He'd intended to bring her to the island and put some distance between them. Giving himself time to assimilate everything. Absorb the reality that she was who she was. A different person. The same person.

And for about twenty-four hours it had worked out that way. He'd kept his distance—gone to the site, stayed in his study.

But then, this afternoon, he'd seen her far below on the beach. He'd seen her taking her clothes off, her pale body gleaming like a pearl against the azure sky and ocean, like some ethereal being. Not human.

Then she'd looked around, taken her underwear off. Stepped gingerly into the water. Then she'd waded further in, ducking under the waves. Apollo had felt like he was intruding on a very private moment and then he'd realised she was in danger of getting out of her depth. And that she couldn't swim.

When he'd reached her his insides had been in a knot and he'd hauled her up out of the water, her slim body far too light and puny against the might of the sea. He'd been angry.

Scared.

He'd also noticed that her eyes were red and he didn't think it was from the water. She'd been crying. Mourning.

He hadn't intended making love to her there and then. But she'd blasted through any resolve to resist her just by looking at him. Never mind being naked, her skin wet from the sea. Red hair in long silken skeins over her shoulders. Like a water nymph sent to tempt him. Or a mermaid.

The more he had of her the more he wanted. It made his skin prickle with a sense of panic. Exposure. The same kind of exposure he'd felt when he'd realised she had been a virgin, because he'd wanted her too much to look for the signs of innocence, and in hindsight they'd been there. He'd just ignored them.

Today had just proved her effect on him.

Dangerous.

He said, 'We didn't use protection today.'

Sophy's hand tightened on the stem of the wine glass. Heat suffused her body again to think of how carnal she'd been on the beach earlier. She barely remembered Apollo putting the dress over her head afterwards, dressing her. Leading her up the steps. Putting her to bed. She'd woken in her room, alone, as the sun had been setting outside.

She'd taken a shower and come out to find Apollo sitting in the dining area, clean-shaven, hair damp, as Olympia had laid the table for dinner. For a moment she'd almost been afraid she'd dreamt up the beach, but the storm he'd mentioned was lashing at the windows now.

They hadn't used protection. Because she'd all but begged him to make love to her.

She fought the rising tide of heat under her skin. Apollo looked at her and shook his head. 'It's amazing that you can still blush...'

That only made her blush even harder. 'It's okay... I'm at a safe place in my cycle.'

Apollo saw the worried look on Sophy's face. She couldn't hide her expressions. He had to acknowledge uncomfortably that he trusted her word.

'It won't happen again.'

Her face was still pink. Her hair was down around her shoulders. She'd appeared for dinner in long loose trousers and a loose silk top. It kept slipping off one shoulder.

The pink leached a little from her cheeks. She said, 'I think you're right, it's not a good idea.'

Apollo dragged his gaze up from where her pale

shoulder was bared. He frowned. 'What are you talking about?'

'Making lo—' She stopped. 'Sex. It's probably not a good idea. Considering everything…'

A visceral rejection of what she'd said rose up from somewhere deep and primal inside Apollo. He might have come here intending to keep his distance but after this afternoon that was an impossibility.

He shook his head and reached out a hand, finding Sophy's across the table and tugging her up out of her chair and over to him. He pulled her down and she landed on his lap, sliding into place like a missing jigsaw piece.

It's just desire, repeated Apollo like a mantra in his head.

He said, 'That's not what I meant.'

Sophy hated the way her heart leapt. 'What did you mean?'

'I meant that I won't be careless again, but we will be making love again. I don't see why we can't make the most of this. The chemistry between us is more powerful than anything I've ever experienced. It's unprecedented for me. But it will burn out. It always does.'

It will burn out. Sophy felt something inside her rebel at that assertion. This feeling that she'd never get enough of him…she couldn't imagine it ever fading away.

As if he could read her mind, he said carefully, 'Sophy, nothing has changed. I am not in the market for a relationship or family. It's not something I ever want to experience. If anything, believing that I might become a father has only confirmed my vow not to have a family. I had a family and I lost them, I won't put my-self through that again.'

Sophy's heart constricted. His words, painful as they were, actually helped to clarify how differently her very similar experience had shaped her. 'I lost my family too…but I know I won't feel whole again until I have a family of my own.'

Apollo tensed under her body and she held her breath. But then he said in a voice devoid of emotion, 'And I'm sure you'll have that one day. With someone else. What I'm offering is very transient. A couple of weeks to explore this insane chemistry before we part ways and get on with our separate lives. Once and for all.'

Sophy knew that she should stand up and step away. Tell Apollo that she wasn't interested in a transient af-fair. She wanted more. She'd always wanted more. It was why she'd still been a virgin long after her sister had lost her innocence.

But Apollo wanted her for now. Maybe that was enough. Maybe she would wake up one morning and not feel this insatiable need. Maybe she would be able to move on. Could she stand up and step back…from *this*? This energy pulsing between them even now?

She knew the answer. *No way.* Memories might be cold bedfellows in the future but she knew she didn't have the strength to walk away. Not yet. He'd been her only constant for the last few turbulent weeks. She needed to feel anchored again. Rooted. Even if it was only temporary.

She slid her arms around his neck. 'Okay, then.'

Apollo smiled and it was a smile of pure male satisfaction as he drew her head down to his and took her mouth in a searing kiss. A promise of what was to come, what he was offering, and she, like a miser, would take it.

CHAPTER TEN

A COUPLE OF days later, Sophy was lying face down in Apollo's bed. The morning sun was streaming in, warm on her bare back. A breeze chased the warmth across her skin.

Her whole body ached pleasurably. Since the other stormy evening, the days and nights had melded into one another, punctuated by moments of carnal pleasure—like last night. Apollo had returned from the site in the early evening. He'd taken Sophy down to the beach and given her another swimming lesson in the sea. They hadn't worn swimsuits, and they'd re-created the other day, except this time with protection.

Then Apollo had taken her back up to the villa and after a leisurely and very thorough shower, they'd eaten and gone to bed. But not to sleep. To discover new heights of pleasure and passion.

Sophy had been so crazed last night, so desperate for Apollo to release her from the sensual torture that she could remember her voice breaking as she'd begged him.

She buried her face in the pillow now and groaned softly, so she didn't hear when Apollo entered the room.

But she felt the bed dip and tensed. A tension that quickly dissolved when a finger trailed down her spine to the top of her buttocks.

She turned her head to meet a cool green gaze. *This* was what kept her from tumbling into fantasy land, this reserve that Apollo showed when he wasn't breaking her apart. The reserve that reminded her that he had rejected her after making love to her the first time. That reminded her that he'd only married Sasha out of a sense of duty and responsibility because he'd believed she was pregnant. That reminded her of his words to her that he didn't *do* relationships.

So, no matter what this was…it wasn't going anywhere. And she had to remember that.

'Kalimera.'

'Kalimera.'

She felt shy. Which was ridiculous. She turned and pulled the sheet up, covering her body. Apollo's mouth quirked as if mocking her attempt to be modest. She wanted to scowl at him.

'You mentioned before that you'd like to visit the site…would you still like to?'

That felt like an age ago now. She nodded. 'Yes, I'd like that.' Then she thought of something. 'Will it be okay for me to be seen here with you?'

'We won't be bothered here. It's entirely private. We'll leave in half an hour.'

Later that morning, Apollo looked to where Sophy was nodding studiously as his foreman showed her around the site. She was wearing those yellow capri pants and the white shirt that tied above her midriff. Wedge shoes.

A hard hat was perched on her head and a plait dissected her shoulder blades.

She could have passed for sixteen if it wasn't for the X-rated memories of how she'd taken him into her body last night, meeting him thrust for thrust, begging, pleading...sending them both over the edge and into a crashing, burning orgasm so intense— *Theos*.

She might have agreed to this transitory affair but he'd seen something in her eyes the other night that had caught at him deep inside. The same place that had been triggered when he'd believed he was to become a father, and when he'd realised that he wasn't as averse to the thought of a family as he'd believed himself to be.

In the aftermath of Sasha's lies, that weakness had been pushed down. Not allowed room to breathe again. Until he'd heard himself telling Sophy the other night that she would have a family one day. With someone else. Not him. He'd said the words and they'd felt like ash in his mouth.

He told himself it was sheer possessiveness of a lover. Nothing more. He didn't want more. Even with Sophy. Especially Sophy.

Apollo saw his foreman put a hand to Sophy's back to guide her over some uneven ground. That sense of possessiveness surged. He closed the distance between them in a couple of long strides, and took Sophy's hand. 'I'll take this from here, Milos, thank you.'

He was aware of Sophy looking up at him and his foreman's bemused expression. He ignored both and led her up to an open piece of ground at the top of a hill. She was panting slightly when they reached it. He let her hand go, and gestured around them. 'This is going to be the site for the solar panels. The resort will be entirely self-sufficient for energy.'

She was turning around, hand up to shield her eyes from the sun. She said, 'Does it have to be just for solar panels? This would be a beautiful spot for an exclusive suite. It would have three-hundred-and-sixty-degree views of the island and surrounding sea. Sunrise and sunset views.'

Apollo looked around and realised she was right. He followed her gaze, which took in the sea and hazy shapes of islands in the distance. The sky was so blue it hurt. Not a cloud in sight. All around them insects and birds chirruped and called. The scent of wild herbs infused the air.

He shook his head, his mouth quirking. 'I've had one of the best firms working on this for a couple of years now and no one came up with that idea.'

'Oh.' Sophy flushed, a dangerous warmth infusing her insides. 'Well, it might be a silly idea. I'm sure it was thought of and discarded for some reason.'

'We'll look at it.'

'Why did you decide to buy an island?' Sophy asked then, taking him off guard a little. Apollo looked out over the sea. 'When we were small, my brother was fascinated by the Greek myths and legends. My mother used to tell them to us at night as our bedtime stories.'

His mouth quirked. 'I found them boring. I was more interested in how things worked. He was the dreamer— he took after our mother. I took after our father. After our parents died and we were shuttled from foster home to foster home, he used to tell me that he couldn't wait to be old enough to leave Athens. Get on a boat and go to all the islands, see the places of the myths and legends. Athens was too harsh for him. He was too sensitive. He fell in with a gang, as much to survive as anything else. Once he started taking drugs…that was it. He was lost.'

Sophy's heart felt sore for Apollo and his brother. 'Why didn't you end up going the same way?'

Apollo shrugged, his eyes hidden behind dark shades. 'I guess I was born more cynical than Achilles. I was more street smart too. I stayed out of the gang's way. He was more susceptible. My father had always encouraged me to study hard, telling me that's how I'd make a life for myself. I put my head down and when I looked up, it was too late.'

The self-recrimination in his voice was palpable.

'You were kids. Your brother was older than you. It wasn't your responsibility to care for him. The adults around you should have been doing that.'

Apollo made a derisory sound. 'Our foster parents were just interested in the money they got from the state to take us in.'

Sophy looked away and out to the horizon again, a little embarrassed at the emotion she was feeling. The fact that he'd done this to honour his brother was beyond touching. The whole site for the resort had touched her—everything was going to be sustainable and designed to make the most of the island's natural resources, which in turn would help grow the local economy.

The resort was going to be seriously impressive and seriously luxurious. Private suites with their own pools, terraces and stunning views would be dotted around a central area where there would be several restaurants, a spa, a gym and shops, showcasing local produce and crafts.

In the main area there would be more rooms, and an infinity pool. Apollo also had plans for self-contained cottages where artists could come and stay in residence for a time—writers, painters, poets. They could apply for sponsorship through the resort and it only just impacted on Sophy now that he must have been thinking of his brother when he'd done that.

'Come,' he said, 'I'll take you to the town. I have a short meeting to attend with the town's council and you can get a coffee and look around.'

She noticed he didn't take her hand this time but she felt his fingers touch bare skin above the waistband of her trousers and it burned hotter than the sun.

Apollo was treated like a visiting celebrity when they reached the small harbour town a short while later. Old men came up to shake his hand, women smiled shyly, bouncing babies on their hips.

He seemed to be embarrassed by the attention, smiling tightly. He took Sophy's hand again, leading her to a shaded leafy square, with little *tavernas* that had seats and tables outside. She was glad of the shade as she was starting to wilt in the hot early afternoon sun.

He spoke to the owner, who answered him effusively, gesturing to Sophy to come and sit down. 'What did you say to him?' she asked, amused by the attention.

'Just to give you whatever you want until I come back. I won't be long.'

She watched him walk off. He was wearing faded jeans and a white polo shirt. The denim did little to hide the firm contours of his buttocks and when the owner came back with a menu, she was blushing.

He gestured towards where Apollo was disappearing around a corner and said something in Greek that Sophy couldn't understand, but she could see the emotion on the man's face and imagined that he was telling her how grateful they were that Apollo had single-handedly breathed life back into this little island. Just because he wanted to honour his brother's memory.

Sophy smiled and put a hand to her chest to indicate that she understood. The man smiled and said in heavily accented English, 'What would you like?'

She asked for a coffee, having developed a taste for the strong tart drink. She noticed that there was bunting up around the pretty square and women were decorating every visible area with flowers.

When they came over to the *taverna*, Sophy jumped up to help them string a garland of flowers over the front of the door. They spoke no English, she spoke no Greek but they laughed and smiled and for the first time in a long time, in spite of her grief, she felt light.

She was dying to know what the flowers were for but her attempts to ask the ladies made them laugh at her mimes. Then she saw them all go brick red and stop talking. They practically bowed down. Sophy had to stop herself from rolling her eyes at their reaction. She didn't have to look to know who was behind her. She could *feel* him.

She might roll her eyes at his effect on the locals but, really, she was no better. He came up alongside her. 'You're helping them prepare for the wedding?'

Sophy looked at him in surprise. 'It's a wedding?'

He nodded. 'The first wedding they've had on the island for a couple of years. It's a big deal…and we've been invited.'

'Oh…' Sophy's heartstrings tugged. She'd love to see a Greek wedding but she didn't expect Apollo would want to bring her with him, as if they were a couple. 'That's okay, they don't know about our…arrangement. You should go, it'll be expected.'

He looked at her and she felt herself flush. Was she being gauche?

'They invited both of us. It's no big deal. Greek weddings are pretty informal in places like this, everyone is invited.'

Now she did feel gauche. 'Oh… Okay, then. That would be nice.'

'I'll show you around.'

Sophy waved goodbye to the ladies and the *taverna* owner and when Apollo took her hand she tried to ignore the hitch in her heart. This was just a fleeting affair. No matter how much she might be falling in love with this lazy, idyllic island.

No matter how much she might be falling deeper in love with the man.

Her feet missed a step and she stumbled. Apollo put his arm around her to steady her. 'Okay?'

She forced a smile. 'Fine.'

Liar.

She couldn't ever afford to forget that she was only here because her sister had gone to this man and told a heinous lie, trapping him into a marriage. He never would have gone after Sophy. She never would have seen him again. She welcomed the dart of pain because this would be nothing compared to the pain she'd feel if she entertained fantasies.

The town comprised of a few artisan shops and a beautiful old Greek orthodox church that was being prepared for the wedding. There was a growing air of excitement.

Apollo led her down another side street and they passed a boutique. Sophy's feet stopped in their tracks. It was a simple boutique but there was a dress in the window that caught her attention. Caught her heart.

It was light blue broderie anglaise. Off the shoulder. The bodice was fitted and it fell in soft folds to below the knees. It was simple and unsophisticated. *Not* the kind of thing Sasha would have chosen in a million years. But she wasn't Sasha. She was Sophy and she wasn't sophisticated.

'You like that dress?'

Embarrassed, Sophy started to walk off. 'No, no, it just caught my eye.'

But Apollo didn't budge. 'It would suit you. Try it on.'

Sophy tried to desist but Apollo was tugging her towards the shop. The saleswoman had seen them too and was opening the door. Too late to turn back. She was obviously delighted that the saviour of the island was frequenting her humble establishment.

They went in and before Sophy could object, she was being whisked off to a changing area.

Apollo paced the floor of the shop. This was something he didn't usually indulge in—dressing his lovers. It would give the wrong impression. But right now he didn't really care. He just wanted to see Sophy in that dress.

He heard a noise behind him and turned. For a moment he felt like he couldn't breathe. He almost reached to his neck to loosen his tie but realised he wasn't wearing one.

He'd seen women in some of the skimpiest and most expensive haute couture but none of them had had this effect on him. The dress shouldn't be having this effect on him. But it wasn't the dress, it was the woman in the dress. She epitomised simple fresh-faced beauty. No adornment.

The bodice hugged her torso, around her high firm breasts and then fell in soft folds to below her knees. Her feet were bare. Her hair was pulled back, highlighting her slim shoulders and neck. He could see where the sun had turned her skin a light gold. She had more freckles.

His voice felt strangled when he said, 'We'll buy it.'

Sophy immediately started protesting but he just signalled to the owner that they'd take it and she whisked Sophy back to the changing area.

When Sophy emerged again Apollo was paying for the dress and accepting it in a bag. She felt conflicted—thrilled to have the dress but weird because he'd paid for it. Sasha had always favoured boyfriends with money who would buy her things and the sheer volume of clothes here and in Athens was testament to how much she'd squeezed out of Apollo.

When they walked out of the shop into the street Sophy said stiffly, 'I really didn't expect you to buy the dress.'

'It looks good on you, wear it this evening at the wedding festivities.'

He was putting his shades on again, oblivious to Sophy's turmoil. She didn't move. 'I want to pay you back for the dress.' She realised she had nothing, and not only that, she would have most certainly lost her job. There was only a meagre balance in her bank account back in England because she'd loaned Sasha money not long before she'd disappeared to Greece with Apollo. The knowledge that she'd most likely funded Sasha's trip to betray her made her feel even more prickly. 'I mean, when I can. I insist.'

Apollo looked at her. 'Fine. Whatever you want. I can get your people to liaise with my people and set up an electronic transfer for the princely sum of thirty euros.' His mouth quirked.

'Don't laugh at me.'

His mouth straightened. He put his hands on her hips and pulled her to him. 'I know you're not your sister, Sophy. You're nothing like her, believe me.'

'You couldn't tell us apart after the accident.'

Apollo arched a brow over his shades. 'Couldn't I? I never wanted her the way I want you.'

He kissed her there in the street, with people passing by. Sophy was aware of whispers and giggles and she couldn't stop her silly heart soaring.

When they returned to the town early that evening, Sophy felt self-conscious in the dress. She'd dressed it up a bit by pulling her hair into a bun on the top of her head and choosing a pair of Sasha's strappy silver sandals.

Apollo was wearing a dark suit and white shirt, open at the neck. He led her down to the smaller square where the church was located and the couple was just emerging from the entrance to loud cheers and clapping. Musicians played traditional Greek music.

Apollo and Sophy stood on the end of what looked like a receiving line of guests to either side of the couple, who passed down, accepting congratulations and good wishes. The bride was beautiful, with dark laughing eyes and long hair. Her husband was tall and handsome. They looked incandescently happy.

When they'd passed down the line, they walked through the town towards the bigger square. Apollo and Sophy followed them. The place had been transformed since earlier that day. Flowers festooned every available surface and fairy lights were strung across the square. Candles flickered on tables.

It was simple, rustic, humble and beautiful. Sophy knew Sasha would have hated it. She loved it.

Apollo was greeted and feted like a VIP. They were seated at a table for dinner near the bride and groom's table. A steady stream of people came up to converse with Apollo. Sophy was happy to let the occasion wash over her, enjoying the people-watching and lively Greek bonhomie and music.

When dinner had been cleared away, the music stopped suddenly and a line of men got up to dance, including the groom. Everyone turned to look at them. At the last minute they gestured to Apollo to get up and join them. He signalled *no*, but one of the men came over and pulled him up, amidst cheers and applause.

The music started slow and mesmeric, a familiar

Greek song, a traditional dance. Apollo was near the middle, near the groom. The men started dancing, slowly, in time to the music, arms around each other's shoulders.

Apollo did the slow deliberate steps with perfect precision, a smile on his face. He looked younger all of a sudden. Less intense. It made Sophy's heart swell, thinking of what he'd told her about his parents dancing. Maybe his father had taught him and his brother this dance?

The music got faster and the steps more intricate, Apollo's torso and hips twisting. He was so dynamic and handsome that Sophy didn't have to look around her to know that every gaze was trained on him. Probably even the bride's.

By the time the music built to a crescendo everyone was on their feet clapping and cheering. The men bowed. Then it was the women's turn, led out to dance by the bride.

One of the women grabbed Sophy's hand and pulled her up. She was shaking her head, laughing, but they ignored her. She caught Apollo's eye and shrugged helplessly.

Apollo watched Sophy being pulled away to dance. Her face was shining and she was laughing, trying to do her best to keep up with the steps of the dance. She stood out with her red-gold hair and blue eyes. Pale skin. She'd kicked off the high-heeled sandals and was in her bare feet.

Physical desire was like a tight knot inside Apollo, winding tighter and tighter. But along with the physical desire was something else, something far more disturbing. A sense of yearning…a need to replace the hollow ache in his chest. An ache he'd ignored for a long time. An ache he couldn't keep ignoring around *her*.

With her questions that struck at the heart of him: *Why did you buy an island?*

A sense of desperation gripped him now. This was just about *sex*. Nothing more. By the time Sophy had picked up her shoes and come off the dance floor Apollo was standing up to meet her.

He took her hand. 'Ready to go?'

She must have seen something of the urgency he was feeling because her eyes darkened and she nodded wordlessly.

Apollo paid his respects to the bride and groom and drove them back to his villa. All was quiet and hushed on this side of the island, only the faintest sounds of the revelry carrying on the light breeze. Sophy's feet were still bare.

They got out of the car and Apollo held out his hand for her. Sophy didn't hesitate. She took Apollo's hand and let him lead her into the villa, dropping her shoes on the way. The need to replace feelings he didn't welcome with the physical reminder of what was between them was overwhelming.

Sophy let Apollo lead her to his room. It was illuminated by moonlight. Standing in front of him, the lingering tipsiness from the wine made her bold. She moved forward and pushed Apollo's jacket off. It fell to the floor.

Then he undid his buttons and opened his shirt, pushing it off his broad shoulders. His chest was wide and powerful. She couldn't resist touching him, running her hands over his skin. His muscles tensed under her fingers and she felt powerful.

He reached for her hair and undid her bun, letting her hair fall down around her bare shoulders. She shivered at the sensation.

He caught her face in his hands and tilted it up to him. His features were stark with need and her insides clenched in reaction. There was something else there, some indefinable emotion. Instinctively Sophy touched his jaw with her hand. 'Apollo? Are you okay?'

Something expressive crossed his face for a second and then it was gone. Replaced by pure unadulterated *need*. 'I'm fine. I just want you. Now.'

She hesitated for a moment, because she sensed that there was some sort of internal battle being fought, but the clamour of her own blood drowned out the need to know. She turned around and pulled her hair over one shoulder, offering him her back. His hands came to the zip at the top of the dress and pulled it down, knuckles grazing the bare skin of her back.

The dress loosened from around her breasts and then fell to her waist. She pushed it off over her hips and it fell at her feet. Now she wore only her underwear.

Apollo came close behind her and she sucked in a breath when she realised that he was totally naked. His arms came around her, hands finding and closing over her breasts. Massaging them, teasing her tight nipples.

Instinctively she moved against him, and she heard an almost feral-sounding growl. Apollo turned her to face him and the electricity crackled between them. Urgency spiked.

He led her over to the bed and she lay down. He

reached for her underwear, pulling them down and off. He came over her, all rippling muscles and sleek olive-toned skin. She opened her legs to him, and he settled between them as if they'd done this dance down through lifetimes and not just in this one.

Sophy lifted her hips towards him, her small hand seeking to wrap around his rigid flesh, bringing his head close to where her body ached for him. For an infinitesimal moment he was poised there on the brink and then he took her hand away and joined their bodies with one powerful thrust.

She was so ready for him. She could feel her inner muscles clamping around him in a pre-orgasmic rush of sensation.

There was no time for slow lovemaking. It was fast and furious, both racing for the pinnacle and reaching it at the same incandescent moment, bodies entwined and locked together in an explosion of pleasure that went on and on. Sophy wasn't even aware of Apollo extricating himself from her embrace or of the way he stood up from the bed and looked at her for a long moment.

A week later, Apollo looked at Sophy across the dinner table that had been set on the terrace of the villa. She was talking to Olympia and the older woman's face was wreathed in smiles as she showed Sophy pictures on her phone of her newest grandchild.

Apollo marvelled at how he had been so blinkered by Sasha's deviousness that he hadn't noticed how different *this* woman was.

People responded to Sophy because she was open and kind. Polite. She was also sexy and utterly addictive. During the past week, Apollo had effectively shut out the world to gorge himself on this woman. But her appeal wasn't waning at all, or burning out. It was burning hotter. Becoming stronger.

He'd been ignoring calls from his office in Athens, to the point where his executive assistant had turned up on Krisakis today to speak to him personally. A visit that had broken him out of the haze of desire, shattering the illusion that he didn't have to engage with the outside world.

An image inserted itself into his mind—Sophy laughing and dancing with the other women at the wedding. The way seeing her like that had opened a great gaping chasm of yearning inside him. A yearning he'd had to eclipse by making love to her like a starving man. A yearning that lingered and caught at him under his skin. Chafing. Unwelcome.

A yearning that had made him careless. For a second time. Something he'd effectively blocked out all week. He was losing control, letting her in too deep.

Olympia was walking away with their plates now and Sophy looked at Apollo, her smile fading at the expression on his face. 'What is it?'

A stone weight made his chest feel tight. But he ignored it. 'We need to talk.'

CHAPTER ELEVEN

SOPHY FOLLOWED APOLLO into his study, her insides in a knot. He'd been distracted since his assistant had visited earlier. There was a spectacular view of the ocean and vast sky, which was currently a glorious pink and lavender colour. But that faded into insignificance behind the man dominating the space.

Apollo rested on the edge of his desk, hands by his hips. Hips that Sophy could remember holding only a few short hours before as he'd—

She blurted out a question to try and distract herself from memories of a week spent indulging in the pursuit of sensual oblivion. 'What is it, Apollo?'

But she already knew. It skated across her skin like a cold breeze. In fact, she'd been aware of it all week, even if she hadn't acknowledged it. The real world was waiting, just in the wings.

Even so, she wasn't prepared when he said tightly, 'When we made love…after the wedding, I didn't use protection that night. I told you I wouldn't be careless again but I was.'

Sophy's insides went into freefall. She hadn't even noticed, hadn't even thought about it afterwards.

Faintly she said, 'It wasn't just your fault. I should have been careful too.' It had been the last thing on her mind during that conflagration. Or during this week, when it had felt like their world had been reduced to this villa, this island. Apollo's bed.

You didn't want to think about anything that would burst the bubble.

No, she hadn't. She'd deliberately shied away from thinking about anything that might break the idyll. She'd let the fantasy become her reality. And now she would pay.

She almost put a hand on her belly but closed it into a fist. She said, 'It's okay. I'm at a safe place in my cycle. I'm sure of it.'

Apollo seemed to absorb that, and then he said, 'My assistant brought your personal things today, including your passport. And Sasha's body is ready for repatriation. My office will arrange everything for her funeral if you just give them the necessary information of where you want her buried.'

The cold breeze turned to ice in Sophy's belly. 'That won't be necessary, I can do all that.'

'I insist. She was my wife, after all. You won't have to worry about costs.'

Sophy swallowed. 'When do we leave?'

'Leander, my assistant, is still on the island, staying in the town. He will come for you in the morning and you will travel back to Athens with him, and then on to London with your sister. You'll be met by an assistant from my London office on the other side, they'll help you make further arrangements.'

Sophy searched for a hint of anything on Apollo's

face or in his eyes, but he'd retreated somewhere she couldn't reach. She'd noticed it when he'd arrived for dinner—when he'd avoided her eye. He'd been shut up in his office with his assistant for most of the afternoon.

'You won't be coming back to Athens?'

'Not just yet. I have some meetings here on the island to do with the construction and I'll travel back the following day.'

A sharp pain lanced her insides.

Her heart.

And also a sense of panic.

As if reading her every passing emotion, Apollo said, 'My assistant in London will make sure you're looked after, Sophy. You won't be left alone.'

If there was one thing Sophy wouldn't be able to bear, it was Apollo's pity or that she was a responsibility to be dealt with. 'That really won't be necessary. I can go back to the flat I shared with Sasha. I'll…be fine.'

Apollo stood up. 'Leander will be here before ten a.m.'

Sophy looked at him, in shock at the speed and efficiency with which he was apparently willing to dispatch her.

'So that's it, then?'

His face tightened. 'I think it's for the best. There's no point in prolonging something that we both know is at an end.'

Sophy felt emotion swelling inside her. If she'd known the last time she'd made love to Apollo was to be the last time, she would have imprinted every second onto her memory. 'You mean, something that never should have started.'

'Sophy…' he said warningly.

But a volatile mix of hurt, anger and fear made her say, 'The truth is that something happened between us that first night, we had a connection, and I think you used my virginity as an excuse to kick me out. To deny it.'

'You were inexperienced. Naive. I wasn't prepared to let you believe it would ever become something more than just sex.'

'Well, I think it was about you just as much as it might have been about me.'

'What's that supposed to mean?'

'I think you're an emotional coward, Apollo. I understand why it's hard for you to trust again. But I've lost my family too and I don't want to shut my emotions up for ever.'

A muscle pulsed in Apollo's jaw. 'Which is why I said to you that you'll go on to meet someone and have a family some day. You want more, Sophy. I don't.'

Sophy felt something inside her crack and break. 'I think you're a liar, Apollo. I think you do want more, but you're too scared to admit it.'

Or maybe he just doesn't want more with you.

Her insides curdled at that thought. Maybe Apollo would trust his heart again some day. When he met someone he couldn't walk away from, or shut out.

He opened his mouth but Sophy held up her hand, terrified to hear Apollo spell out that it just wasn't *her* who could crack the ice around his heart.

Now who's the coward? mocked a voice.

Sophy pushed it down.

'It's fine, Apollo.' She lowered her hand. 'It wasn't

as if you weren't clear about what this was. I'll be ready for Leander in the morning.'

Apollo watched Sophy turn to walk out of his study. At the last moment he blurted out her name. She turned around.

She said nothing. Her face was expressionless. Perversely, Apollo wanted to provoke a reaction.

'You'll let me know if there are any consequences?'

Her face leached of colour. 'You mean a baby?'

Now that he'd got the reaction he just felt hollow. He nodded.

Her mouth was tight. 'I told you, there won't be. I'm sure of it.'

She turned and this time left the room.

Apollo had nothing more to say.

To stop her from leaving.

He was so rigid with tension that he thought he might crack if he moved. *Theos.* Did he want there to be consequences? After everything that had happened?

Her words reverberated in his head, a mocking jeer.

'I think you're a liar, Apollo... I think you do want more...'

He turned around and stared blindly at the view. She was wrong. He didn't want more. He had decided a long time ago what kind of life he wanted and he wasn't about to let one woman change that.

One woman was no match for the demons that haunted him, reminding him of a loss and pain so great he thought he'd have preferred to die with them all.

All he felt for Sophy was physical lust. Nothing more. And that would fade. No matter how much it still burnt him up inside.

* * *

As Sophy's flight from Athens descended through stormy summer skies into London, she took in the unseasonably grey clouds. They mirrored her mood. Volatile.

She was angry with herself for having fallen for Apollo. For having revealed herself so much during that last exchange in his study.

The anger was good—it was insulating her from the sheer terror of stepping back out into a fast-paced world after living in a cocoon for these past few weeks. She knew that not far under the anger her shell was very brittle and fragile.

She had a sister to grieve and a life to re-start. A job to find because, as expected, when she'd rung them from Athens the day before, she'd found out that her position had been filled once she'd disappeared. The fact that they'd been so wholly unconcerned about her disappearance only compounded her sense of isolation now. Sophy shook her head, trying to dislodge that sense of isolation.

She put a hand on her flat belly. She'd not even noticed that they hadn't used protection that night a week ago. But Apollo had. She *was* sure there wouldn't be a baby and she hated herself for the hollow ache that thought precipitated.

Did she really want history to repeat itself, except this time with a real baby?

The plane had touched down. She lifted her hand from her belly. It was time to mourn and bury her sister and try to get on with her life and forget she'd ever met Apollo Vasilis.

Two weeks later, just outside London

'Let us go now in peace.'

Sophy stood by the grave for a moment. She was the only mourner at her sister's funeral. She'd told a few of Sasha's friends but they'd said they were too busy to come.

Sophy was sad, and a little angry—for her sister, in spite of her faults, had deserved better.

She had only barest sensation of prickling on the back of her neck before she heard the priest say, 'Welcome, sir. We've just finished the prayers.'

Sophy looked up and at first she thought she was hallucinating. Apollo looked taller and darker than she'd ever seen him. In a dark grey suit, white shirt and steel-grey tie. Dark shades hid his eyes.

Faintly, she said, 'Apollo…'

He dipped his head. 'Sophy.' He looked at the priest. 'Father.'

The priest came and took Sophy's arm. 'My dear, I'm so sorry. If you ever need to talk, you know where I am.'

Sophy tried to control her suddenly thundering heart. 'Thank you, Father.'

The priest walked away, leaving them alone by the grave. Sophy said, 'I wasn't expecting to see you here.'

Apollo's jaw tightened. 'I had always intended coming but I got delayed. She was my wife…however that came about.'

Sophy clamped down on the dangerous spurt of gratitude and something far more dangerous.

Hope.

'Thank you for your help in organising this.'

'It was nothing. I'll leave you for a moment.'

Apollo walked away and Sophy could see her own funeral limousine and then Apollo's blacked-out SUV. The drivers were talking. Apollo was standing at a respectable distance to give her some time. A gesture that made her feel surprisingly emotional.

She turned her back on him and said a few silent words to Sasha. The last few weeks she'd had to think about a lot of things and her relationship with her sister had been one of them. There was a certain sense of liberation now, but as much as that made Sophy feel guilty, she was also sad that it had had to come at the cost of her sister's life.

Her parents were buried in the same graveyard and Sophy walked the short distance to where they rested in their own plot, laying a flower on their grave.

Then she steeled herself to face Apollo. She turned around, aware of her sober black suit. It was actually the same skirt and shirt she'd been wearing the night she'd met him, and a black jacket. She'd put her hair up in a bun. She felt plain and unvarnished next to his effortless good looks when she walked towards him, where he stood under a tree.

She couldn't see his eyes but she could feel them on her and her skin prickled. She stopped a couple of feet away. He straightened up from the tree.

'Was the other grave your parents'?'

She nodded.

Then he said, 'Can we go somewhere to talk?'

The thought of being alone with him when she felt so raw made her blurt out, 'We can talk here.'

Apollo shuddered visibly. 'If it's okay with you, I've seen enough of graveyards to last me a lifetime.'

She felt a pang in her heart; so had she, come to think of it. She feigned nonchalance. 'Fine…where were you thinking?'

'My apartment in London, it's private.'

Where she'd gone with him the night they'd made love. A penthouse apartment at the top of a glittering exclusive building. The last place she should go with him, but suddenly the lure of seeing him again, however briefly, was too seductive.

'Okay.'

He stepped back and put out a hand for her to precede him to his car. He spoke with the other driver, who left. Sophy got into the SUV.

The journey into town was taken in silence, apart from a couple of phone calls Apollo made. Presumably to do with work. She wondered about Krisakis, how the resort was shaping up. A place she'd never see again.

They pulled up outside Apollo's apartment building and Sophy recognised it. It was bitter-sweet to have her memory back.

The driver opened her door and Sophy got out. Apollo was already standing on the pavement. Tall and gorgeous. Drawing appreciative glances from passers-by. Men and women.

Before, Sophy would have looked at Apollo and compared herself as someone who would fade into the background but she knew she had to stop taking on that role. The one she'd played with Sasha, allowing Sasha to be the noticeable one.

She was never going to set the world alight but she

could own her own space in a way she had never done before.

She walked ahead of Apollo into the building, through the door opened by the doorman. She could remember being here the first time, feeling so awed and excited. Tingling all over. Nervous. She felt as if she'd grown an age since that wide-eyed girl.

Virgin.

The lift took a few seconds and then they were stepping out into the grandeur that Sophy remembered. Lots of glass and plush carpets. Oriental rugs. Massive paintings on the walls. Sleek coffee tables with hardback tomes showing beautiful pictures of Greece and house interiors.

Of course, it had been dark outside the first time she'd been here and now it was bright daylight. And, in fairness, she'd only been interested in looking at one thing. Apollo.

He turned to her now. He'd already shrugged off his jacket and was loosening his tie. 'Can I get you tea, or coffee?'

Sophy held her bag in front of her. 'Just some water, please.'

He disappeared and came back a few minutes later holding a glass of water for her and a small cup of coffee for himself. He gestured around them. 'Please, make yourself comfortable.'

Sophy put down her bag and walked over to one of the windows, which took in the lush green gardens of Kensington Palace nearby. Truly this was a billionaire's address.

He said from behind her in a slightly gruff voice, 'You remind me of the night we met.'

Sophy fought to keep the blush down. She turned around. 'That's because I was wearing these same clothes. Pretty much.' The same clothes she'd put on with shaking hands and with tears blurring her vision after Apollo had summarily dismissed her. For being a virgin.

'How are you doing?'

Sophy's hand gripped the glass. 'I'm okay. I'm starting a new job as a receptionist in a central dentist's office in a couple of weeks.'

Apollo's blood thrummed with heat. A heat that hadn't cooled in Sophy's absence, much to his sense of frustration and a kind of futility.

'Apollo…what is it you want?'

He might have smiled at that loaded question, but it would be a bleak smile. He put the coffee cup down. 'I need to be sure…there are no consequences? After that night?'

His gaze dropped to her waist and he couldn't help but imagine it thickening and growing with his child. Before he could control it, that awfully familiar sense of yearning caught at his guts. *No.* Not what he was here for. Never that. Not even now.

Sophy blinked. He was so terrified of the thought of a baby that he'd come all the way here to check…again? She read his body language and something inside her curled up. *Yes.* He was that terrified.

She got out, 'No. I've had my period since I returned to London. I told you it would be okay.'

There was no discernible expression on Apollo's face

and Sophy was almost sorry now that she hadn't had another answer. To crack that facade.

'Okay…that's good, then.'

Except he sounded almost…disappointed. Sophy shook herself mentally. She was dreaming. She put down the glass in her hand and straightened up again. 'Was that it, Apollo? Because I really should be going now.'

She walked towards him and Apollo caught her hand as she was about to pass him. 'Wait.'

She stopped. She was so close she could smell his distinctive scent and she had to battle the memories threatening to overwhelm her. For a bleak moment she almost wished she could lose her memory again.

'Look at me, Sophy.'

Sophy really didn't want to look at Apollo. She was too full of volatile emotions. He'd only come to make sure she wasn't pregnant. But he wasn't letting her hand go. Reluctantly, Sophy looked up. Her pulse quickened in helpless answer to what she saw in his eyes. Desire.

He said, 'I still want you.'

A sense of desperation and anger that he still had an effect on her made her say, 'Well, I don't want you.'

She tried to pull her hand away but he held on tighter. He tugged her towards him, shaking his head. 'Don't lie, Sophy. Sasha was the liar, not you.'

'How do you know? You barely know me.'

'Don't I? I got to know you when you were your most genuine self. With no memory to inform you, you couldn't be anyone *but* yourself.'

She had never thought of it like that. She was so close their bodies were almost touching. Apollo finally let her hand go. She could have stepped back now but his scent was winding around her, keeping her there like invisible silken bindings.

He brought a hand to her jaw, cupping it. She wanted to turn her face into it, purr like a kitten. She could feel her will to resist Apollo draining away. She'd missed him.

So when he tipped her face up and lowered his head, she let him prove her words wrong. The kiss started out chaste, a touch to the lips, before coming back, firmer, more insistent. Encouraging her to open up to him. After a moment of hesitation she did, unable not to. Apollo swept inside and then she was lost, drowning in a whirlpool of memories and desires she'd tried to ignore and bury in the past month.

She could feel his hands roving over her back, cupping her buttocks. Just before she lost herself entirely, she pulled back, mouth throbbing. 'Apollo…what are we doing… It's over… You never wanted to see me again.'

'This isn't over.'

She pushed herself out of his arms, immediately feeling bereft. She shook her head. 'What are you saying?'

'Why does this have to end when we both still want each other?'

For a wild moment Sophy's heart soared. 'How would that work?'

He said, 'You could move in here, if you like. You said you're working in central London. I'll be in London regularly over the coming months as I've got a project starting up and I need to be on hand.'

Her heart dipped. 'You mean…this is just a temporary thing.'

'Well, for as long as we want each other.'

Her disappointment was so acute that Sophy nearly doubled over. Nothing had changed. He was just looking for an extension of their affair.

Sophy turned and walked back over to the window, not wanting Apollo to see the effect of his words on her. She spoke to the glass. 'So what you're talking about is essentially making me your mistress?'

Apollo looked at Sophy's slender back. He still had the taste of her on his tongue. The feel of her body under his hands.

'You can call it what you like, I'm talking about continuing this relationship.'

She turned around. 'But just the physical side of it. And once that's fizzled out then we get on with our lives?'

Frustration bit into Apollo. 'Can you walk away from what's between us?'

She came closer and to his shock he saw moisture in her eyes. It was like a punch to the gut.

She said, 'No, I can't walk away. But I'll have to. You see, I want more than that, Apollo. Much more. And, unlike you, I'm not prepared to settle for less.'

Panic gripped Apollo. He felt like he was slipping down a cliff-edge with nothing to hold onto. He said, 'How much do you want?'

She looked at him, an expression of shock and then disgust crossing her face. '*No*. I'm not talking about money. I'm talking about *love*. Family. Emotions. All the things you don't want.'

As if money could buy a woman like Sophy. He felt ashamed. A great yawning chasm was opening inside

Apollo—the place where he'd almost lost himself after Achilles had died. When he'd felt so terrified and alone. Abandoned. Sophy was looking at him with those huge eyes, asking him to step into that place.

He shook his head, stepped back. 'I've told you, I can't give you that.'

Sophy felt her heart crack. 'Can't…or won't?'

She wasn't expecting an answer, so she stepped around Apollo and walked towards the corridor leading to the elevator to take her back down to reality.

But she couldn't go without telling him… She turned back and he was looking after her, jaw tight.

She said, 'I love you, Apollo. I fell for you the night we met. I'm so sorry for what my sister put you through, but I'm glad that her actions brought us together because I might never have seen you again.'

She turned and walked out, hoping stupidly that she'd hear her voice or feel his hand on her arm. But there was nothing. She got into the elevator and the doors closed. It descended. She got out and walked forward and out of the building like an automaton.

She went down into the nearest tube station and followed the crowd through the turnstile, not even sure where she was going. She was numb. But she welcomed the numbness, which was protecting her from incredible pain.

You could have stayed…become his mistress.

She shut the voice out. It would have killed her in the end.

She walked towards the signs for the Bakerloo Line, which would take her back to south London. At the top of the escalator, though, she heard a call.

'Sophy!'

No. It was her stupid mind playing tricks. She was about to step onto the escalator and it came again, urgent.

'Sophy, wait. Please!'

She heard a girl near her say, '*I'll* be Sophy if he wants. He's *gorgeous.*'

Sophy turned around. Apollo was standing on the other side of the turnstiles with his hands braced on the sides—as if ready to vault over. Sophy walked towards him, trying not to let a flame of hope spring to life.

He looked wild. She could feel the electric pull between them, even here.

She came closer. 'I won't be your mistress, Apollo. I'm not mistress material.'

He said, 'I don't want you to be my mistress, Sophy… just come back over here, please?'

Sophy was aware of a crowd gathering. People whispering. Slowly, she walked over to the exit turnstiles and came back through. Apollo had tracked her progress from the other side, his eyes never leaving hers. He was waiting for her. Big, solid.

Sophy knew if he asked her again she wouldn't have the strength to say no. She knew she was weak enough to clutch at any more time he would give her to be with him.

She stopped in front of him and he put his hands on her arms. 'I'm sorry,' he said.

'For what?'

'For disrespecting you. And for the ten seconds too long that it took me to remove my head from my—'

A public announcement blared at that moment,

blocking out Apollo's words, but Sophy could guess what he'd said.

She was too full of trepidation to let the bubble of euphoria she felt rise up inside her. 'What are you saying, Apollo?'

'I'm saying that it's too late. Any hope I might have had of protecting myself against the pain of losing you—letting you go in Athens, trying to make you my temporary lover—is well and truly shattered. Because I would prefer to spend one more perfect day with you, if that's all we have, than a lifetime of regret because I was too much of a coward to admit my fears and open my heart.'

Sophy heard someone sigh near them, but Apollo filled her vision. And her rapidly swelling heart. 'Are you saying…?'

'That I love you. Deeply, irrevocably. Infinitely. I fell for you the moment you looked at me for the first time but I didn't know it at the time. All I knew was that I had to have you.'

He tugged her towards him. 'Please…don't walk away from me. Give me a chance.'

Sophy shook her head. Suddenly she was the one who was scared. She whispered, 'I can't do this, Apollo. It'll kill me if you're just saying this to get me back in your bed.'

He kissed her then. In the middle of the concourse of one of London's busiest Tube stations. A deep kiss, full of remorse and pain and…love. A promise.

They broke apart and Apollo looked at her. They were oblivious to the crowd that had formed around them, phones raised.

'All I can do is ask you to trust me. I *do* want more. You've made me want more, and I've denied it to myself, or tried to, but I can't any longer. I want you, Sophy, and I want to spend the rest of my life with you. Will you give me a chance to prove that to you?'

A voice nearby said loudly, 'If you won't, love, I will!'

A giggle of pure emotion burst up from Sophy's belly. Along with hope…a hope that she couldn't push back down. She smiled a wobbly smile. 'One chance.'

His eyes burned like dark emeralds. He took her hand and raised it to his lips. 'One chance is all I need.' He took her hand and led her back up, out of the dark underground and into the light. The sunlight made everything shimmer. It felt like a benediction. A new start. And Sophy took a deep breath and let herself trust.

Sophy looked out over the sight of the city waking up to a brand-new day under a pink dawn. She was wrapped in a voluminous robe and her body felt pleasantly lethargic and sated. She'd left a sleeping Apollo on the bed, his brow smooth in sleep.

She was still trying to absorb what had happened and she couldn't help but feel slightly fearful that it had all been a dream. Or had she projected her love onto Apollo so much that she'd heard what she'd wanted to—and he hadn't actually made those declarations…

'Here you are.'

She tensed against his inevitable effect on her, but it was useless when his arms slid around her waist and he brought his body flush with hers. He said into her ear,

'When I woke up just now, and I was alone in the bed, I thought I'd dreamed it all up. That you were gone.'

Sophy turned around in Apollo's arms and looked up at him. 'I was just afraid of the same thing, that I'd imagined it all…that you hadn't said—'

'That I love you?'

She nodded her head, biting her lip.

'Well, I did. And I do. I love you, Sophy Jones. And if it's all right with you, I'd like us to marry as soon as possible.'

Her heart skipped a beat. 'Was that a proposal?'

He looked worried. 'I can make it more romantic if you like…'

She shook her head and smiled. 'No, that'll do just fine. And, yes, I accept your proposal.'

But then she sobered again. Apollo tipped her chin up. 'What is it?'

She put her hands on his bare chest. He'd pulled on sweats but she had to not let his physicality distract her.

'What I said about a family… I meant that. I do want a family. Children. When you reminded me that we hadn't used protection…for a moment, even though it would have been the wrong thing, I wanted there to be a baby.'

He cupped her face. 'I told myself I didn't want there to be a baby and that's why I was so concerned about *consequences*, but actually I think deep down I was hoping that you might have got pregnant. I had to come to terms with the thought of a baby when I thought Sasha was pregnant and what surprised me was how much I wanted it. In spite of everything I'd been telling

myself for years. Except, in that situation, I compart-
mentalised the baby very separately from its mother.'

'But now…with you… I want it all too. The baby,
you. Us, together. Making a life. It scared me for so
long, the thought of losing someone I love, so I blocked
it out. That's why I was so harsh with you after we slept
together that first night. I knew you'd got to me more
than any other woman ever had. So I used your virginity as an excuse to get you to leave. But I never forgot
about you…and I think eventually the memory of you
would have driven me so mad that I would have come
to find you.

'But then your sister turned up…and I was relieved
I hadn't had to be the one to make a move. Until I realised I no longer wanted you. And then Sasha dropped
her bombshell. I told myself I was glad I didn't desire
you, because then it meant what we'd shared couldn't
have been as amazing as I remembered…but then that
all got blown out of the water…'

Sophy looked at him, finally believing and trusting.
But he said, 'Need more convincing?'

She nodded and started moving her hands down to
his waist. His body hardened against hers. 'Maybe a
little more…just to make sure we're on the same page.'

Apollo scooped her up and carried her back into the
bedroom and put her down on her feet by the bed. He
undid the belt of the robe and tugged it off her body. His
green gaze glittered with barely banked heat as it swept
up and down her body. He muttered, 'I will never get
tired of looking at you, little flame. Or wanting you.'

He kissed her then and she arched into him, pouring
all of her love into the kiss. His sweats got discarded

and they landed on the bed in a tangle of limbs. When Apollo was poised to enter her, Sophy put her hands on his hips. He wasn't wearing protection. She said huskily, 'Are you sure…it's not too soon?'

He bent down and pressed his lips to hers and then he said, 'It's not soon enough, *agapi mou*.'

And Sophy knew, as Apollo joined his body to hers, that he meant every word, and that today was the start of a new life. For them and for ever.

EPILOGUE

Three and a half years later, Krisakis

'MAMA, LOOK! I'M SWIMMING!'

Sophy stood up from the lounger with a slight huff of effort. She smiled and waved at her two-and-a-half-year-old son Ajax, who admittedly looked as if he was splashing more than swimming, being tugged along in armbands by his father.

She plonked a sunhat on her head and went over to the edge of the pool, which was just one of the luxurious features of the Achilles Villa in the Krisakis Resort, which had opened a couple of years ago. This was the villa Sophy had suggested building at the top of the resort and it was the most sought-after for its views and privacy.

As Sophy had predicted, they were inundated with visitors looking to escape the far busier islands around them, and Krisakis was thriving and growing all the time.

Sometimes they themselves needed to escape, and they went out on the yacht that Apollo had bought at the auction those few years ago. He'd named it *Little Flame*, much to Sophy's delight.

She went down on her haunches. 'You are doing so well, my love. Papa is a good teacher, isn't he? He taught me how to swim too.'

Ajax, dark-haired and a handful, as only a child of Apollo could be, broke into giggles. 'Papa teaching Mama to swim—that's silly! You're a grown-up!'

Sophy saw Apollo's smirk and splashed some water at him. He said warningly, 'You'll pay for that, Kyria Vasilis.'

She was Kyria Vasilis again. Except officially this time. They'd got married here on Krisakis in the small Greek Orthodox church. The inevitable media interest in Apollo marrying his widow's twin sister had been handled well by his PR team and it had quickly faded from the news pages.

Sophy stood up now and undid the wraparound kaftan, dropping it to the ground. She saw the way Apollo's eyes narrowed on her and the inevitable flame in their depths.

Her own body—so attuned to his—tingled and fizzed with anticipation. Lord knew, she shouldn't be feeling sexy. She was eight months pregnant and the size of a small hippo but nothing was capable of diminishing their desire. Even Ajax's arrival had been precipitated by Apollo's very sensual brand of trying to 'hurry him along' when she'd been overdue with him.

She went over to the steps that led down into the pool and sat down, relishing the feel of the water cooling her sun-warmed skin. Apollo left Ajax splashing happily in the shallow end and came over to where she was, sliding his arms around her and stealing a kiss. Something they never got away with for long in front of their son.

He pulled back and sat beside her, putting a hand over her belly. The baby kicked. It was a girl. But they were keeping it a secret from Ajax. She put her hand over her husband's and they looked at each other, a wealth of emotion flowing between them.

They'd already been tested by grief when Sophy had lost their second baby at about four months to a miscarriage, almost a year ago now. But that experience had only made their bond even stronger.

Ajax's voice suddenly piped up with an imperious, 'Mama, come here! I want to show you something.'

Sophy smiled wryly at Apollo and moved into the water, swimming lazily over to her son, the way her husband had taught her.

Apollo looked at his wife and son playing and his heart was so full he didn't know how it didn't burst. But it didn't. It just grew and expanded every day. And in another month or so it would expand a lot more.

And what he'd found, thanks to his love for his wife and his family, was that it was always infinitely better to make love the goal. And not self-protection. Because the thought of not experiencing this beauty and love and joy… Well, that was more terrifying than anything.

* * * * *

The Maid's Spanish Secret
Dani Collins

Books by Dani Collins

Harlequin Modern

Untouched Until Her Ultra-Rich Husband

Conveniently Wed!

Claiming His Christmas Wife

One Night With Consequences

Consequence of His Revenge

Innocents for Billionaires

A Virgin to Redeem the Billionaire
Innocent's Nine-Month Scandal

The Sauveterre Siblings

Pursued by the Desert Prince
His Mistress with Two Secrets
Bound by the Millionaire's Ring
Prince's Son of Scandal

Bound to the Desert King

Sheikh's Princess of Convenience

Visit the Author Profile page
at millsandboon.com.au for more titles.

Canadian **Dani Collins** knew in high school that she wanted to write romance for a living. Twenty-five years later, after marrying her high school sweetheart, having two kids with him, working at several generic office jobs and submitting countless manuscripts, she got The Call. Her first Harlequin novel won the Reviewers' Choice Award for Best First in Series from *RT Book Reviews*. She now works in her own office, writing romance.

DEDICATION

For my editor, Laurie Johnson, and the wonderful team at Harlequin in London. Romance novels taught me to chase my dreams and writing for Harlequin Modern was a lifelong goal. Thirty books in, I'm still astonished and eternally grateful that you've made this dream come true for me. Thank you.

PROLOGUE

Rico Montero arrived at his brother's villa, two hours up the coast from Valencia, in seventy-three minutes. He'd been feeling cooped up in his penthouse, hungry for air. He had pulled his GTA Spano out of storage and tried to escape his own dark mood, not realizing the direction he took until he was pulled over for speeding.

Recognizing where he was, he told the officer he was on his way to see his brother—a means of name-dropping the entire family. The ploy had gotten him out of having his license suspended, but he still had to pay a fine.

Since he was literally in the neighborhood, he decided not to compound his crimes by lying. He rolled his way through Cesar's vineyard to the modern home sprawled against a hillside.

He told himself he didn't miss the vineyard he had owned with pride for nearly a decade—long before his brother had decided he had an interest in grapes and winemaking. Rico's fascination with the process had dried up along with his interest in life in general. Selling that property had been a clean break from a time he loathed to dwell upon.

It's been eighteen months, his mother had said over lunch yesterday. *Time to turn our attention to the future.*

She had said something similar three months ago and he had dodged it. This time, he sat there and took the bullet. *Of course. Who did you have in mind?*

He had left thinking, *Go ahead and find me another scheming, adulterous bride.* But he hadn't said it aloud. He had promised to carry that secret to his grave.

For what?

He swore and jammed the car into Park, then threw himself out of it, grimly aware he had completely failed to escape his dour mood.

"Rico!" His sister-in-law Sorcha opened the door before he had climbed the wide steps. She smiled with what looked like genuine pleasure and maybe a hint of relief.

"Mateo, look. Tío Rico has come to see you." She spoke to the bawling toddler on her hip. "That's a nice surprise, isn't it?"

She wasn't the flawlessly elegant beauty he was used to seeing on Cesar's arm, more of a welcoming homemaker. Her jeans and peasant-style top were designer brands, but she wore minimal makeup and her blond hair was tied into a simple ponytail. Her frown at her unhappy son was tender and empathetic, not the least frazzled by his tantrum.

The deeply unhappy Mateo pointed toward the back of the house. "*Ve*, Papi."

"He's overdue for his nap." Sorcha waved Rico in. "But he knows *someone* took *someone else* into the V-I-N-E-Y-A-R-D."

"You're speaking English and you still have to spell it out?" Rico experienced a glimmer of amusement.

"He's picking it up *so* fast. Oh!" She caught Mateo as he reached out to Rico, nearly launching himself from her arms.

Rico caught him easily while Sorcha stammered, "I'm sorry."

If Rico briefly winced in dismay, it was because of the look in Sorcha's eyes. Far too close to pity, it contained sincere regret that her son was prevailing on him for something she thought too big and painful to ask.

It wasn't. The favor he was doing for his former in-laws was a greater imposition, spiking far more deeply into a more complex knot of nerves. What Sorcha thought she knew about his marriage was the furthest thing from reality.

And what she read as pain and anger at fate was contempt and fury with himself for being a fool. He was steeped in bitterness, playing a role

that was barely a version of the truth. A version
that made a sensitive soul like Sorcha wear a poi-
gnant smile as she gazed on him holding his young
nephew.

Mateo stopped crying, tears still on his cheeks.

"*Ve*, Papi?" he tried.

The tyke had been born mere weeks before
Rico's ill-fated marriage. Mateo was sturdy and
stubborn and full of the drive that all the Montero
males possessed. This was why he was giving his
mother such a hard time. He knew what he wanted
and a nap wouldn't mollify him.

"We'll discuss it," he told the boy and glanced
at Sorcha. "You should change," he advised, unable to bear much more of that agonized happiness in her eyes.

"Why—? Ugh." She noticed the spot where
Mateo had rubbed his streaming face against her
shoulder. "You're okay?" she asked with concern.

"For God's sake, Sorcha," he muttered through
clenched teeth.

He regretted his short temper immediately and
quickly reined in his patience. His secret sat in
him like a cancer, but he couldn't let it provoke
him into lashing out, certainly not at the nicest
person in his family.

"I didn't mean to speak so sharply," he managed
to say, gathering his composure as he brought his
nephew to his shoulder. "We're fine."

"It's okay, Rico." She squeezed his arm. "I understand."

No. She didn't. But thankfully she disappeared, leaving him to have a man-to-man chat with Mateo, who hadn't forgotten a damned thing. He gave it one more try, pointing and asking for Cesar, who had taken his older brother Enrique to speak to winemakers and pet cellar cats and generally have a barrel of a good time by anyone's standards.

Mateo's eyes were droopy, his cheeks red, very much worn out from his tantrum.

"I know what you're going through," he told the boy. "Better than you can imagine."

Like Mateo, Rico was the younger brother to the future *duque*. He, too, occupied the unlit space beneath the long shadow of greatness cast by the heir. He, too, was expected to live an unblemished life so as not to tarnish the title he would never hold. Then there was the simple, fraternal rivalry of a brother being that few years older and moving into the next life stage. Envy was natural, not that Monteros were allowed to feel such things. Emotions were too much like pets, requiring regular feeding and liable to leave a mess on the floor.

Rico climbed the grand staircase to the bedroom that had been converted to a playroom for the boys, not dwelling on Cesar's stellar fulfillment of his duty with two bright and healthy children, a beautiful home and a stunning, warmhearted wife.

"There are some realities that are not worth crying about," he informed Mateo as they entered the room. "Your father told me that." It was one of Rico's earliest memories.

Cry all you want. They won't care. Cesar had spoken with the voice of experience after Rico had been denied something he'd desperately wanted that he could no longer recollect.

Cesar had come to reason with him, perhaps because he was tired of having his playmate sent into solitary confinement. Reason was a family skill valued far more highly than passion. Reason was keeping him silent and carrying on today, maintaining order rather than allowing the chaos that would reign if the truth came out.

Doesn't it make you mad that they won't even listen? Rico had asked Cesar that long-ago day.

Yes. Cesar had been very mature for a boy of six or seven. *But getting mad won't change anything. You might as well accept it and think about something else.*

Words Rico had learned to live by.

He was capable of basic compassion, however.

"I'll always listen if you need to get something off your chest," he told his nephew as he lowered them both into an armchair. "But sometimes there's nothing to be done. It's a hard fact of life, young man."

Mateo wound down to sniffling whimpers. He decided to explore Rico's empty chest pocket.

"Should we read a book?" Rico picked up the first picture book within reach. It was bilingual, with trains and dogs and bananas labeled in English and Spanish.

As he worked through the pages, he deliberately pitched his voice to an uninflected drone. The boy's head on his chest grew heavier and heavier.

"Thank you," Sorcha whispered when she peeked in.

Rico nodded and carried the sleeping boy to his crib. The nanny came in with the baby monitor.

Rico followed Sorcha down the stairs saying, "I'll go find Cesar. If Mateo wakes, don't tell him what a traitor I am."

"Actually, I was going to invite you for dinner later this week. There's something I want to talk to you about. Can we go into Cesar's office?" Her brow pleated with concern.

Rico bit back a sigh, trying to hold on to the temper that immediately began to slip. "If this is about me remarrying, Mother has passed along your concerns."

Your sister-in-law thinks it's too soon, his mother had said yesterday, not asking him how *he* felt. She had merely implied that in Sorcha's view, he was in a weakened state. His choice had been to confirm it or go along with his mother's insistence on finding him a new wife.

"This is something else," Sorcha murmured, closing the door and waving toward the sofa. "And my imagination could be running wild. I haven't said anything to Cesar."

She poured two glasses of the Irish whiskey she had turned Cesar on to drinking and brought one to where Rico stood.

"Really?" he drawled, wondering what she could possibly impart that would need to be absorbed with a bracing shot. He left the whiskey on the end table as they both sat.

"Please don't be angry with me. I know I was overstepping, suggesting your mother hold off on pressing you to remarry, but I care about all of you." She sat with her elbows on her thighs, leaning forward, hands clasped. "You may not be the most demonstrative family, but you *are* family. I will never stay silent if I think one of you needs..." Her mouth tightened.

"Sorcha." He meticulously gathered his forbearance. "I'm fine." And, before he had to suffer another swimming gaze of tormented sympathy, he added, "If I were in your shoes, I would understand why you think I'm not, but honestly, you have to stop worrying about me."

"That's never going to happen," she said primly, which would have been endearing if he didn't find it so frustratingly intrusive. "And there may be other factors to consider." She sipped her drink and eyed him over it. Then sighed. "I feel like such a hypocrite."

He lifted his brows. "Why? What's going on?"

She frowned, set down her drink and picked up her phone, stared at it without turning it on. "Elsa, our nanny, showed me something that came up in her news feed."

"Something compromising?" Sorcha would have taken up the concern with Cesar unless— Oh, hell. Had something gotten out from the coroner's report? "Is this about Faustina?" His molars ground together on reflex.

"No! No, it's not about her at all." She touched her brow. "Elsa always comes with us when we have dinner at your mother's. She's acquainted with the maids there and follows some of them online."

At the word *maid* a premonition danced in his periphery. He refused to reach for the drink, though. It would be a tell. Instinctively, he knew he had to maintain impassivity. He couldn't tip his hand. Not before he knew exactly what was coming next.

"To be honest, I rarely check my social media accounts," he said with a disinterested brush of non-existent lint from his knee. "Especially since Faustina passed. It's very maudlin."

"I suppose it would be." Her expression grew pinched. She looked at the phone she held pressed between her palms. "But one way or another, I think you should be aware of this particular post."

Biting her lips together, she touched her thumb to the sensor and the screen woke. She flicked to bring up a photo and held it out to him.

"On first glance, Elsa thought it was Mateo dressed up as a girl. That's the only reason she took notice and showed me. She thought it was funny that it had given her a double take. I had to agree this particular photo offers a certain resemblance."

Rico flicked a look at the toddler. He'd never seen Mateo in a pink sailor's bib and hat, but the baby girl's grin was very similar, minus a few teeth, to the one he had coaxed out of his nephew before the boy's head had drooped against his chest.

"I actually keep my privacy settings locked down tight," Sorcha said. "I've heard photos can be stolen and wind up in ads without permission. I thought that's what had happened. Elsa assured me she never shares images of the boys with anyone but me or Cesar."

The Montero fortune had been built on the development of chemicals and special alloys. Rico had learned early that certain substances, innocuous on their own, could become explosive when in proximity to one another.

Sorcha was pouring statements into beakers before him. A maid. A baby that looked like other children in the family.

He wouldn't let those two pieces of information touch. Not yet.

"It's said we all have a double." His lifetime of suppressing emotion served him well. "It would seem you've found Mateo's."

"This is the only photo where she looks so much like him," Sorcha murmured, taking back her phone. "I looked up the account. Her mother is a photographer."

Photographer. One beaker began to tip into another.

"This is part of her portfolio for her home business. Her name is Poppy Harris. The mother, I mean. The baby is Lily."

His abdomen tightened to brace for a kick. A sizzle resounded in his ears. Adrenaline made him want to reach for his drink, but he only lifted his hand to scratch his cheek—while his mind conjured the forest of lilies that had surrounded them in his mother's solarium as he and Poppy had made love so impulsively.

"Do you…remember her?" Sorcha asked tentatively.

Skin scented like nectarines, lush corkscrews of curly red hair filling his hands as he consumed her crimson lips. He remembered the exact pitch of her joyful cries of release, the culmination of madness like he'd never known before or since.

And he remembered vividly the ticking of the

clock on the mantel as he had sat in his mother's parlor the next morning, an itchy fire in his blood driving him mad. He'd been on the verge of going to look for her because he couldn't stop thinking about her.

Then Faustina had arrived, striking like dry lightning with sheepishly delivered news. Family obligation had crashed upon him afresh, pinning him under the weight of a wedding that had been called off, but now was back on. They would pretend the gap in the parade had never happened.

"Rico?" Sorcha prompted gently, dragging him back to the present. "I know this must be a shock." And there was that infernal compassion again.

He swore, tired to his *bones* of people thinking he was mourning a baby he had already known wasn't his. He was sorry for the loss of a life before it had had the chance to start. Of course he was. But he wasn't grieving with the infinite heartbreak of a parent losing a child. It hadn't been *his*.

And given Faustina's trickery, he was damned cynical about whether he had conceived *this* one.

"Why did you jump straight to suspecting she's mine?" he asked baldly.

Sorcha was slightly taken aback. "Well, I'm not going to suspect my own husband, am I?" Her tone warned that he had better not, either. Her chin came up a notch. "You were living in your parents' villa at the time. Frankly, your father doesn't seem

particularly passionate about any woman, young
or old. You, however, were briefly unengaged."

Rico had long suspected the success of his parents' marriage could be attributed to both of them
being fairly asexual and lacking in passion for anything beyond cool reason and the advancement of
family interests.

Sorcha's eyes grew big and soft and filled with
that excruciating pity. "I'm not judging, Rico. *I
know how these things happen.*"

"I bet you do." He regretted it immediately. It
wasn't him. At least, it wasn't the man he was beneath the layer of caustic fury he couldn't seem
to shed. Sorcha certainly didn't deserve this ugly
side of him. She was kind and sensitive and everything the rest of them didn't know how to be.

She recoiled, rightly shocked that he would de-
liver such a belly blow. But she hadn't risen above
the scandal of secretly delivering his brother's
baby while Cesar had been engaged to someone
else without possessing truckloads of resilience.

"I meant because my mother was my father's
maid when she conceived *me*." Her voice was tight
and strong, but there was such a wounded shadow
in her gaze, he had to look away and reach for the
drink she'd poured him.

He drained it, burning away the words that hovered on his tongue. Words he couldn't speak be-
cause he was trying to spare Faustina's parents

some humiliation when they were already destroyed by the loss of their only child.

"I'll assume if you're lashing out, you believe it's possible that little girl is yours. How she came about is your business, Rico, but don't you *ever* accuse me of trapping Cesar into this marriage. I *left*, if you recall." She stood, hot temper well lit, but honed by her marriage to a Montero into icy severity. "And so did Poppy. Maybe ask yourself why, if you're such a prize, she doesn't want anything to do with you. *I* have an idea, if you can't figure it out for yourself."

She stalked to the door and swung it open, inviting him to leave using nothing more than a head held high and an expression of frosty contempt that prickled his conscience through the thick shields of indifference he had been bricking into place since Faustina had been found.

"I shouldn't have said that," Rico ground out, mind reeling so badly as he stood, his head swam. "I was shooting the messenger." With a missile launcher loaded with nuclear waste. "Tell Cesar what you've told me. I'll let him punch me in the face for what I said to you." He meant it.

She didn't thaw. Not one iota. "Deal with the message. I have a stake in the outcome, as do my husband and sons."

"Oh, I will," he promised. *"Immediately."*

CHAPTER ONE

POPPY HARRIS FILLED the freshly washed sippy cup with water only to have Lily ignore it and keep pointing at the shelf.

"You want a real cup, don't you?"

Two weeks ago, Lily's no-spill cup had gone missing from daycare. Poppy's grandmother, being old-school, thought cups with closed lids and straws were silly. Back in *her* day, babies learned to drink from a proper cup.

Since she was pinching pennies, Poppy hadn't bought a new one. She had spent days mopping dribbles instead, and she'd been *so* happy when the cup had reappeared today.

Unfortunately, Lily was a big girl now. She wanted an open cup. *Thanks, Gran.*

Poppy considered whether a meltdown right before dinner was worth the battle. She compromised by easing Lily's grip off her pant leg and then sat her gently onto her bottom, unable to resist running affectionate fingertips through Lily's fine

red-gold curls. She handed her both the leakproof
cup and an empty plastic tumbler. Hopefully that
would keep her busy for a few minutes.

"I'm putting the biscuits in the oven, Gran,"
Poppy called as she did it.

She scooped a small portion of leek-and-potato
soup from the slow cooker into a shallow bowl. She
had started the soup when she raced home on her
lunch break to check on her grandmother. Every
day felt like a flat-out run, but she didn't complain.
Things could be worse.

She set the bowl on the table so it would be cool
enough for Lily to eat when they sat down.

"The fanciest car has just pulled in, Poppy,"
her grandmother said in her quavering voice. Her
evening game shows were on, but she preferred to
watch the comings and goings beyond their front
room window. "Is he one of your models needing
a head shot? He's *very* handsome."

"What?" Poppy's stomach dropped. It was
completely instinctive and she made herself take
a mental step back. There was no reason to believe
it would be *him*.

Even so, she struggled to swallow a jagged lump
that lodged in her suddenly arid throat. "Who—?"

The doorbell rang.

Poppy couldn't move. She didn't want to see.
If it wasn't Rico, she would be irrationally disappointed. If it *was* him…

She looked to her daughter, instantly petrified that he was here to claim her. What would he say? How could she stop him? She couldn't.

It wasn't him, she told herself. It was one of those prophets in a three-piece suit who hand-delivered pamphlets about the world being on the brink of annihilation.

Her world was fine, she reassured herself, still staring at the sprite who comprised the lion's share of all that was important to her. Lily tipped her head back in an effort to drain water from an empty cup.

The bell rang again.

"Poppy?" her grandmother prompted, glancing her direction. "Will you answer?"

Mentally, Gran was sharp as a tack. Her vision and hearing never failed her. Osteoporosis, however, had impacted her mobility. Her bones were so fragile, Poppy had to be ever vigilant that Lily and her toys weren't underfoot. Her gran would break a hip or worse if she ever stumbled.

There were a lot of things about this living arrangement that made it less than ideal, but both she and Gran were maintaining the status quo, kidding themselves that Gramps was only down at the hardware store and would be back any minute.

"Of course." Poppy snapped out of her stasis and glanced over to be sure the gates on both doorways into the kitchen were closed. All the drawers and cupboards had locks except the one where the plastic dishes were kept. The mixing bowls were a favorite for being dragged out and nested, filled with toys and measuring cups, then dumped without ceremony.

"Keep an eye this way, Gran?" Poppy murmured as she stepped over the gate into the front room, then moved past her seated grandmother to the front door.

Her glance out the side window struck a dark brown bomber jacket over black jeans, but she knew that head, that back with the broad shoulders, that butt and long legs.

His arrival struck like a bus. Like a train that derailed her composure and rattled on for miles, piling one broken thought onto another.

OhGodohGodohGod… *Breathe.* All the way in, all the way out, she reminded herself. But she had always imagined that if this much money showed up on her doorstep, it would be with an oversize check and a television crew. *Not him.*

Rico pivoted from surveying her neighbor's fence and the working grain elevator against the fading Saskatchewan sky. His profile was knife sharp, carved of titanium and godlike. A hint of shadow was coming in on his jaw, just enough to bend his angelic looks into the fallen kind.

He knocked.

"Poppy—?" her grandmother prompted, tone

perplexed by the way she was acting. Or failing to.

How? *How* could he know? Poppy had no doubt that he did. There was absolutely no other reason for this man to be this far off the beaten track. He sure as hell wasn't here to see *her*.

Blood searing with fight or flight, heart pounding, she opened the door.

The full force of his impact slammed through her. The hard angle of his chin, the stern cast of his mouth, his wide shoulders and long legs, and hands held in tense, almost fists.

His jaw hardened as he took her in through mirrored aviators. Their chrome finish was cold and steely. If he'd had a fresh haircut, it had been ruffled by the wind. His boots were alligator, his cologne nothing but crisp, snow-scented air and fuming suspicion.

Poppy lifted her chin and pretended her heart wasn't whirling like a Prairie tornado in her chest.

"Can I help you?" she asked, exactly as she would if he had been a complete stranger.

His hand went to the doorframe. His nostrils twitched as he leaned into the space. "Really?" he asked in a tone of lethal warning.

"Who is it, Poppy?" her grandmother asked.

He stiffened slightly, as though surprised she wasn't alone. Then his mouth curled with disparagement, waiting to see if she would lie.

Poppy swallowed, her entire body buzzing, but she held his gaze through those inscrutable glasses while she said in a strong voice, "Rico, Gran. The man I told you about. From Spain."

There, she silently conveyed. *What do you think of that?*

It wasn't wise to defy him. She knew that by the roil of threat in the pit of her stomach, but she had had to grow up damned fast in the last two years. She was not some naive traveler succumbing to a charmer who turned out to be a thief, or even the starry-eyed maid who had encouraged a philandering playboy to seduce her.

She was a grown woman who had learned how to face her problems head-on.

"Oh?" Gran's tone gave the whole game away in one murmur. There was concern beneath her curiosity. Knowledge. It was less a blithe, *isn't that nice that your friend turned up*. More an alarmed, *Why is he here?*

There was no hiding. None. Poppy might not be able to read this man's eyes, but she read his body language. He wasn't here to ask questions. He was here to confront.

Because he knew she'd had his baby.

Her eyes grew wet with panic, but through her shock, she reacted to seeing her lover, her first and only lover twenty months after they had conceived their daughter. She had thought her brief hour with him a moment of madness. A rush of sex hormones born of dented self-esteem and grand self-delusion.

Since then, her body had been taken over by their daughter. Poppy had been sure her sex drive had dried up and blown away on the Prairie winds. Or at least was firmly in hibernation.

As it turned out, her libido was alive and well. Heat flooded into her with the distant tingles of intimate, erotic memories. Of the cold press of his belt buckle trapped against her thigh, the dampness of perspiration in the hollow of his spine when she ran her hands beneath his open shirt to clutch at him with encouragement. She recalled exactly the way he had kissed the whisker burn on her chin so tenderly, with a growl of apology in his throat. The way he had cupped her breast with restraint, then licked and sucked at her nipple until she was writhing beneath him.

She could feel anew the sharp sensation of him possessing her, so intimate and satisfying, both glorious and ruinous all at once.

She blushed. Hard. Which made the blistering moment feel like hours. She was overflowing at the edges with mortifying awkwardness, searching her mind for something to say, a way to dissemble so he wouldn't know how far he'd thrown her.

"Invite him in, Poppy," her grandmother chided. "You're going to melt the driveway."

She meant because she was letting the heat out, but her words made Poppy blush harder. "Of course," she muttered, flustered. "Come in."

Explanations crowded her tongue as she backed up a step, but stammering them out wouldn't make a difference to a man like him. He might have seemed human and reachable for that stolen hour in his mother's solarium, but she'd realized afterward exactly how ruthless and single-minded he truly was. The passion she'd convinced herself was mutual and startlingly sweet had been a casual, effortless, promptly forgotten seduction on his part.

He'd mended fences with his fiancée the next morning—a woman Poppy knew for a fact he hadn't loved. He'd told Poppy that he'd only agreed to the marriage to gain the presidency of a company and hadn't seemed distressed in the least that the wedding had been called off.

Embarrassment at being such an easy conquest had her staring at his feet as she closed the door behind him. "Will you take off your boots, please?"

Her request gave him pause. In his mother's house, everyone wore shoes, especially guests. A single pair of their usual footwear cost more than Poppy had made in her four months of working in that house.

Rico toed off his boots and set them against the wall. Then he tucked his sunglasses into his chest pocket. His eyes were slate-gray with no spark of blue or flecks of hot green that had surrounded his huge pupils that day in the solarium.

After setting his cold, granite gaze against her until she was chilled through, he glanced past her, into the front room of the tiny bungalow her grandfather had built for his wife while working as a linesman for the hydro company. It was the home where Gramps had brought his bride the day they married. It was where they had brought home their only son and where they had raised their only grandchild.

Seeing him in it made Poppy both humble and defensive. It didn't compare to the grandiose villa he'd been raised in, but it was her home. Poppy wasn't ashamed of it, only struck by how he could so easily jeopardize all of this with a snap of his fingers. This house wasn't even hers. If he had come here to claim Lily, she had very few resources at her disposal. Maybe it would even be held against her that she didn't have much and he could offer so much more.

"Hello," he greeted her grandmother as she muted the television and set the remote aside.

"This is Rico Montero, Gran. My grandmother, Eleanor Harris."

"*The* Rico?"

"Yes."

Rico's brows went up a fraction, making Poppy squirm.

"It's nice to meet you. Finally." Gran started to rise.

Poppy stepped forward to help her, but Rico was quick to touch her grandmother's arm and say, "Please. There's no need to stand. It's a pleasure to meet you."

Oh, he knew how to use the warmth of his accented voice to slay a woman, young or old. Poppy almost fell for it herself, thinking he sounded reassuring when he was actually here to destroy their small, simple world.

Yet she had to go through the motions of civility. Pretend he was simply a guest who had dropped by.

Gran smiled up at him with glimmers of adoration. "I was getting up to give you privacy to talk. I imagine you'll want that."

"In that case, yes please. Allow me to help you." Rico moved to her side and supported her with gentle care.

Don't leave me alone with him, Poppy wanted to cry, but she slid Gran's walker in front of her. "Thank you, Gran."

"I'll listen to the radio in my room until you come for me." Her grandmother nodded and shuffled her way into the hall. "Remember the biscuits."

The biscuits. The least of her worries. Poppy couldn't smell them yet, but the timer would go off any second. She moved her body into the path toward the kitchen door, driven by mother-bear instincts.

"Why are you here?" Her voice quavered with the volume of emotions rocketing through her—shock and protectiveness and fear. Culpability and anger and other deeper yearnings she didn't want to acknowledge.

"I want to see her." He set his shoulders in a way that told her he wasn't going anywhere until he did.

Behind her, the sound of bowls coming out of the cupboard and being knocked around reassured her that Lily was perfectly fine without eyes on her.

A suffocating feeling sat on her chest and kept a vise around her throat. She wanted him to answer the rest of her question. What was he going to do about this discovery? She wasn't ready to face the answer.

Playing for time, she strangled out, "How did you find out?"

If they hadn't been standing so close, she might have missed the way his pupils dilated and his breath seemed to catch as though taking a blow. In the next second, the impression of shock was gone. A fierce, angry light of satisfaction gleamed in his eyes.

"Sorcha saw a photo you posted of a baby who looks like Mateo. I investigated."

Odd details from the last two weeks fell into place. She dropped her chin in outrage. "That new dad at the day care! I thought he was hitting on me, asking all those questions."

Rico's dark brows slammed together. "He came on to you?"

"He said he took Lily's cup by mistake, but it was an excuse to talk to me." Poppy was obviously still batting a thousand where her poor judgement of men was concerned.

"He took it for a DNA sample."

"That is just plain *wrong*," she said indignantly.

"I agree that I shouldn't have to resort to such measures to learn I have a child. *Why didn't you tell me?*" he asked through clenched teeth.

He had some right to the anger he poured over ice. She acknowledged that. But she wasn't a villain. Just a stupid girl who'd gotten herself in trouble by the wrong man and had made the best of a difficult situation.

"I didn't realize I was pregnant until you were married. By then, it was all over the gossip sites that Faustina was also expecting."

It shouldn't have been such a blow when she'd read that. His wedding had been called off for a *day*. Loads of people had a moment of cold feet before they went through with the ceremony. She accepted she was collateral damage to that.

She had been feeling very down on herself by then, though. She ought to have known better than to let herself get carried away. She hadn't taken any precautions. She had been careless and foolish, believing him when he had told her that he and his fiancée hadn't been sleeping together.

The whole thing had made her feel so humiliatingly stupid. She had hoped never to have to face him or her gullibility ever again.

So much for that.

And facing him was so *hard. He* was so hard. A muscle was pulsing in his jaw, but the rest of him was like concrete. Pitiless and unmoved.

"Faustina died a year ago last September," he said in that gritty tone. "You've had ample opportunity to come forward."

As she recalled the terrible headlines she'd read with morbid anguish, her heart turned inside out with agony for him. She had nursed thoughts every day of telling him he had a child after all, but…

"I'm sorry for your loss." She truly was. No matter what he'd felt for his wife, losing his child must have been devastating.

His expression stiffened and he recoiled slightly at her words of condolence.

"My grandfather was quite ill," she continued huskily. "If you recall, that's why I came home. He passed just before Christmas. Gran needed me. There hasn't been a right time to shake things up."

His expression altered slightly as he absorbed that.

She imagined his sorrow to be so much more

acute than hers. She mourned a man who had lived a full life and who had passed without pain or regret. They'd held a service that had been a true celebration of his long life.

While Rico's baby had been cheated of even starting its own.

Rico nodded acceptance of her excuse with only a pained flicker as acknowledgment of what must have been his very personal and intensely painful loss.

Had grief driven him here? Was he trying to replace his lost child with his living one? *No.* The thought of it agonized her. Lily wasn't some placeholder for another child. It cracked her heart in half that he might think she could be.

Before she could find words to address that fear, the timer beeped in the kitchen.

Lily had become very quiet, too, which was a sure sign of trouble. Poppy turned to glance around the doorframe. Lily sat with one finger poking at the tiny hole on a bowl's rim, where the bowl was meant to be hung on a nail.

Firm hands settled on her shoulders. Rico's untamed scent and the heat of his body surrounded her. He looked past her into the kitchen. At his daughter.

Poppy told herself not to look, but she couldn't help it. She was afraid he would be resentful that Lily had lived when his other baby hadn't. Even as she feared he was planning to steal her, she perversely would be more agonized if he rejected her. He had come all this way. That meant he felt something toward her, didn't it? On some level, he wanted her?

His expression was unreadable, face so closed and tense, her heart dropped into her shoes.

Love her, she wanted to beg. *Please.*

His breath sucked in with an audible hiss. He took in so much air, his chest swelled to brush against her back. His hands tightened on her shoulders.

At the subtle noise, Lily lifted her gorgeous gray eyes, so like her father's. A huge smile broke across her face.

"Mama." The bowls were forgotten and she crawled toward them, pulling herself up on the gate.

Lily's smile propelled Poppy through all her hard days. She was Poppy's world. Poppy's parents were distant, her grandfather gone, her grandmother... Well, Poppy didn't want to think about losing her even though she knew it was inevitable.

But she had this wee girl and she was everything.

"Hello, button." Poppy scooped up her daughter and kissed her cheek, never able to resist that soft, plump bite of sweet-smelling warmth. Then she brushed at Lily's hands because it didn't matter how many times she swept or vacuumed, Lily found the specks and dust bunnies in her eager exploration of her world.

This time when Poppy looked to Rico, she saw his reaction more clearly. He was trying to mask it with stoicism, but the intensity in his gaze ate up Lily's snowy skin and cupid's-bow mouth.

Her emotions seesawed again. She had needed this. Her heart had needed to see him accept his daughter, but he was a threat, too.

"This is Lily." Her name was tellingly sentimental, not the sort of romantic notion Poppy should have given in to, but since her own name was a flower, it had seemed right.

Poppy faltered, not ready to tell Lily this was Daddy.

Lily brought her fingers to her mouth and said, "Ee."

"Eat?" Poppy asked and slid her hand down from her throat. "You're hungry?"

Lily nodded.

"Sign language?" Rico asked, voice sharpening with concern. "Is she hearing impaired?"

"It's sign language for babies. They teach it at day care. She's trying to say words, but this works for now." Poppy stepped over the gate into the kitchen and snapped off the oven. "Do you, um…" She couldn't believe this was happening, but she wanted to put off the hard conversations as long as possible. "Will you join us for dinner?"

A brief pause, then, "You don't have to cook. I can order something in."

"From where?" Poppy chuckled dryly as she set Lily in her chair. "We have Chinese takeout and a pizza palace." *Not* his usual standard. "The soup is already made."

She tied on Lily's bib and set the bowl of cooled soup and a small flat spoon in front of her.

Lily grabbed the spoon and batted it into the thick soup.

"Renting the car was a challenge for my staff," he mentioned absently, frowning as Lily missed her mouth and smeared soup across her own cheek.

"Gran said you're driving something fancy," Poppy recalled. She had forgotten to look, unable to see past the man to anything else.

"An Alfa Romeo, but it's a sedan."

With a car seat? Poppy almost bobbled the sheet of biscuits as she took them from the oven. "Are you, um, staying at the motel?"

He snorted. "No. My staff have taken a cottage an hour from here so I have a bed if I decide to stay."

Poppy tried to read his expression, but he was watching Lily, frowning with exasperation as Lily turned her head, open mouth looking for the end of the spoon.

In a decisive move, he removed his jacket and draped it over the back of a chair. Then he picked up the teaspoon beside Poppy's setting and turned the chair to face Lily. He sat and began helping her eat.

Poppy caught her breath, arrested by the sight of this dynamic man feeding their daughter. His strapping muscles strained the seams in his shirt, telling of his tension, but he calmly waited for Lily to try before he gently touched the tip of his teaspoon to her bottom lip. He let Lily lean into eating it before they both went after the next spoonful in the bowl.

Had she dreamed of this? *Was* she dreaming? It was such a sweet sight her ovaries locked fresh eggs into their chambers, preparing to launch and create another Lily or five. All she needed was one glance from him that contained something other than accusation or animosity.

"You said the timing was wrong."

It took her a moment to realize he was harking back to the day they'd conceived her. She could only stand there in chagrined silence while a coal of uncomfortable heat burned in her middle, spreading a blush upward, into her throat and cheeks and ending in a pressure behind her eyes.

He glanced at her. "When we—"

"I know what you mean," she cut him off, turning away to stack hot biscuits onto a plate, suffused in virginal discomfiture all over again. He'd noticed blood and asked if she had started her cycle. She'd been too embarrassed to tell him it was her first time. She was too embarrassed to say it now.

"I should have taken something after." She didn't tell him she had hung around in Spain an extra day, hoping he would come find her only to hear the wedding was back on.

That news had propelled her from the scene, consuming her with thoughts of what a pushover she'd been for a man on a brief furlough from his engagement. Contraception should have been top of mind, but...

"I was traveling, trying to make my flight." Poppy hugged herself, trying to keep the fissure in her chest from widening. She felt *so* exposed right now and couldn't meet his penetrating stare. "I honestly did think the timing was wrong. I didn't even realize I was pregnant until I was starting to show. I had next to no symptoms." There'd even been a bit of spotting. "I thought the few signs I did have were stress related. Gramps's health was deteriorating. By the time it was confirmed, you were married." She finally looked at him and let one hand come out, palm up, beseeching for understanding.

There was no softening in his starkly unforgiving expression.

"I didn't think you would—" She couldn't say

aloud that she had worried he wouldn't want his daughter. Not when he was feeding Lily with such care.

Helpless tears pressed behind her eyes.

He knew what she had almost said and sent her another flat stare of muted fury. "I want her, Poppy. That's why I'm here."

Her heart swerved in her chest. The pressure behind her eyes increased.

"Don't look so terrified." He returned his attention to Lily, who was waiting with an open mouth like a baby bird. "I'm not here to kidnap her."

"What, then?" She clung tight to her elbows, needing something to anchor her. Needing to know what was going to happen.

"Am I supposed to ignore her?"

"No." His question poked agonizing pins into the most sensitive spots on her soul. "But I was afraid you might," she admitted. "I thought it would be easier on both of us if you didn't know, rather than if you did, but didn't care."

Another wall-of-concrete stare, then a clearly pronounced, "I care." He scraped the spoon through the thick soup. "And not only because the maids in my mother's house are bound to recognize the resemblance the way Sorcha's nanny did and begin to talk. She's a Montero. She's entitled to the benefits that brings."

Now he stood directly on Poppy's pride.

"We don't *need* help, Rico. That's another reason I never told you. I didn't want you to think I was looking for a handout. We're fine."

"The day care with the nonexistent security is 'fine'? What happens when it's known her father is wealthy? We take basic precautions, Poppy. You don't even have an alarm system. I didn't hear you click a lock when you opened the front door."

They lived in rural Canada. People worried about squirrels in the attic, not burglars in the bedroom.

"No one knows you're rich. Gran is the only person who even knows your name and I wasn't entirely forthcoming about…who you really are." Poppy gave a tendril of hair a distracted brush so it tucked behind her ear for all of five seconds. "Do you mind if I get her? She takes medication on a schedule and needs to eat beforehand. We try to stick to a routine."

"Of course." He lifted two fingers off the bowl he still held steady for Lily's jabs of her own spoon. "We'll discuss how we'll proceed after Lily is in bed."

CHAPTER TWO

POPPY OPENED THE GATE and set it aside, leaving Rico to continue feeding his daughter.

He had watched Sorcha and Cesar do this countless times with their sons. He'd always thought it a messy process best left to nannies, but discovered it was oddly satisfying. His older nephew, Enrique, had reached an age where he held conversations—some that were inadvertently amusing—but babies had always struck Rico as something that required a lot of intensive care without offering much in return.

Sorcha had pressed her sons onto him over the years, which had achieved her goal of provoking feelings of affection in him, but, like his parents, he viewed children as something between a duty and a social experiment. Even when he had briefly believed Faustina had been carrying his heir, the idea of being a father had only been that—an idea. Not a concept he had fully internalized or a role he understood how to fulfill effectively. Father-hood hadn't been something he had viewed with anticipation the way other creative projects had inspired him.

But here he sat, watching eyes the same color as his own track to the doorway where Poppy had disappeared. A wet finger pointed. "Mama."

"She'll be right back." He imagined Poppy would actually spend a few minutes talking to her grandmother in private.

Lily smiled before she leaned forward, mouth open.

Damn, she was beautiful. It wasn't bias, either. Or his fondness for the nephews she resembled. She had her mother's fresh snowy skin and red-gold lashes, healthy round cheeks and a chin that suggested she had his stubbornness along with his eyes.

A ridiculous swell of pride went through him even as he reminded himself that he didn't know conclusively that she was his. The DNA test off the cup had been a long shot and hadn't proved paternity either way.

Nevertheless, he'd been propelled as much by the absence of truth as he would have been by the presence of it. From the time Sorcha had revealed her suspicion, a ferocious fire had begun to burn in him, one stoked by yet another female keeping secrets from him. Huge, life-altering secrets.

He hadn't wanted to wait for more tests, or hire

lawyers, or even pick up the phone and *ask*. He had needed to see for himself.

Who? a voice asked in the back of his head.

Both, he acknowledged darkly. He had needed to set eyes on the baby, whom he recognized on a deeply biological level, and on the woman who haunted his memories.

Poppy had seemed so guileless. So refreshingly honest and real.

He thought back to that day, searching for the moment where he'd been tricked into making a baby with a woman who had then kept her pregnancy a secret.

He remembered thinking his mother wouldn't appreciate him popping a bottle of the wedding champagne—even though she'd procured a hundred cases that had been superfluous because the wedding had been called off.

Rico had helped himself to his father's scotch in the billiards room instead. He had taken it through to the solarium, planning to bum a cigarette from the gardener. It was a weakness he had kicked years ago, but the craving still hit sometimes, when his life went sideways.

It was the end of the day, though. The sun-warmed room was packed to the gills with lilies brought in to replace the ones damaged by a late frost. The solarium was deserted and the worktable in the back held a dirty ashtray and a cigarette pack that was empty.

"Oh! I'm so sorry."

The woman spoke in English, sounding American, maybe. He turned to see the redheaded maid who'd been on the stairs an hour earlier, when Faustina had been throwing a tantrum that had included one of his mother's Wedgwoods, punctuating the end of their engagement. He would come to understand much later what sort of pressure Faustina had been under, but at the time, she'd been an unreasonable, clichéd diva of a bride by whom he'd been relieved to have been jilted.

And the interruption by the fresh-faced maid had been a welcome distraction.

Her name was Poppy. He knew that without looking at the embroidered tag on her uniform. She stared with wide doe eyes, the proverbial deer in headlights, startled to come upon him pilfering smokes as though he was thirteen again.

"I mean…um…*perdón*." She pivoted to go back the way she'd come.

"Wait. Do you have a cigarette?" he asked in English.

"Me? No." She swung back around. "Do I look like a smoker?"

Her horror at resembling such a thing amused him.

"Do I?" he drawled. "What do we look like? The patriarchy?"

"I don't know." She chuckled and blushed

slightly, her clear skin glowing pink beneath the gold of filtered sunlight, like late afternoon on untouched ski slopes. "I, um, didn't know you smoked." She swallowed and linked her hands shyly before her.

Ah. She'd been watching him, too, had she?

His mother's staff had been off-limits since his brother's first kiss with a maid before Rico had even had a shot at one. He didn't usually notice one from another, but Poppy had snagged his attention with her vibrant red hair. Curls were springing free of the bundle she'd scraped it into, teasing him with fantasies of releasing the rest and digging his hands into the kinky mass.

The rest of her was cute as hell, too, if a bit skinny and young. Maybe it was her lack of makeup. That mouth, unpainted, but with a plump bottom lip and a playful top was all woman. Her brows were so light, they were almost blond, her chin pert, her eyes a gentle yet very direct dark ale-brown.

No, he reminded himself. He was engaged.

Actually, he absorbed with a profound sense of liberation, he wasn't. Faustina had firmly and unequivocally ended their engagement, despite his mother's best efforts to talk her back on board.

His mother had retired with a wet compress and a migraine tablet. He had come in here because he couldn't go home. His house was being renovated for the bride who was now refusing to share her life with him. Driving all the way to his brother's house to get blind drunk had felt like an unnecessary delay.

"I don't smoke." He dropped the empty pack and picked up his drink. "I rebelled for a year or so when I was a teen, but it seemed like a good excuse to talk with Ernesto about football and other inconsequential topics." He was sick to death of jabbering about weddings and duty and the expected impact on the family fortune.

Her shoulders softened and her red-gold brows angled with sympathy. "I'm really sorry." She sounded adorably sincere. "I'll, um, give you privacy to…"

"Wallow in heartbreak? Unnecessary." Faustina's outburst had been the sum total of passion their marriage was likely to have borne. "I don't want to chase you away if you're on your break."

"No, I'm done. I know we're not supposed to cut through here to get to the change rooms over the garage, but I was hoping to catch Ernesto myself. He gives me a lift sometimes."

"Are you American?" he asked.

Her strawberry blond lashes flickered in surprise, her expression growing shy. Aware.

An answering awareness teased through him, waking the wolf inside him. That starved beast had been locked inside a cave the last six months, but unexpectedly found himself free of the heavy chain he'd placed around his own neck. The sun was in his eyes, the wind was ruffling his fur and he was picking up the scent of a willing female. He was itching to romp and tumble and mate.

"Canada." She cleared her throat. "Saskatchewan. A little town with nothing but canola fields and clouds." She shook her head. "You wouldn't have heard of it."

"How did you wind up here?"

"I'd tell you, but I'd bore you to death." Despite her words, a pretty smile played around her mouth and a soft blush of pleasure glowed under her skin.

"I came out here to smoke. Clearly I have a death wish."

After a small chuckle, she cautioned, "Okay, but stop me if you feel light-headed."

Definitely not bored, he thought with a private smile. She wasn't merely a first cigarette years after quitting, either. To be sure he was drawing in this lighthearted flirting with avid greed, but he found himself enjoying her wit. He was genuinely intrigued by her.

"I saved up to trek around Europe with a friend, but she broke her ankle on the second day and flew home." She folded her arms, protective or defensive, maybe. "I tagged along with some students from a hostel coming here, but a few days after we arrived, one of them stole everything I had."

She slapped a what-can-you-do? smile on it, but the tension around her eyes and mouth told him she was still upset.

He frowned. "Did you go to the police?"

"It was my fault." She flinched with self-recrimination. "I gave him my card to get some cash for me one morning. He must have made a copy or something. Three days later he'd syphoned all of my savings and was gone. I had my passport, a bag of raisins and my hairbrush. Losing my camera gutted me the most. It was a gift and my memory card was still in it, not that I'd had the chance to fill it. It was a huge bummer." She summed up with philosophical lightness.

"You're a photographer?"

"Not anymore," she asserted with disgust, then shrugged it off. "At least I had prepaid for a week at the hostel. I asked around and got on with a temp agency. I was brought in to help clean the pool house and guest cottage. Darna liked my work and asked me to stay on full-time in the big house. I've been saving for a ticket home ever since."

"How much do you need?" He reached into his pocket.

"Oh, no!" She halted him, horrified. "I have enough. I just worked it out with Darna that today was my last day. She thought she would need me through the rest of June for—" She halted, wincing as she realized who she was talking to.

Rico let the awkwardness hang in the air, not to punish, but because he was finding her candor so refreshing.

"It seemed like the wedding was going to be really beautiful." She sounded apologetic. "I'm sorry it didn't work out."

He wasn't. That was the naked truth, but he deflected by saying, "I've heard that Canadians apologize a lot. I didn't believe it."

"We do. Sorry." She winked on that one.

Was she sorry?

Rico came back to the tap of a dirty spoon against the back of his knuckles.

Poppy had been twenty-two, disillusioned after being shortchanged on chasing her dreams, yet willing to come home to fulfill family obligations. He had understood that pressure and had confided his own reasons for going along with family expectations.

That affinity had led to a kiss and his feet had somehow carried her to the sheet-draped furniture hidden amongst the jungle of fragrant lilies.

Since learning about Lily, he'd been convinced Poppy had somehow tricked him the way Faustina had, for her own nefarious ends.

That suspicion wasn't playing as strongly now that he was here. Her home was unpretentious, dated and showing signs of age, but neat and well cared for. Her bond with her grandmother and daughter seemed genuine and from the reports he'd commissioned, she was this side of financially solvent. She didn't even have a speeding ticket on her record.

He'd picked up two on his way here, but that was beside the point.

In the past, he had seen what he wanted to see. He couldn't allow himself to be so credulous again.

He made himself take a cool moment to watch Lily's concentrated effort to touch the end of her spoon into the soup and bring the taste to her mouth. She grinned as she succeeded, spoon caught between her tiny white teeth.

He had no proof, but he was convinced she was his. He *had* to claim her.

As for Poppy, he was still absorbing the impact she continued to have on him. He still reacted physically to her. One look at her in jeans and a loose pullover and his mouth had started to water. No makeup, hair gathered into a messy knot of kinks on her head, wariness like a halo around her, yet he'd had to restrain himself from reaching for her. Not to grab or take possession, but simply to *touch*. Fill his hands with the textures of her.

Was her skin as smooth and soft as his erotic dreams replayed? Would her nipples tighten if he licked then blew lightly again? Did her voice still break in orgasm and would that sound once again send pleasurable shivers down his back?

That chemistry was a weakness, one that warned him to keep his guard up, but it didn't deter him from his plan one iota.

In fact, it stoked a fire of anticipation deep in the pit of his belly.

Poppy's tension remained through dinner, even though Rico went on a charm offensive against her grandmother, breaking out levels even Poppy hadn't realized he possessed, asking after her health and offering condolences over Gramps.

"I'm very sorry to hear you lost him. I remember Poppy saying he wasn't well, just before she left Spain."

Poppy released a subtle snort, suspecting he only recalled that detail because she had reminded him of it an hour ago.

He frowned with affront. "I asked you why you weren't using the money you'd saved to see more of Europe. You said your grandparents needed help moving into a care facility."

For one second, she saw glints of blue and green in his irises, telling her he remembered *everything* about that day.

A spike of tingling heat drove sharp as a lance through her. She crossed her legs, bumping her foot against his shin in the process and sending a reverberation of deeper awareness through her whole body.

"We were talking about moving," Gran said, forcing Rico to break their eye contact. "I couldn't look after Bill myself, but having Poppy here bought us an extra year in our home." Gran squeezed her hand over Poppy's, the strength in her grip heart-wrenchingly faint. "He would have faded all the faster if we'd been forced to leave this house. I'll always be grateful to her for giving us that. I don't know what I would have done if she hadn't been here in the months since he's been gone, either. She's been our special blessing her whole life."

"Gran." Poppy teared up. She knew darned well she'd been more of a burden.

"And Lily is ever so precious, too." Gran smiled at the baby. "But it's time."

"Time?" Poppy repeated with muted alarm.

"I'll call your aunt Sheila in the morning," she said of her sister, patting Poppy's hand before she removed her touch. "I'm on the top of the list at that facility near her apartment. I'm sure I can stay with her until a room opens up."

"Gran, *no*."

"Poppy. We both know I shouldn't have been here this winter, making more work for you on top of looking after the baby. You were shoveling the drive on your one day off to get me to the doctor's office. I have no business near that ice by the front steps, either. You're penning up Lily, worrying I'll trip over her. *I'm* worried. No, I don't want to hold you back from the life you ought to be leading."

"This *is* the life I want to lead." Poppy's chin began to crinkle the way Lily's did when she was coming down with a cold and Poppy had to leave her at day care.

"Oh, is your fancy man moving in with us, then?" Gran asked.

"I see where Poppy gets her spark." A faint smile touched Rico's lips. "Poppy and I have details to work out, but you're right that my life is in Spain. I'm here to marry her and take Poppy and Lily home with me."

After a brief, illogical spike of elation, Poppy's heart fell with that bombshell news. Her mind exploded. He wasn't wrenching their daughter from her arms, but she wasn't relieved in the least. She immediately knew this wasn't about her. He'd married for coldly practical reasons the first time. He might dazzle her grandmother with kindness and charisma, but it was a dispassionate move to get what he wanted by the quickest, most efficient means. She shouldn't be shocked at all by his goal or his methods.

"*My* life is here with Gran," Poppy insisted shakily. "She needs me nearby, even if she moves into assisted care."

"Poppy." The fragility of her grandmother's hand draped over hers again. "What I need is to know that when I'm gone, you're settled with someone who will take care of you and Lily. That person ought to be her father." She patted lightly, saying with quiet power, "I know what this would have meant to you."

If her own father had shown up to take her home, Gran meant. The hot pressure behind her eyes increased.

Even so, there was a part of Poppy that simply heard it as her grandmother wishing Poppy would cease to be a burden upon her.

A spiked ball lodged behind Poppy's breastbone, one she couldn't swallow away. It was so sharp it made tears sting her eyes.

"It's obvious Poppy won't be comfortable unless you're comfortable, Eleanor. Give us a chance to finish our talk. Then you and I will discuss your options. I'm sure we can find solutions that satisfy all of us."

Poppy wanted to shout a giant, scoffing, *Ha!* She rose to clear the table.

CHAPTER THREE

POPPY BATHED LILY and put her to bed, not giving her daughter the attention she deserved because her mind was still whirling with Rico showing up and demanding more than his daughter. *Marriage.*

Had she spun that fantasy in her girlish mind? Yes. Even before she slept with him. She had been fascinated by him for weeks, acutely aware of him whether he was making a dry comment or sipping a glass of orange juice. He'd seemed aloof, but in a laid-back way. When she had overheard Faustina going full Bridezilla, shattering a vase and screaming that their wedding was off, Rico had only said in a calm voice, "Let me have the bottom of that. I'll have to replace it."

Deep down, she'd been thrilled that Faustina had ended things. Happy for him.

In the solarium, he'd been that charming man she'd seen tonight at dinner, the one who expressed so much interest in others, it was easy to miss that he gave away very little about himself.

He had told her enough that day, however. Enough that she had been fooled into thinking he liked her. That there was a spark of…*something*.

She'd been wrong. This was the real man. He was severe and intimidating, not raising his voice because he didn't have to. His wishes, delivered in that implacable tone, were sheer power. She instinctively knew there was no shifting him on the course he had decided.

He didn't want her, though. She was merely an obstacle he was overcoming as expediently as possible. Her grandmother would see this marriage as a move toward security, but Poppy refused to trust his offer so easily. What if he got her over there and promptly divorced her? Took her to court for custody? There was no way she could survive without Lily.

Lily settled and Poppy went to the front room. Rico had finished the calls he'd been making and was chatting with her grandmother.

Having him in her home made her squirm. It was her private space where she revealed her true self in faded, toothless photos on the wall next to some of her earliest photography efforts. She and Gran had been working their way through a box of paperback romances that Poppy had picked up at a garage sale and Poppy's latest passionate cover was splayed open on the coffee table.

On the mantel stood Poppy's framed employee

of the month certificate. Her boss at the bus depot had given it to her as a joke. Aside from him, she was the only employee and she was part-time. Gran had had her first good laugh in ages when Poppy had brought it home. Then they'd wept because Gramps would have enjoyed it, too.

Beside the certificate stood a generic birthday card from last month signed, *Love, Mom*. It was the only message besides the preprinted poem.

Rico was seeing far too much of *her* in this space. Maybe gathering ammunition for why his daughter couldn't stay here. A man so low on sentiment wouldn't recognize the comfort in the worn furniture and the value of memory-infused walls.

"The weatherman said it's a good night for stargazing," Gran was telling Rico while nodding at the television. "You might even see the northern lights."

"It's freezing outside," Poppy protested. "Literally." Spring might be a few days away on the calendar, but there was still thick frost on her windshield every morning.

"Bundle up." Gran dismissed Poppy's argument with the hardy practicality of a woman who'd lived on the prairies her whole life. "Your grandfather and I always came to agreement walking around Fisher's Pond. I have the phone right here." She touched the table where the cordless phone lived. "I'll call if Lily wakes and fusses."

Poppy glanced at Rico, hoping he would say it was late and he would come back tomorrow.

"I left my gloves in the car. I'll collect them on my way."

She bit back a huff and layered up, pulling on boots, mittens and a toque before tramping into what was actually a fairly mild night, considering the sky was clear and there was still snow on the ground.

The moon turned the world a bluish daylight and her footsteps crunched after Rico as they started away from the car. He wound a red scarf around his neck as they walked.

"Before today, I had only flown over prairies, never driven through them." His breath clouded as he spoke.

"Were you fighting to stay awake?"

"No, but it's very relaxing. Gives you time and space to think."

She didn't ask him what he'd been thinking about, just took him past the last house on their street, then along the path in the snow toward the depression that was Fisher's Pond.

It was a busy place midwinter. Neighborhood children played hockey every chance they got, but signs were posted now that the ice was thinning and no longer safe. The makeshift benches and lights were gone leaving only the trampled ring around the pond that was popular with dog walkers in summer. Tonight, they had the place to themselves.

"I haven't seen the Milky Way like that, either," he said, nodding at the seam of stars ripped open across the sky. "Not clear and massive like that."

"Rico, I can't go to Spain with you."

"I can hire a live-in care aid." His tone became very businesslike. "Or support her in any facility she chooses. You can be back here within a day if concerns arise. Do not use your grandmother as an excuse to keep my daughter from me."

Wow. She rubbed her mitten against her cold nose, trying to keep the tip of it from growing numb.

"She's not an excuse. She's my family."

He absorbed that, then asked, "Where are your parents? Why has it fallen on you to look after your grandparents?"

"I wanted to." She hugged herself. "They've always been good to me. Even when I came home pregnant."

Especially then. Buying the assisted-living unit would have required selling the house, leaving Poppy without anywhere to live. It had been everyone's wish that they stay together in that house while Gramps was so sick, but Gran was right. They couldn't sustain this. Poppy had been mentally preparing herself for spending the summer clearing out the house. That didn't mean she was ready to move with her daughter around the globe, though.

"Did your parents pass away? Have you always lived with them?"

"I have, but my parents are alive. Divorced. Dad works in the oil patch." She tried not to sound as forlorn as she had always felt when talking about her parents. "He shows up every few months for a week or so, sleeps on the couch and does some repairs. He used to give Gran money sometimes, for taking care of me. I think he gambles most of what he makes. It's one of those things no one in the family talks about, but money has always been an issue with him."

"Thus the divorce?"

"I'm sure that was part of it. Mom had her own issues." She turned from the cleared patch that faced the pond and started on the path around it.

She hated that she had to reveal her deepest shame, but he ought to know it, so he would understand her reasons for refusing to marry him.

"They were really young when they had me. Mom was only nineteen. Not ready for the responsibility of being a parent. My dad brought her here to live with his parents then left to work far away. Mom stuck around until I was two, then she started moving around, living the life she thought she was entitled to, I guess."

"Partying? Drugs?"

"Freedom, mostly." Poppy understood now how overwhelming parenting was, but *she* hadn't dropped her daughter like a hot potato just because it was hard. "She didn't want to be a mom. She wanted to 'explore her potential.'" Poppy air-quoted the phrase. "She tried modeling in Toronto and worked as a flight attendant out of Montreal. She was a music promoter in Halifax, went to Vancouver to work on a cruise ship. Followed a man to India for a year then came back and opened a yoga studio in California. That's how she met her current husband, teaching one of his ex-wives to downward dog. He's a movie producer. They have two kids."

Two sulky, spoiled children who complained about the meals Poppy's mother cooked for them and the music lessons and soccer practices she drove them to.

Poppy tried not to hate them. They were family, but they were also entitled little brats.

"You never lived with her?" Rico asked behind her.

"By the time she was settled, I was starting high school. Bringing me across the border even for a visit was more bureaucracy than she wanted to face. She still hasn't seen Lily except over the tablet. I think she wishes I had never been born. Not in a spiteful way, but she would rather pretend her youthful mistake had never happened."

The path became streaked by the shadows of a copse of trees. She plodded into it, trying not to be depressed by her parents' neglect when they'd left her with such amazing grandparents.

"What I'm hearing is that you wish both of your parents had taken steps to bring you to live with them."

"Is that what you're hearing?" She stopped and turned, thinking her grandparents had been onto something because there was safety in the darkness, where her vulnerability wasn't painted in neon letters across her face. "Because I've come to realize they did me a favor, leaving me with people who tucked me in and told me they loved me every night."

She had surprised him by turning to confront him. He had pulled up, but stood really close. His face was striped by ivory and cobalt.

"Have you told them? Your parents?" she asked.

"I told them she was likely mine, even though the DNA results were inconclusive. I said—"

"What?" Poppy's elbows went stiff as she punched the air by her thighs. "Why did you even *come* here if you didn't *know*?"

"Because I had to know," he said tightly, "Your guilty expression when you opened the door was all the proof I needed."

She was such a dope, confirming his suspicions

before he even *knew*. How did he disarm her so easily again and again?

"What was their reaction?" she asked, focusing on her deeper concerns. The *duque* and *duquesa* had struck Poppy as being aliens in human skin, assimilating on earth well enough not to be detected, but incapable of relating to normal people or showing genuine emotion.

"They asked to be kept informed."

"I see. And is your mother still on the hunt for the next Señora Montero?"

"How the hell do you know that?"

"I'm capable of reading a headline."

"Elevate your browsing choices. Gossip sites are garbage. If you wanted to know what I was doing with my life, you should have called *me*."

"I'm more interested in how your mother is going to react to Lily."

"She'll accept a fait accompli. She's done it before."

When Cesar's indiscretion with Sorcha had resulted in Enrique. But as far as Poppy could tell, Rico's father had barely noticed he had a grandson while his mother had given Enrique tight smiles and offered unsolicited suggestions on how he could be improved. *He looks due for a haircut, Sorcha.*

So Poppy snorted her disbelief. "I've seen what her type of 'acceptance' looks like and it's colder than an arctic vortex."

"Be careful, Poppy."

"That wasn't a cheap shot. I'm saying Lily is far too important to me to set her up to be the subject of criticism and disapproval for the rest of her life. If they're going to treat her like a stain on the family name, I won't take her anywhere near them."

He probably thought she should be grateful he was planning to let her accompany him and her daughter, but he only said, "They're not demonstrative people. There will be no welcome embrace from either of them. Reconcile yourself to that right now. They do, however, bring other strengths to the table. We Monteros look after our own."

"My stepfather can put her in movies if she decides she wants wealth and fame."

"Wealth is not fortune, fame is not standing," he stated pithily. "What sort of future are you planning for her? You'll date, perhaps introduce her to a few contenders and, one day, when you're convinced you're in love, you'll allow another man to raise *my* child without any of the genuine advantages to which she's entitled? In ignorance of her family and the attached opportunities overseas? No. I won't let you deny her what's rightfully hers."

"It's not up to you. And don't say it like that! 'When I'm *convinced* I'm in love.' *I love Lily.* Try to tell me that feeling is a figment of my imagination." She would knock him through the ice. "Do *you* plan to love her? Because, given what I saw of your upbringing, you were never shown how."

A profound silence crashed over them.

"Just as you were never taught to hold your temper in favor of a civil conversation?" Oh, he sounded lethal. The cold in the air began to penetrate her clothes.

"Answer the question," she insisted. "My love for Lily took root the day I learned I was pregnant." It had grown so expansive her body couldn't contain the force of it. It quivered in her voice as she continued. "I won't set her up to yearn for something from you that will never happen. I've been there and it is far too painful a thing to wish onto my child. *You know it is.*"

She had pushed herself right out onto the ledge of getting way too personal. She knew she had, but that was how much her daughter meant to her.

The umbrage radiating off him should have flash-melted the snow and razed the trees, illuminating the skies in an explosion of light.

Even so, she nudged even further by warning through her teeth, "Don't shove your way into her life unless you intend to be there every single moment, in every possible way she might need you to be."

His hands jammed into his pockets and his profile was slashed with shadows.

"You—" Something made him bite off whatever

he had been about to say. He made a sucking noise through clenched teeth, as though enduring the removal of a bullet or something equally wounding. "My brother's sons are not unhappy. He had my same upbringing. He's managed to become quite attached. I would expect to form that sort of connection with my own child."

She was glad for the dark then, because sudden, pitying tears froze to her lashes. His words were such a careful admission that he was fine with not being loved as a child, but would find a way to extend his heart to his daughter.

For that reason alone, for the opportunity to gift him with his child's unconditional love, she knew she would have to allow him into Lily's life.

"Even so…" She folded her arms and squished handfuls of her quilted sleeves with her woolen mittens. She had had a front-row seat to the way his parents' marriage worked and it was…*sad*. They spoke without warmth to each other, as if they were inquiring about a telephone bill minus the anxiety that they might struggle to pay. "What kind of marriage would that be as an example for her?"

"A calm and rational one?" he suggested.

"I don't want rational! I want what my grandparents had." She waved wildly in the direction of the house where she had witnessed deep, abiding love, every single day. "I want pet names for each other and a love that endures through a lifetime."

"You want me to call you red?"

"Don't make fun of me. Or them," she warned. "Gran stayed in that drafty house an extra year for Gramps, because she knew it would break his heart to leave it. Now she can't stand to sleep in it without him there beside her."

"And you want that?" He sounded askance.

"It beats being married to a stranger. Occupying a mausoleum of a house while pursuing separate lives."

"My parents' marriage is an alliance based on shared values. That's not a bad thing if you agree on those values beforehand."

"Speaking from experience, are you?"

Another harsh silence descended. This time she regretted her words. His pregnant wife had died. He might not have loved Faustina, but it must be a very raw wound.

Recalling that, her suspicions of his motives arose again. Maybe he would come to care for Lily, but why was he here now? What did he *really* want?

"Rico… You understand that one baby cannot replace another, don't you?" She knew she had to tread softly on that one, but couldn't hold that apprehension inside her. "If that's why you're here, then no." It broke her heart to deny Lily her father, but, "I won't let you do that to Lily."

He stiffened and she braced herself for his scathing reaction, but it wasn't at all what she expected.

"Faustina's baby wasn't *mine*."

CHAPTER FOUR

THE WORDS WERE supposed to stay inside his head, but they resounded across the crisp air. Through the trees and off the sky. They made icicles drop like knives and stab into the frozen snow.

From a long way away, he heard Poppy say a hollow and breathless, "What?" Her thin, strained voice was no louder than his own had been, but rang like a gong in his ears.

He pinched the bridge of his nose, the leather of his gloves cold. All of him was encased in the dry ice of Canadian winter while his blood pumped in thick lumps through his arteries. His chest tightened and his shoulders ached.

"I shouldn't have said that. We should get back." He glanced the way they'd come, but it was shorter if she would only keep moving ahead on the path.

Thankfully, he couldn't see a soul. They were the only pair of fools out here stumbling through the dark. He waved for her to proceed.

"Rico." Her mitted hand came onto his forearm. "Is that true?"

The quaver in her voice matched the conscience still wobbling like a dropped coin in the pit of his stomach.

"Forget I said it. I mean it, Poppy."

"I can't." She didn't let him brush away her grip on his sleeve. "*It matters.* Tell me."

"If I tell you…" He shifted so he cupped her elbow, holding her before him. "It stays between us. *Forever.* Do you understand?"

He had already said too much, but she was the mother of his child. His *actual* child. He had only tentatively absorbed that knowledge, only enough to know that one way or another he would bring them both back to Spain with him. Marriage was the quickest, most practical means of doing that. Therefore, she deserved to know the truth about his first marriage. As his wife, he expected her to protect his secrets as closely as he would guard hers.

And, damn it, he felt as though he'd been holding his breath for a thousand years. He couldn't contain it one minute longer.

"Her parents found her," he said, overcome with pity for them, despite his bitterness at Faustina's lies. The colossal waste of life couldn't be denied. The unborn baby might not have been his, but he was a decent enough human being to feel sadness and regret that it had been as much a victim as its parents.

"Where?" Poppy asked with dread.

"The garage. It wasn't deliberate. They'd packed bags, had train tickets. She was with her parents' chauffeur, naked in the back seat. They must have made love, perhaps started the car to warm it, then fallen asleep. They never woke up. Carbon monoxide poisoning."

"Oh, my God." She covered her mouth. "That's *horrible*."

"Yes. Her parents were devastated. Still are. They didn't know about the affair. They begged me to keep it under wraps."

"So you've been letting everyone think— How do you know the baby wasn't yours?"

"I had the coroner run tests."

"You told me that day you two weren't sleeping together." She twitched in his grip.

He released her. His palm felt cold, even inside his glove. He was solid ice, all the way to his core, still playing what-ifs in his head.

"Do you think *she* knew it wasn't yours?" she asked tentatively.

"Of course she knew," he spat with the contempt he felt for himself as much as for Faustina. "I had already begun to suspect. As soon as they found her, I knew what she had done. We *weren't* sleeping together. We made love *once* during our engagement. Faustina insisted. Said she wanted to be sure we'd be a good fit. After that, there were excuses. Headaches. Finally she said we should wait until the ceremony, to make our wedding night more exciting."

He hadn't argued. The first experience had barely moved him, certainly hadn't rocked his world the way another very memorable experience had. He skimmed his gaze over Poppy's face, so ghostly in the moonlight.

He'd told himself things would improve with Faustina once they got to know one another. He hadn't realized yet that it was possible to fall into immersive pleasure so profound he could be transported from the world around him. So much so that he made love with a woman he barely knew in the near-public solarium and had thought about her every day since.

He ran his gloved hand over his face. The seam in his palm scraped his skin, allowing him to focus on the rest of the ugly story.

"I believe she learned she was pregnant and slept with me so she could pass the baby off as mine."

"When?"

He knew what she was asking. "A few weeks before she broke things off with me on the day you and I were together."

Poppy rubbed her arm where he'd held her elbow.

"I've since learned that when she left my parents' house, she went straight to her own and told them she had called off the wedding. Her father threatened to disinherit her. They're very faithful and strict, demanded she abide by the agreement. They would have fired the driver if they'd had any inkling of her reason. Maybe even sued him for damages or destroyed him in some other way. Faustina's choice was to live destitute with her lover or crawl back to me."

It was the only explanation for how a stable, well-bred, otherwise honest woman could have behaved in such an underhanded way.

"A week before they died, she used her settlement from our marriage to close on a small house in the north of Spain, near his relatives. That's where they were headed."

"That's so…sad."

"Sad and sordid and I torture myself every day wondering if she would be alive if I'd refused to marry her that next morning."

"Why did you agree? The presidency?" Her voice panged in a way that grated against his conscience. The opportunity to run Faustina's father's company, proving himself in his own arena away from Cesar's shadow, had been the carrot that drew him into the engagement, but it wouldn't have enticed him to go through with the wedding the second time.

"She said she'd just found out she was pregnant, that it was the reason she'd been so emotional the day before. She said the baby was from that *one time*—when I used a condom, by the way. I should have suspected she was lying, but…" Here were the what-ifs. What if he had asked more questions, balked, told her he'd slept with the maid? That he'd *liked* it.

He hadn't done any of that. He'd done his duty by his family. He had done what was expected because, "I thought the baby was *mine*."

"When did you start to suspect it wasn't?"

"The wedding night. She didn't want to have sex. Said the pregnancy was turning her off." Rico had been nursing his own regrets and hadn't pressed her. "She was very moody. Conflicted, obviously. And putting her ducks in a row to leave me. We never did sleep together again. Things grew strained as I realized she was keeping something from me. I put off a confrontation, but it was coming. Then I got the call from her father."

"I'm so sorry, Rico. It's truly awful that you've had to carry this."

"I don't want your pity, Poppy." He curled his hands into fists, straining the seams in his gloves. "I want your silence. I expect it. Not even Cesar knows and we don't keep much from one another. But I swore to her parents I'd keep it quiet."

"What about the company?"

"Her father asked me to stay on as President. He's sickened that she tricked me. I could weather the scandal if the truth came out, but it would destroy them. Despite Faustina's behavior, they're good people. I don't want to hurt them any more than they have been."

"I'll never say a word," she promised.

He nodded, believing her because they were in this together now.

"You understand why I told you? If she had been honest and up front about her situation, I would have helped her, maybe even raised that baby if she had asked me to. I wouldn't have punished the child for her failings." His anger returned, making his nostrils sting. "But I don't appreciate that you have also kept secrets from me, Poppy."

He heard her breath catch as though he'd struck her.

"I will *not* ignore my actual blood. I want *my* daughter."

She took a step back, but he caught her arm, keeping her close and tilting his head to peer through the shadows straight into her eyes.

"You *will* come to Spain. You *will* marry me and we will make this work."

Poppy might have knocked his hand away if she hadn't needed his touch to steady her; his words were that impactful.

"That's a big leap," she managed shakily. "I won't keep you from knowing her, Rico. I see why Lily being yours has extra significance for you." Her heart was aching under the weight of what he'd revealed and she had only just heard it. It had been festering in him for nearly two years. "But you and I barely know each other."

"We know each other," he scoffed gently. "I just told you something I haven't told *anyone*."

And she had shared her heartache over her parents' neglect.

A similar thing had happened that day in the solarium. Their conversation had somehow become deeply personal. Her crush on him had been instant and she'd never meant it to become obvious to him, but for weeks she had longed to talk to him in a meaningful way. She had wanted to find out who he was beneath his shell of gorgeous looks, easy manners and unsmudged armor.

She recalled telling him about that liar of a backpacker who had stolen everything she had, then asked why he had agreed to an arranged marriage.

Why compete with a business rival if a marriage can turn them into a partner? Faustina's very upstanding family would never connect themselves so intimately to any but the most exemplary politician, which polishes my father's already stellar reputation in the upper house of Parliament. Faus-

tina gains the social standing of marrying into a titled family. My mother gets the heiress and the wedding event she envisioned for my brother.

It had seemed so laughably factual. She had asked him what he stood to gain and he'd mentioned running a company he would control, allowing him to pursue ambitions away from working for his brother.

A rational part of her brain had warned her that she deserved someone better than a man bouncing off a broken engagement, but her pride had needed the focused attention of someone so much grander than she was. She had thought the camera thief had genuinely liked her, but he'd been flattering her to blind her. Rico hadn't wanted anything from her except *her*. If he was rebounding after his own rejection, that was okay. It was one more detail that made them equals.

And when their kisses had escalated with passion, she hadn't wanted to stop. His lovemaking had been exactly what she had needed in that moment. Much as she believed she would only marry for love, she had known a soul-mate connection was an elusive thing. Expecting the full package of love and pleasure and a lifelong commitment for her first time wasn't realistic.

It had been enough to have infatuation and a man who ought to be firmly out of her reach, but who brought her entire body to life by simply watching the release of a button on her dress, then lifting his gaze to check in with her as his finger traced a caress against her skin.

She put a halt to recalling the rest or she'd succumb to him all over again without so much as a single protest.

"This is the second time we've spoken," she pointed out, inwardly shaking at how profound their encounters had been. "We made love *once*."

"With spectacular results." His gloved hand took hold of her chin. "I'm not just talking about Lily."

She was so glad he couldn't see her blush, but her helplessness was on full display in her strained voice. "That was... You were relieved you weren't marrying," she accused. "Coming off a dry spell with the first woman you happened across."

"I noticed you before that."

They were close enough that the fog of their breath was mingling.

"I wouldn't have kissed you if you hadn't made a point of telling me you'd finished your last shift and were no longer an employee," he reminded. "The attraction was mutual."

"I didn't make a *point* of it." Maybe she had. He had asked if she wanted to leave and had moved aside, giving her plenty of space to walk past him to the change rooms where she'd been headed when she had bumped into him. She had stayed, eager to keep talking to him. Basking in the glory of being noticed by him.

"Do you ever think about that day?" he asked.

Constantly. She wouldn't admit it, though.

"Hmm?" he prompted, lowering his head. He stopped before he kissed her.

She let her eyes flutter closed and parted her lips in invitation.

He only grazed his mouth against hers, provoking a buzzing sensation in her lips.

She put out a hand, but the knit of her mitten only found the smooth leather of his jacket, too slippery to hold on to.

While he kept up that frustratingly light tickle. His hand shifted to cup the side of her neck, the rough seam on his thumb grazing the tender skin in her throat.

"Do you?" He refused to give her what she wanted until she answered.

Her skin grew too tight for the anticipation that swelled within her. Beneath the layers of her thick jacket, her breasts grew heavy. Her thighs ceased to feel the cold through the denim of her jeans.

"Yes," she admitting on a throb of longing.

He made a noise of satisfaction and stepped so his feet were outside her own. His hot mouth sealed across her lips.

A sob of delight broke in her throat as his hard lips raked across hers, making real all the erotic fantasies she'd replayed in the long nights since leaving Spain. Her arms went up around his neck and he swept her closer still. So close she could hardly breathe.

She didn't care. The thick layers of their coats were a frustration, one that seemed to hold them off from one another. She wanted them *gone*. Wanted passion to take her over the way it had that day, blanking out the world around her with levels of excitement and pleasure she hadn't known existed.

His kiss deepened with greed, as though he couldn't get enough of her, either. She opened fully to him, licked into his mouth and felt his arms tighten around her in response. She ran her hand up past his scarf, pressed the back of his head, urging him to kiss her harder and harder still. She wanted him to mark her. Savage her.

Because he already had.

This passion between them was as destructive as it was glorious. She needed to remember that. Otherwise, she would succumb and wind up far out of her depth again.

As though he recognized the risk as well, he dragged his head up and sucked in a breath, but he didn't let her go.

Panting, she blinked her eyes open. His face was in darkness with a kaleidoscope of colors haloed behind him.

"Look." She seized the distraction to pull herself out of his arms. She wasn't even sure if what she was seeing was real or the leftover fireworks he had so easily set off behind her eyelids.

She staggered slightly as she led him out of the trees. The expanse of sky was bigger than a thousand movie screens above them and the stars had faded behind glowing swirls. Shimmering bands of pink and purple and red danced within the curtains of green. Every few seconds a spear of color shot toward the earth in knifelike streaks. The jabs of color felt so tangible and close, she expected to be struck by one.

"This is beautiful." Rico drew her back against his chest and folded his arms across her collarbone and stomach.

She was still weak from their kiss. She leaned into the wall he made, wondering if he could feel the thump of her still unsteady heart through their winter layers.

"One of my first memories is coming out here with my grandfather," she confided softly. "I asked when my mother was coming back and he brought me out here. I thought he was going to tell me she had died. He said he didn't know if she was coming back, but then he pointed to the sky. I asked what it was and he said he didn't know that, either. That there would always be things in this world we're left to wonder about."

"Gas particles from the sun collide with the earth's atmosphere," Rico informed her.

"Don't ruin it." She nudged her elbow back into his ribs. "It's *magic*. I've taken a million photographs of them, but none capture how amazing this really is. How small it makes you feel."

"I've never seen it like this." His chin touched the top of her head.

"Me, neither." This was the most glorious display she'd ever witnessed and she didn't care that she didn't have her camera. She would never forget sharing this with him: the timbre of his voice vibrating through her jacket, the heat of his breath against her earlobe where it poked from beneath her toque, the weight of his arm across her and the way all those colors glowed inside her even as they danced before her unblinking eyes.

She hesitated then confessed softly, "Gramps brought me out here when I was pregnant, too. I wanted to keep Lily, but I didn't know how I would manage it. It felt too much of an imposition to stay with them. He was upset that he wouldn't be around to look after me and Gran. We had a little cry then saw these lights. He said it was a reminder that even dark nights offer beautiful moments and said that's what Lily would be for all of us if I stayed with them."

Rico's arm tightened across her chest. His voice was low and sincere. "I'm sorry I didn't meet him."

Her chest ached. "I think that's him right now."

A startled pause, then, "I don't believe in things like that, Poppy."

"It's okay." She touched the arm that continued to hold her close. "I do."

"If I did—" His lips pressed to her ear through the knit of her toque. "I think we both know what he's saying."

Her throat grew tight. *Marry Rico.*

He drew back slightly so he could reach into his jacket. When he brought his hand around in front of her, he held a small box. He stayed behind her as he pried up the lid so she stood in the circle of his arms as he offered her the ring.

The band could have been silver or yellow or rose. The diamond caught glints of colored light, blinding her.

Had he really come all this way, not knowing for sure if Lily was his, but brought a ring just in case?

She let him pick up her left hand and tug at the mitten. She took the discarded mitt with her free hand. As though under a spell, she turned to face him.

She tried to think of reasons to persuade him this was wrong or stupid or doomed to fail. Marrying him was all of those things.

But she wanted to marry him. Her compulsion to know him remained. Beneath the anger and armor of indifference was a man who wanted to know his daughter. That meant everything to her.

As the aurora borealis continued to crash silently over them, full of mystical power and spirit voices, she told herself that Gramps wouldn't steer her wrong. He wouldn't tell her to marry Rico if this would ruin her life. He was telling her to say goodbye to her home and family and begin building her new one.

The cool ring caught slightly on her knuckle, then it was on her finger, heavy as the promise it symbolized. Rico's mouth came down to hers again with magnificent heat, burning away her bleak doubts and fears, filling her with hope and possibility.

CHAPTER FIVE

You should have told me sooner. I would have made arrangements. Someone from the family should have been there.

Rico read the text from Pia and swore, then dropped the phone onto the custom recliner beside the one he occupied.

Across from him, buckled into her own, Poppy looked up from distracting Lily with a book. Lily was making noises of dismay at being strapped into her car seat while the view beyond the windows turned to clouds.

"What's wrong?" Poppy asked him.

"A text from my sister, scolding me about the wedding."

"She's upset?" Poppy's expression dimmed.

"That I didn't invite her. I pointed out there hasn't been time."

It hadn't occurred to him Pia would want to come. His parents had urged him to wait for the

DNA results and expressed consternation that he hadn't. Cesar's reaction to his impending nuptials had been a curt text.

Sorcha told me. Congratulations.

Rico had given up at that point and focused on the tasks at hand.

Poppy's gran had been moved to her sister's apartment, where she would occupy a guest room for a few days. Rico had had to push to make it happen, but he had arranged to have her personal items moved into a nearby, private seniors' complex that was so well-appointed, Eleanor had asked him if he'd won a lottery.

Poppy had been anxious about the entire process until she'd spoken with the extremely personable, on-staff doctor who had already been in touch with her grandmother's specialist. A nutritionist had made note of her grandmother's dislike of cumin. Her sensitivity to certain detergents had been conveyed to the housekeeping staff. Eleanor had looked in on the pool where physical therapy sessions were held and checked out the lively games room, approving the entire complex with a delighted nod.

Poppy's father had pointed out that the location in Regina would be easier for him to visit, too. He typically spent half a day driving after his flight landed. Rico had even hired a caretaker to look after the house until decisions had been made on whether to keep it in the family.

The last task had been a brief civil service at the courthouse. Poppy's father had given her away and her grandmother had wept happy tears. They had eaten brunch at an upscale café then climbed aboard his private jet.

Another text rang through, but he ignored it.

"Tell her I didn't even have my mother there," Poppy said.

"I explained why I was keeping it private."

"That wasn't a complaint," she said stiffly, making him aware of how tersely he'd spoken. "I didn't *want* my mother there." She picked up the book Lily dropped, mouth pinched.

Poppy had said she would inform her mother after Rico issued the press release. He'd had enough to juggle in the moment that he hadn't questioned her. Now he did.

"Why not?" Had she been afraid she wouldn't show up? Her mother sounded even less emotionally accessible than his own. At least La Reina Montero maintained appearances.

"I was afraid she wouldn't keep her mouth shut," Poppy muttered crossly. "I agree with you that it's kinder to let your parents inform Faustina's parents and give them a few days to prepare their own statement."

Loathe as he was to bring Faustina into this marriage on any level, he appreciated Poppy's understanding. Having a child Lily's age wouldn't reflect well on his fidelity, narrow window of a called-off wedding notwithstanding. This news would come as a shock to many, including Faustina's parents.

"I didn't mean to speak sharply. I don't usually make mistakes and they've been piling up lately."

For the most part, Rico was a meticulous planner. He had always been taught success was a matter of research and preparation. That lesson had played out as true more often than not and he had heeded its wisdom—right up until he had impulsively made love with his mother's maid.

He had promptly fallen back in line with the precisely orchestrated pageant his first wedding had been, only to discover his wife's betrayal. As resentful as he still was of that, he had to face the fact that if he had refused to marry Faustina when she had come back that next morning, she might be alive and happily ensconced with her lover and child. He wouldn't have the presidency that had seemed like such a delectable consolation prize, but he would have had the first year of Lily's life. Poppy bore some responsibility for his missing that, but so did he.

He had believed his tryst with Poppy was all the bucking of expectations he had needed before settling into the life laid out for him. Even after Sorcha had dropped this earth-shattering news on him, he had attempted to defuse it with surgical care, ordering an investigation and telling no one.

Then the test had come back inconclusive and he had come out of his skin. Mere days later, he had a wife and child. His parents thought he was behaving recklessly and a rational part of him wondered if they were right. He was relying on instinct without concrete evidence or other facts to back it up.

He caught Poppy's affronted glare and heard his own words.

"I wasn't suggesting this marriage is a mistake. But it will cause a tragic death to be splashed across the gossip sites again. *You* will be cast as the Other Woman."

She would be labeled an opportunist and a gold digger. Given her shock at his arrival, he couldn't accuse her of that, but others would.

"I'll look like a faithless husband and a deadbeat father. I'm not proud of any of that. Scandals are not my MO. I'm disgusted with myself for creating this situation."

"And what about Lily? Are you sorry you created her?" The fiery challenge in her expression was quickly schooled as the flight attendant approached to ask after their comfort.

Lily lifted her arms at the woman and pitifully begged, "Oof?"

"She thinks that means up," Poppy explained with a stiff smile. "I guess I was making that noise whenever I lifted her and didn't notice. Button, you have to stay in your seat. I'll apologize now for how miserable she's going to become."

Rico preferred a happy baby over one who was screaming, same as anyone. The baby in question, however, was his. He hadn't fully unpacked that knowledge and very tentatively felt around in the dank spaces within him, looking for the regret Poppy had accused him of feeling toward Lily.

"Our flight should be very smooth until we're over the Atlantic," the attendant said. "She could walk around if you want to let her work out some energy."

"She doesn't walk yet."

"There isn't much she can get into," Rico pointed out, still searching through the bitterness that encased him for resentment that was wrongly aimed at an innocent child. "All the drawers have catches so they won't open midflight."

Poppy peered at the floors. They were as spotless as they ought to be, given the salaries he paid his flight crews.

"You really wouldn't mind?" Poppy asked the attendant.

"Of course not." The attendant was bemused by the question and disappeared to fetch the coffee he requested.

Poppy heard his snort and shot him a frown as she unstrapped Lily. "Why am I funny?"

"This is my plane. If my daughter wants to pilot it through loop-de-loops, it's the crew's job to make it happen." That much he *was* sure of.

Poppy released a small oof of exertion as she pulled Lily out of her seat and stood her on the floor, next to her knee. Then she reached into the toy bag and handed Lily a giraffe. She tossed the half-dozen other toys onto the empty seat next to Rico.

Lily reached for the bag, needing to peek inside to see if more would appear.

"It's empty. They're all there," Poppy told her, pointing.

Lily dropped the giraffe, let go of Poppy's knee and took three toddling steps, completely unassisted.

Poppy gasped and reached out to catch her, but Lily slapped her dimpled hand onto Rico's knee. Her fingers closed like kitten claws into the fabric of his trousers as she steadied herself. Then she cruised around his leg and began examining the array of toys.

Poppy clapped her hand over her open mouth. Her eyes brimmed with excited tears. "Did you see that?" She dropped her hand, but emotion husked her voice.

"Those weren't her *first* steps." It couldn't be. There'd been no fanfare. No announcement over the PA that it was about to happen. It had occurred naturally, as if she'd been doing it all along.

Poppy nodded like a bobblehead doll on the dash of a derby car.

"They were. Just like that. Baby is gone and she's a toddler." She wiped her damp eyes. "I shouldn't be so silly about it. Gran kept saying it would happen any day."

Lily had found his phone amid the stuffed toys and plastic keys. He started to take it from her, but a fierce swell of pride moved his hand to her hair. He faltered briefly then grazed his palm lightly over her fine red hair, downy as a duckling.

She was such a tiny, perfect little human. Recognizing how vulnerable she was made his heart clench in a strange panic. An urge to protect rose in him, but he already knew he wouldn't be sufficient to the task. Not forever. Things would happen beyond his control. Then what? He had instinctively shied from this depth of responsibility, but here it was, thrust upon him, heavy and unavoidable, yet oddly welcome.

How could he not want to shield such a precious young life? How could he ever blame her for existing?

"You don't have to impress me, you know," he told Lily, rueful that he was so button-bursting proud of three little steps.

Lily grinned and held up his phone.

"Thank you," he said politely and pocketed the item, offering a teething ring in exchange. He shifted his attention to Poppy.

"We both could have handled many things better," he told her, clearing his voice to steady it while he mentally allowed the cloak of fatherhood to settle more comfortably over his shoulders. "But I will never, ever regard Lily as a mistake."

Rico gently transferred Lily into a blue crib that likely belonged to Mateo. Rico had said this darkened penthouse in Madrid was used by any member of the family who happened to have business in the capital.

Poppy carefully tucked blankets around her overtired little girl. The first half of the flight had gone well. Everyone had caught a few hours of sleep, but Lily had begun fussing when turbulence forced her to be strapped back into her seat. By the time she had cried herself out and begun to nod off, they were descending and her ears were popping, upsetting her all over again.

"I think she's down for the count," Poppy said with relief as they stepped out of the room.

Rico clicked on the baby monitor and brought it with them into the lounge where he turned on a few lamps. He moved with casual confidence, hardly a wrinkle in his clothes, his eyes heavy-lidded and inscrutable.

"Are you hungry?"

"No. I feel like all I did was eat on the flight." She crossed her arms and hunched her shoulders, hyperaware that they were alone for the first time since they'd stood under the stars that first night.

They were also married.

She had heard him tell the driver to leave their luggage in *his* room, but there was a conversation they needed to have before they shared it. She hadn't figured out yet how to broach it. She wished she could be blasé and sophisticated, but she felt callow and fearful of his reaction. Would he laugh? Look at her with disappointment?

"I…um…wouldn't mind a shower," she murmured, more for a chance to be alone and clear her head.

"Do you want company?" His voice lowered, growing thick with sensual invitation.

Her stomach took a rollercoaster dip and swirl while a wave of heat pushed out from her center, leaving her fingers and toes, nipples and scalp all tingling.

She wanted to laugh at how easily he segued into addressing the elephant, but some of her trepidation must have shown. His expression tightened.

"We don't have to if you're tired."

"It's not that," she murmured, more wired than tired, still trying to come to terms with everything that had happened in such a whirlwind. Drawing a breath of courage, she said, "I'm not sure what you expect."

A brief pulse of surprise, then he said stiffly, "I expect this marriage to include a sexual relationship. I'll never force it, though. And I would normally say a woman doesn't need an excuse for turning me down, but given Faustina's reasons, I'd like to understand yours."

"I'm not turning you down," she said with a small, nervous smile that wouldn't stick. "I expected we'd have sex. When I took Lily for her blood test the other day, I left her with the nurse so I could get an IUD." Sometimes her hair gifted her with the clichéd fiery blushes and now was one of those times. The entire room should have turned bordello red, she glowed so hotly with the admission that she had premeditated having sex with him.

He frowned. "You don't want more children?"

"Not right away." Her cheeks hurt, they were scorched so deeply. "This is a lot to get used to, don't you think? Without bringing a newborn into the mix?"

He tipped his head slightly, acknowledging the point, but a hint of suspicion glinted in his narrowed eyes. Perhaps he saw the rest of the logic that had propelled her decision—a new baby would make it more difficult for her to leave if she had to.

"I want this marriage to work," she assured

him. "But there are things…" Her voice failed her. She cleared her throat. "Things we should discuss before…"

"Health concerns?"

"You mean disease? No! I'm perfectly fine. Are you—?"

"Completely fine," he clipped out. "I was asking if there were complications with delivering Lily that affected you?"

"No. Just the usual leftover imperfections of stretch marks and… Well, you can see I'm still carrying a bit of baby weight. Lily weaned herself three months ago and apparently these aren't going away." She waved at the chest that remained a cup size bigger than prepregnancy.

"I assure you I don't consider any of those things 'imperfections.' Particularly the added curves. Is that the source of your hesitation? You're self-conscious? We can keep the lights off if it will make you more comfortable. I'd prefer it, too. Otherwise my scar from my appendix surgery might turn you off."

"Why would— Oh. All right, I get your point." She rolled her eyes.

He paced closer, which made her freeze in place, skin growing tight with anticipation while nervous butterflies filled her torso, swirling around in every direction.

He touched her chin, coaxing her to meet his

gaze with her own. "We've done this before," he reminded her.

"About that…" She clasped his flat wrist and squeezed her eyes shut. "That's the only time I've had sex. Ever."

She felt the flex in his wrist and the slight increase of pressure in his grip on her chin.

"Open your eyes," he commanded, voice seeming to resonate from the depths of his chest.

She did, meeting his gaze with chagrin. She wasn't ashamed of being a virgin so much as feeling guilty for having misled him that day.

All she could see were his eyes, iridescent almost. Like granite that revealed flecks of precious gems when wet, glints of blue and green in the gray surrounding a giant black pool. His pupils were huge. Atavistic.

Yet skeptical.

"*Ever*," she reiterated helplessly.

Rico couldn't think of another time he'd been utterly speechless. Not that his mind had the capacity to filter any moments other than the one she was referring to. The shyness of her hands squeezing him through his pants and fumbling with his belt.

Enthusiasm counted for more than expertise when it came to lovemaking. If he'd given any thought to her lack of finesse, he had likely imagined she was as overcome as he was. He couldn't say his own performance had been particularly adept, given the stolen nature of their tryst.

He remembered clearly that moment afterward, though, when his lingering pleasure had dimmed because he had feared he had hurt her.

Is your cycle starting?

I guess. Sorry. She'd been mortified.

Don't apologize. At least we're safe from—

He'd been appalled at forgetting the condom. He *never* forgot.

"I don't like lies," he warned her now, lips numb. This news was melting his face off his skull.

"I'm being honest." She winced as though she was squirming inside. "I want to sleep with you, but I don't want you to be..." She swallowed. Her voice remained strained. "Disappointed. *I* don't want to be disappointed."

The word wafted over him, so far from what he might be feeling as to be incomprehensible. Then his ego absorbed the hit.

"Were *you* disappointed that day?"

"No." She withdrew from him a few steps and crossed her arms.

But she had nothing to compare it to. Her lack of experience began to penetrate. Belated concern struck. They'd been quite passionate. "Did I hurt you?"

"No. I mean, a little, but not..." She looked to the ceiling as though seeking deliverance. "I was fine with the discomfort. There were compensations," she added with a small groan of embarrassed irony.

"You felt pleasure?" He had to know. "You weren't faking your enjoyment, were you? Did you climax? Because I thought you did, but—"

"Are we really doing a forensic audit on it?" she cried, face so red it should have been accompanied by five alarms.

"I need to know, Poppy." It was imperative.

"I didn't fake anything! Okay? Quit asking such personal questions."

"How is this too personal? We were both there and I'm making sure we were both *there*. My pride is every bit as delicate as any man's. When it comes to the bedroom, if you're not satisfied, I'm not satisfied. I will make you that promise right now."

She ducked her eyes into her hand. "Thanks. And I'd love to make the same promise, but *I don't know what I'm doing*."

"You don't have to be defensive about it. I'm glad you told me. And your number of past lovers is far less important to me than how many you have *now*." Obviously. "Shall we agree we'll keep it to one?"

She peered at him over her hand, admonishing, but also earnest as she promised, "Of course I'll be monogamous."

"Thank you. So will I." But he was still having

trouble believing she had shelved all her passion once she'd discovered it. "There really hasn't been anyone since me?"

"Who would I sleep with, pregnant out to here?" She set her hand in the air beyond her navel. "I was looking after my grandparents and a newborn. Babies make you want to have a date with your pillow and no one else, trust me."

She looked too uncomfortable to be telling him anything but the truth.

It was starting to impact him that the most profound sexual experience of his life had been with a virgin. He wasn't sentimental, but there was something endearing in knowing he was her only lover.

"Why me?" he asked gently. "Why that day?"

"Because I was feeling like my whole trip had been a bust and I wanted one decent memory to take home with me."

"I was a *souvenir*?"

"I was just a notch on your belt, wasn't I?" she shot back.

His heart lurched and he had to look away, thinking of the way he had obsessed about her ever since. He had tried to relegate her to a notch. Instead, she'd been another persistent what-if.

"It's fine that you were only taking what I offered," she said, hugging herself. "I didn't care that you had all the experience and seduced me. I wanted you to. But now you're only having sex with me because we're married and you're stuck with me. That would be fine if I felt like I was bringing something to the table, but I don't have any sexual confidence because I've only done it *one time*." Her brow furrowed.

Aside from the chaste kiss after the ceremony, he hadn't touched her since their kiss under the stars, but he'd been acutely aware of her every minute since she had opened her door to him. His ears were attuned to each inflection in her voice—the chuckling remarks she exchanged with her grandmother, the loving tone she used when speaking to Lily. He had studied the fit of her jeans, drunk in the scent of her hair, enjoyed the smooth warmth of her hand if their fingers happened to touch. He had noted the way her lips closed over a fork and the little frown that appeared between her brows if she was growing stubborn.

He had spent every night lying awake, recalling their passionate union until he was so filled with ardor, he ached.

He couldn't believe she didn't know that.

But he had taken pains to keep his reaction hidden so as not to let her undermine him with what he perceived as a weakness. He hadn't wanted to admit that he had obsessed about her from the first moment he'd seen her dusting his mother's furniture.

"You have a lot to compare to and I don't want

to start our marriage by falling short of your expectations." She offered a dejected smile. "That's why we're standing here instead of in the shower."

CHAPTER SIX

Poppy felt like a head case and was trying not to apologize for it. Women were allowed to have reservations. To feel conflicted. She might want sex, but she didn't want empty sex. Not this time. Not when she had tried that the first time and discovered she wasn't capable of keeping her emotions out of the experience.

But Rico was her husband and the father of her child and their kisses had reassured her that their lovemaking would be as pleasurable as it had been the first time.

Maybe she was expecting too much.

Was that what he was thinking behind that enigmatic expression? A muscle was pulsing in his jaw as though he was trying to crack nuts with his teeth.

"I haven't been with anyone else, either," he finally said.

"Oh, please." Disappointment in him descended like a curtain while her heart latched a little too hard on to that outrageous statement. "It's been nearly two years!" He could have his pick of supermodels. He'd gotten the maid with a wink and a smile, hadn't he?

"I already told you that I slept with Faustina *once*. Weeks before you." He opened his eyes to scowl with affront at her distrust. "I didn't cheat on her, and given the way my marriage ended, I haven't been feeling very amorous."

She found that believable, actually.

"Until very recently," he added pointedly, pretty much flinging sexual awareness at her and leaving her coated in it. "All of which could impact *my* performance. You're not the only one with high stakes here."

"Oh, I'm sure we're on exactly the same level of nerves," she muttered sarcastically.

He relaxed slightly, eyeing her. "Do you think about it?"

"What? Sex?" The whole world tilted like a magnifying glass. One moment certain things had loomed large, now all of that went out of focus while a bright ray of heat singed into her bones. "With you, or…?"

"Anyone. But sure, me."

She was *not* going to admit that she thought about him *all the time*. "I can't believe you're asking me these things."

"This is exactly the sort of conversation a husband and wife should be able to have."

"Do *you*?" she challenged.

"Think about you? Of course. I've often recalled our lovemaking and imagined doing things with you that we didn't have time to enjoy."

He was admitting to fantasizing about her. And he wasn't flinching in the least. He was staring right into her eyes and making *her* think of things she wished they'd done.

His brow went up in a light challenge.

She swallowed, hot all over.

"I imagine you're in the shower with me. For instance," he provided in a drawl that somehow pulled all her nerve endings tight. "If you're looking for a seductive move, I guarantee you an invitation to join you will always pique my interest."

She narrowed her eyes. "I don't appreciate you making fun of me."

"I'm not joking," he assured her, but amusement lurked around his mouth.

"Fine," she said with annoyance. "Let's move this to the shower, then."

"Poppy."

His voice caught like a hook in her heart, pulling her around without even touching her before she could hurry down the hall.

She caught her breath. If he said he didn't want to, she might lose her nerve and never find it again.

"What?" she demanded when he waited until she quit spinning her gaze around the room in avoidance and made herself look at him.

"This isn't a test." His voice grew grave. Tense. "If you're not ready, say so."

"I said I want to!" She waved in the direction she'd been headed.

He came toward her, brows raised in a mild scold. "You're nervous. Maybe instead of barreling into the shower, we should slow down."

"I want the awkwardness over with," she admitted, bordering on petulant.

He gently peeled her hands off her elbows and held them in a loose grip. "But if I'd been in less of a hurry last time, I might have noticed you were new to this. *I* want to be sure you're with me every step. Why don't we start with a kiss?"

"Really?" She rolled her eyes toward the ceiling. "Fine. If that's what you want."

"Humor me." He stepped in and stole a single kiss, one of those deliberately light ones that made desire soak through her like gasoline.

She shifted lightly on her feet, instantly restless, but not in a hurry to go anywhere. "You could try that again."

He did, lingering. Taking his time finding the right fit, playing with levels of pressure.

While she shyly returned his kiss, her whole body became sensitized to everything around them. The lamplight chasing them toward the hall, the scent of faint cologne against his cheek and the slight rustle of their clothing as they stopped holding hands and reached to touch. Her hand came to rest on the fabric of his shirt, curling into a fist that crushed the fine linen while her mouth moved with tremulous passion beneath his, encouraging him.

That bashful invitation seemed to test his control. He growled and deepened the kiss. His hands found her waist and drew her fully against him.

All the memories she had convinced herself were fantasy were becoming real. He was here. She was in his arms, in his home. This was her new life. It was too much. A small cry sounded in her throat.

He lifted his head. Both of them tried to steady their breath.

She suddenly remembered him saying, *You deserve better than the lowlife who took your camera.*

She had known she did, but she hadn't believed she deserved him. Not for more than a brief hour. At the time, she had countered, *She didn't deserve you, either. I hope you find someone better.* She had wanted him to see *her* as an option. To *want* her.

Did he? She could tell he was affected by their

kiss, but he was pulling himself back under control as she watched.

This was the true source of her apprehension. That she would lose herself to his touch again and whatever grip or autonomy she had over her life would slip away. After their first time, even before she had learned she was pregnant, she had known her life would never be the same. Every other man would be compared to him and fall short.

After tonight, he would know he could do this to her. He could break down her barriers without effort, own her body and soul. Her eyes began to sting at her defenselessness.

His hands moved soothingly across her lower back. His eyes had gone more blue than gray and were shot with sparks of green, hot as the center of a flame. As he slowly drew her in again, he made a noise that was a question.

She settled gladly against him. Melted into him.

If she had had the strength of mind, of willpower, she might have balked. But she wanted this. She craved his touch like she'd been sucked into quicksand and suddenly found the vine that would pull her free.

He lowered his head and took another thorough taste of her, long and lazy and luscious. The stab of his tongue acted like alcohol, shooting pleasurable trickles of heat through her veins. She grew loose of limb and warm and weak. She moaned softly and curled her arms around his neck, encouraging him.

He settled into a passionate kiss, not aggressive, but full of confidence. Unhurried and possessive. Seductive.

She quit thinking about whether she was being reckless or not skilled enough. She let herself sink into the play of his mouth across hers and simply feel. Feel the hardness of him with her whole body as she rose on her tiptoes. Feel the silk of his hair with her fingers and the faint abrasion of chin stubble as he twisted his head and swept his tongue across hers.

She immersed herself in the feel of *him*. The sweep of his hands across her back and down to her hips, the iron thighs holding steady as she leaned into him. The erotic hardness of his erection pressing into her abdomen, telling her she was affecting him.

The knowledge he was aroused sent arrows of answering lust deep into her belly. Lower. Each bolt was tipped with flame, burning her hotter as their kisses went on until she was melting and dripping with anticipation. Making pleading noises without conscious awareness of it.

The scoop of his hands under her backside surprised her, but her legs locked around his waist as he lifted her. She found herself nose to nose with him.

"Hold on." He looked as though he commanded armies, his face a mask of sharp angles as he carried her down the hall.

She clung across his shoulders, and buried her face in the masculine scents against his neck. She nuzzled his throat and lightly bit his earlobe, smiling when she made all the muscles in his body flex in reaction.

His hands tightened against her backside and she chuckled with feminine power, thrilling, then falling—

She gasped and let go to put out her hands, but he caught her with strong arms across her back, bending with her, coming with her and covering her as she landed gently on the mattress.

Barely any light had followed them into the room. They'd forgotten the baby monitor, but Lily was across the hall. Poppy would hear her—but dearly hoped she wouldn't.

She glanced toward the en suite.

"We'll get there," he murmured of the shower, propping himself over her on one elbow. "This is nice for now." His legs were tangled with hers, his hips heavy on hers. With his free hand, he popped the first button on her top. *"Sí?"*

She smiled shyly, not sure what she was supposed to agree to. He could undress her if he wanted to, but this was the furthest thing from "nice." It was exhilarating and dangerous and consuming. It was everything she wanted.

And there was something awfully sweet about a man who wanted to seduce her when she was already there.

"You have to answer, *cariño*." His fingers came up to comb tendrils of hair away from her face.

"Sí," she whispered.

"Perfecto." He stroked the backs of two fingers down her throat and finished opening her shirt, revealing her breasts in her demicups.

She tried to open his shirt, but, like the first time, had none of his skill. His buttons were small and tight. Impossible. He brought his hand up and brushed hers away then swept his hand in a sharp yank that tore off buttons and ripped holes.

She gasped. "You didn't have to do that!"

"I did," he assured her, catching her hand and bringing it to his hot chest. "I've waited a long time for your touch."

His words sent her heart into a spin. She greedily brushed aside the gaping edges of his shirt and claimed his taut skin. The texture of his chest hair played against her palms and his breath sucked in when she skimmed the heels of her hands across the tight points of his nipples.

He said something in Spanish that she didn't have the wherewithal to translate, but his hand slid across her waist, making her realize he had finished releasing her buttons and now took his time exploring all the flesh he had bared. He made a circle against her quivering belly, stroked his thumb across the bumps of her ribcage, then traced the zigzag stitching on the bottom of her bra.

She should have bought something better. Her underclothes were boring beige, purchased from a big box store. He didn't seem to mind. He drew circles on the soft cups. There was no padding. She felt his touch almost as if she was naked. Her nipples stood up against the thin fabric, waiting for more. Begging for it.

Time stood still. His smile of pleasure was almost cruel as he teased her. She didn't realize she was furtively raking her thumbs across his nipples until his fierce gaze came up to hers and he said in a low growl, "Two can play that game, *preciosa*."

With a casual flick of the front closure, her bra released and he brushed the cup aside. His nostrils flared as he took a moment to admire her blush-pink areoles and the turgid nipples atop them. Then he dipped his head, catching her nipple in his hot, damp mouth, devouring her.

She bit back a cry and arched, barely able to withstand the burn and rush of blood that made the tips unbearably tight and sensitive before he began to pull and tease and scrape with his teeth.

She bit her lip and thrust her fingers into his hair, but he didn't let up. He continued his delicious torture until she writhed against him, hips lifting in ancient signals of willingness.

He rose to kiss her mouth, drowning her in pure sensuality before he moved to her other breast, keeping his hand on the first, circling his thumb on the wet, taut button in a way that sent currents of desire straight through her. She grew wet with yearning. She was both embarrassed and becoming desperate, alternately trying to squeeze her thighs together and open them with invitation.

His legs were pinning hers, though, keeping her beneath him in a sensual vice where she couldn't escape the pleasure he was bestowing on her. She finally clasped the sides of his head and dragged his mouth up to hers again. She pushed her tongue between his lips, flagrant and uninhibited.

Take me, she begged with her kiss.

He groaned, shifted. Got his hand between them and released her jeans. He made another sound of deep satisfaction as he pushed his hand into her open fly, covering heat and damp cotton. His touch was wickedly skilled, rocking as he eased his touch deeper into the notch of her thighs, until she was lifting into the pressure of his palm, streaks of glorious pleasure arcing through her back. Only then did he slide a finger beneath the placket to brush her skin, leave her pulsing, then returning to soothe. Incite.

"I thought it was my imagination, the way you

reacted like this," he said against her throat, deepening his caress in a way that was exquisitely satisfying, yet a profound tease.

"Rico." Growing mindless, she ran her hands over his chest and sides beneath his open shirt and across his back, arching to feel more of his naked skin with her bare breasts.

"Show me you weren't faking. Show me I can make it happen for you."

His trapped hand was making her wild. She moved with his touch, unable to resist the lure of the pleasure he offered. His mouth went back to her breasts and that was it. Seconds later she fell off the edge of the earth, but went soaring into the ether.

As cries of culmination escaped her parted lips, he lifted his head and covered her mouth, kissing her with rapacious hunger that she returned with greed.

She gave up trying to open his belt and tried to worm her hands under it.

He was speaking Spanish again, swearing maybe. His hand caught her chin and he licked into her mouth as if he couldn't get enough of her. Then he made a pained noise as he lifted enough to jerk his own belt open and release his pants.

They moved in unison, pulling away to yank and divest and kick their pants off their legs. Naked, they rolled back into one another, near frantic.

This was how it had been that other time. There was no stopping this force. It was stronger than both of them.

And knowing he was as helpless to it as she was made it okay.

As he settled himself over her, however, she felt his tension. The care he took as he settled his hips low between her thighs and braced his weight on his elbows. She could feel his exertion of will over himself and by extension, her.

His whole body shook with the effort, but there was clarity behind the passion that glazed his eyes.

"Rico." She closed her eyes against that betrayal, wanting him to fall back into the miasma with her. She slid her touch between them, seeking the shape of him. So taut and smooth, damp on the tip, tight at the base.

His breathing grew ragged, telling her she was lacerating his control.

"Poppy." His voice reverberated from somewhere in his chest, ringing inside hers. "Open your eyes."

She didn't want him to read how anguished she was. How her soul was right there, seeking his as her body yearned for the impalement of his flesh. It was too much.

"Let me see you."

She opened her eyes and time slowed.

"Take me into you," he commanded, biting at

her chin, using his powerful thighs to spread hers apart.

She guided the tip of him against her folds, parting, distantly thinking she ought to be more self-conscious, but she was only joyful. She was *aching*. She needed this slick motion of him against her sensitive button of nerves. She hummed with pleasure, growing wetter. Needier. She gloried in the pressure as he slowly forged into her, so hot as to burn her slick, welcoming flesh.

And sweet. Oh, the sweet, sweet easing of the ache as he invaded. The breadth of him was exactly as she remembered it. There was even a moment of distress when she thought he was more than her body could accept. Her fear eased within the next heartbeat as he settled and pulsed within her.

They were both quaking.

She thought he might have asked her if she was all right, but she only pulled him into a kiss. This moment was utterly perfect. She never wanted it to end.

But after a few drugging kisses, he began to move and she remembered now that pleasure was music on a scale, some notes sharper than others, but every single one a necessary part of the beautiful whole.

There was the smoothness of his skin across his shoulders, the power in them so delicious against the stroke of her palms. There was the friction of his waist against her inner thighs as her legs instinctively rose to hug him. The stretch of tendons at her inner thighs somehow added to the sweet tension that gripped her.

There was his mouth, dragging new, glorious sensations against her throat and jaw, then sucking her earlobe and making her scalp tighten before he kissed her, letting her taste the blatant sexuality in him. There was the silk of his hair grazing her cheek when he sucked a love bite against her neck. The moans they released were the chorus to their dance and the colors behind her closed eyes were matched only by the erotic sensations streaking through her whole body as he thrust and withdrew.

The sensations where they joined were particularly acute. No friction or tenderness, just shivering waves of joy that began lapping closer together, coiling tension within her until the intensity became unbearable.

"Rico." She writhed beneath him, fingernails digging into his buttocks, aching for more of him. Harder. *Deeper.*

"Only me." He held her face between his hands. Possessive, no question, but she thought she tasted wonder in the graze of his lips across hers. A strange reverence that sent quivers of joy through her whole being.

"Only you," she agreed. But she didn't think

she could stand this level of tension. Trembles of arousal shivered over her, alarming in their intensity. "It's too much."

"Bear it," he said with a savage flash of his teeth. "Feel what we do to each other."

He moved in heavier strokes, her slippery heat gripping him instinctually, making the friction all the more acute and glorious. She gasped in breathless need as the universe opened with infinite possibility. Her hips rose to meet his and his shoulders shuddered with tension as he held back. Waited for her. Waited.

His eyes were black, his cheeks flushed. They were both coated in perspiration. She wanted to tear the flesh from his bones, she was at such a screaming pitch of arousal.

Then she tightened convulsively in the first notes of release. His control cracked. He moved faster, the bed squeaking beneath them. She didn't care about anything but the purposeful thrusting that was driving her so close to the edge she was ready to scream with agony. Anticipation. Craven demand for satisfaction. Her thighs clamped around his waist and her arms clung to his shoulders. She was ready to beg.

He made a feral noise and pushed his hand under her tailbone, tilted her hips and struck a fresh spear of sensation through her, throwing her soaring off the cliff, her climax so profound she opened her mouth in a soundless scream, gripped in the paroxysm of complete ecstasy.

While his own body clenched and shuddered over her. Within her. His eruption became an intimate complement to her own, extending her pulses of pleasure so they simply held each other tight, letting the convulsions, the clenches and twitches and fading pulses of aftershock wash over them again and again.

CHAPTER SEVEN

POPPY WOKE DAZED and tender and alone. She sat up, looking for the baby monitor without finding it. It was daylight. The clock said 9:10 a.m.

She looked at the pillow, but even though both of their suitcases were still standing near the foot of the bed, his pillow was undented.

After making love, they had dozed, caught their breath, then made love again. She had a vague recollection of him leaving after that. She hadn't been able to move or even ask where he was going, but apparently he hadn't come back.

Which put a hollow ache in her chest.

Waking alone felt like a terrible start to their marriage. She had thought his passion meant he wanted her. After soaring through the heavens most of the night, she was juddering back to earth, landing hard as she realized he might want her physically, but that was all.

She put on yesterday's clothes and scowled at her pale face in the mirror. Her hair stuck out like shocks of lightning and she couldn't even get a brush through it. She wanted to check on Lily before she showered, though. She grabbed the mass together in a fat ponytail and walked out in search.

A glance into the room where Lily had slept showed the single bed had also been slept in. Her heart panged at the evidence he hadn't had insomnia. He'd preferred to sleep apart from her. Were they to have a marriage like his parents? One based on "shared values"?

They shared two things—a child and passion. It might be enough to build on, but relationships were a two-way street. If he was going to put literal walls between them, they didn't stand a chance.

Telling herself this was only Day One and she needed to give this time, she continued to the lounge.

She found Rico on the sofa, reading his tablet and nursing a coffee. Lily was on a blanket nearby, working her way through a box of unfamiliar toys. She gave a scolding cry when Poppy appeared and held up her arms, demanding a cuddle where she rested her head on Poppy's shoulder while Poppy rubbed her back. Lily was a resilient little thing, but they both needed the reassurance of a hug after facing all these recent changes.

"Why didn't you wake me when she got up?" She hid behind their daughter, mouth muffled against Lily's hair while she kept her lashes lowered, too nervous of what she might see in his eyes to meet his gaze.

"I wanted to let you sleep." His voice rasped across her nerve endings, waking her to sensual memory without any effort at all. Maybe it was the words, the suggestion that he had worn her out—which he had.

"She's had toast and banana," he added. "The housekeeper is making us a proper breakfast. It should be ready shortly."

"I could have cooked."

"We pay her to do it."

Lily pointed at the toys and Poppy set her down to continue playing.

"Thank you." Poppy hugged herself. "I'm not used to anyone getting up with her. Gran could keep an eye on her if my back was turned, but Lily was getting too heavy and fast for her to do much else."

"A potential nanny is meeting us in Valencia. You can look forward to sleeping in every day, if you want to."

"I can look after my own daughter." Especially if she wasn't working. That part was bothering her. Her income had been piecemeal with a small, but reliable paycheck from working part-time at the bus depot and occasional top-ups with school portraits and the odd headshot or boudoir shoot. Now she was reliant on Rico. It was way too much like being a burden. Again.

"There will be many occasions when you'll have to be at my side without her. You'll want the consistency of a regular caregiver."

"What do you mean, 'many'?" She finally looked at him, but he only raised his brows in mild surprise.

"Do you need a paper bag to breathe into? Why are you looking so shocked?"

"Because I thought you would go to work and maybe I'd find a job around your hours and we would eat dinner together, watch TV and go to bed like normal people."

He sipped his coffee. As he set it aside, he revealed a mouth curled into a mocking smile.

"This is my normal. Whether you work is entirely your choice. I know many power couples in which both spouses hold down high-profile positions."

Maybe not the bus depot, then.

"I also know many women, including my mother and Sorcha, who make a career of running a household, planning charity fund-raisers and attending events in support of their husbands."

"How charmingly old-fashioned." She meant antiquated and patriarchal.

The deepening of his smirk told her he knew perfectly what she was saying.

"As I say, my normal. If you do intend to work, we'll definitely need a nanny. At least that much is settled."

Poppy wanted to stamp her foot in frustration. She couldn't go after him about doing his share on the childcare front, though. Not when he'd gotten up with Lily on his first morning with her, letting Poppy sleep in.

"I've booked a stylist to come by in an hour or so." His gaze went to her bare, unpolished toes and came back to her electrocuted hair.

Her hand went to the seam in her distressed jeans. "Why?"

"I'm introducing you and Lily to my parents this evening."

"I've met them," she reminded with an urge to laugh, because it was such a gross overstatement. She had stood behind Darna on three occasions without garnering even a glance as Darna had nodded understanding of the duquesa's orders. Rico's father had once held out a dirty glass as she walked by, not even looking at her, let alone thanking her for taking it.

"The press release will go out while we're there. I expect a few photographers will gather at the gate. You need to look the part."

"Paparazzi are going to want photos of *me*? Really?" She crossed one foot over the other and hugged herself. "How are your parents going to react to that?"

"By presenting a united front. That's why we're having dinner there."

"*Presenting* a united front," she repeated. "That tells me how sincerely they'll welcome me at their dining table, doesn't it? And then what?" She thought of all the gossip sites where she'd seen pictures of him with Faustina, then snapshots of his grim expression as he put her in the ground. "Rico, I can't do this," she realized with sudden panic. "I'm not prepared. You know I'm not."

"That's why I've called a stylist. You'll be fine."

To her horror, tears of frustration and yes, fear, pressed into her eyes, but the housekeeper came in and invited them to sit down to the breakfast she had prepared.

Poppy had to suck up her misgivings and let her new life unfold.

"You look beautiful," Rico said sincerely. "If you could drop the wide-eyed terror, you'd be flawless."

His attempt to lighten Poppy's mood fell flat.

Her stylist had understood perfectly the effect Rico wanted and had spent a good portion of the day achieving it.

Poppy wore a bronze slip with a lace overlay embroidered with copper roses. It was simple and

feminine, sophisticated yet held a decidedly innocent flair. Her hair had been meticulously coaxed
into tamer waves then gathered into a "casual"
chignon suitable for a low-key dinner with family.
Her makeup was all natural tones and her heels
were a conservative height.

By the time he'd offered the jewelry he'd bought
her, she'd looked like a dog that had been at the
groomers so long she'd lost her will to live.

Now the fresh-faced nanny, who couldn't be
more than a year over Poppy's age, suggested carrying Lily into the villa so their daughter wouldn't
stain or snag Poppy's dress.

Rico agreed and Poppy shot him a glance of betrayal then fell into step beside him, mouth pouted.

Her angry dismay plucked at his conscience like
a sour note on a string. He kept telling himself that
she had already seen the workings of his family
from an insider's perspective. None of this should
be a surprise to her. And this was how it *was*. He
couldn't pretend their life would be anything different. That would be a lie.

Even so, he sensed she'd put up a wall between
them and it rankled. Which was hypocritical on
his part because he'd taken steps to withdraw from
her last night, after their lovemaking had left him
in ruins.

What should have been a sensual celebration of
a convenient marriage had become a conflagration

that had turned him inside out. He had been right back to that interminable family dinner after his encounter with Poppy two years ago. Cesar and Sorcha had turned up—an engagement Rico had completely failed to recall had been scheduled. They'd eaten in polite silence while his mother had stiffly come to terms with Rico's wedding being off. She had already been floating the names of alternatives and a timeline for courtship.

Rico had sat on the pin of a land mine, wanting to rise from the table and go after Poppy. He hadn't seen a way in which he could even sustain an affair with her, though. As he'd eaten what might have been sawdust, facts had been reiterated about his father's prospects in the next election. The importance of certain alliances had been regurgitated.

Rico wasn't so shallow as to value money and appearances and power over all other things, but he understood how possessing those things allowed him and his family to live as comfortably as they did. All the actions he took were about them, never only himself.

So, even though his engagement had been broken, even though he was sexually infatuated with his mother's maid, another bride would be slotted into place very quickly. The show must go on.

There had been some relief in living up to those expectations, too. As earth-shattering as his encounter with Poppy had been, he had instinctively recognized how dangerous that sort of passion was. How easily exposure to a woman who provoked such a deep response within him could dismantle him. Turn him against the best interests of his family and even impact him at a deeper level. A place even more vulnerable than the injuries of bruised ego and broken trust that his first wife had inflicted on him.

That premonition was playing out. His daughter had been the excuse, but the lure of Poppy had drawn him halfway around the world. He hadn't waited for tests to prove they should marry. He had accomplished it with haste and dragged her back here as quickly as he could.

Last night had proved to him they were still a volatile combination. Afterward, he'd felt so disarmed, so *satisfied* with having blown up his own life, he had had to leave her to put himself back together.

If Lily hadn't awakened a few hours later, he might very well have succumbed to temptation and crawled into bed with Poppy again.

He couldn't let her have that kind of power over him. That was what he kept telling himself. He had to keep control of himself or there would only be more scandal and disruption.

But he loathed that stiff look on her face.

It was too much like the ones on his parents' faces as they entered the small parlor where Faustina had once thrown down a vase like a gauntlet.

He ground his teeth, wishing at least Pia was here, chronically shy and uncomfortable as she might be. His sister was off studying snails or some other mollusk in the Galápagos Islands, however. Cesar had taken Sorcha and the boys to visit Sorcha's family in Ireland. There was nothing to soften this hard, flat evening for Poppy.

"My father, Javiero Montero y Salazar, Excelentísimo Senor Grandeza de España, and my mother, La Reina, the Duque and Duquesa of Castellón. You both remember Poppy." He wasn't trying to be facetious, but it came out that way.

His mother smiled faintly. "Welcome back."

Poppy was so pale he reached for her hand. It was ice-cold.

She delicately removed it from his hold and gave Lily's dress a small tug and drew the girl's finger from her mouth, smiling with tender pride. "This is Lily."

His parents both took a brief look at their granddaughter and nodded as if to say, *Yes, that is a baby*.

"A room has been prepared upstairs," Rico's mother said to the nanny, dismissing her and Lily in a blink.

The light in Poppy's eyes dimmed. It struck Rico like a kick in the gut.

This is who they *are*, he wanted to tell her. There was no use wishing for anything different, but he could still hear the thread of hurt and rejection in her tone as she had told him about her parents never coming back for her.

He wanted to take her hand again, reassure her, but at his mother's invitation, she lowered to perch on an antique wing chair, hands folded demurely in her lap.

Champagne was brought in; congratulations were offered. Poppy's hand shook and he neatly slid a coaster under her glass before she set it on the end table.

His mother very tellingly said, "I imagine you're still settling in. We'll move into the dining room right away so the baby can have an early night."

This evening would *not* be a drawn-out affair. The rush was a slight, but Rico didn't want to subject Poppy to their company any longer than necessary so he didn't take issue with it.

The first course arrived and Poppy tried offering a friendly smile at the butler. It was countered with an impassive look that made her cheerful expression fall away. She blinked a few times.

The staff would talk to her when his parents weren't around, he wanted to tell her. This was how they were expected to act with guests and she shouldn't take it as a rejection.

His father cleared his throat.

Poppy glanced at him with apprehension. Rico briefly held his own breath, but his father only asked Rico about the progress he'd made on some alloy research.

Annoyed, Rico was forced to turn his attention to answering him, which left his mother to make conversation with Poppy.

"I'm told you enjoy photography, Poppy. How did your interest come about?"

Poppy shot him a look, but he hadn't provided that tidbit. This was also who his mother was. She would ferret out any item suitable for small talk that would avoid addressing more sensitive horrors like the fact Rico had messed with the maid, had an illegitimate child and brought them into the villa as "family."

Poppy spoke with nervous brevity. "When I was ten, my grandfather asked me to help him clean the basement. We came across his father's equipment. My great-grandfather was a freelance photographer for newspapers."

"What type of newspapers?" his mother asked sharply.

"Mother." Rico quit listening to his father and gave the women his full attention.

"The national ones," Poppy replied warily, sensing disapproval. "Sports, mostly. The odd royal visit or other big event. I was intrigued so my grandfather closed in a space and showed me how the development process worked."

"You should have shown me." Rico was ridiculously pleased to hear she shared the same spark of curiosity that had drawn him into chemical engineering.

"I haven't used it in years. We quickly realized the cost of chemicals and paper wasn't sustainable. I switched to digital photography."

"Metol or hydroquinone," Rico's father said in one of his stark interjections, as though he'd retrieved a file from the dusty basement of his own mind. "Sodium carbonate and sodium sulfite for proper pH and delay of oxidation. Thiosulfate to fix it. None are particularly expensive, but there's no market for the premixed solutions. We got out of it years ago."

"Only niche artists are using them, I imagine," Poppy murmured.

"Speaking of art," his mother said with an adept pivot from boring science. "I'm attending an opening in Paris next month. I imagine you'll be decorating a house very soon. What sort of pieces might you be looking for?"

Poppy looked as though a bus was bearing down on her.

"It's early days, Mother," Rico cut in. "We'll talk more about that another time."

At this point he was only looking as far as getting through this evening.

The meal passed in a blur of racking her brains for the names of Canadian politicians who might have said something brilliant or stupid lately and trying to look as if she knew how to eat quail in gazpacho. Poppy was infinitely relieved when they left and went to Rico's Valencian penthouse.

This wasn't a family property. It was his own home, purchased after Faustina had died. It was luxurious and in a prime location with a pool and a view, but it was a surprisingly generic space, tastefully decorated in masculine tones yet completely without any stamp of his personality.

She dismissed the nanny, put Lily to bed herself, then moved into the bedroom to kick off her heels and sigh with exhaustion.

Rico came in with a nightcap for each of them.

She immediately grew nervous. It had been a long, trying day, one that had started out with a rebuff when she'd woken alone. That sense of foreboding had grown worse as his stylist had spent hours turning her into some kind of show pony.

She suspected she had disappointed anyway. As he set down his own drink and loosened his tie, she had a sick, about-to-be-fired feeling in her stomach, much like the one she'd had when she'd lost her first babysitting job after accidentally letting the hamster out of its cage.

"Well?" she prompted, trying to face the coming judgment head-on.

"I thought it went well."

She strangled on a laugh. "Are you kidding?

I've never spent a more horrendous two hours and twenty-three minutes in my life."

"You were there, then." He shrugged out of his jacket.

"Don't make jokes, Rico." She stared at him, but he wasn't laughing. Uncertain, she asked, "Was that really a normal dinner for you? The way it's been your whole life?" She had thought her own mother awful for calling in lame efforts at nurturing with insincere apologies from afar. His parents had displayed zero remorse as they had openly dismissed his newfound daughter.

"Don't be ridiculous," he said with scathing sarcasm. "I didn't sit at that table until I was twelve. Children are invited to the dining room when they know how to eat quietly and speak only when spoken to."

She thought of the way Lily squealed and slapped her tray and wore more food than she ate. But even Gran with her old-fashioned ideals about child-rearing had always insisted that dinner was a time for the whole family to come together.

"Why are they *like* that?"

He stripped his tie and threw it away with a sigh. "My father is a scientific genius. He only speaks logic and rational debate. Emotion has no effect on him. It's one of the reasons he makes a genuinely good politician. He reads and considers policy on its own merit, not worrying about his popularity or future prospects. Mother was born with a title, but no money. She had to marry it and prove she was worth the investment. Having brought herself up this far, she refuses to backslide. And, after thirty-five years of my father's lack of sentiment, she's abandoned any herself."

"That sounds so empty. Is she happy?"

"They set out with specific goals and achieved them. They are content, which is the standard to which we've been taught to aspire."

She searched his expression. "And you're *content* with that?"

"Why wouldn't I be? My life is extremely comfortable." He peeled off his shirt, revealing his gorgeous chest and tight abs.

She swallowed and turned away, annoyed with herself for reacting so promptly to the sight of him.

"Is that why you agreed to an arranged marriage the first time? To maintain the status quo?"

"Yes. I was expected to do my part in preserving the life we all enjoy." His voice was suddenly right behind her, surprising her into lifting her gaze to the mirror.

He lightly smoothed his hand across her shoulders, grazing an absent caress against her nape as he ensured no tendrils of hair would catch as he unzipped her.

"How angry are they that Lily and I ruined everything?" She braced herself as she held his gaze. "Be honest. I need to know."

"They don't get angry." He sounded mild, but she thought she caught a flicker of something in his stoic expression.

"What about you? You were angry when you showed up at my door."

"And I wound up telling you something I had sworn to take to my grave. Heightened emotions don't help any situation."

"What does that mean?" With a niggling premonition, she began unpinning her hair, not wanting to remove the gaping dress and be naked when she was beginning to feel defenseless. "I want to fit in, Rico. I want to be a team player and know what to say about decor and houses and all those different people she was talking about. But along with not being prepared to live at this level of wealth, I'm wired for emotion. Don't expect me never to get angry. Or to stop feeling."

His cheek ticked and she could hear the thoughts behind that stiff mask. *Don't expect me to start.*

Which made her angry. Furious that she'd spent every minute since he'd shown up on her doorstep having her emotions bombarded until they were right there, under the thin surface of her skin, tender and raw, while he had somehow used tonight's endurance event of a dinner to shore up his shields so he was more withdrawn than ever.

"That's what you want, though, isn't it?" she realized, appalled to see her shimmering nascent hopes for deeper intimacy disappearing faster than she could conjure them. "You want me to learn not to care. To feel nothing. Certainly I shouldn't aspire to happiness, should I?"

"Happiness is achieved by keeping your expectations realistic. That's a proven fact."

It was such a cynical thing to say, it physically hurt her to hear it.

"What about desire?" In a small stab at getting through to him, she let the dress fall off her arms. She stepped out of it before tossing it onto the foot of the bed. "Do you want me to quit feeling *that*?"

"That's physical." He let his gaze rake slowly down her pale form from shoulder to thighs, jaw hardening along with his voice. "And you're starting a fight for no reason."

"I'm sorry you feel that way," she said facetiously. "I'm going to shower. Would you like to join me? Yesterday it was one of your many fantasies, but maybe you *feel* different today."

His eye ticked and she knew he was sorry he had ever told her that. Did she feel guilty for using it? Not one bit.

She slid her panties down and left them on the floor.

It was a bold move, one far beyond her experience level. If he left her to shower alone, she would probably drown herself in there, but she desperately wanted to prove to both of them that she had some kind of effect on him. Some means of reaching through that armor of his.

She moved into the bathroom and stepped into the marble-tiled stall, bigger than the porch on Gran's bungalow.

He came into the bathroom as the steam began to gather around her. He dimmed the light so the gilded space became golden and moody and he stripped off his pants.

She watched him, reacting with an internal clench when she saw he was aroused.

When he came into the shower, she lost some of her moxie and turned her face into the rain of warm water from the sunflower head above her.

His cool hands settled on her hips and his thumbs dug lightly into the tops of her butt cheeks. "You have a gorgeous ass."

"Even with the dimples?" Her heartbeat was unsteady.

"Especially with." He took hold of the wet mass of her hair, holding her head tipped back while he scraped his teeth against the side of her neck. "I will always accept this invitation, Poppy. But you had better know what you're inviting."

She gasped. The sensations he was causing were cataclysmic. All her senses came alive. He settled his cool body against her back, his chest hair lightly brushing before the warm water sealed them together. His hard shaft pressed into the small of her back and her buttocks tightened in excited reaction. Her breasts grew heavy, her loins tingled. The humid air became too heavy to breathe and her bones melted like wax in the sun.

Blindly she shot a hand out to the slick wall and wound up leaning both hands there while her hips instinctively tipped with invitation.

"What are you trying to prove?" he growled, slapping one hand beside her own on the wall.

Nothing. She was reacting, pure and simple.

He briefly covered her like any male mounting his mate and his teeth sank lightly against her nape again. His free hand splayed across her abdomen, then roamed her wet skin to cup her breast.

In a sudden move, he pulled her upright and spun her so the world tilted around her. She found the hard tiles against her shoulders. His knees nudged between hers and his thighs pinned hers. He bracketed her head between his forearms and touched his nose to hers before he claimed the kiss she was starving for.

He held nothing back, wet mouth sliding across hers with carnal greed, slaking her thirst after this arid day. She flowered. She opened and ran with dewy nectar. She unfurled her arms around him and twined them across his back, lifted her knee up to his hip and invited him into her center.

Rocked and tried to make him lose control the way she continued to abandon hers.

"Let's talk about your fantasies, hmm?" His hands caught her wrists and pinned them beside her head while his tongue slithered down her neck and licked into the hollow at the base of her throat. "What do you want?"

He drew back slightly and gazed down on her with unabashed hunger.

"Rico." She turned her wrist in his grasp and shifted with self-consciousness. Her nipples stood up with blatant, stinging arousal. She brought her foot back down to the floor, but his feet were still between hers.

"Did you ever touch yourself and imagine it was me?" He dropped one hand and drew his fingertip through her swollen folds, looking down again as he languidly caressed her. "Did you want to *feel* my hand here?"

She was immediately disoriented, glad for the hard wall at her back as she rose into his touch and draped her arm across his shoulders, seeking balance.

"Tell me," he commanded between kisses. "Tell me or I'll stop."

"Yes," she gasped.

He rewarded her by bending to suck one nipple, then the other, driving further spikes of pleasure into that place he continued to tease. A keening noise sounded and she realized it was her, unable to express her agonizing climb of desire in any other way.

Now he was on his knees, licking at her. Splaying her and gently probing and circling and driving her to the brink of madness. She realized distantly that she had her hands fisted in his wet hair, that she had completely abandoned herself to him. To the exquisite pleasure he relentlessly inflicted upon her. Within moments, cries of ecstasy tore from her throat, filling the steamy, hollow chamber.

He ran his mouth all over her thighs and stomach, soft bites that claimed his right to do so as she stood there weakly, heart palpitating, breath still splintered.

He stood and snapped the water off, staring at her while she leaned helpless and overwhelmed. Outdone.

Meeting his gaze was like looking into the sun, painful in its intensity. Painful in how blind and exposed she felt, but she couldn't look away. Couldn't pretend he hadn't peeled her down to her core until she was utterly at his mercy.

While he remained visibly aroused, but in complete control.

"The way we make each other feel is a hell of a lot more than many couples have. Recognize that. Be satisfied with it."

She wasn't and never would be.

But when he held out a hand, she let him balance her as she stepped out onto the mat. He dried her off and took her to his bed, where he satisfied her again and again and again.

CHAPTER EIGHT

RICO WOKE IN the guest bed he'd been using all week and listened, thinking Lily must be stirring. He ought to be sleeping more heavily considering the quantity and quality of sex he was enjoying, but his radar remained alert to the other occupants of his penthouse.

He listened, thought he must be imagining things, started to drift off then heard the burble of a video chat being connected. The volume lowered.

He rose, already wearing boxers in case he had to go to Lily. His door was cracked and it swung open silently, allowing him to hear Poppy's hushed voice reassuring her grandmother.

"No, everything's fine. I couldn't sleep and thought this would be a good chance to chat without a baby crawling all over me. How are you settling in?"

"Same as I told you yesterday," her grandmother said wryly. "You're the one with the gadabout life. What have you been up to?"

He stood and listened to Poppy relay that the nanny had taken Lily for a walk today while she had pored over properties with a real estate agent. He'd been going in to work each day, but taking her out at night. She mentioned this evening's cocktail party where he had introduced her to some of his top executives and their wives.

She made it sound as though she had had the time of her life when she'd actually been petrified and miserable, not that she'd been obvious about it. He knew how she behaved when she was comfortable, though. She laughed with Lily and traded wry remarks with her grandmother.

That woman was making fewer and fewer appearances when she was with him, however, which was beginning to niggle at him. He glimpsed her when they made love. She held nothing back in bed, but tonight she had disappeared quickly after they had wrung untold pleasure from each other. She had rolled away and her voice had pulled him from his postcoital doze.

"Will you check on Lily as you go?"

"Of course." He had told himself he was glad she'd kept him from falling asleep beside her. His will to leave her each night grew fainter and fainter, but staying seemed the even weaker action. He wasn't Lily, needing his cuddle bear clutched in his arm in order to drift off.

He wasn't sure what he had expected from this

marriage. When contemplating his first to Faustina, he had anticipated following his parents' example. Like his siblings, he had been raised to keep his emotions firmly within a four-point-five and a four-point-seven. Not a sociopath, but only a few scant notches above one. He had never been a man of grand passions anyway and had been comfortable with the idea of a businesslike partnership with his spouse.

That certainly hadn't worked out. Given the betrayal and drama he'd suffered at Faustina's hands, he had wanted this marriage to conform to that original ideal.

It didn't. Poppy didn't. He kept telling himself she would get used to this life, but seeing her natural exuberance dim by the day was eating at him. He didn't know what to do about it, though. This was their reality.

"Dinner will be served soon. I have to start making my way or it will be cold by the time I arrive," Eleanor said with a papery chuckle.

"Okay. I love you. I miss you." She ended the call, but didn't rise.

He was growing cold standing there, but didn't go back to bed. He could see her shoulders over the back of the sofa. They rose slightly as she sighed deeply. Her breath caught with a jag. She sniffed.

A terrible swoop of alarm unbalanced him. The

embarrassed moment of walking in on something personal struck, yet he couldn't turn away and leave her to it.

As her shoulders began to shake and she ducked her head into her hands, beginning to weep in earnest, a rush of something indefinable came over him. A sharp, shimmering, deeply uncomfortable *ache* gripped him. It was so excruciating, it made him want to close himself in the guest room and wait for it to pass.

But he couldn't turn his back on her while she was like that. A far stronger compulsion pushed him down the hall toward her.

"Poppy." Her name scratched behind his breastbone. At some level he understood he was responsible for this misery she was exhibiting. He had some scattered thoughts of all that he was providing her, but he knew she didn't care about those things. She was a complex, emotional creature and it struck him how completely ill-equipped he was to handle that.

She lifted a face tracked with silver and made an anguished noise, clearly mortified that he was seeing her this way. Again he thought to give her privacy, but he couldn't let her suffer alone. This was his fault. That much he understood and it weighed very heavily on him.

"Come." He gathered her up, the silk of her pajamas cool against his naked chest.

"I don't want to make love, Rico. I want to go *h-home*." The break in her voice rent another hole in him.

"Shh." He carried her to the bed where he'd left her a few hours before and crawled in with her to warm both of them. He told himself that was what this was, even though the feel of her against him had the effect of pressing a cut together. It didn't fix it, but it eased some of the pain. Slowed the bleeding and calmed the distress. "It's okay," he murmured.

"No, it's not." Her words were angry, despairing sobs. "I'm so homesick I hurt all the time. At least the last time I was stuck here, I made friends, but no one will talk to me."

"Who's refusing to speak to you?" he asked with sharp concern.

"*Everyone*. The staff. They only ask me if I want something, never joke or make me feel like they like me. They're only being polite because you pay them to be."

"That's not true." He suddenly glimpsed how isolated she must be in her new position and cursed himself for not recognizing it would be so acute.

"I have nothing in common with *your* friends. They talk too fast for me to even understand them. You're Lily's father and I want her to know you, Rico. I know I have to stay here for her sake, but why does the nanny get to take her for a walk while I have to go to stupid parties? I hate it here. I hate it so much."

"Shh," he soothed, closing his hand around the tight fist on his chest and kissing her hard knuckles. "This is going to be an adjustment for all of us."

"How is this an adjustment for *you*? You're completely unaffected! I can't do this, Rico. I *can't*."

His neck was wet and her hair stuck to the tear tracks, keeping that fissure in him stinging. He rubbed her back, trying to calm her while her desolation shredded his ability to remain detached.

There are some realities that are not worth crying about, he had told Mateo a few weeks ago. He'd been taught to believe no one would care, but he *did* care. Not the generic regard of one human for another, but a deeper, more frightening feeling he didn't know how to process.

Everything in him warned that he should distance himself, but he couldn't ignore her pain.

He knew what he had to do. It would cost him, but he would do it. This anguish of hers was more than he could bear.

Poppy woke from the dense fog of a deep sleep to hear Rico's morning voice rasping on the baby monitor.

"We'll let Mama sleep this morning."

The transmission clicked off, but as Poppy

rolled onto her back and straightened her limbs, she discovered the warm patch beside her on the bed.

He had stayed the night? She was chagrined that he'd caught her in the middle of a pity party, but she hadn't been able to hold it in any longer. She had tried, honestly tried not to care about all of those things.

She did care, though. She was lonely and out of her depth. Her only friend was the daughter she had to share with a nanny who adored her, but whom Poppy was growing to resent by the day.

She threw her arm over her eyes, trying not to spiral back into melancholy. They had appointments to view properties today, she recalled. She could hardly wait to have a bigger house to get lost in, and more staff to treat her like some kind of visiting foreign official.

A few hours later, she was beside Rico as he drove a shiny new SUV up the coast. Poppy had understood the property agent would be driving them to view potential homes, but she didn't complain. It felt nice to be just the three of them for a change.

"You should have told me to bring my camera," she murmured, quite sure she would have a kink in her neck from swiveling her attention between the sunny coastal beaches and the craggy hillocks interspersed with picturesque ancient villages. "I'm used to staring at wheat and sunflower fields on long drives."

"Think about what sort of space you want for your studio as we look at potential homes. I'm sure a darkroom could be built into just about any corner of a house, but give some thought to how that will fit with our day-to-day living."

"A darkroom! I told you, that's expensive." She wouldn't mind a studio, though.

"As it turns out, I happen to have money. If that's where your interest lies, pursue it." He turned into a private road that lacked a for sale sign and wound through a vineyard.

"There's no money in photography." Not the sort his level of society expected a woman to make if she was going to pursue a career over home-making.

"I don't expect you to make money. Do it for yourself. Be an artist."

"You're going to be my patron? Don't pander to me just because I acted like Lily last night." She spoke to the window to hide her embarrassment.

"I'm not. I want you to be happy."

That swung her around because no, he didn't. He had specifically told her to settle.

He might have recalled that conversation, too. His expression grew stiff as he braked and threw the vehicle into Park.

Poppy glanced around. "I don't see the agent."

"It's not for sale. This is Cesar and Sorcha's home."

"Why didn't you tell me we were meeting them today?" She glanced down at the pantsuit she'd put on hoping to look the part of a rich man's wife viewing villas as if she knew what such a man needed.

"You look perfect." He stepped out. "They don't know we're coming so they'll be equally casual."

"Why don't they know we're coming?" she asked as he came around while she was opening the back door to get Lily.

"You're supposed to wait for me to come around and open your door for you," he chided.

"I know how to open my own car door. I also know how to look after my own daughter." She brushed him away from trying to reach in, then grunted as she released Lily and took her weight, dragging her out. "What I don't know is how I'm supposed to behave when you drop me on relatives who don't know I'm coming."

Lily squinted as Poppy drew her from the car and buried her face in Poppy's neck.

"I'll keep her," Poppy murmured as Rico tried to take her. It was pathetic to hide behind her daughter, but she needed Lily's sturdy warmth to bolster her.

A maid let them in and the view took her breath as they moved from the foyer to a front room where huge picture windows overlooked the Mediterranean.

"Tío!" A young boy of about four ran in wearing red trunks and nothing else.

Rico picked him up. "You remember Enrique? Cesar's eldest?" he asked Poppy.

"You've grown," she murmured. *"Bon dia,"* she added in the small amount of Valencian dialect she knew the family used among themselves.

"Say hello to Poppy and Lily," Rico prompted him.

"Hola. ¿Cómo estás?" Enrique asked with a confidence beyond his years.

Rico gave Enrique's backside a pat. "You're wet. How are you swimming? It's too early in the year."

"I got in to here." Enrique touched his belly button.

"And now you're eating your lunch," Cesar said, strolling in wearing crisp linen pants and a shirt he was buttoning. He nodded to send Enrique back outside.

This was the most relaxed Poppy had ever seen Cesar, but he still projected a chilly formality not unlike the duque and duquesa. In fact, he greeted his brother with a look that bordered on hostile.

"You've lost your drop-in privileges with my family." It was a very civil, *Get the hell out.*

Because of her and Lily? Because they were a stain on the family name?

With a muted noise of distress, Poppy closed her arms protectively around Lily and looked to the door.

Rico glanced at her with concern then scowled at his brother. "Now you've gone and hurt *my* wife's feelings."

Cesar frowned at her. His gaze dropped to Lily and his frown eased.

"Whose feelings?" Sorcha came up behind her husband. She was blond and effortlessly beautiful in a summer dress with a forget-me-not print. Daywear diamonds sparkled in her ears.

"Poppy." Her surprise warmed into a welcoming smile that sent the first trickles of relief through Poppy's defensively stiff limbs. "And here's Lily." Sorcha came right up to them and gave Lily's elbow a tickle. She tilted her head to meet the gaze Lily shyly kept tucked into Poppy's neck.

"Will you come see me? Let me introduce you to your cousins?" Sorcha held out her hands. "They'll share their lunch with you. Are you hungry?"

Lily went to her. Who could resist the promise of food and the warm lilt of an Irish accent?

"Thank you, darling. That's quite a compliment." Sorcha cuddled her close, then glanced at Rico. Her tone dropped to permafrost. "*You* can wait in the car."

"I deserve that," Rico said with tense sincerity. "I regret the hurt I caused you. I wouldn't interrupt your weekend, but Poppy needs you, Sorcha. Will you help her? If not for me, then for her sake and Lily's? Please? I know how you feel about family."

"That's below the belt!" Sorcha tucked her chin, looked as though she wanted to punish him further, then gave a little sigh. "Since you've brought me this *very* precious gift—" She snuggled Lily more securely onto her hip. "I will forgive you. *This one time*." She smiled at Poppy without reserve. "And of course I'll help you any way I can. I would have called you later this week." Another dark look toward Rico. "I didn't want to wait until our gala next month. I'm so glad you're here. Come join us."

"What did you do?" Poppy hissed at Rico as he fell into step beside her.

"Said something that doesn't bear repeating." To her surprise, he took her hand and wove their fingers together, giving her a little squeeze. "But Sorcha knows what you're up against. Let her be your guide."

It struck her that this had been hard for him. She doubted it was in his nature to ask for help any more than it was in hers. He and Cesar were obviously on rocky ground, but he had invaded their family time for her sake.

"Please tell Chef we're four adults and three children for lunch now," Sorcha said easily to the hovering butler.

"Champagne," Cesar added, holding Sorcha's

chair as she lowered with Lily and kept her in her lap. "Boys, this is your cousin, Lily. Can you say hello and welcome her and Auntie Poppy to the family?"

Enrique began to giggle. He pointed his fork at Cesar. "That's Papi."

Poppy smiled. "Maybe you'll have to call this one Tío Mama now." She thumbed toward Rico as he helped her with her own chair.

Enrique nearly tumbled out of his, laughing at the absurdity as he repeated, "Tío Mama."

Poppy bit her lip with remorse, suspecting she'd released a genie that wouldn't go easily back into its bottle. She called on one of Gramps's favorite tricks for getting through to a child who had a case of the sillies. She leaned over and spoke very softly so Enrique would have to quiet to hear her.

"My grandfather used to tell me it was okay to tease your family with a funny name when you were alone, but you have to remember to be respectful when you're with others. Will you be able to do that?"

Enrique nodded and clamped his smile over his fork, eyes full of mischief as he looked at Rico.

"Sorry," Poppy mouthed as she caught Sorcha's amused glance. "You have a very beautiful home," she added, glancing at the placid pool and the profusion of spring blooms surrounding it.

"Thank you. We're extremely happy here." Sorcha looked to her husband for confirmation, but her smile reflected more than happiness. Even two years ago it had been obvious to Poppy these two were deeply in love.

While Rico wore his customarily circumspect expression.

"I want one of those," Cesar informed Sorcha with smoky warning, nodding at Lily where she sat contentedly in Sorcha's lap, fist clenched around a spear of juicy peach.

"Let's keep this one." Sorcha pressed her smile to the top of Lily's head. "She's exactly what we've been thinking of."

"We should probably try making our own before we resort to stealing."

"Picky, picky. But if you insist, I'll have my people talk to your people. Schedule a one-on-one for further discussion."

"Really?" Rico drawled of the flirty banter. "In front of the children?"

"They've walked in on worse," Cesar muttered, rising as the butler arrived with the champagne. "Learn to lock doors," he advised while Sorcha looked to the sky.

The lunch passed with easy chatter and the wiping of sticky fingers.

"I'm so glad Rico brought you today," Sorcha said later, after a travel cot had been found for Lily and she'd been put down for her afternoon nap while the men took the boys into the vineyard. Sorcha sobered. "I'm very glad he went looking for you. Are you angry with me?"

"For telling him? No." Poppy crossed her arms. "I'd been thinking about doing it. Things were complicated at home so I put it off, but it's all worked out." For Gran and Lily. Her? Not so much.

"I'm sorry for interfering. I know how hard that decision can be, but I couldn't let him miss out on Lily. He shut right down after Faustina. My heart broke clean in half for him. I'm so happy to see the way he's taken to her."

Poppy nodded dumbly, shielding her gaze with a glance toward the floor so Sorcha couldn't read the bigger story in her eyes.

"He wants to be a good father. I was afraid of… Well, nothing, I guess," Poppy admitted ruefully. When it came to Rico's feelings for Lily, she had every confidence their bond would only continue to grow.

"But?" Sorcha prompted.

"It's hard." Her throat thickened and she felt tears pressing behind her eyes. "This is all really hard. Rico and I don't have what you and Cesar did. The years of familiarity and caring."

Sorcha choked on a laugh. "Do I make it look like it was easy for us to get where we are? That is quite a compliment and good on me for selling that image, but no. I assure you that what we have was achieved through blood, sweat and tears. Years of loving my boss, if you want the truth. Which is how and why Enrique came about," she added dryly. "But like the rest of his family, Cesar had kicked his heart under the sofa and forgotten about it. So there will definitely be some heavy lifting required to find Rico's. I'm sorry to tell you that." Sorcha sobered. "But I think it's understandable, given what he's been through."

Sorcha thought she knew what Rico had been through, but he wasn't nursing a broken heart over a lost baby. That was what made this so hard. This wasn't a matter of mending his heart. Or finding it. It was a matter of him wanting to give it to her. And he didn't.

But she only nodded again, protecting the secret Rico had entrusted to her.

"It will all be worth it, Poppy. I promise you," Sorcha said with a squeeze of her arm. "In the meantime, you have me. I'm happy to help you navigate this new world. When I was in your position, I needed help, too. One of these days we'll go shopping with my friend Octavia. She really does know how to make all of this look easy. For now, let's go to my closet. I'll show you what is absolutely essential. Try not to faint."

Poppy could feel Rico's heart slowing to lazy slams beneath her breast. Her sweating body was splayed bonelessly across him. She knew she ought to move, but he stroked his hand down her spine and traced a circle on her lower back, making her shiver. She clenched around him in a final aftershock of ecstasy.

He turned his head, brushing his lips against her temple in what she took as a signal to move. As she started to pry herself off him, however, his arms closed more firmly around her.

"You can stay right here all night," he murmured lazily.

"Don't you want to go to the guest room?"

His arms dropped way from her. She rolled off him.

"Do you want me to?" All the indolent warmth disappeared from his tone.

"No." Her voice was barely audible. "But why are you staying? Because you feel sorry for me?"

"No. Why would you think that?"

"You slept with me last night because I was crying."

"I came to bed with you because you were crying. I stayed because I wanted to."

"You didn't want to those other nights?"

A sigh.

"Rico, I keep telling you I've never done this before. This might be how you normally conduct a sexual relationship, but it's not the way I thought marriage was supposed to be."

He bit off a laugh. "This isn't normal. That is the problem, Poppy." He sighed and repeated more somberly, "That is the problem."

Even she, with her limited experience, understood that their passion was exceptional. She had climaxed three times before he'd clasped hard hands to her hips and bucked beneath her, releasing with a jagged cry. She imagined she would have fingerprint bruises under her skin and perversely enjoyed having such an erotic reminder linger for days.

Sex was the easy part. Talking to him, catching him alone and digging up the courage to speak her mind and face difficult answers was the hard part. But she made herself do it.

"Is that why you haven't wanted to sleep with me? Too much sex? Am I being too demanding?"

He blew out a breath that was amused yet exasperated. "No. Although I fear for our lives on a nightly basis."

"Please don't make jokes, Rico. I need to understand. You're the one who said I should keep my expectations realistic. Tell me what realistic looks like because I don't *know*."

"I don't know, either," he admitted after a moment. "That's why I'm not processing this any better than you are. I thought our first time was an anomaly. It wasn't. It's shocking to me how powerfully we affect each other. It doesn't matter that you just spent an hour wringing me out. I want you again. *This isn't normal.*"

"I don't like it, either! I hate that you can snap your fingers and I fall onto my back."

He threw his arm over his eyes and released a ragged, self-deprecating laugh. "I'm the one who was on his back tonight, *corazón*. In case you hadn't noticed."

"It's not very comforting to hear that when you're clearly annoyed by it. Why does it bother you so much that we react this strongly?"

Another silence where she thought he might ignore her question. Finally he admitted, "Passion is dangerous. You know that Cesar was in a car crash some years ago?"

"I only know what's online about it."

"Mmm. Well, it happened after he slept with Sorcha. Directly after. I'd always been aware he had a physical infatuation with her. He didn't give in to base urges any more than I ever thought I would, but that day he did. And he decided the passion they shared was worth blowing up his life for. Mother was pushing him toward an arranged marriage. He went to Diega and told her he wouldn't be asking her to marry him. We don't know if he was overwrought or what, but he skidded off the road after he left her and nearly died."

Part of her panged with empathy. For all his

habitual detachment and his recent disagreement with Cesar, Rico was as close to his brother as he was capable of being with anyone. It must have been a terribly worrisome time for him.

But what she also heard was that he really did think the passion between them posed a mortal danger—which equally told her he would hold her at arm's length because of it.

"It's not like I'm doing this on purpose, you know." She rolled away. "I'm a victim, too."

"I know." He followed her, dragging her into the spoon of his body. His voice tickled hotly through her hair. "I'm realizing that uncontrollable passion isn't only a crazed act in a quiet solarium. It's a hunger that refuses to be ignored. I'm not a dependent person, Poppy. I don't like being unable to suppress a craving that isn't a *need*. But I don't see the sense in hurting you, making your assimilation here more difficult because I'm displeased with myself."

It was hardly a declaration of love, but he didn't want to hurt her. It was something. She relaxed deeper into the bend of his body.

"You *are* trying to kill me," he accused, aroused flesh pressed to her backside.

She rolled to face him, stretching against him in a full-body caress.

"Maybe this is our normal."

"Maybe it is. Let's hope we survive it."

* * *

Over the next few weeks, Poppy tried to think of this new life as something she could do, rather than something that was being done *to* her. It helped to take the wheel, even if she wasn't sure where she was going. She began reviewing the week's menu with the housekeeper and making additions to the shopping list. She toured several properties and told Rico why she felt some of them wouldn't suit—one had a distinct perfume in the air from the fertilized fields next door, another had rooms that were very closed off from one another.

Rico was dead set on getting a vineyard again and wanted a pool. Poppy mentioned she'd prefer to be close to Sorcha and Lily's new cousins, to which he said, "Of course. That's the area I'd prefer as well."

She even sat down with the nanny and cleared the air. Poppy admitted this was all new to her and she sometimes felt threatened. Ingrid confessed to feeling she wasn't working hard enough and that's why she kept stepping up, trying to take Lily off her hands. By the time they finished their coffee and cake, they'd worked out the fine points of a long-term contract, both of them relaxed and smiling.

Rico continued dragging her to dinners and networking events, but they went more smoothly after she began taking Sorcha's advice and asking the other wives for recommendations on things like shoe boutiques and hair stylists. Their responses went in one ear and out the other, but at least they seemed to warm to her.

"Let me know when you need an interior designer," one said at one point.

"We have to find a house first. That's proving a challenge," Poppy admitted with genuine frustration.

Twenty minutes of sharing her wish list later, the woman offered a lead on a property that was farther up the coast from Cesar's villa. It wasn't officially on the market, but rumor had it the family needed the money and would accept the right offer.

Rico made a few discreet inquiries and they viewed it the next day.

"I asked Mother if she knew anything about it. She said to be careful when we open the closets," Rico told her as they stepped from the car.

"Skeletons?" Poppy asked, but her smile wasn't only amusement. Despite the clear signs of age and neglect, a covetous joy rang through her as she took in the stone house, instantly falling in love with the tiled roof and cobbled walkway and darling gated courtyard where she imagined Lily safely playing for hours.

Arches down the side formed a breezeway that wrapped around both levels then overlooked the pool—which needed repair and filling—but it offered a view of the Med that rivaled Cesar and Sorcha's.

Inside, the rooms were desperate for updating. Rico went a step further and said, "This floor plan should be completely reconfigured."

"When are they moving out?" she asked, looking at the furniture draped in sheets.

"They've already taken what they want. We would buy it as is. Mother will know which collectors to call to get rid of most of this."

The scope of the project was enormous, but Poppy was strangely undaunted. In fact, as she discovered a spiral staircase, she excitedly scooted up it. The small rooftop patio looked in every direction for miles and doubled as a sheltered place for intimate dining, utterly charming her.

"We could build out this direction," Rico said, firmly holding on to Lily as he leaned to see off the side. "Perhaps put a guest cottage at the edge of the orange grove."

There were other fruit trees along with a flower garden and a plot off the kitchen for a small vegetable garden, something Poppy's grandparents had always had when she'd been young. It became too much for all of them in later years, but the idea of Lily eating fresh strawberries gave Poppy such a sense of nostalgia and homecoming, she had to swallow a cry of excitement.

"Everything is pollinated by the bee hives in

the lower corner," Rico informed her, referring to some notes on his phone. "Apparently we would have our own honey."

Poppy blinked. "Why do I love the idea of keeping bees?"

"I don't know, but I'm intrigued, too."

As they walked out a lower door to view the hives, Rico nodded meaningfully at an exterior door. "Wine cellar."

She knew what he was driving at and shook her head, not wanting to get her hopes up. It was too perfect already. "You'd need it for wine, wouldn't you?"

They entered a big, dim room filled with nearly empty racks. While he glanced at the labels on the handful of bottles left behind, she explored the rear of the cellar, discovering a narrow, windowless room with a low ceiling. A few shelves held empty glass canning jars, suggesting it was a root cellar. A bare bulb was the only light.

Poppy was overwhelmed by what seemed like her birthday, Christmas and every other wishmaking day come true. She began arranging her future darkroom. The tubs would go there, the enlarger there. She might cry, she wanted this so badly.

"Am I wrong or is this everything we want?" Rico was carrying Lily and followed Poppy into the narrow room.

This was everything she could ever wish for herself and her daughter. The only thing she could want after this was her husband's heart.

Her own took an unsteady tumble as she realized how deeply she was yearning for that when every other part of their marriage was slotting into place.

Then he slid his free arm around Poppy and scooped her in for a quick kiss, sending her emotions spinning in another direction.

"Well done."

"We haven't seen the bees yet," she pointed out, wobbling between delirious happiness and intense longing. She worried often that his feelings toward her were still very superficial, but if he was willing to give her this—not just the castle above it, but the space to explore the creativity inside her—surely that meant he cared for her on a deeper level?

"By all means, let's go see the bees," Rico said magnanimously, oblivious to her conflict. "If there are birds to go with them, I'm sold."

"Your daddy thinks he's funny," she told Lily, trying to hide her insecurities.

"Da." Lily poked him in the cheek.

"Dada, yes." He caught her hand in his big one and kissed the point of her tiny finger. "You're as smart as your mama, aren't you?" He kissed Poppy again. "Yes?"

She shakily nodded.

Rico called to make an offer before they left. A week later, Poppy added meetings with interior designers and landscape contractors to her already busy weeks.

Even with those small successes, she was hideously nervous when she finished dressing for the Montero gala. It was an annual event, one that Sorcha and Rico's mother hosted on alternate years. Sorcha had told her what she had spent on her own gown and said, "Match it. This is your debut as a Montero." Then she had sent her favorite designer to the penthouse to consult with Poppy.

Poppy turned in the mirror, feeling like the biggest fraud in the world. Who was that woman? Had she gone too demure? The gown had a high neck and cap sleeves, but the fitted bodice accentuated her curves. The top was a very dramatic gold satin with a floral pattern in carmine and saffron and chestnut. The skirt was an A-line in crimson silk that moved like pouring paint, graceful and luxurious, following her in a small train even after she put on five-inch heels.

Her final touch was an art deco bracelet the stylist had recommended. Poppy, neophyte that she was, hadn't realized the stones were genuine sapphires and topaz and the gold twenty-four karat until the woman had looked up from her phone with excitement.

"Your husband signed off on it. He *does* want to make a statement, doesn't he?"

Poppy had smiled wanly, head swimming at what she'd accidentally bought.

She felt light-headed now as she walked out to the lounge, wondering what he would make of all of this, especially her hair. It had been straightened to within an inch of its life, then a slip of gold ribbon woven through a waterfall braid around her crown.

Rico paused with his drink halfway to his mouth.

She wrinkled her nose and took a slow turn, corkscrewing the skirt around her. *Super sophisticated, Poppy. Don't try that again.* She gave it a small ruffle to straighten it then stood tall, facing him again.

He hadn't moved.

"What's wrong?" She started searching for the flaw.

"Absolutely nothing." He set aside his drink and came to her, lifted the hand with the bracelet. "You look stunning."

"Really? Thank you. You look really nice, too." A tuxedo, for heaven's sake. She covered her racing heart. "Are we solving an international crime this evening?"

Someone was definitely targeting his heart. Rico almost said it, but it was too close to the truth.

She looked up at him and he read the sensual awareness that was always there between them, ready to be stoked into flame. There was a glow from deeper within her, too. One that was wide and bright and hot, like the sun about to rise behind the mountains and pierce through him.

It was beautiful, making him catch his breath in a strange anticipation, but he made himself break eye contact and move them out the door.

He was still trying to find the middle ground between providing Poppy the supportive attention she craved and maintaining some sort of governance over himself. He recalled chiding his brother once for having affection for Sorcha. *You don't want to admit you have a weakness where she's concerned.*

It was a weakness. Not only of character. It was a vulnerability that could be exploited so he steeled himself against allowing his affections to run too deep.

Even so, he found himself eager to show her off. He'd never been one of those men who wore a woman like a badge of virility, but apparently, he was capable of being that guy.

The pride swelling his chest and straining the buttons of his pleated shirt wasn't really about how Poppy made *him* look, though. Hell yes, he stood taller when he escorted her into the marquise behind Cesar's villa. But he stuck close to her not to be seen with her, or even to protect her—which he would in a heartbeat if anyone stepped out of line.

No, he was enjoying watching the way her confidence was blossoming. He couldn't change his world to make it easier for her to fit into it, but seeing her grow more comfortable with these trappings pleased him. *Eased* him.

She smiled and greeted couples she had already met and calmly ignored the occasional sideways glance from people still digesting the gossip that Rico Montero had married the mother of his love child.

She even showed less anxiety when they caught up with his parents, exchanging air kisses with his mother and speaking with genuine enthusiasm about the new house. She had clearly been studying at Sorcha's knee because she then asked his mother, "Would you have time next week to review the floor plan with me? Sorcha assures me I'll need the space for entertaining, but I don't want the front room to feel like a barn."

"Email my assistant. I'm sure she can find an hour for you."

It sounded like a slight, but the fact his mother was willing to make time for her was a glowing compliment.

"You're building a darkroom," Rico's father said.

"Yes." Poppy faltered briefly with surprise, then

tried her newfound strategy on him. "I wondered if you could advise me on where best to source the chemicals?"

"Your husband can do that."

Rico bit back a sigh. He held Poppy's elbow cradled in his palm and lightly caressed her inner arm while saying, "It's not always clear whether my father is genuinely interested or merely being polite." *Be polite*, he transmitted with a hard look into his father's profile.

"Rico," his mother murmured, her own stern expression reminding him they were all aware of his father's limitations. And they were in *public*.

"I am interested." Rico's father frowned, being misinterpreted. "Keep me apprised of your progress," he ordered Poppy. "I'd like to observe the process when you're up to full function. La Reina, I've seen people we ought to speak to."

"Of course." They melted into the crowd.

"Wow," Poppy said as they moved away. She slapped a bright smile on her face, but he saw through to the woman who felt ground into the dust.

"This is why the house you found us is so perfect." He stroked her bare arms. "It's even farther away from them than this one."

Her hurt faded and her mouth twitched. "That's not nice."

"No. And you don't realize it, but he was being

as nice as he gets. His asking to observe you is quite the commendation."

"Really?" She dipped her chin, skeptical.

"Mmm-hmm. If I cared about scoring points with my parents, I would be high-fiving you right now."

"We could dance instead," Poppy suggested. "What's wrong?"

"Nothing." Except he'd just recalled the steps he was taking that, as far as scoring points with his parents went, would wipe him to below zero in their books. He would owe future favors. *That* was the cost of giving in to base feelings like passion and infatuation.

So he wouldn't.

"Let's dance," he murmured and drew her onto the floor.

CHAPTER NINE

POPPY WAS FALLING for Rico. Really falling. This wasn't the secret crush of a maid for a man who hadn't even noticed her. It wasn't the sexual infatuation of a woman whose husband left her weak with satisfaction every night. It wasn't even the tender affinity of shared love for their daughter, although what she was feeling had its roots in all of those things.

This was the kind of regard her grandparents had felt for each other. She knew because she began doing the sorts of little things for Rico that they used to do for one another. If he tried a particular brandy while they were out, and liked it, she asked the housekeeper to order some in. When discussing the decor of his home office in the new house, she had the designer track down a signed print of his favorite racecar driver, now retired but still revered.

And when she had an appointment to spend the morning looking at photography equipment, she impulsively called Rico's assistant and asked if her husband had plans for lunch. He was pronounced available so she booked herself as his date and made a reservation, dropping in to surprise him.

His PA, a handsome man about her age whom she was meeting in person for the first time, rose to greet her. He looked startled. Alarmed. Maybe even appalled.

"Senora Montero. You're early." He smoothed his expression to a warm and welcoming smile. "I'm Anton. So good to meet you. Why don't I show you around while Senor Montero finishes his meeting?"

Poppy might be a country girl at heart, but she knew a slick city hustle when she was the victim of one. She balked, heart going into free fall. All her optimistic belief that she and Rico were making progress in their marriage disintegrated. One dread-filled question escaped her.

"Who is he with?"

Before Anton could spit out a suitable prevarication, the door to Rico's office cracked. He came out with an older couple. Everyone wore somber expressions.

Rico's face tightened with regret when he saw her. Anton offered a pinched smile of apology. He moved quickly to the closet where the older woman's light coat had been hung.

The older couple both stiffened, clearly recognizing her while Poppy's brain scrambled and somehow made the connection that they must be Faustina's parents.

The brief anguish she had suffered mildewed into horror. Rico wasn't meeting some Other Woman. *She* was that reviled creature.

How did one act in such a profoundly uncomfortable moment? What should she say? All she could conjure was the truth.

"I wanted to surprise you," she admitted to Rico, voice thick with apology. "I didn't realize you would be tied up." She thought she might be sick.

Rico introduced her to the Cabreras. Neither put out their hand to shake so Poppy kept her own clutched over her purse, nodding and managing a small smile that wasn't returned.

"The woman you 'dated very briefly when your engagement was interrupted,'" Faustina's mother said with a dead look in her eye.

"I'm very sorry," Poppy choked, reminding herself that they had lost their only child and would hurt forever because of it.

"I'm sure you are," Senora Cabrera said bitterly. "Despite gaining all the prestige and wealth my daughter brought to this marriage. What do *you* bring except cheap notoriety and a bastard conceived in adultery?"

Poppy gasped and stumbled slightly as Rico scooped her close, pressing her to stand more behind him than beside him.

"The hypocrisy is mine. Don't take your anger out on Poppy." His tone was so dark and dangerous, she curled a fist into the fabric of his jacket in a useless effort to restrain him, fearing he would physically attack them. "Leave innocent babies out of this altogether."

A profound silence, then Senora Cabrera sniffed with affront. Her husband clenched his teeth so hard, Poppy could have sworn she heard them crunching like hard candy behind the flat line of his lips.

"I've given you some options," Rico continued in a marginally more civilized voice. "Let me know how you'd like to proceed."

"Options," Senor Cabrera spat. "None that are worth accepting. This is hell," he told Rico forcefully. "You have sent us to hell, Rico. I hope you're happy."

The older man whirled and jerked his head at his wife. She hurried after him. Anton trotted to catch up and escort them to the elevator while Rico swore quietly and viciously as he strode back into his office.

Poppy followed on apprehensive feet, quietly closing the door and pressing her back against it. She watched him pour a drink.

"I am *so* sorry. Anton didn't tell me they would be here or I wouldn't have come. I asked him not to tell you I was dropping in. This is all my fault."

"I knew you were coming." He threw back a

full shot. "I thought we would be finished an hour ago. It went long—you were early. Bad timing." He poured a second. "Do you want one?"

"It was that bad?" She wondered how many he'd had before talking to the older couple. Maybe she ought to make some espresso with that machine behind the bar.

"It was difficult." He poured two glasses and brought them to the low table where melting ice water and full cups of coffee sat next to untouched plates of biscotti. He set the fresh glasses into the mix and threw himself into an armchair.

She lowered herself to the sofa, briefly taking in the classic decor of the office with its bookshelves and antique desk. A younger version of Senor Cabrera looked down in judgment from a frame on the wall. She felt utterly helpless. Deserving of blame, yet Rico wasn't casting any, just slouching there, brooding.

"What sort of options did you give them?" She hated to ask, sensing by their animosity his suggestions hadn't been well received.

"I told them I was stepping down."

"From being president?" A jolt went through her. It was the last thing she had expected. "Why?"

"I have to." He frowned as if it was obvious. "I had my parents prepare them for it when they informed them about you and Lily. I've stayed to keep things on an even keel, but today I gave them the alternatives for transitioning me out of the chair."

She could only blink, remembering what he had told her in the solarium the day Faustina had broken his engagement. Poppy hadn't meant to pry, but she had admitted to not understanding the appeal of an arranged marriage. She had been compelled to ask what he would have gained.

I was to become president of Faustina's father's chemical research firm. Cesar and I work very well together, but this would have given me a playground for my personal projects and ambitions. My chance to shine in my own spotlight.

He'd been self-deprecating, but she had sensed a real desire in him to prove something, if only to himself. She completely understood that. It was akin to what drove her interest in photography.

"What will you do?" she asked now.

"Go back to working under Cesar. There's always room for me there."

But it wasn't what he wanted. "You married Faustina so you could move out from his shadow. You have your own ambitions."

"I'll find another way to pursue them." He flicked his hand, dismissing that desire.

"But—" She frowned. "What happens with this company? Do they become your competitors again?"

"One option is to leave this enterprise under

Cesar's direction. Another would be for us to sell this back to them at a discounted price. They'd be gaining a much more lucrative business than when I took over." He muttered into his glass. "So I think that's what they'll choose."

"How much would it impact you if they do? Financially, I mean?" Her blood was congealing in her veins. They'd just bought a house. Not a cute bungalow in a small prairie town that a union wage could pay off in twenty years, but a mansion with acres of grapes and the sort of view that cost more than the house. Her palms were sweating. "Why didn't you tell me this was happening?"

"Because it doesn't affect you. The sting in the pocketbook will be short-lived, some legal fees and a return of some stocks and other holdings. I'll have to restructure my personal portfolio, but our family has weathered worse. Things will balance out."

She could only sit there with a knot of culpability in her middle.

"Rico, I hate that I brought nothing to this marriage. I didn't know I was going to *cost* you. Not like this." Her eyes grew hot and she braced her elbows on her knees to cover her eyes with her palms. "I've been spending like a drunken sailor. I just ordered equipment for— I'll call them. Cancel it." She looked for her purse.

"Poppy." He leaned forward and caught her wrist. "Don't take this the wrong way, but a few thousand euros on photography equipment isn't going to make a dent in what's about to change hands. Cesar and I have discussed how to finance this. You and I are perfectly fine."

"But this is my fault! Now he's going to hate me, too. Sorcha will stop being my friend. I'm sorry, Rico. I'm so sorry I slept with you and ruined everything."

Her words hit his ears in a crash, like the avalanche of rocks off a cliff that continued roaring and tumbling long after the first crack of thunder, leaving a whiff of acrid dust in the air.

They came on top of words spoken by Señora Cabrera that had made him see red. *A bastard conceived in adultery.*

That was not what Lily was. Their attack against Poppy had been equally blood boiling and now *Poppy* was expressing regret over their daughter's conception?

"Don't you *dare* say that."

Maybe it was the alcohol hitting his system, maybe it was the pent-up tension from his meeting releasing in a snap. Maybe it was simply that he was confronted with Poppy's emotions so often, he was beginning to tap into his own, but rather than suppress his anger, he let himself feel it. It raged through him because her words *hurt*.

"I told you I will never regard Lily as a mistake

and don't you ever do it, either." He threw himself to his feet, trying to pace away from the burn of scorn that chased him. "I would give up every last penny I possess so long as I can have her in my life."

Damn, that admission made him uncomfortable. He shot her a look and saw her sit back, hand over her chest, tears in her eyes. She was biting her lips together, chin crinkling.

Was he scaring her? He swore and pushed a hand into his hair, clenching hard enough to feel the pain of it, trying to grapple himself back under control.

"Thank you, Rico," she said in a voice that scraped. "I hope you know that's all I've ever wanted for her. Parents who love her. Not all of this." She flicked a hand around the room.

"I do know that." He swallowed a lump from his throat, but it remained lodged sideways in his chest. He felt pried open and stood there fighting the sensation.

"But I'm starting to see that you and your family support a lot more people than just me and Lily. It shouldn't be such a revelation to me. When I needed a job, your mother gave me one and I was grateful. Now I can see that this lifestyle you're protecting has value to more people than just you. That's why it's upsetting to me that I'm undermining it. I think I'd feel better about it if you'd at least yell at me."

"I'm not going to yell at you." Was he angry? Yes. About many things, but none that mattered as much as his daughter. "My career ambitions and the bearing our marriage has had on them are insignificant next to what I've gained through this marriage. *You brought our child.* There's nothing else you could have brought that comes close to how important she is to me."

There was a flash of something like yearning in her eyes before she screened them with her lashes. She reached to pluck a tissue from the box and pressed it under each eye.

"It means a lot that you would say that. I struggle with exactly what they said. Every day." Her mouth pulled down at the corners. "Feeling like I snuck in through a side door, using my daughter as a ticket. I feel like such an imposter." She sniffed.

"Stop feeling that way," he ordered, coming over to sit beside her, facing her. "It's a terrible thing to say, but I can't imagine Faustina showing our baby the same sort of love that you show Lily. I'm lucky my child has you as her mother."

Her eyes grew even bigger and swam with even more tears. Her mouth trembled in earnest.

"Please don't cry. You're making me feel like a jerk."

"You're being the opposite of a jerk. That's why I'm crying."

She had worn her hair in a low ponytail today

and half of it was coming loose around her face. He wound a tendril around his finger, thinking of how often he saw her wince and pry Lily's fist from the mass, never scolding her for it.

How could anyone resist this mass, though? He dipped his head to rub the ribbon of silk against his lips. Watched her gaze drop to his mouth and tried not to get distracted.

"There's something I've been wanting to ask you," Rico began.

Her gaze flashed upward, brimming with inquisitive light. "Yes?"

Unnatural, fearful hope filled him even as he second-guessed what was on his tongue. He couldn't believe these words were forming inside him. Not as the next strategic move in the building of the Montero empire, either. Not in reaction to what outsiders said about their marriage. No, this was something that had been bubbling in him from the earliest days of their marriage, something he didn't want to examine too closely because it occupied such a deep cavern inside him.

"Rico?" she prompted.

"With the house almost ready, I keep thinking we should talk about filling more of those rooms."

Her pupils threatened to swallow her face. "Another baby?"

"I know you wanted to wait." He let go of her hair and covered the hand that went limp against his thigh. He pressed his lips together, bracing himself for rebuff. "If you're not ready, we can table it, but I wanted to mention it. My relationship with Pia and Cesar—we're not as close as some, but I value them. I realize many things contribute to the distance between you and your half-siblings, but the age gap is a factor. That's why I thought sooner than later would benefit Lily."

He heard his upbringing in the logic of his argument and recognized it as the defense tactic it was. If he kept his feelings firmly out of the discussion, there was no chance they would get trampled on.

Poppy blinked and a fresh tear hit her cheek, diamond bright. "Are you being serious? You want to make a baby with me *on purpose*?"

The magnitude wasn't lost on him. Marriages could be undone. Property could be split. The entanglement of a child—*children*, if he had any say in it—was a far bigger and more permanent commitment.

"I do."

"You didn't tell me there's such a thing as a babymoon," Rico said a month later as they toured the empty rooms of their villa, inspecting freshly painted walls, window treatments and light fixtures. Furniture delivery would start next week.

"You'd have seen one by now if you had ever

changed a diaper," she teased. "Instead of handing Lily off to the nanny."

Rico's mouth twitched, but he only drew her onto the private balcony off their master bedroom. It made her feel like the queen of the world to stand there looking so far out on the Mediterranean she was sure she glimpsed the cowboy boot of Italy.

"Besides, we're not there yet."

After a visit to the doctor a couple of weeks ago, they were officially "trying." Today, Rico had asked the designer about setting up a nursery *when the time comes*. The woman had cheerfully promised a quick turnaround on redecorating the room of their choice. "Most couples take a babymoon for a few weeks so we aren't disrupting their daily life," the woman had added, then had to explain to Rico what it was.

"We never even had a honeymoon," he pointed out now.

"There's been a lot going on. A lot for Lily to adjust to. I wouldn't want to leave her even now, when we're about to move into this house and change everything again."

"We could take her with us."

"I think that's called a family vacation, not a honeymoon."

"You're full of cheek today, aren't you?" He gave one of her lower ones a friendly squeeze. "We could take the nanny so we get our alone time. Really put our back into the honeymoon effort. See if we can't earn ourselves a babymoon."

She chuckled. "So romantic." But she kissed him under his chin, ridiculously in love when he was playful like this—

Oh. There it was. The acknowledgment she'd been avoiding. Because if she admitted to herself that she was fully head over heels, she had to face that he wasn't.

"Romance is not my strong point, but sound logic is."

He gathered her so her arms were folded against his chest, fingertips grazing his open collar, but his words echoed through the hollow spaces growing wider in her chest.

"The transition is almost finished with the Cabreras," he continued. "Cesar has some projects he wants me to take the lead on in a couple of months. I won't have much downtime once I'm knee-deep. This is our window for a getaway. Let's take it."

"If you want to," she murmured, thinking she ought to feel happy. Excited. But she only felt sad. She felt the way she had as a child, wishing her mother and father wanted her. It shouldn't have mattered. She'd been loved by her grandparents.

But she'd still felt the absence of it from people she thought *should* love her.

And she felt it again now.

"What's wrong?"

"Nothing," she lied, conjuring a smile. "Where…? Um…where would you want to go?"

"I don't know. Somewhere that Lily would enjoy and you could play with your new camera. Maybe we could tie in a visit to your grandmother at the end. I know you're missing her."

"You wouldn't mind?"

"Of course not. I wish she would agree to come live with us here. You know you can visit her anytime. I'll come with you as often as I can."

"Thank you." A tiny spark of hope returned. Whenever he doted on her, she thought maybe he *was* coming to love her. Tentative light crept through her. "Okay. Let's do it."

Two weeks later, they were riding elephants through the rainforests of Thailand.

"This is not camping," she told him when they arrived at the hidden grotto where sleep pods were suspended in the trees. "Camping is digging a trench around your tent in a downpour at midnight so you don't drown in your sleep."

"I think this is 'glamping,'" the nanny murmured in an aside as the pod she would share with Lily was pointed out to her. "And *thank you*."

They dined on rare mushrooms and wild boar, coconut curry soup and tropical fruit with cashews. When they fell asleep, replete from lovemaking, the wind rocked their pod and the frogs crooned a lullaby. They woke to strange birdcalls and the excited trumpet of a baby elephant as it trampled into a mud pool.

Poppy caught some of the elephant's antics with her new toy, a Leica M6. She switched out to her new digital camera to catch some shots of Lily to send to Gran then held her as she fed the baby elephant, chuckling as Lily squealed in delight.

A click made her look up and she found Rico capturing them on his phone.

"New screen saver," he said as he tucked it away.

Poppy flushed with pleasure, in absolute heaven. She began to think she really was living happily-ever-after, cherished by her husband, making a family with him. Her life couldn't be more ideal.

Then, as they came off their last day in the forest to stay a few days at a luxury beach resort on the coast, she discovered that, for all their success the first time, they weren't so lucky this time. She wasn't one-and-done pregnant.

It wasn't even the light spotting that had fooled her with Lily. She had a backache and a heavier than normal case of the blues.

Plenty of women didn't conceive right away. There was no reason she should take it this hard. She knew that in her head, but her heart was lying there in two jagged pieces anyway.

Rico came into the bedroom of their suite as she was coming out of the bathroom.

"I sent the nanny to the beach with Lily. We—"
He took off his sunglasses and frowned. "What's
wrong?"

He wore a T-shirt and shorts better than any
man she'd ever met. The shirt clung to his sculpted
shoulders and chest and his legs were tanned and
muscled. One of her favorite things in the world
was the scrape of his fine hair when she ran the
inside of her thigh against his iron-hard ones.

Everything about him was perfect.

And she wasn't. She hadn't even gotten this right.

"It's not working. I'm not pregnant."

"Oh." He was visibly taken aback. "You're sure?"

She bit back a tense, *Of course I'm sure*, and
only said, "Yes." She turned her back and threw
sunscreen and a few other things into a beach bag.

"But it only took once last time."

"I know that." She drew a patience-gathering
breath. "I don't know why it didn't happen." She
blinked, fighting tears. "But it didn't and there's
nothing I can do about it."

"Poppy." He touched her arm. "It's fine. We're
having fun trying, right? Next time."

She didn't want him to be disappointed. That
would make her feel worse. But it didn't help to
hear him brush it off, either. She dug through her
bag, unable to remember if she'd thrown her book
in there.

"You go. I'll catch up."

"Poppy. Come on. Don't be upset. This isn't a test that we have to pass or fail."

"Not for you it isn't. For me? Yes it is. Every single day! Either I bring value to this marriage or I'm just a hanger-on."

"I have *never* meant to make you feel like that."

"I feel like that because that's what I *am*." The rope handle of her bag began to cut into her shoulder. She threw the whole works onto the floor, standing outside herself and knowing this was toddler-level behavior, but there was poison sitting deep inside her. The kind that had to come out before it turned her completely septic. "At least when I was looking after my grandparents, I was *contributing*. You don't need me to look after Lily. The nanny does most of the work."

"You *love* Lily. I told you that's all—"

"Yes! I love her. That's what I bring. The ability to give you babies and love them. Except now there's no baby." She flung out a hand.

"We've just started trying! Look." He attempted to take her by the shoulders, but she brushed him off and backed away. "Poppy. I don't know much about this process, but I do know it takes some couples a while. There is no need to be this upset."

"I *want* to be upset!" She hated how backed into a corner she felt. She pushed past him and strode to the middle of the room only to spin around and confront. "But I'm not allowed to be upset, am I?

There's no such thing as emotion in your world, is there? I'm supposed to fit into a tiny little box labeled Wife and Mother." She made a square with her hands. "And uphold the family image, except I'll never be able to do that because I'm forever going to be a blotch."

"Calm down," he ordered.

She flung out a hand in a silent, *There it is*.

He heard it, too, and sighed. He gave her a stern look. "You're not a blotch. We've been over all of this. You contribute. I don't know why you struggle to believe that."

"Because I've been a burden my entire life, Rico. My grandparents were planning to do things in their retirement. Take bus tours and travel and *see* things. Instead, they were stuck raising me."

"It didn't sound to me like that was how your grandmother felt."

"That's still how it *was*. That's how I wound up working in your mother's house. I couldn't bear the thought of asking them for money when they'd supported me all those years. Then I came home and bam. Pregnant. Back to being a parasite. Gramps didn't want to sell that house because he was afraid I would go broke paying day care and rent. I was supposed to pay Gran back after all those years she took care of me, but now you're supporting her. *And* me. That feels *great*."

"You are not a parasite. Eleanor is my daughter's great-grandmother. I *want* to look after her. And you."

"See, that's it." She lifted a helpless hand. "Right there. You don't want to look after *me*." She pressed her hand to the fissure in her chest where all her emotions were bleeding out and making a mess on the floor. "You want to look after Lily's mother. Exactly the way they took in their son's daughter for his sake. You don't want *me*, Rico."

"You're upset. Taking things to heart that don't require this much angst."

Her heart was the problem. That much he had right. It felt like her heart was beating outside her chest.

"Do you love me?" she asked, already knowing the answer. "Do you think you're ever going to love me?"

Her question gave him pause. The fact a watchful expression came across his face as he searched for a response that was kind yet truthful was all the answer she needed.

"Because I love you," she admitted, feeling no sense of relief as the words left barbs in her throat. Her lips were so wobbly, her speech was almost slurred. "I love you so much I ache inside, all the time. I want so badly to be enough for you—"

"You are," he cut in gruffly.

"Well, you're not enough for me!" The statement burst out of her, breaking something open in her. Between them. All the delicate filaments that had connected them turned to dust, leaving him pallid. Leaving her throat arid and the rest of her blistered with self-hatred as she threw herself on the pyre, adding, "This isn't enough."

His breath hissed in.

"At least my grandparents loved me, despite the fact I'd been dumped on them. But I waited my whole childhood for my parents to want me. To love me. I can't live like that again, Rico. I can't take up space in your home because your children need a mother. I need more. And what breaks my heart is knowing that you're capable of it. You love Lily. I know you do. But you don't love me and you won't and *that's not fair*."

He let her go.

He shouldn't have let her walk out, but he didn't know what to say. He knew what she wanted to hear him say, but those words had never passed his lips.

From his earliest recollection of hearing the phrase, when he realized other children said those words to their parents, he had instinctively understood it wasn't a sentiment his own parents would want to hear from him. They weren't a family who said such a thing. They weren't supposed to feel it. Or *want* to feel it.

So he let her walk out and close the door with a polite click that sounded like the slam of a vault, locking him out of something precious he had only glimpsed for a second.

Which seemed to empty him of his very soul.

He looked around, recalling dimly that he'd thought to enjoy an afternoon delight before joining their daughter on the beach for sand castles and splashing in the waves.

Not pregnant. He had to admit that had struck harder than he would have expected. It left a hole in his chest that he couldn't identify well enough to plug. He knew how to manage his expectations. He'd spent his entire life keeping his low, so as not to suffer disappointment or loss. Despite that, he was capable of both. He wanted to go after Poppy and ask again, *Are you sure?*

She was sure. The bleak look in her eyes had kicked him in the gut. He wasn't ready to face that again. That despair had nearly had him telling her they didn't have to try again ever, not if a lack of conception was going to hit her so hard it broke something in her.

He wanted a baby, though. The compulsion to build on what they had was beyond voracious. How could Poppy not realize she was an integral part of this new sense of family he was only beginning to understand?

Family wasn't what he'd been taught—loyalty and rising to responsibility, sharing a common history and acting for the good of the whole. That was part of it, but family was also a smiling kiss greeting him when he walked in the door. It was a trusting head on his shoulder and decisions made together. It was a sense that he could relax. That he would be judged less harshly by those closest to him. His mistakes would be forgiven.

Forgive me, he thought despairingly.

And heard her say again, *You're not enough for me.*

He was still trying to find his breath after that one. He knew how it felt to be accepted on condition, better than she realized. The gold standard for approval in his childhood had been a mastery over his emotions. Tears were weakness, passion vulgar. He should only go after things that made sense, that benefited the family, not what he *wanted*.

Do you love me?

He didn't know how. That was the bitter truth.

He would give Poppy nearly anything she asked for, but he refused to say words to her that weren't sincere. How the hell would he know one way or the other if what he felt was love, though? He hadn't had any exposure to that elusive emotion, not until his brother had gone off the rails with Sorcha, causing his parents to shrink in horror, further reinforcing to Rico that deep emotions prompted destructive madness.

Love had *killed* Faustina, for God's sake.

He hated himself for hurting Poppy, though. For

failing her. The sick ache sat inside him as he went out and looked for her. She wasn't on a lounger under the cabana with the nanny, watching Lily play in a shaded pocket of sand.

He moved to stand near them, scanning for Poppy, figuring she would turn up here eventually.

It took him a moment to locate her, walking in the wet sand where waves washed ashore and re-treated. Was she crying? She looked so desolate on that empty stretch so far from the cheerful crowd of the resort beach.

She wasn't a burden. It killed him that her parents had let her grow up feeling anything less than precious. She brought light into darkness, laughter into sober rooms.

She had brought him Lily—literally life. He glanced at his daughter. She was batting down each of the castles the nanny made for her. The most enormous well-being filled him whenever he was anywhere near this little sprite. Poppy shone like the sun when she was with Lily, clearly the happiest she could possibly be.

That was why he wanted another baby. He didn't know how to express what he felt for Poppy except to physically make another of these joy factories. With her. He wanted her to have more love. The best of himself, packaged new and flawless, without the jagged edges and rusted wheels. Clean, perfect, unconditional love.

From him.

He swallowed, hands in fists as he absorbed that he may not know how to love, how to express it, but it was inside him. He would die for Lily and if Poppy was hurting, he was hurting.

He couldn't bear that. Not for one more minute.

He looked for her again, intent on going after her.

She had wandered even farther down the beach, past the flags and signage that warned of—

He began jogging after her, to call her back.

Long before he got there, the sea reached with frothy arms that gathered around her legs and dragged her in. One second she was there, the next she was gone.

"Poppy!" he hollered at the top of his lungs and sprinted down the beach.

One moment she was wading along, waves breaking on her shins. Without warning, the water swirled higher. It dragged with incredible strength against her thighs, eroding the sand from beneath her feet at the same time. The dual force knocked her off-balance and she fell, splooshing under.

It shocked her out of her morose tears, but she knew how to swim. She mostly felt like an idiot, tumbling like a drunk into the surf. As she sputtered to the surface, she glanced around, hoping no one had witnessed her clumsiness.

As she tried to get her feet under her, however,

she couldn't find the bottom. She was in far deeper water than she ought to be. As she gave a little dog paddle to get back toward the beach, she realized she was being sucked away from it. Fast.

Panic struck in a rush of adrenaline. She willed herself not to give in to it. This was a rip current. She only knew one thing about them and that was to swim sideways out of it.

She tried, but the beach was disappearing quickly, making her heart beat even quicker. Her swimsuit wrap was dragging and tangling on her arms. When she tried to call out for help, she caught a mouthful of salt water and was so far away, no one would hear her anyway.

Terrified, she flipped onto her back, floating and kicking, trying to get her bearings while she wrestled herself free of the wrap and caught her breath.

Think, think, think.

Oh, dear God. She popped straight and the people were just the size of ants. Had anyone even noticed she'd been swept out? She looked for a boat. Were there sharks? *Don't panic.*

She was beyond where the waves were breaking. This was where surfers would usually gather, sitting on their boards as they watched the hump of waves, picking and choosing which to ride into shore.

She didn't know how to bodysurf, though. It was all she could do to keep her head up as the waves picked her up and rolled toward the beach without her.

Treading water, she saw nothing, only what looked like a very long swim to shore. She thought she might be on the far side of the current that had carried her out. A crosscurrent was drifting her farther toward the headland, away from where she'd left Lily on the beach.

Lily. She tried not to cry. Lily was safe, she reminded herself.

This was such a stupid mess to be in. She had picked a fight with Rico then walked away to sulk. Why? What did she have to complain about? He treated her like a queen. No one she knew took tropical vacations and rode elephants and slept in five-star oceanfront villas with butler service to the beach.

I'm sorry, baby, she said silently as she began to crawl her arms over her head, aiming for the headland that was a lot farther than she'd ever swum in her life. A few laps in a pool were her limit. Just enough to get her safety badge when she was ten. *I'm sorry, Rico. Please, Gramps, if you can hear me, I need help.*

Rico absconded with a Jet Ski, scaring an adolescent boy into giving it up with whatever expression was on his face. The only words he'd had in him had been a grated, "My wife."

Her coral wrap had been his beacon as he raced to the family with the Jet Skis. Now it was gone.

He ran the Jet Ski along the edge of the riptide, gaze trying to penetrate the cloudy water, searching for a glint of color, of red hair, terrified he'd find her in it and terrified he wouldn't.

He sped out to where the head of the current mushroomed beyond the surf zone, dissipating in a final cloud of sand pulled from the beach. Still nothing.

Dimly he noted two surfers and a lifeguard from the resort joining his search, zigzagging through the surf.

He had to find her. *Had to.*

In a burst of speed, he started down the far side of the rip and had to fight the Jet Ski to get back toward the current. Another one, not as strong, ran parallel to the beach. He realized she might have been drawn toward the headland. It was a huge stretch of water to get there.

Despair began to sink its claws into him.

Bill, help us out, he silently begged her grandfather's spirit.

A glint above the water caught his attention. A drone?

He looked toward the beach and saw the operator waving him toward the headland.

Using the drone as a beacon, he gunned the Jet

Ski that direction, searched the chop of waves. *Please, please, please.*

A slender arm slowly came out of the water. It windmilled in a tired backstroke, slapping wearily on reentry.

Swearing, he raced toward her. The resignation in her eyes as she spotted him told him how close she'd been to giving up. He got near enough she put a hand on the machine, but he had to turn it off and get in the water with her to get her onto it, she was that weak.

She sat in front of him, trembling and coughing, breaths panting and heart hammering through her back into his own slamming in his chest. She hunched weakly while he reached to start the Jet Ski again. He shifted her slightly so he could hold on to her and steered it back to shore.

He was shaking. Barely processing anything other than that he had to get them to dry land.

"I'm sorry," she said when he got to the small dock where the startled family had gathered with damned near every living soul in Thailand.

The crowd gave them a round of applause. The nanny stood with Lily on her hip, eyes wide with horror at the barely averted catastrophe.

"Oh, Lily," Poppy sobbed, and hugged her daughter, but Lily squirmed at her mother's wet embrace.

A lifeguard came to check on Poppy.

"Have a hot shower. You'll be in shock. Lie down and stay warm. Drink lots of water to flush the seawater you drank."

Rico nodded and took her into their villa, bringing her straight into the shower and starting it, peeling off their wet clothes as they stood under the spray.

"I'm so sorry," she said, feeling like she was drowning all over again as the fresh water poured like rain upon them.

He dragged at the tie on her bikini top only to tighten the knot. He turned her and she felt his fingers between her shoulder blades, picking impatiently at the knot.

"I wasn't paying attention. It was stupid. I'm really sorry. Please don't think I did that on purpose. I was upset, but I wouldn't leave Lily. I know she needs me."

"I need you!" he shouted, making her jump.

She turned around and backed into the tiles, catching the loosened top so she clutched the soggy, hanging cups against her cold breasts.

"You scared the hell out of me. I thought—" His face spasmed and she saw drops on his cheeks that might have been from the shower, but might have been something else. "What would I do without you, Poppy?"

He cupped her face and the incendiary light in

his eyes was both fury and something else. Something that made her hold her breath as he tenderly pressed his thumbs to the corners of her mouth.

"I wanted to go looking for you the day after the solarium. Do you know that? I didn't know where to start. Ask the staff? It was too revealing. Try to catch you at the hostel? The airport? You hadn't told me the name of the town where you lived, but I imagined I could find out. I didn't want to wait that long or travel that far, though. Not if I could catch you before you left."

He was talking in a voice so thick and heavy with anguish it made her ache.

"It was an irrational impulse, Poppy. We don't have those in this family. I couldn't admit to *myself* how attracted I was. I couldn't let anyone else see it, not even you. I had to live up to my responsibilities. After Cesar, *I* had to show some sense. It was better to let you go. *But I didn't want to.*"

Her mouth trembled. "Then Faustina took away any choice you might have."

"Yes." He moved his hands to lift the bathing suit cups off her chest and high enough to pull the tie free from behind her neck.

Her hair fell in wet tendrils onto her shoulders. He drew her back under the spray, took a squirt of fragrant body wash in his palm and turned her to rub the warm lather over her back and shoulders, working heat into her tired, still trembling muscles.

"Everything in my world went gray. Through the wedding, into my marriage and after she was gone. I didn't care about anything. I had achieved maximum indifference." His hands dug their soapy massage into her muscles, strong and reassuring. "Then Sorcha told me you might have had my baby. I tried to approach the situation rationally. I did. But the test came back inconclusive and I got on the plane. I had to see you. I had to know."

"What if Lily hadn't been yours?"

He turned her. A faint smile touched his mouth. "Can you imagine? There I was spitting fire and fury and you might have said she was Ernesto's."

"The seventy-year-old gardener? Yes, he's always been my type."

He turned her to settle her back against his chest. He ran his firm palms across her upper chest and down her arms, not trying to arouse, but the warmth tingling through her held flickers of the desire that always kindled when they were close.

"I have a feeling it wouldn't have mattered if she wasn't mine." His voice was a grave rumble in his chest. A somber vow against her ear. "I can't see myself turning around and going home just because I happened to be wrong. One way or another, you were meant to be here in my life. I was meant to be Lily's father."

She swallowed, astonished. Shaken. Questioning whether this man of logic really believed in fate.

"You're talking like your bohemian wife who thinks her grandfather can talk to her through the stars."

His hand slowed and his chin rested against her hair. "You think I didn't ask him for help? Did you see the drone above you?"

"No. But that would be a tourist, not Gramps."

"It was in the sky, Poppy. I was begging him for some sign of you."

He turned her to face him.

Her arms twined themselves around his neck because they knew that was where they belonged. Lather lingered to provide a sensual friction between their torsos.

"I love you." He stared deeply into her eyes as he spoke, allowing her to see all the way to the depths of his soul. To the truth of his statement. "I'm sorry it took something like this for me to say it. To *feel* it. In my defense, it was there—I just didn't know what it was."

She tried to hold it together, but her emotions were still all over the place. Her mouth trembled and tears leaked to join the water hitting her cheeks. "I love you, too." Her voice quavered. "I shouldn't have said you weren't enough. I was upset."

"I know." His gaze grew pained. "Maybe instead of 'trying,' we'll just see. Hmm? I don't want you to think our marriage hinges on whether we have another baby. I love *you*."

"Okay. But I really do want your baby." The yearning and disappointment was still there, but as she let her head rest on his shoulder, the hollowness eased. The darkness was dispelled by the light of his love.

"Me, too." He pressed his wet lips to her crown. "And when the time is right, I'm sure we'll have one."

Weeks later, Rico crowded her to scan the strips of negatives with her.

"I want the one I took of you in front of the waterfall," he said.

Poppy never minded the touch of his body against hers, but, "You're here to tell me how your father will behave. Act like him and pick something he might like."

His parents were coming for an early dinner, their first visit to the finished house. Sorcha and Cesar had plans elsewhere so it would be only the four of them. They would show them the beehives and the wine cellar and, at the explicit request of the duque, Poppy would demonstrate her darkroom.

"The waterfall is a good shot," Rico said, not backing off one hairbreadth. "The ripples in your hair mirrored the path of the water. I've wanted to see it since I took it."

It was poorly framed and crooked, but she could fix that.

Actually, it was a decent shot, she decided, once the negative was in the enlarger. It was perfectly focused and the light was quite pretty, dappling through the jungle leaves. It was taken from behind her. She sat up to her waist in the water, looking toward the waterfall. She had been wearing her bikini and the strings were hidden by the fall of her hair so she looked like a naked nymph spied in her natural habitat.

"I am not showing this one to your father."

She had already run test strips from this batch so she set her timer and switched the overhead light to red. Then she set the paper for exposure.

"How long do we have?" His hands settled on her waist.

"Not long enough." The timer went off and she chuckled at the noise of disappointment that escaped him.

She moved the paper into the developer bath and gently rocked until the second timer pinged. She moved the paper to the fixing bath, explaining as she went.

"This last one is water, to wash off the chemicals." She left the image in the final bath.

"See? It's great," he said.

"It is," she agreed, washing her hands and drying them. "*Now* ask me how much time we have."

"Enough?"

"It shouldn't stay in there more than thirty minutes." She closed one eye and wrinkled her nose. "But we shouldn't stay in *here* more than thirty minutes or we won't have time to get ready for our guests."

"I can work with that."

"I know you can," she purred throatily and held up her arms.

He ambled close, crowded her against the counter beside the sink then lifted her to sit upon it. "Have I told you lately how much I love you?"

Every day. She cradled his hard jaw in soft hands, grazing her lips against the stubble coming in because he hadn't yet shaved. "Have I told you lately that you make all of my dreams come true?"

Maybe not all. They were still "seeing," not "trying," but their love was tender and new. They were protecting it with gentle words and putting no pressure on it with expectations they couldn't control.

"I want to," he said, hands slowing as he ran them over her back and up to pull the thick elastic from her hair. "I want you to be happy."

"I am. So happy I don't know how to contain it all." She skimmed her fingers down to his shirt buttons, good at this now. She smiled as she spread the white shirt. It glowed pink in the red light. She slid light fingers across the pattern of hair flat against thick muscle and drew a circle around his dark nipples.

"Me, too," he said, skimming the strap of her sundress down her shoulder and setting kisses along the tendon at the base of her neck. "I didn't know happiness like this was possible. That it was as simple as opening my heart, loving and allowing myself to be loved. You humble me, being brave enough to teach me that."

This was supposed to be a playful quickie, but his words and the tenderness in his touch were turning it into something far more profound.

"This is what I wanted the day we made love the first time. I wanted to know the man you didn't show to anyone else. Thank you for trusting yourself to me." She held his head in her hands, gazed on the handsome face that she read so easily these days. She pressed her mouth to his.

He took over, gently ravaging in a way that was hungry and passionate and reverent. She responded the way she always did, helplessly and without reserve. She trusted herself to him, too, and it was worth that risk. Their intimacy went beyond the right to open his belt or slide a hand beneath her skirt. His touch was possessive and greedy, but caring and knowing. Hers wasn't hesitant or daring, but confident and welcomed with a growl of appreciation.

He slowed and gazed into her eyes, not because

he sensed she needed it, but because, like her, he sensed the magnitude of the moment wrapping around them. Their love would grow over time, but it was real and fixed and imprinted into their souls now. Irrevocable. Unshakable.

They moved in concert, sliding free of the rest of their clothes, losing her panties to a dark corner, drawing close again and *there*. He filled her in a smooth joining that set hot tears of joy to dampen her lashes.

"I love you," she whispered, clinging her arms and legs around him. "I love when we're like this. This is everything."

"Mi amor," he murmured. "You're my heart. My life. Be mine, always."

They moved in the muted struggle of soul mates trying to break the limits of the physical world and become one. For a time, as they moved with synchronicity, mouths sealed and hands chasing shivers across each other's skin, they were nearly there. The rapture held them in a world where only the other existed, where the culmination was a small death to be eluded before the ecstasy of heaven swallowed them whole. Golden light bathed them as they held that delicious shudder of simultaneous orgasm.

Slowly it faded and they drifted back to the earthly world. Poppy came back to awareness of the hard surface where her backside was balanced, the leather of Rico's belt chafing her inner thigh. One bared breast was pressed to his damp chest, his heart still knocking against the swell. His breathing was as unsteady as hers, his arms folded tightly across her back, securing her in her precarious position. She nuzzled her nose in his neck and licked lightly at the salty taste near his Adam's apple.

Within her, he pulsed a final time. She clenched in response.

"I may have a small fetish for the scent of vinegar and sulfur for the rest of my life," he teased, nuzzling her hair. "That was incredible."

She suspected they might have a small something else after this, but she didn't say it. It was only a feeling. An instinct. A premonition she didn't want to jinx.

It proved true a few weeks later.

"Really?" Rico demanded with cautious joy. "It's absolutely confirmed? Because—"

"I know," she assured him, understanding why he was being so careful about getting attached to the idea. She had been wary to believe it, too, despite missing a cycle and having a home test show positive. "But the doctor said yes. I'm pregnant."

He said something under his breath that might have been a curse or a murmur of thanks to a higher power. When he drew her into his embrace, she discovered he was shaking. She felt his chest swell as he consciously took a slow, regulated breath and let it out.

"You're happy?" she guessed, grinning ear to ear, eyes wet as she twined her arms around his waist.

"I want to tell the whole world."

"Most people don't tell anyone until after twelve weeks."

"Can I tell Lily?"

That cracked her up. "Sure. Go ahead."

After a frown of concentration, Lily grabbed a doll by the hair and offered it to Poppy. "Baby."

"Pretty much how I expect my mother to react," Rico drawled. "But at least you and I know what an important occasion this is. Where should we go on our babymoon?"

"I was thinking exotic Saskatchewan?"

"To see your Gran? Excellent idea. But first, come here." He drew her into his lap and kissed her. "I love you."

"I love you, too."

They kissed again and might have let it get a lot steamier, but Lily stuck an arm into the cuddle and said, "Me."

"Yes, I love you, too. Come on." Rico scooped her onto Poppy's lap and kissed the top of his daughter's head. "I don't know where we'll put the new baby, but we'll find room."

EPILOGUE

One year later...

POPPY WATCHED RICO carefully set their infant son in her grandmother's welcoming arms while Poppy's heart swelled so big, she thought it would burst.

"Sé gentil," Lily cautioned her great-grandmother with wide eyes.

"English, button," Rico reminded her, skimming his hand over the rippling red-gold waves. He called Lily button and angel and he called Poppy flash and treasure and keeper of my heart.

"Be gentle," Lily repeated in the near whisper they'd been coaching her to use when her little brother was sleeping. She was two and a half and talking a blue streak in two different languages, sneaking in a little Valencian and the Swiss nanny's French here and there.

"I will be very gentle, my darling," Gran said with a beaming smile and damp eyes. "Will you stand here beside my chair while your mama takes our picture?"

Rico stepped out of the frame, waited while Poppy snapped, then took the camera so she would have a few of her with her grandmother and the children. She didn't let herself wonder how many more chances she would get for photos like this, only embraced that she still had the opportunity today.

"He's beautiful," Gran said, tracing her aged fingertip across the sleep-clenched fist of Guillermo, named for her husband, William. "And heavy," she added ruefully.

"He is," Poppy agreed, gathering up Memo, as Lily was already calling him. Poppy kissed his warm, plump cheek. "Two kilos more than Brenna—that's Sorcha and Cesar's little girl. She's only a couple of weeks younger."

"Brenna is, is, is—" Lily hurried to interject with important information, but hit a wall with her vocabulary.

"Your cousin, sweetheart."

"My cousin," she informed Gran.

"You're very lucky, aren't you? To have a little brother and cousins, too."

"Mateo is bossy."

"Mateo might express similar opinions about his cousin," Rico said with dry amusement, waving Poppy to sit on one end of Gran's small sofa.

He took the other and patted his knee for Lily to come into his lap.

Lily relaxed into his chest, head tilted to blink adoringly at her daddy. "Can I see Mateo?"

"In a few days. We're visiting Gran and then we're going camping. Remember?" Poppy said.

"And buy Mateo a toy," Lily recalled.

"That's right. Before we go home, we'll buy toys for him and Enrique."

"And Brenna?"

"And Brenna," Poppy agreed.

"You were so homesick when you first went to Spain. Now look how happy you are." Eleanor reached out her hand to Rico. He took it in his own. "Thank you for making her smile like this."

"Thank *you*." He secured Lily on his lap as he leaned across to kiss Gran's pale knuckles. "We still have a room in Spain for you," he told her for the millionth time. "It's very warm there."

"I'm too old for migrating around the world like a sea turtle," she dismissed with a wave of her hand. "I have my sister and my friends here. But you're sweet to keep asking."

They stayed through the dinner hour so Gran could show off her great-grandchildren and handsome grandson-in-law.

"Poppy is becoming famous for her photography," Gran made a point of announcing over dessert. "There was a bidding war at the auction."

"It was for charity," Poppy said, blushing and downplaying it. "Rico's brother was being nice, topping each bid."

"Don't be modest. That's not what happened at all," Rico chided. "Cesar was incensed that people kept trying to outbid him. My sister-in-law wanted it and he wanted her to have it."

"It was so silly," Poppy said, still blushing. "I could have printed her another."

"They wanted the only one and now they have it," Rico said. The negative had been signed and mounted into the frame. "Poppy has an agent and is filling out her portfolio. We expect she'll have her first show next year. We're heading north in the morning, hoping to catch the aurora borealis."

The whole table said, "Ooh."

The next night, they were ensconced in a resort that billed itself as one of the best places for viewing the northern lights. Their children were abed, the nanny reading a book by the fire and Poppy and Rico were tramping through the trees to a lake that reflected the stars and the sky.

The world was still and monochromatic under the moonlight, the air crisp with the coming fall. They stood holding hands a long moment, absorbing the silence.

"Well, Gramps," Poppy murmured. "We haven't heard from you in ages. Care to say hello?"

Nothing.

"I vote we pass the time by necking," Rico said.

"I always have time for that," Poppy agreed, going into his arms.

His lips were almost touching hers when she sensed something and opened her eyes. She began to laugh.

"There he is."

Rico looked above them and couldn't dismiss the appearance with science. Like love, it was inexplicable, beautiful magic.

* * * * *

The Vows He Must Keep
Amanda Cinelli

Amanda Cinelli was born into a large Irish Italian family and raised in the leafy green suburbs of County Dublin, Ireland. After dabbling in a few different career paths, she finally found her calling as an author after winning an online writing competiton with her first finished novel. With three small daughters at home, she usually spends her days doing school runs, changing diapers and writing romance. She still considers herself unbelievably lucky to be able to call this her day job.

DEDICATION

For Keith, the hero of my own love story.

CHAPTER ONE

VALERIO MARCHESI AWOKE to the thunder of his own heartbeat, his senses taking in the complete darkness that surrounded him and the feeling of cold sweat on his skin. It was not the first time he had awoken in a state of panic in the past six months. His physician had called it post-traumatic stress, and like countless others had sympathised with him for his ordeal. He didn't want their damn sympathy.

Gritting his teeth, he fought through the fog left by the entire bottle of whisky he had downed the night before and reminded himself why he'd completely sworn off drinking in recent months. As he came fully to consciousness and tried to sit up, he became instantly aware of two things.

One, judging by the soft clearing of a throat nearby, he was not alone in the room. And two, he couldn't move his upper body because he had been tied to his own bed.

Any remaining effect of the alcohol in his system instantly evaporated. The room was dark, but he could just about make out the blurry outline of his luxury yacht's master cabin around him. Both of his wrists had been tied to the ornate wooden headboard on either side of his head, using what felt like soft fabric. He tested the bonds, black panic snaking up his back like wildfire, followed by the swift kick of fury.

He would die before he allowed this to happen again.

'Good, you're awake.'

A female voice cut across the shadows.

'I was just debating if I should throw some water over your head.'

The woman's voice silenced his growls momentarily as his brain scrambled to differentiate between the danger of his past and in the present moment. Drawing on some recent meditative practice, he inhaled deeply past the adrenaline, focusing his mind to a fine point. The woman's voice sounded familiar, but Valerio couldn't quite place it other than to note that it was English, upper class, and deathly calm. Nothing like the rough-hewn criminals from his memories, but one never knew.

'What the hell is going on here?' he demanded gruffly. 'Show your face.'

Heels tapped across the wooden floor, the dim light from the curtain-covered windows throwing her shape into relief. She was tall, for a woman, and had the kind of exaggerated full-figured curves that made his spine snap to attention. A knot of awareness tightened in his abdomen, catching him completely by surprise. At thirty-three years of age, he'd believed himself long past the kind of embarrassing loss of control usually attributed to youth. But it seemed he hadn't been around a woman in so long, apparently *anyone* was going to ignite his starving libido. Even someone who was possibly attempting to hold him hostage.

It was a strange kind of twist, considering his most recent brush with captivity had been the catalyst for his self-imposed isolation from society. Had his broken mind moved on to finding some kind of thrill in the possibility of danger?

He pulled at the headboard once again, a sharp hiss escaping his lips at the burn of the fabric on his skin. The sheet that only partially covered his nude body slipped further down the bed.

'You're only going to hurt yourself by struggling.'

'Well, then, cut these damn ropes off,' he growled, trying and failing to keep the edge from his voice. 'I don't keep money here, if that's what you are after.'

A soft laugh sounded out, closer this time. 'I'm not here to rob you, Marchesi. The ropes are for my own safety, considering the night we've just had.'

'Your safety...?' He tried and failed to process her words, feeling the tug of a memory in his mind.

He knew that voice.

Soft hands brushed against his skin as the woman gently adjusted the sheet over his body. Another shiver of awareness heated him from the inside out. It had been so damn long...and her familiar scent was all around him, tugging at those memories. He breathed her in greedily, feeling the warm blend of sweetness and musk penetrate his chest, melting some of the ice that seemed permanently lodged inside.

A soft lamp was flicked on beside the bed without warning, the sudden golden light making him wince with pain. The woman came into focus slowly, a watercolour of long ebony curls and flawless dark caramel skin. Recognition hit him with a sudden jolt, his eyes narrowing, and all anxiety was suddenly replaced by swift, unbridled anger.

'Dani.'

'Only my friends get to call me that, Marchesi.'

Daniela Avelar narrowed her eyes, pulling a chair closer to the bed and lowering herself down elegantly, as though sitting down to afternoon tea.

'You made it clear the last time I saw you that you are *not* my friend.'

Guilt hit him in the gut even as he fought to remain outraged. Memories assailed him of the last time they had spoken. Six months ago he had delivered the most painful speech of his life, marking the death of his business partner at a memorial ceremony. His best friend. Her twin brother.

Duarte Avelar had been shot dead right in front of him, after they'd both been taken hostage after an event in Rio de Janeiro and kept at gunpoint for two weeks, deep in the slums of the city. The story had made global news. He'd been lamented as a hero for surviving. He alone knew the truth of what had happened.

He had forced himself to hold it together throughout his friend's memorial service on a rainy morn-

ing in the English countryside. He had tried to speak
words that would honour the sacrifice Duarte had
made to save his life. But eventually he'd lost his grip
on control and had torn out of the church as if the
fires of hell had been at his heels, needing to get away
from all the sympathetic stares and unbearable grief.

But Dani had run after him, standing in front of the
door of his chauffeur-driven car. Daniela Avelar—a
woman who prided herself on being one of the best PR
and marketing strategists in the business, and who had
always seemed to look down her nose at him and his
wild playboy lifestyle. She was a woman who never
asked anyone for help, not even her own brother, but
she had begged him to stay. She'd held on to his arm
and begged him to tell her the truth of what had happened in Brazil…to let her help him.

He had scraped together enough composure to
growl at her, telling her that knowing wouldn't make
anything different. That it wouldn't bring Duarte back.
Then he had got into his car and driven away, pretending not to be affected by the sight of the tears streaming down her cheeks.

Shame was a familiar lead weight in his solar plexus
even now.

In the lamplit room, Daniela crossed her legs, drawing his attention to the spindly-heeled shoes on her
feet. She had been working for Velamar as their PR
strategist for years, so he was used to her trademark
pinstriped trousers and perfectly pressed blouses, with
their delicate ribbons tied at the throat. But on this
cream-coloured confection the collar was undone, the

ribbons hanging limp and creased as though someone had grabbed them and held them tight in their grip.

She looked tired, though she was trying hard not to let it show. But he could see the faint dark shadows under her eyes, the tightness around her mouth. He wondered if grief had stolen her perfect polished image and grace, just as it had stolen his carefree nonchalance.

'Do you have any idea how long I've been trying to find you?' She met his eyes without fear or hesitation—an easy feat considering she had him half naked and trussed to a bed.

'I'll admit that of all the ways you could have got my attention this is quite creative, if not a little insensitive.' He spoke easily, pulling at the bonds and feeling them slide slightly to one side. The knots were strong, but not strong enough. She might be about to inherit part-ownership of Velamar—one of the most exclusive yacht charter companies in the world—but she was no sailor.

Valerio ignored the pull in his chest at the thought of the brand he had built from the ground up, the work that had once given him purpose and pride. 'Did you ever think that maybe I didn't want to be found?'

'You walked away from your responsibilities, Marchesi.'

'My company is in good hands.'

'*Our* company is in brilliant hands—considering I've been running it alone for six months.'

She sat and surveyed him like a queen on her throne,

which was not inaccurate considering the Avelar family name was practically royalty in their native Brazil.

'But your employees don't respond to my own particular brand of authority, it seems. They're practically begging for the return of their playboy CEO and his infamous parties.'

'Final warning. Untie me and get the hell off my yacht, Daniela.'

'You don't remember anything about last night, do you?' She raised one brow, watching him with curiosity and the faintest ghost of a smile.

Valerio looked around the room once more, the pain in his head sharpening. The last thing he remembered was storming out of his brother's sprawling villa in Tuscany after an embarrassing display of temper and popping open the first alcoholic beverage he could find. He'd drunk alone and brooded silently in the back of his chauffeur-driven car the entire way to where his yacht had been moored in nearby Genoa.

He'd always known that yesterday would be a difficult day, considering he'd avoided his family for so long, but he'd thought he'd done enough work on himself to get through a couple of hours in their company. He had expected pity and tiptoeing around him. He hadn't been prepared for their anger. Their judgement. They didn't know anything about what he'd gone through…what he'd done. All they cared about was the precious Marchesi image and the worrying rumours that he'd gone insane.

His rages were unpredictable, and tended to fog his memory, so he didn't remember much. But he was pretty sure he had smashed a few of his brother's expensive vases on his way out.

Wincing, he tried to sit up more fully against the wooden headboard, only managing a couple of inches before he inhaled sharply against the sudden throb of pain that assaulted his cranium. What had been in that whisky?

'Don't move too fast. The doctor gave you a mild sedative.'

'You *drugged* me?'

'You tried to take on my entire security team one by one. You were in some kind of a trance. We couldn't…' She swallowed hard. 'You weren't yourself.'

Growling, he pulled hard against the bonds once more. A satisfying creak sounded from the wooden beam above him. He saw the first glimmer of unease flicker in her eyes.

'This was the only way I could think of to make you listen.' She stood up, her eyes darting to the door at the opposite side of the room. 'I didn't mean for it to go this far… I didn't think you were as out of control as your brother said.'

'You spoke to Rigo?' His brother—the damn idiot. He had promised Valerio that if he accepted the invitation he would keep his appearance in Tuscany to himself. But then, Valerio hadn't planned on causing such a scene. Once again, he'd lived up to his reputation of being the reckless wild-card Marchesi brother.

The shame burned his gut.

Daniela cleared her throat. 'Look, I've been patient. I've given you more than enough time, considering what happened, but now it's time for you to come back. The board members are not happy with my choices as acting CEO. There's a motion in place to sell off my brother's design projects and pull out of a large chunk of our charity commitments, and I'm the only one blocking their way.' She pinched the bridge of her nose, a deep sigh escaping her chest. 'This kind of unrest is bad news. With the pressure of the new *Sirinetta* launch coming up, I just don't have time for it.'

Her words rang in his mind, fuelling his anger and disbelief. Nettuno Design was Duarte's brainchild—an offshoot of the Velamar brand—and the maritime engineering firm had created the very first *Sirinetta* mega-yacht. It was the yacht that had launched their modest luxury yacht charter firm right up into the upper echelons of society five years ago. It had been the catalyst that had brought them in contact with figures of royalty and power across the globe, and wealth beyond their dreams.

'So you decided to kidnap me to tell me this?'

She narrowed her eyes on him with barely restrained irritation. 'A second meeting is being held the day after tomorrow in Monte Carlo, with more board members flying in. I have information that they are planning to vote me out.' She took a deep breath, meeting his eyes. 'I need your help. I need you to get over whatever this is and come back.'

'I know it's not technically official, but *I* named you acting CEO in place of both me and Duarte,' he gritted out, his friend's name sounding wooden and unfamiliar in his mouth. 'They can't vote you out. They're bluffing.'

'Considering Duarte is about to be declared legally dead, and what with all the recent rumours in the press about your mental instability... I'm afraid they can.'

Valerio froze, the news sending his blood cold.

Duarte's official death certificate had not been issued—he'd made sure of it. As executor of the estate, he'd specifically given the authorities more time before Daniela could legally inherit all her brother's assets.

And now she dared to barge on to *his* yacht and calmly make demands while she was sitting on a bombshell of this magnitude? *Dio*, she had no idea what this meant.

Oblivious, she continued. 'Apart from the fact that our reputation is being pulled under the proverbial bus...they know I'm not qualified. I mean, to be honest, I know it too. I'm a PR strategist—not a leader or a figurehead. I've never done this before.'

'Let me free,' he growled.

'Not until you agree to come to the meeting.'

She folded her arms under her breasts, the movement pushing up her ample cleavage and making the blood roar in his ears.

'Daniela... I'm warning you. You have no idea what's going on here, so let me off this bed right now.'

'I'm quite aware of what's going on in my own company. *You're* the one who's been MIA for months on end, and I can't risk you disappearing on me again.' She closed her eyes briefly, opening them to lock on his with intent. 'I don't care if you hate me for this. I will do whatever it takes to save my brother's legacy.'

She claimed that *he* was the only one who could save the company? The man she had once called a frivolous playboy? She had no idea what he had been uncovering over the past six months. Hell, he wasn't even sure *he* knew.

What he did know was that she wasn't the only one who was prepared to do whatever it took to save something. But the person he'd been trying to save seemed intent on putting herself in danger, again and again.

Anger gave him an extra spurt of energy, and the last knot that bound his wrists slipped free.

Like a coiled spring, Valerio launched himself off the bed.

Dani felt a shocked scream rise in her throat but she refused to let it free—refused to believe that this man whom she had known for almost half of her thirty-one years on the earth would ever actually harm her.

But this was not the Valerio she had watched from afar—the playboy reprobate who'd bedded half the socialites in Europe and charmed everyone he met with his pirate's smile and his wild thirst for adventure. It was as though any trace of light in his deep blue eyes had been snuffed out.

Before she had a chance to run, he had grabbed her by the wrists to stop her. He pulled her to face him but she shoved him back, the movement accidentally sending them both tumbling down onto the bed, with her body landing directly on top of his.

Large hands moved to grip her waist and she inhaled sharply at the feel of his skin as it seemed to burn through the fabric of her shirt. She shifted position, trying to stand, but her movements somehow only served to press her even harder against him.

'*Dio*, stay still,' he cursed, his voice sounding strangled and raw.

It seemed a lifetime ago that Dani had fantasised about exactly this kind of situation. Her foolish teenage self had once dreamed of having Valerio Marchesi look at *her* the way she had seen him look at a parade of beauties, while she'd watched awkwardly from the sidelines. But he had long ago made it clear that there was no way he would ever look at her as anything but his best friend's chubby, boring, know-it-all twin sister. The annoying third wheel to their perfect partnership.

No, there was nothing sexual that she could see in the barely controlled fury glittering in his eyes now, as he stared up at her. He seemed to inhale deeply as her hair fell over her shoulder, forming a cocoon of ebony curls around them. His hands flexed just underneath her ribcage, his eyes lowering to where the buttons on her blouse had come undone, revealing the far too large breasts threatening to spill over the plain white lace of her sensible bra. And still his hands tightened, holding her still and stopping her retreat.

'Let go of me. What do you think you're doing?'

She was furious, her knees moving directly towards the part of him where she could cause the most damage. Not that she *wanted* to hurt him, but he was being completely unreasonable—and she refused to accept that she had lost the upper hand now, after all her careful planning, simply because he had more brute strength.

He easily controlled her, pinning her legs with his own and pulling her arms directly above her head.

'What do *I* think I'm doing?' He repeated her question, a harsh bark of laughter erupting from his chest as he grabbed both her wrists and tied them to the headboard he had just freed himself from. 'I believe there is an English expression... Turnabout is fair play?'

Dani was breathing heavily with the exertion of trying to fight him. She didn't see his plan until she was already tied in place. Disbelief turned quickly to anger as she tried and failed to pull herself free.

'Thrashing around like that really isn't going to help either of us. Especially considering our position and my lack of clothing.'

Dani became completely still, looking down to where their bodies were melded together. Her legs in the dark wool of her designer trousers were wrapped around the bare skin of his torso. She felt her cheeks heat up, perspiration beading on the back of her neck. He said he was unaffected, and yet just a moment ago she had moved her hips and she could have sworn she'd felt...

Suddenly he moved. With an impressive flex of

muscle, he slid his large body out from underneath her with surprising ease, gently laying her down on the pillows before moving out of her vision.

'I understand that you have some anger towards me…' His voice sounded husky, and he was slightly out of breath from his exertions in freeing himself. 'But, whatever this game was tonight, know that it was out of line.'

'I'm not playing a game. I told you that I had to have you restrained for your own safety and mine. You were threatening to kill your own bodyguard, for goodness' sake, and we couldn't snap you out of it.'

She tried to lift her head to look at him, but on seeing a flash of tall, naked male, she returned her head to the pillows with a thump.

'Maybe so. But you're trying to manipulate me. To force my hand. Maybe in the past I might have seen the humour in all this…but I am not that man any more.'

'Where are you going?' she asked innocently, remembering that while she might have temporarily lost the upper hand in this battle, she was far from losing the war.

'I am going to walk out of here and leave you to think about your actions for a while.'

He flicked on the full lights in the room and she watched as he walked towards the doorway, then suddenly stood still. Her body tensed in the long silence, and she imagined the look on his face as he realised his mistake. Because they were not on his luxury yacht in Genoa. They weren't even on Italian soil.

He let out a dark curse in Italian and Dani felt an unruly smile threaten at the corner of her lips. She listened as his footsteps boomed across the luxury wooden floor of the cabin and out into the hallway.

He might not remember the events of last night but she did—with painful clarity. She remembered having Valerio's own personal bodyguard help her carry his boss onto the brand-new, not officially launched *Sirinetta II* mega-yacht that she'd commandeered, and then sending the man on a fool's errand to the doctor in town so that she could order the captain to sail off into the night.

She waited for Valerio to return, realising that it was impossible even to attempt to look ladylike while she was sprawled face-down on a bed, her arms pinned at an awkward upwards angle as they were.

'Where the *hell* have you brought me?'

His voice suddenly boomed from the other side of the room and the door of the cabin banged open on its hinges, making her jump.

'Back so soon? I've had barely four minutes of my time out. Hardly enough time to think about my actions.'

He came to a stop beside the bed. Dani turned her head on the pillow and allowed her eyes to travel up his impressive form. Mercifully he had donned the clothing she had grabbed from his yacht's cabin during their swift exit. The dark blue jeans fitted him perfectly and the plain black T-shirt was like a second skin, moulding to his impressive biceps. The rumours of his mental state were yet to be confirmed, but he certainly hadn't stopped working on his infamous abs since he'd gone into exile, that was for sure. If anything, he'd kicked it up a notch.

'I'd say we're cruising somewhere near Corsica.' She met his intense gaze without showing her unease. 'I decided to multitask and give you a tour of the new model while we discussed our approach for this meeting. And before you get any ideas, the wheelhouse is locked down and the captain has been ordered to refuse entry without my passcode. Company policy.'

'You…' He took a step away, pinching the bridge of his nose. 'You had me drugged and loaded onto one of my own company's yachts. And then you turned my own crew against me?'

'*Our* crew.' She smiled sweetly. 'You forget that I've got quite familiar with all the staff in our employ over the past six months, *partner.*'

'Order them back to land. Now.'

He leaned over her, one hand braced on the headboard beside her. His breath fanned her ear, sending gooseflesh down her neck. Evidently being tied up and ordered about was something her inner self got a dark thrill out of, regardless of the fact that the man giving those orders was a selfish bastard who had abandoned her when she'd needed him most.

No, she corrected herself, he had abandoned *his company*. The company that *she* was going to inherit half of once her brother's estate was released, as well as countless other assets and properties—thanks to his death. And that was without the inheritance she'd already got after their parents' accidental deaths seven years before.

If she had still been the praying kind, she would have thought that someone somewhere up above had really taken a dislike to the Avelar family. But she no longer believed in anything but cold hard facts, and right now keeping her brother's prized Nettuno Design a part of the company was what she needed to focus on.

Valerio and Duarte had had countless other investments, but they had spent twelve years building Velamar from the ground up. Was he just going to sit back and allow his work to be poached by the vultures? Not on *her* watch.

'You can leave me tied up here as long as you like. I won't make the order.' She flexed her fingers, feeling a slight numbness creeping in from her position.

'Dani—'

'I told you not to call me that,' she snapped. 'Use my proper name. You and I are business partners now and nothing more.'

'Do business partners usually tie each other up naked and watch from the shadows?'

'I wasn't watching you.' She bristled, hating the way that her skin immediately turned to gooseflesh at his words and hating the sinfully erotic image they created. She closed her eyes, praying he couldn't see. That he didn't notice the ridiculous effect he still had on her, no matter how much she'd believed she'd got past it.

'It's pretty clear that you were sitting there in the

dark, waiting for me to wake up. What were you thinking about all that time, Daniela? The company? Or was there a small part of you that enjoyed having me at your mercy?'

He crouched low, sliding a lock of hair from her face, and waited until she met his gaze. Dani swallowed hard, fighting the urge to lick her suddenly dry lips.

'You shouldn't have followed me. You could have just emailed me the details of the meeting. But you didn't trust me to show up, did you? Bastard that I am...' He let his fingers trail along her face, smoothing her hair behind her ear. 'You found me and saw me at my worst. The runaway playboy, the raging madman in the flesh. Tell me that you didn't relish the opportunity to punish me, to ensure I didn't have an easy escape. Tell me you didn't enjoy it, Daniela.'

She bit her lower lip, knowing that he was just playing a game. Trying to make her uncomfortable enough to make her order the yacht back to land and let him cut his responsibilities all over again.

She turned her face, opening her eyes to meet his directly and summoning all the strength she had. 'There is nothing enjoyable about watching you give up and walk away from everything you've worked so hard to achieve,' she said boldly. 'You could have died in Rio too, but you didn't. I thought that might have made you see life as more precious than you did before, that you might take things more seriously. But you've just been running away, pretending that nothing's happened.'

Valerio's hand dropped as though she had burned

him. In a way, she supposed she had. Guilt momentarily pulled at her subconscious, but she pushed it away, knowing that she was doing what she needed to do. Lucky for her, she knew exactly what to say to keep Valerio Marchesi at a distance in order to protect herself. She always had. But right now she needed him on her side more than she needed him to get away from her.

She felt his hands on hers as he silently loosened the ropes at her wrists. She worked herself free as quickly as she could, noting that his knots were skilled. He had been a sailor practically from birth, after all. The blood rushed quickly back into her hands as she sat up, rubbing at her wrists, and saw that he had moved to the other side of the room. He stood completely still, looking out of the window to the blackness beyond. There was no moon tonight— nothing to light their way in the night. Only dark clouds and the subtle sheen of the waves that surrounded them.

'I know all too well how precious life is, Daniela. If you think I've been running away, then you really don't know me at all.' Valerio's voice was cold and distant, bleak. 'If you think that I could ever hope to forget what happened… If you think I haven't gone over and over every single second…' He shook his head as he turned to face her, and a look of complete darkness seemed to cast a shadow over him.

Dani felt emotion burn her throat. She wished she could take her words back but knew it was done. Since Valerio had left her alone at Duarte's funeral all those months ago, she had been filled with a rage of her own. *He* had been the one to return from their trip alive after weeks of being presumed dead. *He* had been the one to refuse to tell her the full details of what had happened, only revealing that Duarte had been killed shortly before Valerio had escaped.

Her twin had been murdered and she'd had no idea. There had been no sudden shift in the cosmos, no supernatural feeling of loss or pain. Instead she had felt nothing. And that feeling of disconnected numbness had continued for the past six months as she had thrown herself into keeping the company running smoothly.

'I'm sorry. I didn't mean to be so harsh.' She breathed past the emotion in her throat, wishing she'd chosen her words more carefully. 'But it doesn't help that I don't know anything about what happened other than—'

'It doesn't matter.' He cut across her, pure steel in his voice. 'I'll be there at the meeting. I'll say whatever you want me to say.'

'You will?' She paused, struggling to make sense of his sudden shift from outraged to passive. Yes, her words had been harsh, but...

'I will come to Monte Carlo with you because it's what Duarte would want.' He took a step forward. 'But in return I need you to do something for me.'

'You're giving *me* terms?' She tilted her head. 'I should have known there would be a catch.'

He folded his arms across his chest in a pose filled with dominance and attitude, but his voice quavered slightly as he spoke. 'I have one condition, yes, and I need you to trust me that it's necessary and non-negotiable.'

'Is this a security thing?' She took in the tension in his posture, the way his fists were pulled tight by his sides. 'I have taken on board all the terms you laid down with that crazy security team before you disappeared. I never go anywhere without their protection.'

'You think I haven't been checking in over the past six months?' He shook his head, his voice deepening with some unknown emotion. 'I may not have been here, but I didn't run away. I need you to understand that. There were things I had to do before I could…' He frowned, turning slightly to look out across the murky water through the window. When he began speaking again, his voice was deeper. 'When we realised things were going to end badly in Rio…I made a promise to him that if I survived I would keep you safe.'

Dani felt a lump in her throat, but pushed it away, reminding herself that getting emotional would only put her in a vulnerable position. He wanted her to trust him? Valerio hadn't even tried to keep whatever promises he'd made—he had blocked her out and walked away at his earliest convenience, preferring to process his grief alone. Or more likely in the company of expensive whisky and a string of beautiful women across the globe.

She had learned the hard way that she could only rely on herself. Folding her arms tightly across her chest, she didn't bother to hide the ice that crept into her voice. 'Just outline your terms, Marchesi.'

His jaw flexed menacingly, and a hardness entered his gaze as they stood toe to toe in the darkness of the master cabin. When he finally spoke, the huskiness was gone from his voice and had been replaced by a hint of that sultry charm she remembered.

'The board believe that Velamar is weakened because of my absence…that I am unreliable and unstable. If you want my presence to be of any benefit, then we need to show them a better angle. If I get off this yacht tomorrow, my only term is that you stay by my side. That we stand together as a couple.'

'Of course. I'm the PR guru here. I can find a good spin for all this, if that's what you're worried about.'

She frowned at his use of the word 'couple'—a strange expression for their partnership. Still, she forced a smile, hardly believing the upward turn this venture had taken. An hour ago she had been terrified of what he might do after her actions tonight. She had taken a risk, forcing his hand this way. For now, she was happy to have him firmly on the side of the company and getting his mind back into the game.

'I presumed you would be more averse to the idea of us being together.' Valerio raised one dark brow, shrugging a shoulder as he moved to open the door. 'It's settled, then. We will announce our engagement first thing in the morning.'

CHAPTER TWO

VALERIO MOVED AWAY from Daniela's frozen form and walked quickly down the hallway. A part of him longed to turn around and reveal the full truth of their situation—the real reason he had promised to keep her safe, the truth behind his disappearance from society and the reason it needed to be this way. He had told himself he was biding his time, gathering all his facts. He hadn't expected the imminent issue of Duarte's death certificate to completely force his hand this way.

He focused on some deep and steady breaths as he emerged into the open-plan living space of the yacht's accommodation deck.

He remembered attending the initial meetings for the *Sirinetta II* just before they'd left on their trip to South America. It had been one of Duarte's most innovative design projects yet. His senses felt over-loaded by the bright and airy interior, with its open-plan spaces and natural blond wood design. He knew from memory that the endless smooth surfaces were an illusion, and in fact filled with discreet touch cabinets and modern technological gadgets.

'What did you just say?'

Daniela's voice had risen an entire octave, and her flashing amber eyes filled with disbelief as he looked over his shoulder.

Her cheeks were flushed with the warmth of the force of her anger at his proposal. Well, technically he hadn't proposed so much as *declared* their engagement... He winced inwardly. Probably not the best way he could have done things.

Turning away from her, he touched a panel and grabbed a bottle of water from one of the discreet built-in fridges that slid out from behind the wood. 'We can make the announcement in the morning papers if you get on it now. You are the PR guru, as you said. I assume you have contacts who can word it to make it all appear as romantic as possible.'

'Valerio, we are *business* partners—our alliance is solid enough without turning it into some kind of media circus.'

'Did you or did you not say that rumours surrounding my disappearance from the public eye have cast doubt on my stability?'

'I—I am experienced with appeasing doubt.' She stammered a little over her words. 'It's been my job to control Velamar's public image for the past seven years and I'm quite good at it without resorting to outright lies and...and pageantry!'

'My terms are that we release the news that we are engaged. That is non-negotiable.'

He took a long drink of water, trying to shake off the feeling of adrenaline still running riot in his veins. He was always like this after a bad night—he felt on edge for days. But now, knowing that someone had pushed to have Duarte declared legally dead even when he had made every effort to hold it off... He had to act now. He had to be ready.

Dani was silent for a long time, a frown marring her brow as she shook her head slowly from side to side. 'I don't buy it. What aren't you telling me?'

Valerio walked out onto the open-air deck, gritting his teeth at the sound of her heels as she instantly followed him. Of *course* she wouldn't just meekly accept his terms and move forward; this was Dani, after all.

He closed his eyes and inhaled a deep breath of cold sea air into his lungs. He wasn't ready for this— for any of it. He needed to get off this yacht and find some breathing room while he built himself up to step back into his old life. Daniela thought she knew everything he had been doing for the past six months. Yes, he was broken, but not in the way that she thought. Despite public opinion, he was far from losing his mind. He had never had a more single-minded focus.

But that focus was entirely set on revenge.

'Valerio...' She appeared at his side, her expression a mixture of confusion and concern. 'Talk to me. Please.'

She believed him to be mad... Let her think that. Maybe then he would be able to shield her from the true monster he had become. Before all this he had been a good man. He might even have deserved a woman like her. Not that he had ever truly considered having her. He had always known she was off-limits to him. His friendship with Duarte had been worth more to him than any pleasure he might have got from pursuing any inconvenient attraction he may or may not have had. She was and would always be his best friend's sister.

Untouchable.

Now he was just the man who had let her down in so many ways. He'd known that she disliked him before, but now that he'd abandoned her to run Velamar for months without explanation... It was his own fault if she hated him, and perhaps that was a blessing in disguise. The man who stood beside her right now was nothing but darkness and regret. If hating him would keep her safe from getting too close, he'd bear every moment of the burn from her wrath.

He turned away from her, bracing his hands on the railing and looking down at the inky foam of the midnight waves as they crashed along the side of the yacht.

'You made your demands, Daniela. Now I have made mine. I'm willing to forgive your actions tonight so long as you agree to my terms without any further questioning.'

'Your terms being the immediate announcement of a fake engagement?' She was incredulous, her chest rising and falling with outrage.

'Not just an engagement.' He turned to face her, noticing once again how much warmth her eyes held.

He could almost feel the heat emanating from her, along with that intoxicating scent she wore. The galloping of his heart seemed to slow when he considered the deep golden-brown depths of her eyes.

'You will be my wife.'

As he spoke the words and saw the shock turn to anger in her eyes, he felt a strange calm settle within him. He had known for six months that it might come to this. He had known that she would fight him every step of the way. And now, seeing her ablaze with fury and outrage, he thought maybe she would withstand the burden of being tied to him. He had to believe that. He had no other choice.

Dani stood frozen, her mouth refusing to form words, as Valerio took a step forward.

'A long time ago Duarte told me to keep the hell away from you unless I planned to marry you.' Valerio shook his head, looking out at the darkness that surrounded them. 'I doubt he ever thought things would come to this.'

'This is ridiculous.'

Dani turned and walked inside, needing to move away from him. He had no idea what he was saying. How hurtful it was on so many levels. Even when she'd moved back to London and become engaged to another man, she'd fought not to let herself think of him. She growled in her throat, marching into the living area and reaching for her laptop—only for a large male hand to close over hers, stopping her.

'Valerio, stop. Let me show you my plans and we can discuss this rationally.'

'Your brother knew the kind of guy I am. He knew the perfect way to ensure I would never touch you.'

'You never *wanted* to touch me!' She practically growled it. She felt heat rise into her cheeks at her own words…at the hint of years of hidden feelings under the surface.

He opened his mouth as if to speak, then paused. For a moment there was nothing but weighted silence between them and the sound of the waves outside the open door.

Valerio cleared his throat, waited until she met his eyes. 'The day before Duarte was killed, we planned an escape. He told me that if anything happened to him and I survived, I was to keep you close. To give you my name and protect you.'

'I don't need a husband for protection. That is *my* choice. Not his.'

Dani fought against the lump of emotion that tightened in her throat at the thought of her brother instructing his best friend to care for her. He must have known that she would never agree to this kind of archaic showing of duty, or whatever it was.

Valerio turned away briefly, pushing his hands through his hair. 'I swore to him. I promised that I would follow his wishes. And I spent the last six months…'

Dani looked up at him, seeing a strange look in his eyes. 'You spent six months…what? Trying to find a way out of it? *That's* what it was all about?'

'No…you don't understand.'

'I think I understand far more than you do, Marchesi.' She picked up a small bag from under the desk and threw it onto the low sofa between them. 'I'm done here. I apologise for wasting your time tonight. Believe when I say I wish I hadn't bothered. The code for the wheelhouse is in that bag, along with your mobile phone. Order the Captain to take you wherever you need, so long as you're off this yacht by morning.'

'This won't just disappear because you order me away. I'm coming to Monte Carlo. You say you need me for this board meeting, so I'll be there.'

'I'll find another way. I always do.' She fought to keep her voice level, to hide her hurt and anger under the professional veil she wore so well. 'Pretend tonight never happened. Consider yourself officially relieved of your duties to Velamar. To me. All of them.'

She didn't wait for his response before she walked away, not stopping to take a breath until she had her cabin door firmly closed between them and she was sure that he hadn't followed her.

Then she closed her eyes tight and sank back against the door, allowing herself a single moment to feel the blinding pain of knowing how little Valerio Marchesi had ever cared about her.

'I can't believe you didn't take a photograph. I'd pay good money to see either one of the Marchesi brothers all tied up.' Hermione Hall waggled her brows seductively from across the terrace table of their favourite little Monte Carlo café.

Dani rolled her eyes, playing with the remains of her omelette as she struggled with the knot that had formed in her stomach and had refused to shift since the night before. Her best friend of eighteen years usually always knew just how to pull her out of a dark mood, but her night with Valerio had shattered all the careful control she had worked so hard to achieve over the past few months. She felt completely off balance.

Hermione was no stranger to difficult situations, being the child of an infamous Los Angeles talent agent who had stolen money from half of Hollywood. They'd met as teenagers, on their first day at boarding school in England, when Hermione had stepped in to defend Dani from a group of name-calling older girls. Together they'd become untouchable, unrepentant overachievers all the way through college, supporting one another through the loss of parents, bad relationships and sanity.

Now that Hermione was one of the most in-demand personal stylists in Europe, they didn't get to see one another very often, but their emails were long and never short on salacious details.

Hermione called over a waiter and ordered a caramel-drizzled waffle from the extravagant dessert menu, declaring it a celebration after hearing Dani's heavily edited version of the events of the night before.

Dani shook her head. 'You're completely overlooking the part where he just assumed he could announce our engagement. Along with the rest of his little speech about keeping me safe by *marrying* me. I mean…who even *thinks* like that? Apparently "safe" is just another word for "away from my own sources of power and independence".'

'I don't know… Daniela Marchesi has got a nice ring to it.' Hermione smirked.

'You're taking far too much enjoyment from my outrage.'

'Sorry—a drop-dead gorgeous Italian, whom you used to have a gigantic crush on, is now back to run his own company, which might allow *you* to finally get back on track with starting your own PR firm.' She took a sip of her tea, her tone dry. 'Oh, and he apparently wants to marry you too. How utterly *terrible* all this is.'

Dani looked away from her friend, ignoring the tension in her body as she remembered that her own consulting work had come to a standstill since she'd taken the helm at Velamar. No one knew that she had signed a lease on an office in London just weeks before the awful news from Rio—that she'd finally been poised to quit her job at Velamar and launch her own firm.

But, truthfully, it had been easier to cancel all her plans and throw herself into the heavy workload that had come with being a stand-in CEO. There was less time to think, less time to feel…

Hermione continued to chatter, trying to lighten the mood in her usual way. 'With those eyes and that insane body…I wouldn't turn down *any* kind of dark and brooding proposal from Valerio Marchesi—that's all I'm saying.'

'I'm sorry that I don't share your love of dramatic romance. And I get it that he's a little paranoid since… since everything that happened in Rio. But I'm not in danger. This isn't Regency England and I am not on the market for a protector.'

She frowned as her phone buzzed with an email notification from the head of the Velamar events team.

Subject: You might be interested in this.

The email showed the guest list for the modest cocktail party she had planned for some select guests to get a sneak preview of the *Sirinetta II* later that evening. Dani frowned, her eyes scanning down the list with increasing disbelief.

A shocked huff of laughter escaped her lips. It seemed that Mr Hotshot CEO had decided to dive right back into work.

The numbers for the 'small and intimate' gathering had now tripled, and contained the names of some of the wealthiest people in Monaco, including philanthropists, celebrities and even a few members of European royalty. It was no secret that the Marchesi family had connections, but seriously…

The arrogance of the man! For him to just march over and amend details of an event that *she* had planned and executed without even asking…

The curse words that escaped her lips were very

unladylike, sending even wild-mannered Hermione's eyebrows upwards.

'He believes he can just reappear and completely railroad an event that I've been planning for weeks! I bet he doesn't even think he's done anything wrong.'

She stabbed her index finger at the phone screen, beginning to type an email to inform her team that she didn't need to see the guest list, as she wouldn't be attending. Let the returned 'Playboy Pirate' explain her absence to his guests—let him try to make the same kind of connections and collaborations that she did at such events. He thought he could just swoop in and do everything? She would leave him to it.

Hermione interrupted her thoughts, bending to look at the email over her shoulder and letting out a low whistle. 'That's a lot of prime potential new clientele. What are you going to wear?'

'I won't go.' Dani bit her bottom lip. 'If he refuses to treat me like an equal partner in this company, then I don't see why I should jump to host this event by his side.'

'Correction, you *will* go. Because you *are* an equal partner in the company and a professional one at that. You'll go and you will tell him exactly where he can stick his proposal. Along with giving him a clear outline of the kind of treatment you will be expecting from now on.' Hermione opened up her small tablet computer and began clicking rapidly. 'I've got the perfect dress I've been saving for you—you just need to get the perfect date. And before you ask, I already have plans tonight.'

Dani knew her friend was right. The problem was that Valerio would also know that she couldn't *not* attend, and that grated on her nerves. 'If I do go, I won't need a date. I was the one to plan the thing originally, so I'm technically the hostess.'

Hermione had a familiar glimmer of mischief in her eyes. 'You don't *need* one…but imagine what kind of statement it would make for you to walk into that party with the one man that Valerio Marchesi truly despises by your side.'

'You don't mean…?' Dani felt her eyes widen as she let out a puff of shocked laughter. 'I couldn't bring *him*. It would cause a riot. Besides, it's pretty late notice…'

'You think Tristan Falco isn't going to jump at the chance to gatecrash that party?'

Dani frowned, knowing her friend was right.

'You want to put Marchesi in his place, don't you?' Hermione waggled her brows. 'Time for you to introduce the ace up your sleeve. Show him that you're not playing nice. You make the call—I'll go and assemble my wonder team. That man has no idea who he's messing with.'

Hermione dropped a quick kiss on her cheek and breezed away, leaving Dani staring down at her phone, which was still open on the guest list.

She walked to the railing of the restaurant's terrace, looking out at the pink and orange clouds painted along the sky… The sun would start setting soon— she didn't have the luxury of waiting around. If she was going to put up a fight, she had to go to this event.

Tomorrow she would come up with a new angle and figure out how to save Nettuno from being sold off. As for tonight...

She opened her phone and scrolled down to the name of a man she had never thought she would call again. A smile touched the corner of her lips as the number rang and a deep male voice answered. Within moments she had confirmed her scandalous date for the evening, silently marvelling at Hermione's evil genius.

It seemed that Cinderella *would* attend the ball after all, but she would not be waving the proverbial white flag and dancing with Prince Charming.

Tonight she would make Valerio Marchesi realise just how wrong he had been to underestimate her.

The paparazzi were gathered eagerly around the gates of Valerio's luxurious Monte Carlo villa, waiting for the first public photograph of the Playboy Pirate's return and an exclusive opportunity to see what had become of their tragic hero.

Valerio had planned to give them their show—to depart in his usual extravagant style, driving one of his prized sports cars. But at the last moment he had chosen to have his bodyguard drive one of the Jeeps, instructing him to exit the rear gate so that he could slip past the cameras.

He had told himself that he was adding to the mystery—that he was playing up to the media circus and fanning the flames of gossip. It was all good publicity, after all. He was building up to a grand return on his own terms. But the reality was that he had stopped himself from booking the first flight out of Monaco at least three times since walking off the yacht into the dawn light that morning. If it hadn't been for the threat to Dani, he'd have gone. But he knew he had to be here—knew he had to ensure her complete safety.

He had stood in the marina, looking up at the now unfamiliar city that had once been one of his many playgrounds, and he had felt like an impostor. He was playing the part of Valerio Marchesi, but he had no interest in that life any more.

It all seemed so hollow now, as he looked back at the way he had lived. He had gone from one extreme to the next, proving himself in daring sailing challenges, throwing the wildest parties and seducing the most beautiful women. Life had just been one big adventure after another, with nothing ever big enough to satiate his appetite for more. Until everything had suddenly become tasteless and the thought of sailing or seducing had seemed just a waste of energy better spent on his investigations.

His old life seemed like a distant memory—like the life of a stranger. But if he was no longer that version of himself...he had no idea *who* he was...

When he arrived at the party, his first priority was to ensure that Velamar's private marina was securely locked down. The elite security team he had hired six months ago had been expertly trained by the best in the business and they knew exactly where they needed to be. He stepped onto the main entertaining deck of the massive yacht to see that some of the guests had already arrived. A small swing band had set up on a small platform, and the intrusive bouncing melody of the music provided a perfect background for a night that would likely be filled with uncomfortable conversations and questions about his time away.

For the first time in months he wished he could down a few drinks as he was approached by several acquaintances all at once. But he'd long ago learned that drinking only made him feel worse. He needed to be in control of his senses, of his mind.

The party filled out quickly, and soon enough the entire room was watching him, the curiosity in their gazes mixed with the familiar sympathy he'd come to expect in the days immediately after his rescue. Hushed conversations began, ensuring that anyone who was *not* aware of the events that had put the scars on Valerio Marchesi's face and the growling darkness in his eyes was soon informed.

He had never lacked confidence about his looks—he knew that even despite the minor scarring and his leg injury he was still attractive enough. Some women would probably find it thrilling, seeing such a dramatic reminder of his fight for survival. They would build it into the fantasy of him as a rugged adventurer, like in the stories the media had loved to spread. But having so many eyes on him was a stark reminder of everything he would never outrun.

He would always be the scarred hero to them—someone both to pity and admire. None of them knew the truth of what had happened. None of them had lived through it.

But now was not the time to show weakness—not when he had important work to do. Being born a Marchesi meant he had been introduced to instant fame and pressure even before he could walk. He had chosen a different path from the family business, but he still used the lessons he had learned from his father every day. *When you feel weak, walk tall and look them in the eye.* So he met each set of curious eyes without hesitation, ignoring any mention of his absence and filling each conversation with talk of the latest yacht they planned to launch.

'Ah, here comes Daniela.' One of the members of the Velamar board craned her neck to look past him. 'Good grief—is that Tristan Falco on her arm?'

Every set of eyes in the small group around him snapped towards the steps at the opposite end of the long entertaining deck.

She wouldn't… Surely she would have the sense not to…

After seeing a series of nervous furtive glances towards him, Valerio gritted his jaw and turned to see for himself.

CHAPTER THREE

TIME SEEMED TO come to a standstill as his eyes sought Dani across the crowd. She was shaking hands with one of the politicians he'd invited, the wide smile on her ruby-red lips a world away from the indignant anger he'd last seen on her face.

He was powerless to look away, and the tightness inside his chest loosened as he watched her tilt her head back and laugh. She didn't even have to try to be the perfect hostess—it just came naturally.

As he looked on, the crowd tightened and gathered around her, vying for her attention. And even if he hadn't already been treading a fine line with his control, seeing Tristan Falco by her side had him fighting the insane urge to growl.

There wasn't a single person on this yacht who didn't know of his long-standing rivalry with the heir to the Falco diamond fortune. He shook his head, biting his lower lip to stop himself from laughing at such a deliberate power-play. Clever, infuriating woman. For some reason she was trying to provoke him…

As though she'd heard him, the object of his

thoughts met his gaze across the sea of guests. Almost in slow motion, she raised her champagne glass in a toast, an unmistakable smirk on her full lips.

Schooling his own expression to one of mild interest, he raised his own in response and began to move slowly across the deck towards her. He could see her eyes shifting towards him at regular intervals as he got closer, her hand moving first to push an errant curl behind her ear, then to touch the delicate necklace at her throat.

He noticed that she had trapped her ebony curls high on her head, only letting a few hang free. It was impossible not to see how the style accentuated the long, bare expanse of her neck and shoulders, but likely that had been her aim. She was a confident woman—surely she knew how her appearance captivated the crowd around her.

He didn't know much about fashion, but he knew that she had chosen perfectly in the emerald-green concoction encasing her curves. He felt his throat turn dry as the shimmering material moved, revealing a modest slit up to the smooth skin of one thigh. Reflexively, he forced his gaze back to her face. She seemed to sparkle in the light as she moved away from the small crowd around her, taking a few steps in his direction to close the final gap between them.

'My compliments on your stellar work today, Mr CEO,' she said tightly, her charming smile still firmly in place as she waved politely at a couple of guests who passed them.

'I assumed you wouldn't mind my input on this

event's inadequate guest list, seeing as you were so eager to have me back.' He fought the urge to smirk as her eyes sparked fire at him.

She took a delicate sip of her champagne, giving him an icy glare over the rim. 'If you had given me your input *before* making your sweeping changes, you might have found out that there was a strategic, brand-specific reason for my tiny guest list.'

'If you'd answered any of my calls today, maybe I could have done that.'

'Well, maybe I was too busy recovering from your ridiculous...*proposal*.' She lowered her voice to a hiss, her eyes darting around as she uttered the last word as though it were some kind of demonic chant.

Valerio couldn't help it then—he chuckled under his breath. There was absolutely nothing funny about any part of their situation, but some long-buried part of him was really enjoying this verbal sparring.

It had always been like this between them—from the first time they'd met as teenagers, when she'd come to watch Duarte in a sailing competition at their all-boys boarding school. Even when she'd joined Velamar he'd used to start fights with her at events just to draw out this...*fire*. At one point he'd started to wonder if she was avoiding him, and that had only made him try harder to provoke her—before Duarte had mistaken his playful jabs at her as interest and moved the entire PR and marketing division to their London offices. He'd said it wasn't because of that, but Valerio had known better.

The terse silence between them was broken by

the arrival of a wide-smiling Tristan Falco at Dani's elbow. 'Marchesi, you seem to have forgotten my invitation tonight. Luckily your partner was in need of a fine male escort.'

'I wasn't aware that you were in town.' Valerio extended his hand to the other man, not missing the way Dani's eyes widened with surprise. 'I've never had the chance to thank you since the last time we spoke.'

A serious look came across the other man's features. 'It was nothing. I hope you took my advice.'

Valerio exhaled on a sigh, reflexively crossing his arms over his chest as he nodded brusquely. 'I did.'

'Am I missing something here?'

Dani's voice was hard as stone between them. Her hand was on her hip, her eyes narrowed as she looked from one man to the other. Tristan was the first to speak, sliding his arm over her shoulders and pulling her in close.

'It's a private matter between us guys.' He smiled in his trademark way. 'I met up with Marchesi a couple months back while I was in Rio.'

'Rio?' Dani fired that amber gaze Valerio's way briefly, then turned back and fluttered her lashes up at Tristan. 'How lovely. What did you guys get up to in lovely Rio?'

Valerio tensed, hoping Falco would have the good sense to stop talking. Despite his invaluable help, the man was still a thorn in his side. Even looking at him now, with his big meaty arm slung over Dani's shoulders, it made him want to throw a punch in his pretty-boy face and launch him bodily off the yacht.

After a long, painful silence it seemed Dani had realised that neither of them planned to elaborate further on the matter. But she didn't fire off another smart retort. Instead Valerio watched as a brief glimmer of hurt flashed in her eyes. Her lips thinned for a moment and she made a big display of looking around the party. Then she smiled—a glorious movement of red-painted lips and perfect teeth that seemed to hit him squarely in the chest.

'Excuse me, gentlemen… Some of us have work to do tonight.'

Valerio was powerless to do anything but watch as she retreated in the direction of the bar, stopping here and there to greet her guests cheerfully, as though nothing had happened at all. He cleared his throat, turning back to see Falco pointedly raising one eyebrow.

'Why do I feel like I'm interrupting something?' the other man drawled.

'Just a professional disagreement.' Valerio cleared his throat and took a long sip from his glass. 'None of your concern. Also, she's off-limits to you.'

'Professional?' Tristan Falco laughed. 'Right…and that's why you looked like you wanted to throw me overboard when you saw her with me.'

'There's still time if you don't stop talking,' Valerio said, gritting his teeth.

Falco raised both hands in mock surrender, leaning back against the wall to survey the crowd in his usual calculated way.

Valerio tried to ignore the pang of guilt in his gut.

He hadn't wanted Dani to find out that he'd been back
to Brazil at all. And he certainly hadn't wanted her
to find out like that.

She didn't know anything of the past six months of
his life because he'd been trying to protect her from
the worry that would come with the knowledge that
he was still actively pursuing the men who had taken
him and Duarte in Rio. That he had been knee-deep
in a dangerous criminal underworld of corrupt poli-
tics and blackmail as he tried to piece together the
events that had led to his best friend's death.

It had been pure chance that Tristan Falco had
been in Rio at the same time. He'd saved Valerio from
being arrested, drunk and ranting, after another lead
had turned out to be useless.

The other man had cleaned him up and offered him
some solid advice. *No more booze. Hire profession-
als to do the digging.* He'd also put Valerio in contact with a discreet and highly qualified clinician to
help with the psychological aspects of his recovery.
And he'd shared some of his contacts to help Valerio
dig into the backgrounds of some of the men he suspected of involvement. The diamond heir had become
an unlikely ally in his fight for justice.

Valerio took the first opportunity to move away
in search of his unhappy business partner. He had
made his peace with Falco, but that didn't mean he
was suddenly able to tolerate his company for longer
than necessary.

He moved through the crowd, hating how uneasy
and wooden he felt when he stopped to converse

with his guests. His smile felt too tight, his shoulders heavy. The old Valerio would have been in his element here, not counting down the minutes until it would be acceptable for him to slip away.

This conflict with Daniela had got under his skin. Clearly she was annoyed by his actions today—which, honestly, he'd expected. He hadn't planned to triple her guest list, but it added to his mission to draw attention to his social standing and good connections. An unstable CEO would hardly host a party for all of Monaco's elite, would he? Plus, he'd been frustrated at her reaction to his proposal. He felt an urgency to his plans now and he needed her to stop fighting him.

The trouble was, he didn't want to reveal the full truth of her situation and scare her away. He had planned to find a balance tonight, to give her just enough incentive to co-operate and accept his proposal. She was no fainting little miss, that was for sure—especially considering she had quite literally kidnapped him to ensure she got him to Monte Carlo.

But his plans for tonight had not involved having her completely furious with him. He needed her by his side. It was the only way he could keep her safe.

Discomfort had him running a finger along the rim of his collar, fighting the urge to rip off his tie and open a few buttons. He had chosen the open decks of the yacht deliberately, knowing that confined spaces were one of his triggers. But it seemed that even having the entire night sky above him was not enough to stop the familiar tingle of hyper-awareness from creeping up his spine. Every loud bark of laughter and clink of glassware brought a shot of tension painful enough to have him gritting his teeth.

A movement on the opposite side of the sea terrace caught his eye. One of Daniela's security men, conferring with the rest of the team with a worried look on his face. Valerio moved forward, the tension mounting in his gut like a furnace.

One brief exchange of words with the men was enough to confirm his worst fear.

She was missing.

Dani had moved away from the crowd initially just needing a moment to herself. That moment had turned into a quarter of an hour as she'd wandered through the yacht in search of privacy. Finally she'd emerged onto an open sea-view terrace at the stern, breathing a sigh of relief to find it empty but cursing herself for not grabbing another glass of champagne or some canapés. She hadn't eaten a lot after her brunch with Hermione, and already she could feel the buzz of alcohol in her head. She'd always been a lightweight.

From their current position, she could see the lights of Monte Carlo twinkling like fiery diamonds above the water. She could see the glow of the iconic Monaco Naval Museum and the Grimaldi Forum in the distance. Such beauty would usually bring her a sense of calm, but nothing seemed able to rid her of the restless feeling that had plagued her all day.

Her late entrance to the party had been calculated to ensure the maximum effect of the majestic, glittering emerald gown Hermione had provided. Its designer was a new hot name on the Paris runway, his trademark exclusive material a blissfully comfortable stretch velvet that had actual diamond fragments threaded throughout.

The piece was heaven for the more curvaceous women of the world, like her. It moulded to her body like a second skin and flared out slightly just below her knees in a delicate flounce. And the *pièce de résistance* to complement her perfect ensemble was the man she'd had on her arm.

What on earth had she been thinking, bringing Tristan Falco? Everyone else on the yacht had watched that ridiculous display of thoroughly masculine camaraderie between him and Valerio with a mixture of appreciation and curiosity. She had heard whispers—one person wondering if this finally meant a partnership of the two brands was in the works… another dreamily wishing that *she* could be in the middle of the two hunks.

Dani didn't know what bothered her more: all those women drooling over the two men or the fact that most of the guests would attribute any future partnership between Falco Diamonds and Velamar to Valerio's presumed genius.

Dani had been approached by Tristan numerous times in the past few months about a possible collaboration between their two brands. It was no secret that Valerio had firmly declined his numerous offers in the past, even though it made perfect business sense for the two to join forces, considering the strong history already present between Falco Diamonds and the other members of the wealthy Marchesi family.

The soft clearing of a throat brought her back to the moment. She turned, expecting to see that Valerio had followed her, but instead she was met with the sight of a thin man with a shock of salt-and-pepper hair that seemed vaguely familiar. There was a kind of meanness in the smile he gave her, and a shrewdness in the way he scanned the empty deck area with a seeming lack of interest.

'*Boa noite*, Senhorita Avelar.'

His voice was reedy, as though he smoked twenty cigarettes a day. A few steps closer and the odour that drifted off his expensive suit confirmed her theory. She held her breath as the man leaned forward to place the customary kiss on her right cheek.

'Angelus Fiero—I'm an old friend of your father's and a silent member of the board.' He smiled, extending a flute of champagne towards her. 'I hope you don't mind me following you?'

She accepted the glass, pasting a polite smile on her face and ignoring the shiver of unease in her spine. He took a seat directly across from her on a low cushioned bench that bordered the delicate curved rail of the deck.

'You seem to be taking your job as CEO very seriously. I have heard of your divine talent. Ruling with an iron fist and a perfect smile. Turning things from rotten wood into finely polished oak,' he said cryptically, with a strange glimmer in his eyes. 'Tell me…

is it a new company protocol to bypass a direct order from the executor of someone's will?'

Dani paused, the champagne flute inches from her lips.

'I'd bet Marchesi has no idea that *you* were the one to apply for Duarte's death certificate, has he?'

Dani initially fought the urge to shout that Valerio was not her keeper. But then her logical brain processed the man's words and she didn't speak, her mind utterly frozen in confusion. Who *was* this man, with his all too knowing eyes and his knowledge of top-secret information?

There was no proof that she'd been the one to file the request for Duarte's death certificate—she'd used a notary and the company name as a group entity. Not that she'd been planning to keep it a secret—not until Valerio's furious reaction, anyway. She'd planned to tell him eventually.

She couldn't really explain her urge to have the limbo of her brother's death put into legal black and white. It had been an intolerable hum of sadness and a slow bubble of frustration—like an itch under her skin that she couldn't scratch. She'd known she couldn't wait around for Valerio to return and decide to accept that Duarte's death was a reality.

But now, on this dark, secluded part of the yacht, a part of her became suddenly painfully aware of the fact that she had put herself in a vulnerable position, out here alone without any of her security team.

Fiero stood up, taking a few steps to close the gap between them. Dani fought the urge to stand and run, taking note of his distance from her and feeling the weight of the empty champagne glass in her hands. She was alone, but she was not incapable of self-defence. She straightened her shoulders, meeting his gaze with what she hoped was a perfectly calm expression.

'I came here tonight to give you a warning. If you value your life, stop digging into things that don't concern you.'

Dani inhaled sharply at the threat, watching as the older man turned to walk away.

His route was suddenly barred by the arrival of three security guards in the doorway and a thunder-faced Valerio, who took one look at Daniela's ashen face and immediately cornered their guest.

'Marchesi.' Fiero spoke calmly, placing a ciga-rette between his lips and lighting it. 'Nice to see you again. Is there some sort of problem?'

'I don't know yet.' Valerio looked the man up and down, his fists clenched at his sides. 'Daniela?'

Valerio said her name softly, but with a stern under-tone that had her snapping out of the daze she was in. 'Everything is fine,' she heard herself say. 'Let him go.'

She was vaguely aware of Valerio ordering the se-curity men to escort Fiero back to the party and keep a close eye on the man. He waited until they were alone on the deck, then took a few steps towards her, crossing his arms in that way he did when he was in-tensely annoyed by something.

It amazed her that she could still tell his mood just by observing his body language, considering how little they had seen one another in the past few years. She was lucky he couldn't do the same with her, or he'd know just how absolutely terrified she felt. A shiver ran down her spine as she looked up at the thunderous expression on his face.

'Disappearing alone without protection—have you lost your mind?'

'We're on a yacht.' She rolled her eyes. 'Also, I'm a grown woman, Valerio. Not a child for you to keep track of and scold,'

'Even a child would know not to risk its own safety by wandering off alone into the darkness.'

He blocked her path when she tried to move away, placing one hand on her arm.

'Why did you come out here, Dani? What could Angelus Fiero possibly have to say to you?'

Her mind kept replaying those words over and over on a loop.

'If you value your life.'

'If you value your life.'

She felt the heat of Valerio's hand on her arm, sinking into her skin like a brand. She tried to draw on her anger at him for disappearing, for leaving her to run Velamar alone while she tried to hide her own grief. She shouldn't feel this urge to fall into the safety of him when he had done nothing but give orders and trample on her work in all his six-foot-four and ridiculously handsome glory.

He had kept his newfound peace with Tristan Falco from her, and his apparent trip to Rio, and God only knew what else. He made her utterly furious.

She tried to remember all the reasons she might throw at him for why she had walked out…other than the fact that she'd needed to get away from him and the way he made her feel completely off balance. But now, with his simple touch burning against her arm, she was powerless even to control the erratic beating of her own stupid heart.

He frowned down at his hand on her arm, dropping it away as though he hadn't realised he was touching her.

'He was just expressing his condolences in person for our loss. He couldn't come to the memorial service.' Dani felt the lies fall easily from her lips, guilt pressing at her conscience as she turned and began walking back through the yacht towards the faint strains of the string quartet and the sound of laughter.

'Stop running from me. I need to speak with you alone.' He easily moved around her in the darkened study and blocked her way. 'You arrived here tonight with that womanising fool on your arm without any thought other than angering me.'

'Why would I care what you think, Valerio? You clearly don't do the same for me.'

'You don't see a slight problem with bringing a date to your *fiancé's* event?'

Dani froze in disbelief, the word 'fiancé' coming from his lips sending her blood pressure into overdrive. The man had lost his mind entirely.

'Again this ridiculous promise you made? Valerio… I've already made it quite clear what I think about your proposal. It's completely unnecessary.'

She took a step backwards, needing to put physical space between them. No one made her quite as angry as he did. No one else could manage to get under her skin and surpass her control.

'I'm not some damsel in distress who needs your protection. Until this morning I was acting CEO of the company we share equal ownership of. I've been at the helm of Velamar for six months while I gave you the time you needed to recover.'

'I don't think you're a damsel in distress. You are the strongest woman I've ever met. I just need you to trust me that we need to do this.'

'It doesn't make sense. I wouldn't let Duarte make this choice for me if he were alive. And I won't be accepting it from you, either.'

'This isn't about how capable you are. This is about your safety.'

Suddenly her anger fell away and she looked at him. Took in the tension around his mouth, the shadows in his eyes. She remembered his reaction when she'd told him that Duarte was soon to be declared legally dead. She had seen something entirely different then. He hadn't just been angry… He'd been afraid. For *her*. And then her mind replayed the look on his face as he'd arrived just now with the three guards in tow, asking her if there was a problem.

'Look…I haven't been truthful about what I've been doing for the past six months. You thought I was in hiding while I recovered and I let you believe that because it's partially true. I have been isolated and angry and dealing with…with what happened.

Tristan Falco witnessed my own methods of dealing with it first-hand and gave me some good advice.'

'No more lies and avoidance. Tell me the truth. Why do you need me to agree to this so badly?' As she asked the question, her legs felt weak, and an odd twisting sensation started up in her stomach.

He smoothed a hand down his face, closing his eyes for a long moment as though fortifying himself.

'Duarte knew that he was in danger when he went to Rio alone. He didn't expect me to follow him. All I know is that he was being blackmailed. I couldn't get a full picture of who was behind it or what had gone down before I arrived and everything went to hell, but I do know that he was trying to neutralise an imminent threat…to you both.'

Dani felt the breath completely leave her chest as she sat down on a nearby chair, looking up at him with disbelief. 'If I'm in danger… If they've already got Duarte…'

'Daniela, look at me.' He knelt down, gripping her chin between his fingers and forcing her to meet his eyes. 'I won't let anyone hurt you. I've spent months trying to find another way to help because I knew you would hate this. The only thing I'm sure of is that it has to do with part of your inheritance. The land and properties in Brazil.'

'They can have it—I never wanted any of it.' She breathed in, feeling her pulse careening out of control. This was insanity—utter madness. She'd give everything away…every single cent. Nothing was worth the loss she'd endured. *Nothing*.

'I thought of that.' Valerio spoke softly, as though he feared he had fully tipped her over the edge. 'But it's complicated. We're talking about decades of your parents' work in creating affordable housing there. Tens of thousands of innocent tenants who stand to be displaced. Acres of protected land being put at risk.'

Tens of thousands... Dani closed her eyes and felt a tremor within her.

Her father had been an only child, sole heir to the wealthiest, most corrupt landowner in Brazil. When his old man had died, her *papai* had been newly married to his very liberal-minded English wife. Together they had wasted no time in setting out on a crusade to turn the majority of their expensive, undeveloped inner-city land into rent-controlled housing initiatives for disadvantaged families. It had been revolutionary, and it had angered a lot of wealthy developers by the time they'd started on the city of Rio.

'Dani...' Valerio said. 'As a married couple, we can create an iron-clad prenuptial agreement that ties all your assets to mine. We need to make them untouchable, so that there's no valid reason for anyone to target you. My family name, the legal power it holds... It's like a fortress. Duarte knew that. He'd planned for it if his efforts didn't succeed.'

Dani shuddered, the reality of her situation settling like a frost on her skin. She and her brother had been targeted for something they had no control over. She had never asked to be born into this life... She hadn't asked for her entire family to be taken away from her in a matter of years.

She felt her throat contract painfully as she tried to force breath in and out.

'Do you understand now why it needs to be this way?' he said softly, coming round to look into her eyes. 'I need you to stop fighting me on this. I need you to put your trust in me and let me keep you safe.'

She couldn't meet his eyes. This was all far too much to handle without the effect he had on her added to the mix too.

She simply nodded once. 'I'll do it.'

'I'm sorry I couldn't find another way.'

She tried not to wince at his words. Tried not to imagine his horror when he'd realised he was going to have to shackle himself in matrimony to a woman he could barely tolerate. A woman he seemed to actively avoid even though they'd been working for the same company for years.

'You don't need to pretend that this is what you want. It is what it is, Valerio.' She stood up, smoothing down her dress in an effort to compose herself even as her voice shook. 'We need to get back to the party or they'll start talking about us... Although I suppose I'm going to have to get used to that if I'm about to marry you.'

Something glittered in his eyes as she said those words. Whether it was relief or dread, she didn't take the time to find out. She needed to get away from the strange intimacy of being here in the darkness with him. Back to the safety of the party, to networking, putting on a show.

'You will have to get used to a lot of things.' His gaze drifted away, his jaw tightening. 'We both will.'

Dani smiled tightly, turning and walking along the corridor, then up the stairs to the entertaining deck. She heard him following silently behind her, but didn't pause until they were safely on the sidelines of the dance floor, where the music made it slightly harder to hear him without leaning in.

'I'm making our announcement here…tonight.'

His voice travelled slowly across the din of music and voices, and Dani frowned, his meaning taking a moment to sink in. Her eyes widened as he moved to step away, and her fingers clutched at the sleeve of his jacket to stop him.

'If you're talking about what I think you are…'

He moved close, dipping his head to speak close to her ear. 'We are on a superyacht, filled with the most famous people in Europe. If we want news of our engagement to travel fast, then there's no time like the present.'

Dani shook her head, hardly believing what a turn the evening had taken. 'Okay…but there's no need for it to be a big deal. It doesn't have to be a spectacle.'

'You know it does.'

He smiled, and for a moment she got a glimpse of his old self. Mischievous and eager to cause a stir.

'I'm going to make sure the whole world knows you are about to become my wife.'

CHAPTER FOUR

'Oh, God…' Dani breathed, staring up into the azure blue depths of his eyes and praying that she could maintain her composure. She looked around at the beautiful people surrounding them, oblivious to the fact that her entire world had shifted on its axis. 'We can just make the announcement tomorrow somewhere…please.'

'This needs to be convincing, Daniela.'

His voice was gravelly and low in her ear, making her skin prickle. She knew he was right. This was the kind of guest list, with the kind of publicity reach, that could undo every single bit of questionable press Velamar had got in the past six months. It was the perfect way to take control of the media narrative while also taking steps to secure her safety. She tried not to imagine the backlash—the sniped remarks about why a man like him would choose her.

She prided herself on being self-sufficient. On having walked away from her ex because he'd assumed that she would change her iron-clad life plan to fit around him. And now here she stood, contemplating entwining her life and everything she owned with the one person she had sworn never to trust again. This wild, reckless playboy had somehow become the only solid land within reach in a dangerous sea.

She shook her head, hardly believing what she was about to do. 'Okay, but…but you need to get down on one knee,' she breathed, hardly believing the words coming out of her mouth.

'Are you organising my proposal?' His eyes sparkled with mirth. 'Do you have a preference for which knee I use?'

'Be serious. Just… It's more romantic that way.'

One dark brow rose in disbelief, and for a moment she expected him to argue. But then he raised both hands in mock surrender and took a step backwards.

A single gesture to a nearby server gave a signal that he wished to grab everyone's attention. Somewhere nearby silverware was clinked gently against a glass and a lull fell over the party, the string quartet slowing their melody to a stop. Dani felt her heartbeat pound in her ears as Valerio met her eyes and then lowered his impressive frame gracefully down onto one knee.

Dani tried not to be hyper-aware of the dozens and dozens of stunned eyes and gasped breaths as everyone became glued to the tableau unfolding in their midst. It was one thing to be in business mode amongst them, but this was so far out of her comfort zone she almost felt like taking her chances overboard. Never mind her lifelong terror of swimming in the open sea—anything was preferable to feeling this exposed.

Valerio looked up at her, and for a moment, Dani

forgot to breathe. This painfully gorgeous man was every woman's dream. It was almost too much to take in the sincerity on his handsome features as he cleared his throat and reached for her hand. And she had never understood the term *fluttering* when it came to heartbeats, but there was no other way to describe the strange thrumming in her chest as Valerio gently lowered his lips and pressed a featherlight kiss against her fingers.

'This will come as a shock to many of you, but Daniela and I have been keeping a large part of our life private for a long time now.' Valerio's voice sounded huskier, his accent more pronounced, and his eyes never wavered from hers as he continued. 'Darling, I know we said we would wait, but I want to share this moment with our guests. Daniela Avelar, will you do me the honour of becoming my wife?'

Dani was painfully aware of the silence around them. She nodded, her chin bobbing up and down like a puppet on a string, forcing a wide smile and praying that she didn't look as terrified as she felt. Applause began to resound around them as their guests cheered and fawned over them.

She swallowed hard, her eyes widening as she noticed the small velvet box he had produced from his coat pocket. The ring inside was an antique canary-yellow diamond that she knew instantly would match the gold heirloom wedding band she had inherited from her mother.

She tensed at the realisation that he had come so prepared for this moment. Had he been so sure that she would agree to this madness? Suddenly, the huge guest list made even more sense.

Her hand shook against Valerio's warm skin as he slid the ring onto her third finger. It was a perfect fit.

He stood, his eyes darkening with some strange emotion as he pulled her against his hard chest and buried his face next to her ear. 'I'm going to kiss you now, Daniela. Try to pretend you're enjoying it.'

His arm tightened around her waist as his lips easily found hers. The kiss was initially just a gentle press of skin against skin. Dani tried to remain impartial to the searing heat of the large male hand on her hip and at the nape of her neck, but she shivered reflexively at the contact. He was so…*large* all around her…he somehow made her feel small.

She was being ridiculous. She needed to keep a level head here. But when the delicious scent of his cologne enveloped her, she couldn't help her own reflexive movement and she traced her tongue along the seam of his lips. It had been so long since she'd been kissed that her body seemed to jolt with electricity as a mortifying groan emanated from deep in her throat.

Valerio seemed to stiffen at the noise, and for a moment she fully expected him to move away. He would know that she wasn't just pretending. But instead he pulled her even tighter against his body, deepening the kiss and giving back just as good as he got. His movements were much more skilful than her own shy ones, and his lips and tongue moved slowly against hers in such a perfectly seductive rhythm she quickly lost the ability to think straight.

She had never been kissed this way. It was as if she'd spent her life believing she knew all there was to know about her own body and now he was just tearing everything down.

Her mind screamed at her to slow down, to stop falling for this act they were putting on, but her body flat-out refused to listen. Already she could feel herself become embarrassingly aroused, heat spreading through her like wildfire. She reached up and spread her fingers through his hair, down to the warmth of his nape under the collar of his shirt, needing to feel more of him under her fingertips.

When her nail accidentally scraped his skin, the groan that came from deep in his throat shocked her to her core. It was quite possibly the most erotic sound that she had ever heard in her life.

Of course he would choose that exact moment to rip himself away from her. His eyes were wide with a mixture of shock and anger, and he watched her for a long moment, both of them breathing heavily as they became aware of their surroundings once more.

Dani fought the urge to pull him straight back, then felt her cheeks heat with embarrassment at how quickly she'd lost control. The whole thing had probably lasted no more than a minute and yet she felt as though time had ceased to exist.

The swing band resumed their music with a loud, jazzy celebratory number, and the guests began gathering inward, everyone bustling over to give them their good wishes. Flutes of champagne were handed out and soon they were swept away on an endless stream of toasts and congratulations.

And all the while Dani was painfully aware of the man by her side, of every small touch of his hand at her back or dip of his head to speak close to her ear.

She thanked the heavens when he finally moved away to another group of people, feeling as if she was pulling air into her lungs after being underwater. It had been far too long since she'd had any contact with a member of the opposite sex, she thought. She felt as though every nerve-ending in her body had been lit up like a firework. And now the mad urge to seek him out in the crowd every few minutes plagued her consciousness. She couldn't concentrate, couldn't relax with these knots in her stomach.

A few glasses of champagne later and she was significantly less wound up, but the exhaustion of the past twenty-four hours was crashing down on her like a freight train.

The more distinguished guests disappeared once they'd docked back at the marina, leaving a younger, energetic crowd, who seemed to be only just getting started on their evening of partying.

Just as she began to wonder if anyone would notice if she slipped away to bed, she felt two warm hands slide around her waist from behind.

'I think it's time for me to take my fiancée home,' Valerio said, addressing the small gathering of remaining guests over her shoulder.

'No, I can go alone. You should stay—' She turned

towards him, gently removing his hands from their possessive grip on her hips.

He simply tightened his hold, a low chuckle coming from deep in his throat as he leaned down, his lips so close to her ear it sent another eruption of shivers down her spine.

'That's not how a newly engaged couple should behave. At least try to act like you can't wait to get me to bed,' he said quietly, and then he raised his voice to address their remaining guests. 'I believe Falco mentioned wanting to host an after-party back at his place—isn't that right?'

Tristan Falco, who had been sitting with a beautiful blonde actress, stood up, a teasing smile on his lips. 'Considering I've just put in an order for one of these wonderful vessels, I think I'll stay on board tonight—if that's all right with you?'

'Stay as long as you need.' Dani smiled. 'If you have any problems, I'll be sleeping just down—'

'She'll be unavailable because we're going home.' Valerio cut across her, one hand caressing her shoulder as he spoke. 'Please take your time and enjoy the rest of your night.'

With barely a moment to protest, Dani felt herself deftly manoeuvred away from the group and across the empty entertainment deck.

'Valerio, I'm not going home with you. For goodness' sake…all my things are here,' she finished weakly, a mixture of champagne bubbles and exhaustion weighing heavily on her brain's ability to function.

'I've already had them moved to my villa.'

She paused at the edge of the dance floor, narrowing her eyes up at him. 'I get it that I should be grateful that you're helping me. But the next time you decide to organise something that involves my active participation and *my* personal things, I'd appreciate if you clear it with me first.'

'Dani...'

He began to protest, but she'd suddenly had enough of talking for the night. She stepped around him, moving down the lamplit ramp and into the dark confines of his chauffeur-driven car before he could see how completely unravelled she'd become.

If silence was a weapon, Daniela Avelar wielded it with damning precision. Valerio had spent the entire drive from the marina to his coastal villa on edge as she faced away from him. He'd expected her outrage at his heavy-handed behaviour, but this passive silence was something he had never experienced from her. It was unnerving. They still had things to discuss about their arrangement.

Once they were safely inside the foyer, he steeled himself for a showdown—but his housekeeper appeared and offered to show her to her room. Dani practically ran up the stairs away from him before he could wish her goodnight.

He fought the urge to follow her, to force her to meet his eyes. To acknowledge him in some way. They were about to be married, for goodness' sake, and she was acting as if he was some kind of villain, trying to take away her freedom. Didn't she see that everything he'd done had been with *her* at the fore-front of his consideration?

And then there was that kiss…

He shook his head. He wasn't going to think about the kiss. They'd both known it was just a part of the act they were putting on. It wasn't *her* fault that he'd responded as he had…like a starving man with his first taste of sustenance… He'd wanted to devour her.

His body responded to the memory so powerfully that he jumped when his phone began to ring and shook him from his erotic thoughts. Looking at the number on the screen, he steeled himself for more bad news.

The call from his private investigations team took less than five minutes and told him everything he'd already suspected. Someone on the board at Velamar had applied for Duarte's death certificate without any clearance from him.

He felt a sick twist of nausea in his gut at the re-alisation that someone close to Velamar was behind all this. He remembered the look in Angelus Fiero's eyes as he'd moved away from Daniela on that dark-ened deck earlier. How pale she'd looked. He needed to share this information with her…ask her if Fiero had mentioned anything suspicious.

He thanked his housekeeper as she locked up for the night, then shrugged off his jacket and folded it over a nearby chair before climbing the stairs. To his surprise, the door to the main guest room was slightly open, a glow of golden light shining out onto the dark-ened hallway. She was still up.

He paused outside. He needed to press her further about Fiero… He had a feeling that there was something she wasn't telling him. And it had nothing to do with wanting to ask her why she had kissed him back so passionately. Or the fact that the memory of the way her fingers had slid up through his hair refused to shift from his mind.

He knocked once on the door, opening it a little more, then froze as he took in the sight before him. Dani sat fully dressed on the chaise in the corner of the room, her tablet computer glowing on her lap but her head thrown back at an angle in peaceful sleep.

Guilt assailed him; she probably hadn't got much sleep with all the dramatics the night before. She must have been exhausted and yet she hadn't complained once.

She would ache in the morning if he left her in her current position… He took a few steps closer, clearing his throat in case he startled her. 'Dani…?'

She didn't move. She looked as utterly composed in sleep as she did when she was awake—no snores escaped her lips, and even her legs were tucked perfectly to one side.

He gently tapped her shoulder, repeating her name once more. She was completely out.

Making a snap decision, he set her computer aside and lifted her from the chaise, depositing her gently on top of the bed. Her eyes drifted open, her hands moving up to touch his face.

'You kissed me tonight…' she slurred softly, eyes half closed.

'I did,' he said stiffly, removing her hands and pushing her down to the pillows so that he could pull up the bedcovers and leave.

'I usually hate kissing,' she mumbled. 'But you're really good at it.'

'You're not so bad yourself.'

'It's okay. I know I'm terrible. I'm awful at everything bedroom-related—it's a curse of some sort.' She made a sound halfway between a giggle and a hum.

Valerio froze, staring down at her as he processed her nonsensical words. 'What makes you think that?'

'My ex was very honest. Oh, wait—you're supposed to take off my dress.' She closed her eyes, raising her arms above her head. 'I can't sleep in it. Hermione will kill me.'

'I draw the line at undressing unconscious women, even to save a designer dress.'

He'd gritted his teeth at her mention of her ex, but now he sucked in a breath as her hands began pulling at the hem of the dress and moving it upwards. He averted his eyes, steeling himself against the flash of delicious caramel skin in the lamplight. A tiny squeaking sound caught his attention, and he looked back to find her trapped inside a swathe of green fabric, her hands fumbling over her head.

Of course she wore no bra.

Cursing, Valerio pushed her hands away, then gently pulled the gown the rest of the way up over her shoulders and arms. The tension in his body mounted with the effort of trying not to notice the delicious curves revealed with every pull of the fabric. He averted his eyes as much as possible, fighting the flare of heat in his solar plexus at an unavoidable glimpse of a tiny pair of lacy red knickers.

Biting his bottom lip, he quickly covered her with the bedsheet and sat back, his breath coming fast, as if he'd just run a marathon. He was not any better for that three-second sight of her naked breasts. He imagined they would spill over his palms, perfect twin globes, with dusky tips just begging to be kissed. His heartbeat thundered in his ears, a fine sheen of sweat was forming on his brow, and his blood pressure was likely rising through the roof.

But then Dani sighed, and he couldn't stop himself from looking down at her as she stretched out like a cat in sunshine. He had never seen her so still. The woman was a force of nature—always on the move. He wondered when she'd last taken a vacation, or even a day off.

He eased back, planning to slip out, but she opened her eyes again, narrowing them on him.

'I want to kiss you again.' She reached for him, her fingertips sloppily tracing the column of his throat where his shirt hung open.

'I can't tell if you're drunk from too much champagne or overtiredness.' He tried to ignore the rush of pleasure her words gave him, knowing that the sober Daniela would be mortified. 'I need to go.'

'Don't leave me.' She opened her eyes more fully, their whisky-gold depths suddenly shimmering. 'Just lie here for a little while.'

Valerio felt the air in his lungs go cold at the vulnerability in her eyes. He had only ever seen her cry once, in the entire time they had known one another.

He sat back down on the bed, taking her hand in his and pressing her fingers to his lips. 'I'll stay a moment if you promise to sleep.'

Her eyes drifted closed and she sighed, the evidence of her sadness trailing from the corner of her eyes and down her cheeks. 'Everyone always leaves...' she whispered, half asleep.

Valerio felt something deep inside him crack at the pain in her words and he reached down to wipe the moisture from her cheek. He closed his eyes, inhaling once before looking down at her sleeping form. 'I'm not going anywhere.'

He shed his shoes, wincing at the stiffness in his injured leg as he lay back on the bed alongside her sleeping form. His fiancée had revealed far more tonight than she would likely have preferred.

He thought of her words—'my ex was very honest'. His fists tightened by his sides and he resisted the urge to wake her and demand to know exactly what her idiotic English lawyer ex had said. He had never met the man, couldn't even recall his name, but he had heard enough from Duarte to know that Dani deserved more.

Still, the violence of his outrage on her behalf was enough to stop him in his tracks. But it was entirely appropriate for him to feel protective towards the woman he'd vowed to protect, wasn't it?

There had been nothing 'appropriate' about his reaction to their kiss earlier. Nothing innocent or protective in the way he'd fought the urge to haul her towards him and devour her. Claim her as his own in front of the entire party—including Tristan Falco.

But he knew that he was not the kind of man she deserved, either. She needed someone whole. Someone who didn't abandon her and keep secrets. He had always been happy to live the life of a bachelor, thinking that maybe one day he might settle down. But now he knew that day would never come.

He wasn't built for family life the way his father and brother were. The Marchesi men were known for their reliable leadership and level-headedness. Somehow Valerio seemed to have missed out on that genetic component and that had always been fine with him. He was the wild one...the joker.

Cursing under his breath, he closed his eyes and saw again Daniela's golden gaze meeting his as he slid that ring onto her finger. For that split second she hadn't looked as if she hated him quite as much.

They both knew that even if it was only a legal arrangement this marriage needed to look real. Neither of them could afford any bad press, and the distraction of their supposed romance would work in their favour. He needed to make sure she understood what that meant. He needed to know she understood that while she might deserve better, for now he was the only man she would be seen with.

Forcing himself to look away from her sleeping form, he rested his head back against the pillows. He would stay until he was sure she was asleep—surely he owed her that much?

Not for the first time since he had woken up to see her furious form twenty-four hours before, he wondered how on earth his life had become so complicated.

Dani awoke with the most painful headache of her entire life, inwardly cursing whoever had thought endless flutes of champagne was a good idea—then realised that it had, in fact, been her. She rolled over in the bed, freezing, and realised she was wearing only her underwear. Not only that—she wasn't alone in bed.

Valerio lay on his back, one arm behind his head as he slept. Fuzzy memories of him helping her to bed came to her, making her flush with embarrassment. She had practically ordered him to take her clothes off and then begged him to stay. Good grief, had she really told him about the things Kitt had said to her?

She stared at his sleeping form for a long while, noting the deep frown line between his brows and the sharp staccato of his breathing. There was nothing peaceful about the way this man slept—it was as though he were in pain. Even as she watched, he kicked out one leg at some invisible form, and a deep rumble sounded from his chest.

She sat up, clutching the covers to her bare breasts, and laid one hand on his chest. His hand shot up to grab hers so fast she jumped with fright.

It seemed one moment she was staring at him, the next he was gripping her shoulders painfully tight and pushing her onto her back. He loomed over her, caging her with his arms, and for a moment she felt a flash of unease at the zoned-out look in his eyes.

She pushed at his chest, feeling the silk of his shirt and the heat of his hard muscles under her fingers. It was like trying to shift a hulking great pillar of marble. Had he always been this physically defined? She tried to find words, only managing a tiny gasp in the tense silence.

He watched her through hooded eyes, barely controlled violence in the tension of his shoulders. But when she let out a small whimper from the force of his grip, something finally seemed to shift in his eyes, as if he had only just awoken.

'*Dannazione*…never touch me while I sleep,' he rasped.

'You…you're the one in my bed.' She pursed her lips, all too aware of her lack of clothing and the intimacy of their position. The thin sheet was the only thing covering her body from his gaze.

Her mind went back two nights, to when he'd attacked her bodyguards on his yacht in Genoa. He had been awoken from sleep then too. His eyes had been wild and unfocused, as though he had been possessed.

'Did I hurt you?' he asked quietly, his eyes scanning the bare skin of her arms as though he expected to see something terrible there.

She watched as he swept his fingers up her arms, seeing the faint red skin on her shoulders from his grip. He tucked his fingers under her chin, gently tilting her face up to look at him.

'No, you were just startled. It's fine,' she said shakily. 'I'm fine.'

His head momentarily sagged against her, his forehead pressing gently on her collarbone as he let out a long, shaky breath.

'Do you see now? This is why I stayed away for so long. Every damn time I feel like I'm getting it all under control…'

She felt every breath he took fanning gently against her skin. It was shockingly intimate.

All too soon she felt him pull away. He sat up on the side of the bed, leaving her shivering at the sudden loss of his heat. She wanted to ask him what he was talking about, if these moments of trance-like behaviour happened often. But she feared him shutting down, freezing her out again. She needed to wait for him to open up, no matter how much she craved to know what had happened to him during those awful weeks and the months that followed.

She sat up, moving beside him and fighting the urge to cover one of his large hands with her own. She couldn't stop wanting to touch him, to be near him. It was ridiculous—she was supposed to hate the man.

'Look…you don't have to tell me any details. But you didn't hurt me, okay?'

He stood up, hissing briefly as he straightened his leg. Avoiding her eyes, he set about buttoning his shirt. 'Those marks on your shoulder say otherwise.' He looked back at her, cursing under his breath. 'Don't worry. I won't let it happen again.'

Dani frowned, realising that was the opposite of

what she wanted. She had been surprised to wake up to find him in bed beside her, but it had been the kind of surprise that sent shivers down your spine, not fear. She had worried that he might be able to sense her response to having him there with her, but stopped now she saw the familiar look of detachment cover his handsome features.

She could understand him being angry, and possibly embarrassed by whatever she had witnessed, but the complete blankness that had descended over him made her grip the blanket tighter across her chest.

'You'll join me for breakfast on the terrace.' He avoided her eyes, and his words were more of a command than an invitation. 'I'll leave you to…get dressed.'

His movements were stilted, the injury in his leg more pronounced as he stalked over to the doorway and disappeared without another word.

CHAPTER FIVE

When Dani emerged from her room, she was freshly showered and dressed for the office in one of her favourite dusky pink shirts, which she'd paired with form-fitting, lightly flared dove-grey trousers. The meeting wasn't taking place until late afternoon, but she had some files to prepare and some facts to confirm. Valerio's presence was only a small part of her attack plan. She never walked into anything without considering every possible angle, and today was going to be no different.

The housekeeper showed her out to an impressive marble dining terrace, bathed in golden morning sunshine and surrounded by creeping vines full of beautiful spring wild flowers. Valerio was drinking a steaming cup of coffee and staring blankly out at the hustle of Port Hercules below in the distance. His dark brow was furrowed when he turned to acknowledge her, standing to pull out a chair. She wasn't used to such small, chivalrous gestures. It made her slightly uncomfortable. But she knew he'd been raised in Italian high society—it was likely just second nature.

She avoided his eyes, thanking his housekeeper with a wide smile when she appeared with a platter of fresh fruit and a fresh pot of water for tea before disappearing again.

'I remember you don't drink coffee.' Valerio looked across at her, his eyes slits of stormy blue under his furrowed brow. 'I've had a selection of teas ordered in. I don't know if they're any good.'

'Thank you. That was very thoughtful.'

Dani felt a glow of warmth bloom in her chest, then instinctively pushed it away, remembering that she was trying to keep her guard up. But a small part of her whispered that Valerio had never been purposely unkind to her in the past—only indifferent. It wasn't *his* fault that she'd been attracted to him. If he was trying to make a gesture of goodwill, she should accept it.

She made a show of admiring the fine bone china teapot and selected her favourite brand of English breakfast tea. They passed a few moments in companionable silence, with the buffer of the usual city sounds forming a background.

'We need to discuss our living arrangements,' he said, then waited a moment, frowning at her stunned silence. 'I'm aware that you haven't yet permanently occupied any of the homes that will form your inheritance. My villa is not the most convenient location, but it has a large study you can use for your consulting work.'

Dani felt something tighten in her throat as she looked down at the ring on her left hand. She had been so preoccupied with today's meeting she'd foolishly thought they would just brush past the fact that they were now engaged to be married.

'Valerio…we haven't even talked about the logistics of this arrangement yet and you're already saying you want me to move in here with you?'

'Yes—as soon as possible.' He looked away, his jaw tighter than steel. 'Obviously we won't share a bedroom, but living under one roof will be better for your safety as well as for keeping the appearance of a normal marriage.'

Dani marvelled at the utter madness of his words. 'We both know that there is nothing "normal" about this marriage. But from a PR point of view, I suppose I agree.' She sat back, running a finger along the filigree rim of her teacup. 'I've still got a lease on my apartment in London, but that can be easily fixed. And I won't need your study, as Velamar is my only priority for the time being.'

'Good.' He paused, meeting her eyes as he processed the end of her statement. 'Wait…you've stopped taking on any independent clients? Why would you do that?'

'It's kind of hard to be the sole leader of a global brand and still find time to fly around the world on consulting contracts with unpredictable time frames.' She squared her shoulders. 'I made a conscious choice to focus on Velamar for my own reasons.' She spoke with a clear edge to her tone. 'Just as I will continue to do so now that I'm inheriting the responsibility.'

Valerio pinched the bridge of his nose sharply.

'Dani, I didn't think through leaving you the sole responsibility of Velamar while I was gone. You have to know I would never have allowed you to sacrifice your own career in order to step in for me.'

'Well, then, it's a good thing I didn't need your permission, isn't it?' She cleared her throat, pouring more tea into her cup. 'I'm not here to discuss my career decisions. Please can we just continue with the discussion at hand?'

For a moment he looked as though he fully intended to start an argument. But then he exhaled on a low growling sigh and braced two hands on the balcony ledge. 'We will live here, then, for the time being. For obvious reasons, we will both need to remain unattached while this arrangement is in place. Will that be a problem?'

'*You're* the notorious womaniser.' She raised one brow in challenge. 'If anyone will struggle with discretion, it won't be me.'

He seemed annoyed at her comment, his eyes darkening to a storm. 'I'm not talking about my wife indulging in discreet affairs—I'm talking about you abstaining from them completely. Just as I will.'

She froze at his use of the word 'wife', baffled at the sudden intensity in his gaze and the effect it was having on the knot in her stomach.

She hadn't been trying to insult him—it was no secret that he liked to date a variety of beautiful women. He hadn't been photographed with anyone since the accident, but likely he'd just been discreet. She seriously doubted that his name and the word 'abstinence' had ever been uttered in the same sentence.

'Dani, you know how this needs to look to anyone who is watching. I wish that I could have found any other way...'

'Yes, yes—I get it that you're making a huge sacrifice by marrying me.' She was surprised herself at her own flash of annoyance, and saw his eyes widen in response. Softening her voice a little, she avoided his curious gaze. 'Fine. So I move my stuff in with you and there will be no sordid photographs in the press of me with a string of lovers. Understood.'

'Good.' He was still watching her, his strong, tanned fingers idly twirling a spoon through his second cup of espresso. 'I'm glad we understand each other.'

Dani ignored the flush of awareness that prickled along her skin at the effortlessly sexy tone of his voice. Being around Valerio Marchesi so much was already causing mayhem on her nerves and she was agreeing to *marry* the man? Suddenly she felt caged in by all the unknowns about this arrangement and her ability to survive it.

'Is there a time frame for all of this?' she asked as nonchalantly as she could manage. 'I mean to say... how long do we actually need to stay married?'

His eyes darkened. 'Already dying to be free of me, *tesoro*?'

She inhaled sharply at the endearment, noting that he seemed slightly unnerved by his own words as well. He pulled gently at the collar of his shirt as though it had suddenly grown too tight.

The tense silence between them was interrupted by soft footsteps in the doorway to the kitchen. His housekeeper moved towards them, announcing an urgent phone call from Valerio's brother on the landline.

'Take the call. I've got to get to the office anyway,' Dani urged.

'This conversation is far from over, Dani.' He stood, unbuttoning the top buttons of his shirt. 'I'll pick you up for lunch. You can brief me on the meeting.'

And with a barely audible curse under his breath, he excused himself, disappearing inside with swift, thundering steps.

Dani watched him go with a mixture of relief and disappointment. *'I wish that I could have found any other way.'* Just what every woman wanted to hear from her fiancé. He had sounded as if he was prepping himself for a walk to the gallows.

His brother had probably got wind of the news and was calling now to put a stop to such madness. She shouldn't be hurt by Valerio's coldness. This was business. This was a formal transaction—a professional arrangement and nothing more. From his standpoint this was simple and clear-cut. *He* wasn't tied up in knots by complicated feelings and emotions the way she was.

She thought back to all the times she had dreamed of her own wedding day. She cared little about the actual day itself—more what it represented. Commitment, love, a family of her own and a home filled with happy memories. Deep down she craved the love and devotion she'd seen while growing up.

Her parents had adored one another and had always put their children's welfare before their own. They'd traded in their lofty social scene in Brazil when she was ten years old for a simple life in the English countryside. She had always imagined herself doing the same for her own children some day— that was why she had said yes when her ex, Kitt, had proposed after only six months of dating…even when a small voice in her head had told her to slow down and think it through.

But when her career had skyrocketed, she had realised that the high-powered work life she craved wasn't easily compatible with the traditional family life she had once dreamed of. At least that was what Kitt had said when he'd given her his ultimatum. He'd told her that her ambition and refusal to compromise was ruining any chance they had of a future.

Maybe this kind of business arrangement was the closest thing she would ever get to a real marriage. Maybe it was time she faced the fact that her life was never going to be the stuff of fairy tales and maybe that was okay. She loved her work. She was committed to taking care of the legacy her family had left behind, to doing them all proud.

Faking a happy marriage to a man who would never see her as anything but an obligation was a small price to pay for her safety.

It had to be—she had no other choice.

* * *

The rest of her morning was a blur, starting with an unplanned meeting with her regional team about some issues that had arisen with their plans for the Monaco Yacht Show. Usually she didn't enjoy playing CEO at meetings, but for once she threw herself into the role, thankful for a slice of normality.

Work had always been a source of calm for her during times of difficulty. Her parents had taught her the value of hard work, ambition and charity, ensuring that neither of their children became entitled trust fund brats. After Duarte had dropped out of college at nineteen, to live the wild life with Valerio, she had thrown herself into graduating with top honours and had then gone on to do the same in her master's degree in Public Relations and Strategic Communications.

When their parents had died so suddenly, in that car accident seven years ago, she'd jumped at Duarte's offer to be Velamar's PR and marketing strategist. She had been the one to help them turn their modest success into an empire. She was more than capable of public speaking and turning on the charm but, being naturally introverted, preferred to do her work from the shadows as much as possible. She did not possess her twin's natural ability to attract people to her with an almost gravitational pull. Duarte had been the wall she had always leaned on and hid behind.

Pushing away the overwhelming sorrow that always accompanied any memory of her twin, she threw herself into a few hours of preparation for the meeting that lay ahead, praying that Valerio would have the good sense to arrive early so that she could prepare him.

But afternoon came without him and she made her way alone to the large boardroom on the top floor of the building, frowning at the eerily empty space. Even the surrounding offices were empty. A feeling of unease crept into her stomach as she tapped a button on her phone, calling her personal assistant.

'Dani, thank God you called. I just saw one of the secretaries for two of the board members…' The young woman gasped, as though she'd been running.

'Are you okay? What's wrong?'

'They moved the meeting!' her PA exclaimed. 'They moved it to Valerio Marchesi's villa and deliberately chose not to pass on the memo to you.'

Dani felt her fist tighten on the phone until she heard a crunch. Thanking her overwrought PA, she slammed the device down on the table.

He'd moved the meeting and hadn't called her. Damn him.

She had asked him to do one thing—one simple favour… But, as usual, Valerio Marchesi did what he wanted to do and only ever on his own terms. Heaven forbid the man should ever take her advice or think of someone other than himself.

She wanted to fight—she needed a win of some sort. Maybe then she might start to feel something again other than this restless void of work and sleep.

Embracing the hum of adrenaline in her veins, she raced towards the elevators.

* * *

Valerio sat at the top of the long marble dining table and surveyed the six men and three women seated around him. He told himself that he'd chosen to change the location of the meeting to his own home at the last minute because it would give him an advantage—not because he needed the option of retreat if he lost control. And he knew the board members wouldn't be able to resist the chance to find out where he'd disappeared to. To discover if the rumours of his madness were true.

Just to keep a little mystery on his side, he'd spoken very little as they'd commenced their professionally catered lunch, and had given short, clipped answers to their many questions. But his unease had grown as the minutes had turned into an hour and there had been no sign of his fiancée.

Daniela was never late.

He wanted a single-minded focus on finding out who had pushed for Duarte's death certificate, but now he could hardly concentrate.

After ordering one of his guards to find out where she was, he sat back and tried to focus his anger on discovering which of these people, with their greed and lack of patience, had put Dani in danger.

But of course no one else knew the truth behind the seemingly random events that had transpired in Brazil. No one who was still alive, anyway.

Angelus Fiero stood up from his seat near the top of the table, slicking back the neatly oiled salt-and-

pepper hair atop his head. Valerio had never met the
man in person before last night…

'Marchesi, I'm afraid my flight plans have changed
and I need to leave. I'm needed back in Rio sooner
than I thought. But I believe I speak for all of us when
I say that I'm very relieved to see you return to work.'

Valerio swallowed his final mouthful of crème
brûlée, narrowing his eyes at the man with barely restrained menace. Around him, the other board members continued in their heated discussion about the
success of their new Fort Lauderdale headquarters
and their expansion throughout the Caribbean and
South America.

Angelus Fiero had been their very first investor,
back when they had started up and had needed capital
to bulk up their fleet offerings. An old friend of the
Avelar family, he had been trusted with managing the
family's affairs in Brazil after their move to England.

'Please, allow me to see you out.'

Valerio stood, prowling slowly beside the table
until he stood so close to the other man he could see
a tiny vein throbbing at his temple. He had amassed
enough experience over the past six months to know
when someone wasn't telling the full truth.

As they walked side by side towards the entrance
hall, Fiero made small talk about the latest yacht de-
signs. Valerio barely heard a word—he was too busy
mentally cataloguing what he knew of the man's character. He had briefly suspected Fiero's involvement in
the kidnap after he'd returned from Brazil and started
his investigations, but he hadn't found a single mo-

tive or link. The man was comfortably wealthy, he had no debts or enemies, and he didn't stand to gain anything from Duarte's death other than the headache of managing the company's reputation and a slew of uneasy investors.

'I was surprised that Daniela didn't join us for lunch today.' Fiero paused in the hallway to don his coat and hat. 'She has to know that half of the board are pushing to have her voted out.'

'Quite a stupid move on their part,' Valerio drawled, 'considering Daniela is about to become officially one of the wealthiest women in Europe, thanks to an anonymous push for Duarte's death certificate to be released. *You* wouldn't happen to know anything about that, would you?'

Another man might have missed the sudden flicker in Fiero's pale blue eyes. He masked it well, subtly clearing his throat and pasting a grimace on his face.

'You should direct your suspicions elsewhere,' he said. 'I've been a good friend to this family.' He shook his head in a perfect show of grief, placing one hand on his chest, where a small gold cross lay over his tie. 'I have information that the death certificate is to be issued at the start of next week. Quite unusual, considering they never recovered the body...did they?'

Valerio felt his fists tighten, and nausea hit his stomach as memories threatened to overcome him. The old man knew something—he could tell by the way he narrowed his eyes, tapping lightly on his hat as he moved towards the door. There was no way to know if he was on the right track, but it was enough for him to place Fiero firmly back on the list of those possibly involved.

He said goodbye to his newly reinstated suspect, closed the door and took in the violent tremor in his hands that had already begun to creep up his forearms at two words. *The body.* The memories were coming hard and fast. The sharp smell of gunpowder was in the air… Blood soaked the ground around his feet.

He swore he could feel every pump of blood in his chest as he started walking, counting backwards from one hundred. He never knew when one of these bouts of dream-like panic would hit, and he'd long ago stopped trying to fight them off or cure them with whisky. Like his scars, he felt they were a permanent part of him.

He reached the nearest bathroom quickly, slamming the door shut just as black spots swam in his vision and forced him to his knees.

CHAPTER SIX

DANI SANK BACK into the alcove under the steps up
to Valerio's impressive villa and cursed under her
breath. Angelus Fiero had just disappeared into a
sleek black car and driven off—which meant she'd
likely missed her chance to talk to him. The rest of
the board would still be inside, though. Likely being
entertained by their prodigal playboy CEO.

Adrenaline fuelling her, she barely waited for the
door to be opened by a member of staff before moving quickly through the house, following the sound
of raised voices. At a set of large double doors, she
paused, pressing her ear against the wood.

'I'm just saying the majority of our clients are
male,' someone was saying loudly. 'They flock to
us for the promise of the brand. The iconic image of
two powerful, handsome playboys who never settle
for less than the best.'

'Duarte and Valerio were the dream team…' A
strong female voice sounded out above the others.
'I can't help but feel that Duarte's sister's talents are
better kept…behind the curtain, you know?'

'We can't dispute the effectiveness of her marketing strategies—she's had some great ideas,' someone chided gently from further back in the room.

'Yes, but what good are ideas in a company figurehead when she has all the charisma of a wet blanket. She's *boring*,' a male voice sneered, inciting a rumble of laughter that Dani felt pierce through the thin layer of bravado she'd arrived with.

Any belief she'd held on to that only a small portion of the board wanted her gone instantly disappeared. She felt her cheeks heat, her heart rate speeding up in the uncomfortable way she knew all too well. Old scars burst open. Damn them for making her feel this way. Damn them for seeing her brother as perfect and her as a poor replacement.

Someone cleared his throat behind her, making her almost jump out of her skin.

'Eavesdropping, are we?'

Valerio stood braced against a door frame on the other side of the hall—how long he'd been standing behind her was anyone's guess.

She straightened, rubbing her palms on the front of her trousers. 'It's impossible to eavesdrop on a meeting I am entitled to attend.'

'I had the notification of the change in venue sent hours ago. It's not my fault you're late.' He glowered down at her, the expression on his face strangely blank, his eyes unfocused.

'Well, that "notification" was purposely kept from me.' She moved to sidestep him, only to have him hold on to her elbow and gently manoeuvre her back.

Something wasn't right, she realised. He seemed on edge. There was a sheen of sweat on his brow and he was just a little paler than his usual olive tone. She stopped herself from enquiring, though, remembering how defensive he had been about his behaviour that morning.

Her pulse skipped a little as she looked back towards the door, feeling dread creep in at the thought of walking in and facing those men and women after hearing what they really thought of her.

Valerio tipped his head slightly, listening to the voices still perfectly audible through the door.

'Daniela Avelar is not his usual type.' A man laughed. 'She's frumpy and she frowns too much. No sex appeal, you know?'

'He may be marrying her, but we need to make it clear that Marchesi alone as CEO is our best move forward,' someone else said, inciting a loud murmur of assent from the others.

Dani felt Valerio stiffen beside her, heard a shallow gust of breath leaving his lungs. Mortification threatened to overcome her, but she stood strong, plastering a smirk on her face as she turned to face him with a shrug.

'They've been singing my praises, as you can hear. Clearly they *adore* me.'

'Lose the sarcasm,' he gritted out, bracing one large hand on the door frame. Tension filled his powerful body, as though he were suddenly poised for battle. 'I'll put an end to this. I won't allow them to discuss you this way.'

'You assume that I plan to just walk away?' She raised one brow, stepping past him and inhaling a deep, fortifying breath. She disliked confrontation, but that didn't mean she was incapable of fighting her own battles.

Without warning, she slammed the door open and strode into the room, leaving Valerio momentarily frozen in the doorway behind her.

'Someone forgot to invite the boring temporary CEO to lunch, it seems.' She threw a glance around as she took a seat at the head of the table and folded her arms across her chest.

Multiple pairs of eyes landed on her, widening. Some looked down at the remnants of their coffee, spread out on the dining table along with their files and spreadsheets.

'I'd like to know who kept the change of venue from me.' She spoke with calm assertion, narrowing her eyes as one of the men cleared his throat and sat forward.

'Miss Avelar, there must be some mistake...'

'There have been many mistakes made.' Dani shook her head, pursing her lips. 'Shall I begin listing them?'

She slid a folder from her briefcase, opening up the file she'd prepared in advance the moment she'd realised a coup was in the works. She had evidence here to remove at least four board members for a variety of infractions that violated the company's code of ethics. And as she read out her first statement, the room was completely silent.

Footsteps sounded from the doorway. Daniela paused for a moment, watching as the man most of them truly wanted as their CEO finally entered the room. All eyes shifted to him, as if silently begging him to intervene, to stop this woman from tearing apart their plans.

Dani swallowed hard as his eyes met hers across the room. The impressive expanse of his shoulders was showcased in a simple white shirt with an open collar. She felt a thoroughly inappropriate flash of lust and instantly chided herself. He *had* to know how impressive he looked, damn him. He wouldn't look out of place on a Parisian runway. She knew that her larger frame would *never* be compared to a super-model, but she certainly wasn't frumpy.

She waited a heartbeat as he silently took a seat at the opposite end of the table, but instead of cutting short her speech, he simply nodded and motioned for her to continue.

A gruelling hour followed, during which four members of the board were put on temporary suspension and the table became filled with more tension than ever. Dani handed out sheets advising some further steps she wished to take regarding the future management of their design branches and charity assets, but decided to leave the actual decision making to a future meeting. Slow and steady was sometimes the best course of action.

Valerio had been reserved throughout the whole process, only answering when directly spoken to. A strange tension seemed to emanate from him, and every now and then she caught his eyes on her, burning with something dark and unrecognisable. Uncomfortable, she lost a little steam towards the end of her speech, and was almost relieved when he finally spoke up and commanded the room.

'I'd like to address some of the comments I have overheard,' he said. He spoke calmly, but with a gravelly hardness to his tone. 'Firstly, our brand is based on experience, reliability and being ahead of the market—not on a room full of aging business execs who have an opinion on the sex appeal or charisma of those who lead it. Secondly, you will not pass further comment on the details of my relationship with my future wife or debate the reasoning for our marriage. She may be graceful enough not to retaliate against such nonsense, but I am not bound by the same brand of polite restraint.'

Dani shivered as his eyes met hers for a split second.

Exhausted, she was relieved when Valerio began to take charge of escorting the others out. She walked over to the large windows and caught sight of her reflection in the glass. Her trousers were wrinkled and her wild curls seemed to have grown even wilder than usual, but she didn't care. She felt powerful after the surprising success of the afternoon, despite the awful comments she'd overheard.

It seemed like a lifetime ago that she had spent so much of her energy trying to reduce her curves and bumps, trying to squeeze into waist-slimming corsets and spending hundreds of euros on having her thick Latina curls chemically straightened. She'd been obsessed with looking like the hordes of slimmer businesswomen with their designer suits and pin straight styling.

After her failed almost-jaunt down the aisle and subsequent break-up with Kitt, something had clicked inside her and she'd started working to accept the body she had. The one she'd been born with. She was done with being shamed.

Valerio returned to the room, closing the door behind him with purpose. Evidently the meeting was not entirely concluded. She sat down again.

'That was very well done,' he said sincerely, bracing his hands on the dining table. 'But it makes what I'm about to say even more difficult.'

She froze, taking in the darkness of his eyes, and felt trepidation churn in her gut.

'I'll be stepping back into my role as CEO of Velamar and I want you to take a step back. Maybe recommence your plans to start up your own firm.'

Stunned, she met his eyes. 'What the—?'

'I asked you to trust me.' His voice was sincere. 'I need you to take a step back from the spotlight for a while…until I have a few things in order.'

'You mean you don't want me leading the brand either? What a shocker.' She fought the urge to slam her hand down on the table. 'I will not allow you to put my brother's legacy at risk with your own shallow prejudice.'

'*My* prejudice?' His brows knitted together. 'They're

the ones with ridiculous closed ideas of sex appeal and whatever else. I defended you.'

'You might as well have agreed with them. You're doing exactly what they want—getting me out of the picture so they can start picking this company apart like a damn chicken bone. You can't do this.'

In one single sentence he'd washed away all her self-doubt and made her feel appreciated for her talent. And then he'd ruined it all by railroading over her authority and making decisions for her once again.

'I can.' He stood slowly, stalking towards her like a predator. 'I am the only legal chief executive of this company. I appointed you as temporary CEO in my absence and I have the power to revoke that appointment.'

'You. Bastard.' She stood her ground even as he towered over her.

'Perhaps.' He shrugged. 'But if you trusted me you'd believe me when I say I have my reasons.'

He allowed his gaze to wander down her face… and further. She felt the heat of his eyes sweep along her chest and abdomen, right down to her toes. She took a step back, the urge overpowering her.

'If you think I agree with any of the things they said about you and your…assets… Clearly you have no idea what the meaning of sex appeal is, either.'

Her breath caught in her throat. Her mind was whirring, trying to find a clever retort to his words. He had to be trying to unnerve her, to make her leave. She felt hot shame rise within her, along with that damn pulse of awareness that refused to leave her every time he was in her vicinity. He was a beacon of sexual energy and, like a pathetic moth to his flame, she was completely unable to stay away.

'I've just been informed that Duarte's death will be certified in a matter of days,' he said. 'We don't have time for this back and forth.' He reached for the remnants of his coffee, downing the last of the liquid with a hiss of satisfaction. 'I need our marriage taken care of and tied up legally before your inheritance is unlocked. We could be married in St Lucia by Monday morning if we leave tonight.'

'St Lucia?' She repeated the words slowly, her shoulders tensing as she began to prepare all the reasons why she couldn't just up and disappear to the Caribbean without making plans for the business.

Then she remembered he'd technically just fired her from the only job she currently had. She had no reason not to go.

'I'm not your enemy, you know.' He spoke softly.

'I know.' She sighed. 'Right, I guess we're eloping, then.' She made a weak attempt at a smile. 'We've got a new base being built there. I've been monitoring the building work remotely, via our management team on the ground, but I'd love the chance to go and do a walk-through.'

'Should I be offended that your first thought is how to turn our romantic Caribbean wedding into a chance to get some work done?' He seemed irritated, gathering papers from the table and then thrusting them back down with a huff of breath.

'It's not a wedding,' she said quickly, frowning

at his strange change in mood. 'It's an elopement. I don't understand why you're on edge—snapping as though you're angry with me for all this.'

'I'm not angry with you, Dani…' he growled, turning to walk towards the door. 'I'm angry that you've been put in this situation. And I'm angry that you still refuse to trust me. But really I'm always on edge—so maybe you'd best get used to that.'

Valerio had just ended a painful phone call with his mother—his second family intervention of the day—when their car arrived on the runway beside the sleek Marchesi family jet. He felt a nervous twitch in his stomach as he watched Dani walk across the Tarmac ahead of him, in her perfect form-fitting trousers and flowy blouse.

She was polite, greeting the in-flight attendant as she stowed their bags and accepted some light refreshments. He gestured to the seat across from him and noticed her face tighten as she moved into it, her posture screaming with tension.

Just as he planned to apologise for his abrupt behaviour after their meeting, his phone rang again.

Seeing his brother's name show up on the display, he cursed aloud and jammed his finger on the screen to block the call. Ramming one hand through his hair, he closed his eyes and huffed out a loud breath filled with frustration.

'Is there a problem?' his fiancée enquired with a raised brow.

For a moment he considered not answering her

question at all. But then he remembered the promise he'd made to himself as they'd driven in silence to the airport—to at least *try* not to be so closed off and abrasive with her. She was going to be his wife... They were going to be sharing a lot more time together. He needed to put some effort in to his behaviour.

Reluctantly, he sat down across from her and met her eyes. 'You saw that I got a call from my brother earlier today, followed quickly by one from my mother? We haven't been on the best terms since I came back from Brazil. I've been distant, and now they've found out about our engagement through the media... Needless to say, my family are not happy about our elopement plans.'

Dani frowned. 'Of course they're not. I never even thought of how they might see this. Do they know all the details?'

He frowned. 'My brother knows a bit, but I've told him not to tell our parents the full truth. I can't tell them about the danger, not when my mother is such a worrier. They think it's a real marriage.'

He thought back to the sound of worry in his brother's voice on the phone. Rigo Marchesi had never been one to give his little brother an easy time, but after the display Valerio had put on at that christening dinner... Well, he couldn't remember all the details, but he was pretty sure that he deserved the scorn in his brother's voice. His entire family had believed him dead for two weeks and had been overjoyed at his return—only to be shut out and ignored for months on end.

They didn't realise that it was better this way.

'I won't pretend to understand what you've been working through these past months, *fratello*,' Rigo had said, 'but this seems quite sudden. I've been around you and Dani many times. She hates your guts and she is possibly the only woman I've ever witnessed being utterly immune to your charms.'

'No one is immune to my charms.' Valerio had answered easily. 'It's not like that. It's more like a business arrangement between us.'

'Now, where have I heard that before...?' Rigo had laughed out loud.

Rigo and his wife, Nicole, had married years before, as the result of a media scandal. Rigo had sworn his marriage was in name only, and yet now they were the picture of married bliss, with two small daughters and another on the way.

Across from him, Dani cleared her throat, pulling him back to the present. 'Valerio, if this is causing problems for your family, we should find another way. We can find someone with similar financial power and influence that we can trust.'

'Someone like Tristan Falco?' The venom-filled words were out of his mouth before he could stop them.

'I wasn't thinking of Tristan, but now that you say it, he might be a good fit.'

Valerio tensed. *Over his dead body.*

'I wouldn't trust anyone else—and neither should you. My family will get over it.'

He stood up, stretching his lower back muscles and pouring himself a glass of cold water to try to calm his nerves.

He had to admit that not once had he thought of his parents' reaction to his sudden nuptials. Amerigo and Renata Marchesi were not fiercely traditional, and they had always pushed their sons to choose their own path in life. But his mother was understandably hurt.

Once again he was a disappointment. Even when for once he was being selfless in his actions. He had nothing to gain from shackling himself in marriage other than protecting Daniela from harm and fulfilling his promise to her brother.

A small part of him spoke up, pointing out that so far he seemed to have been a lot more preoccupied with their living situation and ensuring she was by his side. He should have been working more on investigating possible perpetrators—like Fiero.

He leaned down, pinching the bridge of his nose sharply. '*Dio*, why is everything so damn complicated?'

Truthfully, he'd been relieved to talk things through with his older brother earlier. Rigo had been by his side at every important moment in his life—the day he'd dropped out of college, the day he'd told his father that he didn't want to be a part of the family business, and the day he'd cut the ribbon on the first company premises. Rigo had always offered impartial advice and support. He had always been a rock no matter how heavy the storm.

But his father was another story. Amerigo Marchesi had always hoped his two sons would run the family business together, but Valerio had never coped well behind a desk. He had been a wild teenager and an even wilder adult, taking on whatever ridiculous challenges life threw at him. He had once thrived on adrenaline and risk—now he spent his days obsessing over one woman's safety. The irony was not lost on him...

When Dani suggested they talk through some of the details of the new base they were going to visit in St Lucia, he jumped at the chance to shut his brain off by listening to the progress she'd made on the project. It was impressive—more impressive than anything he and Duarte could have planned. She was a marvel at organising, and seeing details no one else did.

When she finally yawned, and said she was going to try to sleep for the rest of the flight, he almost asked her to stay and tell him more. Something about her presence soothed him and made him feel less adrift. But in the end he let her go with a single nod.

Once he was alone he felt a familiar restlessness settling into his bones. The last time he'd been in St Lucia had been a few days before the accident with Duarte. They had been finalising the purchase of their new premises there when Duarte had told him that he needed to go to Brazil for a couple of days to sort out some business. At the last minute Valerio had decided to follow him as a surprise, so they could celebrate their expansion plans.

Valerio tried in vain to shut himself off to the memory...tried to block out the anger and regret. He'd spent months torturing himself for not realising that something was up with his best friend, that the man had been preoccupied and taking mysterious phone calls in the middle of important meetings. He'd clearly been under some unseen pressure, but Valerio had believed his excuse that he was just 'in a situation' with a woman.

Duarte had been an intense guy at the best of times—it had been easier for Valerio to look away and focus on growing their empire.

Regret washed over him, and once again he fought the urge to ask his fiancée to come back and discuss more business plans. She would likely jump at the chance. She loved to talk about work, and he could simply lose himself in her soothing presence.

Then he cursed himself for his own selfishness, hoping he might relax enough to sleep but knowing it was completely hopeless that he would ever feel at rest.

When Dani awoke, a number of hours later, she found Valerio sleeping soundly on his recliner in the main cabin. She walked over to stand beside him, fighting the urge to cover him with a blanket. He had told her never to touch him while he slept and she wasn't about to overstep that boundary, no matter how much she wanted to soothe the beast that roared in him.

Frowning, she took a seat at the opposite end of the cabin and successfully busied her fretful mind by reading over some of the finer details of their new Caribbean expansion. She might not be a fully active CEO, thanks to his demotion of her, but she had been the one to put the work into the planning of this base and she wasn't about to let him go in unprepared. She was able to separate her emotions from her professional work.

She thought of Valerio's urging her to focus on her independent contracts and how success had felt when it had been on her own terms. It had been hard work, a lot of travelling, and impossible to forge any kind of relationship in such a transient role. But that was what had drawn her to the work in the beginning— it had been the perfect balance. She had spent half her time working with her brother and the other half travelling solo.

But even though she had believed she was content, something had felt strangely lacking. The travel had grated on her sleep schedule, and she'd felt no desire to see any of the cities she'd landed in, preferring just to get her work done and sit in her rented apartment or hotel room watching romantic comedies and eating cold pizza from the box.

The lack of travel in the past six months while she had been running Velamar had been a welcome change of pace, but it still hadn't quite eased the restlessness that had long plagued her.

In the months before Duarte's death, she had been drawing up plans to start her own PR firm—something she had always dreamed of. Initially she had believed that she needed more experience or larger jobs—that no one would take her seriously until she had proved herself on a grand scale. But bigger jobs and more respect had come and still she'd held back.

Now she was about to be the co-owner of a global yacht charter firm and about to marry her business partner.

Unable to focus on work any more, she set about tidying away the items that Valerio had left out on the table. A photograph slid from his wallet onto the floor and she picked it up, frowning as an image including herself stared back at her. She remembered that day. The picture had been taken at the very first charity yacht gala she had planned six years ago. Just a few months before she'd moved to London and met Kitt.

Duarte stood centre stage, looking straight into the camera, while Dani and Valerio stood either side of him. Dani's hand was outstretched towards her brother's best friend as though she was mid-punch. She sighed, seeing that look in her eyes that she remembered so well. But she couldn't quite place the expression on Valerio's face…

Embarrassment, perhaps?

Had she been that obvious?

She scrunched her face up, cursing how terrible she had always been at disguising her emotions. Even now, did he know how utterly infatuated she had been with him? Could he tell that she still struggled with that pull of attraction?

She let her eyes wander from the photograph to the

real-life, grown-up version of the man. He lay completely relaxed, his strong jaw in profile, showcasing
the kind of chiselled designer stubble that most male
models would have killed for. His arms were crossed
over his broad chest, where the material of his shirt
strained over the taut muscles that lay underneath.

She imagined what this flight might have been like
had they been a real engaged couple on their way to
a romantic whirlwind elopement. That version of her
wouldn't have thought twice about sliding onto her
sleeping fiancé's lap and running her fingers along
his perfect jaw to wake him with a sizzling kiss…
And maybe that kiss would have led to the kind of
mile-high aeroplane chair sex she had only ever read
about in magazine confession columns.

Just as she allowed herself to imagine the mechan-
ics of such an act, the Captain chose to announce
their descent. Valerio woke with his familiar knee-
jerk rapid awareness. His eyes landed on her and Dani
felt herself freeze as though she'd been caught with
her hand in the proverbial cookie jar.

His gaze seemed curious, and she wondered if her
erotic daydreams were somehow painted across her
forehead. She felt far too warm as she cleared her
throat and slid into the seat across from him, avert-
ing her gaze as she commented all too loudly on the
picture-perfect view of the island of St Lucia below.

Their first stop was the office of a very prestigious
local attorney, to ensure that the documents their
company lawyer had filed in application for a mar-

riage licence had been received. They were assured
that all was going to plan, and that the short ceremony would take place in two days' time, as per the
legal waiting period during which they must not va-
cate the island.

Dani ignored the twist of nerves in her gut at the
idea that in a mere forty-eight hours she would be
legally wed to the silently brooding man by her side.
He had been distant since their argument, his brow
permanently marred by that single worry line in the
centre. At one point she had almost reached out to
smooth it down—had even had to pull her hand into a
tight fist and marvel at how ridiculous she was being.

They left the attorney's office and walked the short
distance to the marina, where Velamar's sleek new
Caribbean base was in the final stages of being finished. The building was single-storey, in traditional
St Lucian style, with an enviable frontage of the large
marina, which housed the beginnings of their sleek
new fleet of charter yachts and catamarans.

'Well, what do you think?'

Dani crossed her arms as Valerio silently took in
the bright, modern entrance foyer. The interior was
still a mess of plastic coverings and unfinished paint-
work, but the majority of the structural modifications
had been completed exactly according to her orders.

Valerio was silent, his eyes seeming to take in every
small detail as he moved around the large space. He
craned his neck upwards to the feature chandelier
hanging above their heads and let out a low whistle.

'I had it commissioned by a local artist.' Dani

spoke quickly, before he tried to comment on the possible price of such a frivolous item. 'I used local tradesmen for everything—including furniture design. I figured it was good for our global image, as well as making a statement about our commitment to being a part of this community—not just another big company setting up shop.'

'It's genius. This design is the perfect blend of our brand mixed with a St Lucian flavour.' He shook his head. 'You're perfectly on schedule too, by the looks of things. We've never managed that on any of our projects before.'

She fought the impulse to make a snarky comment about how she *was* just that good—about how he was making a mistake by removing her from her CEO duties. Instead she let his compliment sit for a moment, then replied with a simple thank-you. It was very adult, for the pair of them. Very professional.

More than once she caught him watching her from the corner of her eye as she spoke to the small management team who had been running things on-site. They were jumping over one another, eager to show the progress that had been made in readying the base for the first launch in the upcoming season.

Valerio seemed oddly distant now, allowing her to take the lead on the walk-through while he stood to the side and listened.

She suggested they take the team to dinner, to show their appreciation of their hard work, and was delighted when Valerio booked a sleek little boutique restaurant on the harbour that served the most delicious lobster she had ever tasted. He stepped easily into the role of charming CEO as he regaled the small table with entertaining stories from the company's early days, starting up in Monaco, and the various catastrophes they had endured.

She felt an enormous sense of pride in her company— and then froze, wondering when on earth she had begun thinking of it as hers and not Duarte's. It was as if hearing that his death was about to be confirmed had forced her to start accepting that he was not coming back to claim what should have always been his.

She found herself struggling to keep up with the jovial conversation during the rest of dinner, and fell into silence on the short drive up the coast to the villa Valerio had leased for the weekend.

It was nestled high on the side of a hill in a small inlet, with a short private beach visible between the cliffs below. The house itself was a warm peach-coloured creation of concrete and salvaged wood, surrounded by beautiful potted trees. Wild flowers grew up its façade, along with green foliage along the windows.

She stepped out of the car, breathing in the warm sea breeze. There wasn't a sound around them other than the chirping of birds and the muted crash of the waves on the wind. It took her breath away. It was as if her own personal postcard fantasy of an island paradise had been dreamed into life.

But even such a spectacular panorama couldn't cut through the heavy cloud that had come over her. Grief was a strange thing. It seemed to disappear then pop back up when you least expected it.

She followed Valerio as he led the way past the front door, following a lamplit paved path around the side of the house. The manicured gardens stretched for what seemed like miles around them, sloping gently down towards a sharp cliff edge. Whoever had designed this space had ensured a perfect symmetry between the smooth curving lines of the house and the natural beauty of the landscape.

Her heart felt both happy and sad as she inwardly acknowledged that her brother would have loved it.

'This place is magical,' she breathed softly as she wandered around to a sprawling terrace at the rear of the villa, which stretched out from the cliff face on what seemed like stilts, dug down into the rock itself. It was quite literally as if you could walk right out into the clouds from here.

At this northernmost point of the island, the Caribbean stretched out endlessly to one side, the Atlantic Ocean in the distance on the other. On a clear day, she'd bet you could see all the way to the neighbouring island of Martinique.

'I'm glad you like it.' Valerio had a smile in his voice as he spoke, stopping at the polished wooden balustrade beside her. 'I was thinking that, instead of the courthouse, we could just get married right here.' When she was utterly silent, he continued awkwardly. 'I have my security team on-site... It would be easier to contain. Plus, I thought it might be a bit of a nicer view than stacks of paperwork and musty bookshelves.'

Dani felt every romantic cell in her body light up

from the inside out, the idea of saying her vows in such a place making her eyes water. But then she remembered that they weren't real vows, and that she wasn't to be a real bride in this picture-perfect setting. That the reason he had to keep her safe was because someone wanted to hurt her.

She felt herself deflate like a helium balloon coming down from the heavens. As beautiful as this place was, no amount of dressing it up would make this wedding any less painful.

CHAPTER SEVEN

VALERIO WAS PUZZLED by the sudden change in Dani as she simply nodded and murmured something non-committal about his idea sounding 'nice'. He pursed his lips, ignoring the sinking disappointment in his gut at her reaction.

He wasn't sure why he'd hoped she would be happy with the setting—they both knew that this was just a quick formality that needed to be done. It really didn't matter if they signed their licence and said their vows by the side of a road—only that the legalities were seen to.

He watched as she wandered down the terrace, briefly taking in the impressive pool area, then moved inside the house to explore. Valerio kept a few steps behind her as she looked around, commenting on the vibrant colours of the potted plants and the flowers around each room. For the most part, the rented house was decorated in neutral tones of white and grey. It was lacking an owner's touch of personality.

The kitchen looked like a relatively new addition, as did the state-of-the-art surveillance system and security room. The privacy and safety of the house had been one of Valerio's main concerns when booking, and he had advised his two guards to take shifts in the guest cabin at the gate. He wasn't going to take any chances.

'I'm going to go unpack my stuff…maybe take a shower.'

She wandered away through the house and Valerio watched her go, a feeling of unease within him. She was unhappy—he had seen it in the set of her mouth all the way through dinner. He had respected her silence in the car with difficulty, wanting to give her space in whatever bothered her, but he had also wanted to stop the car and demand she tell him what was wrong.

But it wasn't his place. He wasn't the man for her to confide her innermost feelings to…to lean on when she was sad. If he started blurring those lines, who knew what would come falling down next? Distance wasn't just wise with Dani; it was absolutely necessary.

Ignoring the sudden increase of tension in his spine, he moved to the fridge and found it fully stocked, as requested. Fresh fruit and pre-cooked gourmet meals lined the shelves—enough to keep them going for a couple of days while they waited for the paperwork to go through.

Suddenly, the idea of sitting around waiting for the formalities of their elopement just didn't sit right with him. If they had any hope of making this work, they needed to get back on the same team. He needed her to trust him, and not to feel like a coiled spring in his company.

Suddenly, he knew exactly what to do.

The tiny beach restaurant was a hidden gem Valerio had heard about on the east side of the island. Dani had initially worried aloud that her simple turquoise shift dress might make her feel underdressed, but that had been before Valerio had revealed that he'd booked out the entire venue for their exclusive use.

'There's no one else here,' she whispered as they were seated at a small table overlooking a pebbled beach. Small lanterns lit the way down to the shore and a light scent of salt was in the cool night air. 'I understand we need to be cautious, but it's so quiet.'

He nodded towards an area at the edge of the deck and watched as she turned and saw the duo of island musicians setting up under a string of fairy lights. Soon the sound of a steel drum and a rhythmic guitar began to flow through the air. She smiled as she closed her eyes and swayed a little.

'You should do that more often,' Valerio said silkily, taking a sip of his soda water and lime to distract himself from the hum of attraction that had refused to shift since she'd walked down the stairs in that flowy knee-length dress. She shifted and crossed one leg over the other, revealing a long, smooth expanse of perfectly curved skin. He cleared his throat, looking up to her face and away from those damn thighs. 'I want you to enjoy these few days here. Take it as a chance to recharge before we have to return to reality.'

'Or at least the new appearance of reality.' She smiled again.

'Exactly.'

The corners of his mouth tipped up slightly and for the first time he felt the urge to laugh. It was enough to stop him for a moment, before he caught himself. He'd had a hard time too, he reminded himself. Maybe they both deserved to feel a little freedom while they were here.

'You're starting to look serious again,' she commented, one brow raised.

'I was just thinking…maybe it's time we called a truce. Let's enjoy a few days off the grid, so to speak. No arguments or work. No serious talk.'

A simple handshake sealed the deal and they entered into a pleasant flow of conversation until their food arrived then drifted into companionable silence as the delicious food and great music added to their lighter mood.

Their waiter was a kind-faced older man, who saw the ring on Daniela's finger and insisted that the band play a slow number for them to dance to.

Valerio stood, extending his hand to her and forcing a smile as she stood up and moved close. The music had a soft, seductive rhythm, and he found himself forgetting all the reasons why he shouldn't be enjoying this, why he shouldn't pull her close and pretend they were just another couple on an island adventure.

He breathed in the scent of her hair and heard the softest sigh escape her lips.

'I didn't expect you to be a good dancer.' She spoke near his ear, her breath fanning his skin. 'I should have known you'd be good at everything.'

'You think I find everything easy?' He subtly moved even closer, moving his hand on her back and leaning forward. 'I stepped on every dance partner's toes at events when I was a teenager. My mother made me go to dance lessons twice a week for six months. I was an embarrassment.'

She laughed deep in her throat as he dipped her into a flamenco-style twirl, tipping her back over his arm. 'Well, you certainly overcame your awkward phase.'

Their eyes met for a long moment, their breath coming a little faster from their exertions. Valerio found himself wondering if he should suggest they kiss, to maintain the appearance of being a happily engaged couple. But really he just wanted to kiss her again. Wanted to see if it was his sex-starved brain that had elicited that first reaction from him after their first kiss or…if it was just simply her.

As he began tipping his head down towards her, a shout from behind them caught his attention.

They both turned and watched as one of the security guards ran down the beach and into the water towards a small boat. A single man was in the vessel, a black boxlike item in his hands. Valerio turned himself in front of Dani, shielding her with his body as he shouted for the other guard to follow.

After a few tense moments of shouting and confusion, it was revealed that the man was just a local fisherman who hadn't been told of the restaurant's private hire. The guards and Valerio quickly apologised to the man, and to the restaurant owner, who had been quite distressed by the commotion.

'Get back to the car,' Valerio growled, guiding her away from the dance floor by the elbow.

'Valerio, it's okay. It was just a mistake.'

'This entire impulsive evening out was a mistake.' He shook his head. 'I can't even keep you safe for one day. I need to get you back to the house now. Just… please don't fight me on this.'

Dani didn't fight him. She barely even spoke on the drive back to the villa, knowing that Valerio needed time to cool down after the adrenaline rush of the false alarm. She had been scared too, but he had moved swiftly from fear and protective mode to anger towards himself. She was beginning to see a pattern with him. Did he have a hero complex? Or was he hiding something about himself?

An email on her phone caught her attention as they entered the large open-plan living area of the villa.

'The board have accepted my plans for Nettuno and the charities.' She frowned. 'But I never got the chance to send them my files before you asked me to step back.'

'I sent them.' He turned to her, both hands in his pockets. 'I looked into your plans further after the meeting and I knew they were the best course of action. You'll get full credit, and I'll keep you in the loop on everything regarding Duarte's projects.'

'Valerio…that means more than you know—thank you.'

'You don't need to thank me. I should be thanking you for being so good at what you do. I'm being honest when I say I wouldn't ask you to take this step back if it wasn't important.'

She nodded once. 'And you still won't tell me exactly why?'

Valerio's gaze became instantly defensive and he prepared to turn away.

'No arguments, remember?' she said quickly, knowing that she needed to take a different tack. This was a business deal, after all—why shouldn't she employ one of her oldest moves? Entertain the opposition… keep them close. 'I'm not going to launch into a fight, if that's what you're thinking. I want us to keep to our deal. A weekend of fun, starting now.'

She moved to one of the sideboards she'd investigated earlier, returning with a deck of cards. 'How do you fancy your odds?'

'Poker?' He raised one brow, picking up the deck and shuffling the cards with seasoned practice. 'You sure you're up to playing me?'

'You forget that I've been schmoozing your clientele in Monte Carlo these past few months. I've become quite a pro.'

'We don't have any chips.'

He shuffled the cards again, dancing them easily between his hands with the lightest touch. She watched his movements, transfixed by how effort-lessly he manipulated the deck. The man was good with his hands…

Clearing her wandering thoughts, she sat up straighter. 'I used to play without chips with Hermione back in college. We sat up all night, creating this stupid game where you get a forfeit instead of chips, while we were supposed to be studying for exams.'

'A forfeit?' His eyes met hers across the table. 'Like Truth or Dare?'

'More like Truth or Lies. You have to ask awkward questions and try to get the other person to lie or refuse to answer. But be warned: I'm pretty good at this.'

The premise of the game was simple enough: a crazy mix-up of various card games that only Hermione could have concocted. Each player had the chance to steal cards by challenging the other to answer a question or make a statement, then determining if the answer was the truth or a lie. The problem was, as the game went on for a few rounds, Dani realised that some of the questions Valerio was asking were quite inappropriate.

'How many lovers have you had?' he asked boldly.

Dani answered honestly, praying she didn't blush with embarrassment as she admitted she had only ever been with Kitt. Valerio's eyes burned into hers, widening with disbelief as he declared it a lie, and she shook her head, taking her share of his cards as her forfeit.

'How many lovers have *you* had?' Dani asked

when it was her turn, trying and failing to keep a straight face.

Valerio pursed his lips, counting the fingers on both hands, then reaching for a pen and jotting down some sums. 'Let me see. Carry the two…multiply by seven… Roughly in the low hundreds.'

'Okay, well, I'm just going to say that's true.' She shrugged, pretending not to care about his answer.

'Lie.' His eyes sparkled as he took her cards. 'I'm actually quite discerning about who I take to bed, despite the tabloid rumours. You have a low opinion of me.'

Dani smirked. 'Well, what *is* the number, then?'

'Ah-ah, that's not a part of the game.'

He laughed as she groaned her annoyance.

'What's your biggest fear?' he asked on the next turn, his gaze strangely focused on her and a slight curve to his mouth. He was enjoying this, she thought.

'That's an easy one. The open sea,' she said easily, schooling her features.

When he guessed that she was lying, she shook her head, grabbing yet more of his cards.

'You're serious? You work at a yacht charter company and you're afraid of the open sea?' He let out a bark of laughter.

'I'm just afraid of swimming in it—not sailing. I don't like to sail myself, but I trust the boats.'

She sat back as they played another hand, feeling his eyes on her the entire time. The next time her turn came up, she felt the effect of the wine kicking in, along with a new sense of bravado. She asked him some questions about his childhood, his decision not to join his father's company—everything she could think of that she'd always wished to ask.

'What's your most shameful secret?' he asked on his next turn, laughing when she grimaced at his question. 'You know the rules: you have to give an answer or you forfeit.'

'Well, unlucky for you, that's an easy one for me.' She met his gaze, throwing out her best poker face. 'I have never had a proper orgasm.'

His brow furrowed, his eyes narrowing on her for one intense moment before they widened in a mixture of surprise and anger.

'You have to say if you think it's true or false,' she said, but she was instantly regretting her flirty answer, wondering what on earth had possessed her. 'Or we can just move on.'

The air was still and silent between them, except for the sound of insects chirping and waves crashing against the cliffs nearby. She pursed her lips, sitting up and flicking her hair over her shoulder.

'Forget that one. I'll give you the cards and let's just move on.'

A long exhalation escaped Valerio's lips. Dani looked up to see his hands in tight fists on his lap.

'*Madre di Dio.* I knew that pompous lawyer was beyond useless. You actually believe that you are somehow defective because of that idiot?'

'It's not always the man's fault, Valerio. And it's kind of a sensitive subject,' she said tightly. 'Draw your next hand, please.' She heard the ice in her voice—it was a sore subject for her. But she wasn't about to discuss it over some stupid card game.

'Even if it's true—which is up for debate—you're telling me he made you believe that it was your fault? That you can't—?'

'I said draw your next hand.'

The next round was more heated, with Dani using her best tricks to ensure she won. She knew she was a damn good card player, even if it was an utterly ridiculous game.

She met his eyes across the table. 'Time for your most shameful secret, Mr Marchesi. And it had better match mine.'

Valerio sat back in his seat, still feeling the tension within him from her revelation. He wiped a hand down his face, wishing they'd never started playing this game. She was just giving him as good as she got—she had no idea how many secrets he held in. But she had asked to know before…about Rio. Maybe this was his chance to share his burden with her. He only hoped she would be able to handle it.

'Valerio, you don't have to answer,' she said quickly, obviously taking in the change in him. 'I'll choose a different question.'

'You answered yours,' he said simply. 'I have no problem continuing to play by the rules. My most shameful secret is easy. Most people believe me to be some kind of hero, but the reality is that I'm the opposite. I'm a coward. It was my fault that your brother was killed and I will never forgive myself for that.'

'Valerio…' she breathed.

'No. You asked me for the truth once before, and I walked away. You deserve to know how he died.'

An unbearable pity was there in her deep brown eyes as she nodded once and gestured for him to proceed. He felt her attention on him like the warm heat of the sun, watched her delicate hands folding and unfolding in her lap as she waited. They both knew this wasn't just a game any more.

'I followed him to Rio when he asked me not to. We were attacked by a van full of men and taken,' he began, hearing his own voice sounding out perfectly clear in the night air, as somewhere deep inside his chest ached. 'I woke up in a shipping yard, surrounded by men in black hoods. They roared questions in a Portuguese dialect that I couldn't even begin to understand. Duarte was tied up beside me for a while but then they separated us. They were far more interested in him than me.' In his mind, he remembered the solemn look on Duarte's face as he apologised for dragging him into such a mess… He swore he would get them both freed. That he had a plan, but he made him vow to protect Dani if anything happened to him.

But for days on end they had tortured him and Duarte in turn, in front of each other, never allowing him to speak, only Duarte, using their loyalty to one another against them.

'Days passed… They tortured me for fun. I didn't have anything else they needed. I had already offered them money… After they broke my knee and I could no longer fight back, they got bored. Then they mostly just left me alone in the dark.'

He heard a sob and looked up to see that Dani had covered her face with her hands, but he had to finish this while he could. He owed her this story, even if he knew it might break her to hear it. He hoped she was strong enough.

'Eventually they lost their patience. A man brought Duarte in and held a gun to my head. Someone asked in English how much his friend's life was worth. But one of the guards who I hadn't seen before turned his gun on the others. He freed us both before they killed him. I had a gun in my hand but I hesitated. I had the chance to end it and I didn't. They shot Duarte by accident. I saw the panic in their eyes once they realised. They debated shooting me too but got disturbed by someone outside and just knocked me out instead. When I woke up, Duarte's body was gone and so were they.'

Valerio remembered staggering out of that shipping yard. He was found on the street. When the police came, they found tracks leading to the dock—evidence that a body had been dumped in the water. Washed out to sea. They'd dragged his friend's body away, denied him a proper burial.

He shook his head as if coming out of a daze.

'You know the rest.'

He felt a warm weight on the seat beside him and felt himself cocooned in the soft comfort of her intoxicating scent. She leaned her head against his shoulder, her sharp breaths telling him that she was crying even though she hid her face.

'Thank you,' she said simply, and then she allowed the silence to stretch on for a long while. She seemed to know instinctively that he couldn't speak any more, that he needed to just...*be*...for a moment.

No matter how many times he allowed himself to access those memories, they always seemed to hit him with the same force. The look on Duarte's face as he'd realised they weren't getting out of that shipping yard alive. The look of pure hatred in the masked men's eyes as they'd tried again and again to beat him into submission.

Every single moment was like a pinprick in his skin, every vision a reminder of what he might have done differently, how he might have saved his friend's life if he'd not hesitated that split second.

After a long time Dani sat up and turned to him, her eyes a mess of smudged make-up.

'Lie,' she said, an echo to their earlier game.

'Is that your attempt at a joke?'

'I would never joke about what you went through. You came back alive—you survived the unimaginable. But the way you tell that story... It's as though you feel you were to blame for my brother's death. As though you could have saved him if you'd done something different. You're lying to yourself. Punishing yourself for surviving.'

Valerio looked away, his jaw tightening with anger. 'You have no idea what you're talking about.'

'I know that you're a good man. That you would

have done what you believed was right. You were under so much pressure—'

'Stop.' He stood up, fury and resentment choking him, making him want to lash out. 'You blame me for his death just as much as everyone else. Are you telling me you have never wondered how I survived when he was clearly the more experienced fighter? You think I don't know what people say about me behind my back? You've had the luxury of grieving him without knowing the details, without having them permanently etched in your memory as a life-long torture. Do you think you can just pull me out of my life, tie me to a bed and order me to get back to work…go back to living my life? Do you think I can just switch any of this off?'

He laughed, harsh and low.

'I'm done with this game.'

Dani stood up, walking quietly to the door back into the villa. She paused, turning back for a moment to meet his eyes. When she spoke her voice was surprisingly calm and soft in the aftermath of all the venom he'd just thrown at her.

'Valerio… I know you're angry. But there is no luxury in grief, no matter what side you stand on. We both loved him. And I know that I pushed you to come back, but I'm not sorry. I get it that there are parts of you that are broken and scarred from your experience. But I just need you to know that I don't blame you for his death. I never did. And you might have wanted to die in that dark shipping container, but I am thankful every single day that you came back.'

The door to the house closed softly behind her, leaving Valerio to sit alone in the darkness, feeling the result of his own stupid temper and guilt surrounding him like a dark cloud. He took a step forward, willing himself to storm after her and demand that she be angry. Demand the hatred he deserved.

But he remained frozen for a long time, his mind fighting to swim up from the fiery pit of anger it had succumbed to. It was at times like this, when the blackness came over him, when he wondered how there was anything of him left at all.

Valerio kept out of Dani's way the next morning, not even passing comment when she holed herself up in the study at the villa and he spied her hard at work on her computer. She needed to take a break and some time to relax, but she wasn't going to listen to him— not after he had been his usual difficult self last night.

He hardly even remembered half of what he'd said, he'd been so set on telling her the story of what had actually happened in Brazil.

He found his own computer and sat down in the dining room, logging on to the Velamar system for the first time in months and taking in the vast amount of work he'd been neglecting. It was no surprise Dani hadn't had any time for her independent contracts— he'd left her alone to handle all this.

He spent the day through to the afternoon methodically sorting through emails and project outlines, sales projections and marketing plans. He immersed himself in the work, surprised when it fuelled the drive in him rather than making him feel trapped at a desk like it usually did.

His mind felt focused—as if he had unburdened it a little just by sharing his darkness with Dani. But guilt assailed him. He needed to swallow his pride and apologise for his behaviour. For all his behaviour over the past few days. He was about to be her husband, and even if it was in name only, he didn't want to let her down.

'I'm still committed to our agreement of a weekend off, even if you're not. So I'm going to go for a swim before it gets dark.'

Like a mirage, she had appeared in the doorway of the dining room, a towel wrapped around her and the black strings of a simple bikini top visible at her nape.

Cursing himself for his instant flare of arousal, he glared down at his computer, waving a hand in her direction. He listened to her footsteps pad away, closing his eyes at the distinctive sound of a towel hitting a smooth surface before there was the splash of water.

His mind conjured up a vision of her smooth, dark curves gliding through the cool water in the setting sunlight. His groin tightened in response, all the blood in his body rushing south. He snapped the computer shut, looking up at the ceiling and shaking his head. This was what happened when he ignored his body for so long. He was like a teenager around her. She would be horrified to know of his lack of control.

He tried to get back into his work but his concentration was shot. So he sat in painful silence, listening to the sound of her moving through the water on the other side of the terrace doors.

Suddenly a muffled scream came from far away, jolting him from his thoughts. He frowned, tensing. When a second scream sounded out, he jumped from his seat and started running.

He reached the pool to see Daniela frozen in the centre, her eyes wide with terror as she pointed towards the wooden bridge over the water.

He followed her finger, his eyes instantly landing on what was possibly the most gigantic snake he had ever seen. The reptile was olive green in colour, with black markings along its length which almost matched the entire span of the bridge.

As Valerio watched, its heavy body moved and became partially submerged in the water towards its tail end. He looked closer, seeing a small alcove under the bridge filled with tiny movements. This mother snake was protecting her young. She didn't move again, but was clearly aware of the woman who had interrupted her peace. Tiny black eyes were focused solely on Dani, and Valerio felt his chest tighten at the sight of her fear.

'Do you think you can swim to the edge?' He spoke softly, ready to move if the snake did. Judging by its size, it was one of the island's native boa constrictors—non-venomous, but who knew how it might react if it sensed a threat?

Dani laughed—a panicked, breathy sound. 'I can't move at all. I've tried.' She groaned. 'It's watching me.'

'Okay, I'll come and get you.' He pressed his lips

together, stepping out of his shoes. 'It won't hurt you. The only poisonous snakes on this island are a lot smaller than this large lady.'

'Lady?' she squeaked, incredulous. '*I'm* a large lady—*that* is a gigantic reptile. Seriously, I'm in mortal danger here and you're being *respectful* of that thing?'

Valerio waded into the pool with slow, purposeful strokes. He reached her side in seconds, placing a finger against her lips. 'Careful. She might hear you and take offence.'

'Stop messing around.' She clutched at him, her hands shaking as she latched on to his wet shirt and folded her body against his.

He felt a low groan escape his lips as his body roared to life at the delicious contact.

'I'm sorry… Did I hurt you?' she breathed, her attention still largely focused on the snake.

Get it together, Valerio.

He sliced at the water to move them both closer to the edge. Now was definitely not the time to be losing his grip on his rediscovered libido. She was afraid, and she was trusting him to get her out of the pool safely, so he was going to do just that.

He began to lift her onto the lip of the pool, then instantly regretted it as she froze and clung to him even tighter. 'Don't *lift* me!' She pushed a hand at his chest.

Valerio growled with irritation. '*Dio*, again with the worrying. I have lifted you before and, believe me,

I was not even slightly hampered by your size. You honestly have no idea how perfect these curves are.'

Her eyes went wide. 'I meant…don't lift me out where the snake can get me.' She began to blush a bright pink, her body suddenly softening in his arms. 'But…thank you.'

He froze for a long moment, just looking into her brown eyes, feeling her heartbeat thudding against his chest through the wet fabric of his shirt. He was an idiot. An absolute idiot.

His forehead dipped to press against hers as he fought the insane urge to kiss her. But he knew that if he kissed her now he would want more. He would want as much as he could have of her…as much as she was willing to give.

And where would that leave them? He had promised himself that the first time had been the last, that this was how it needed to be. And yet every time they were alone together it seemed like the most natural thing in the world to have her in his arms.

Thank God for the water around them, or she'd be all too aware of the nature of his thoughts.

'Valerio…'

She shifted against him, her thighs tightening on his hips as she tilted her face slightly. Her lips brushed against his, soft and wet, and he felt the ravenous beast within him roar with triumph. Surely, if she was starting it, it would be rude to stop her?

His arms banded around her, pulling her chest flush against him as he plundered her mouth, deep and hard. He felt her nails on his back as she moved against him, heard the sound of her groans as he pushed her back against the side of the pool.

With one hand he gripped her hair, tilting her head back and gaining deeper access, deeper control of the kiss. The darker forces in his mind screamed at him to take her right here in the water and to hell with the consequences. But it seemed Dani had different ideas. She stiffened in his arms, pushing him away with surprising force.

'I'm sorry…' he began, readying himself for the inevitable argument.

'No, Valerio… The snake moved again. I heard a splash.'

He turned, and sure enough, the reptile was now fully submerged in the water. He lifted Dani up with ease, doing his best to ignore the deliciously wet curves under his hands. Once he'd lifted himself out too, they both looked down at the impossibly long, dark shape in the water.

'I'll call Animal Control in the morning. Our snake friend has a nest of babies under that bridge that need to be taken somewhere a little bit safer.'

Dani shivered at the word 'babies', stepping backwards, away from the pool. 'I swear, I'll never swim peacefully again.'

That made two of them, he thought wryly, but for entirely different reasons.

The cool evening breeze cut uncomfortably through the wet fabric of his clothes. He needed a hot shower and a lot of distance between them to get his head in order.

Making a snap decision, he pulled off his soaked shirt and hung it over a chair, doing the same with his trousers. The outside shower was tucked into a wall on the terrace of the villa. It was fully stocked with toiletries and had a cabinet filled with towels. It seemed the rental company had thought of almost everything—except checking for hidden families of snakes, of course.

When he emerged from the shower, he hoped Dani would have gone inside. But she sat waiting for him on a sun lounger, with a towel wrapped around her body. A wet pile of fabric lay on the ground beside her. Her discarded bikini.

Valerio gritted his teeth, wishing he had taken his shower inside and then locked himself in his bedroom. Being a coward was infinitely preferable to this kind of sexual torture. If she had any idea what her mere presence was doing to him, with her damp curls hanging over her bare shoulders and the way she watched him through her lashes with a look of uncertainty on her beautiful face...

He tightened his fists, searching for control, hating it that she made him ache for all that he couldn't have. And he was finally admitting to himself that he did want to have her—not just because of sexual frustration or circumstance. He wanted *her*.

'You said you were sorry.' She spoke softly, standing up to face him. 'About that kiss. But I'm the one who kissed you this time. I didn't even ask. Surely I'm the one who should be apologising.'

'You don't need to apologise. I'm the one who

needs to apologise. My behaviour towards you has been unacceptable from the moment I came home,' he said, cursing himself as her eyes widened and she took a step towards him.

He raised a hand between them, holding her at arm's length.

'I'm sorry for how I spoke to you last night. I'm sorry I can't be…what you need. But we both know why we need to keep things professional here. My priority is keeping you safe, and that includes keeping you safe from me too. You've seen the way I am. I can't even be woken from sleep without becoming a danger.'

'That's ridiculous. You would never hurt me, Valerio.'

'You have no idea who I am. Not any more,' he rasped, his eyes lowering to take in the towel she clutched to her chest. 'I'm the man who promised to keep his best friend's sister safe. Then kissed her for the first time in front of an audience and had to stop himself from lifting her up like some kind of brute and carrying her off to the nearest bed. And if there hadn't been a damn snake in that pool, the same thing would have happened ten minutes ago. I have no control over myself around you.'

'Well…that would have certainly got everyone's attention…'

'This isn't a game any more. In two days you are going to be my wife…' He swallowed hard, trying to ignore the way her eyes darkened to deep burnished amber in the low glow of the setting sun. 'But I'm going to find the people behind all this, and once I'm sure you're safe—'

'What, Valerio?' She spoke quietly. 'You'll leave again? What a surprise.'

'I'll have our marriage annulled and you can get on with your life.'

'What life? I've spent the past two years working myself to the bone.' She ran a hand through her curls, taking a few steps away from him to compose herself. 'At least with you I feel…'

'What do you feel?' he asked, feeling himself itching to move closer, to coax this fire between them until it burned them both.

'I don't know…' Dani began, twisting the white towel in her hands, suddenly unable to look at him as she spoke.

Was she really going to be honest? She had kept her feelings for Valerio Marchesi under lock and key for so long it would be no effort at all to lie and agree to his sensible plans for their sensible marriage of convenience.

But she was tired of being sensible. She was tired of putting on a show of being strong and self-contained all the time.

'I don't think I have ever heard you speak in so many unfinished sentences,' he said.

'You said that I have no idea who you are any more,' she said, standing up and looking down at him. 'I think we're both different people now. Changed people because of events that neither of us had any control over. We've both been alone and we've learned how to cope with the unknown in our own way. I don't want to be alone any more, Valerio.'

He looked up at her. 'You're not alone. I'm here with you.'

'You're not,' she said quietly, feeling her bravado falter slightly but pushing on. 'Not really. And if I marry you, that means sharing a home with you, sharing my entire life with you… I can't be around you all the time in these intimate situations and not be affected. I'm just not that good an actress.'

'Are you saying you don't want to be around me?' He raised a brow.

'I do,' she said quickly, looking down at the ground and cursing herself for how badly she was getting her point across. 'God, I really do… That's the problem.'

Valerio stood up, closing the gap between them with a single step. 'We're not just talking about marriage any more, are we?'

'Look…I understand that this has never been something you wanted.' Dani spoke fast, praying she wouldn't lose her nerve. 'But I need to be honest. I'm really attracted to you. More than I've ever been to anyone else. It's quite inconvenient, considering that we're planning a marriage built on nothing more than business and friendship, but…I just wanted to have that out in the open.'

His fingers pressed against her lips, silencing her. 'Are you proposing to amend the terms of our contract, Miss Avelar?' He wrapped his hand around the towel, pulling her towards him until they stood chest to chest. 'How much more do you want?'

'I don't know,' she said breathlessly. 'How much are you willing to give?'

He answered her with his lips on hers, his hands spanning her waist and pulling her against him—hard. '*Dio*, I thought I was already crazy with wanting to have you. But now…with this mixture of pretty blushing and the throwing around of business terms…'

His lips trailed down her neck, his hands sliding down to cup her bottom through the towel. Dani moaned low in her throat, the power of speech slowly leaving her.

'Do you want me to make love to you, Daniela?' he whispered next to her ear, his hands kneading her skin gently.

'Yes… God, yes.'

He pulled back, an expression of awe on his face as he cupped her jaw and looked deep into her eyes. 'This will complicate things.'

'Only if we let it.' Her voice shook as she spoke. 'We're both adults. We know what this is.'

'I don't have any protection.' His brow furrowed, his hands tightening on her as though he feared his words might make her run away. 'I haven't been with anyone since before Brazil, and I don't really go around carrying condoms in my wallet. But I've had my yearly check-up since and I know I'm clean.'

'Me too—and I've had an IUD for years.' She pressed her hand to his cheek, hardly believing they were having this conversation. 'I don't want to think about this as a complication. I don't want to *think*, Valerio. I just want to do what feels right.'

CHAPTER EIGHT

His eyes darkened, his hand moving to the front of the towel, spreading over it slightly. His fingers trailed over the bare skin of her stomach. 'Tell me... does this feel right?'

She answered with a moan.

He continued his exploration, his touch sending her skin into an explosion of sensation. Her legs felt weak as he reached the edge of the bikini bottoms she had yet to remove, smoothing his hand down over her sex through the thin, still damp fabric. She bit down hard on her lower lip, tilting her head back as he licked a path of fire along the side of her neck.

She had never enjoyed sex in the past—she'd always been so consumed by her negative body image and her pesky inability to reach an orgasm. But her mind seemed unable to worry about that now, as he slid his fingers under the fabric and along the slick seam between her thighs.

'How about this?' he murmured softly against her skin, his teeth nipping at the area just below her ear.

Her answer was incoherent as she clung to him

while he performed some kind of magic with his fingers. She had never felt such intensity from a simple touch before. Every slide of his hand sent fresh waves of pleasure shooting up her spine and down her legs.

Soon she was moving against him, powerless not to join his sensual rhythm. Her eyes widened in disbelief as she felt herself tightening around his fingers. The shock momentarily stopped her rhythm, her legs shaking beneath her as her mind got in the way of her pleasure.

'Do you want me to make you come, Dani?' he purred next to her ear.

'It's okay. I don't usually…' she breathed, her chest tightening. 'I mean, I've only ever been able to do it a few times by myself. And it takes far too long.'

Valerio pressed his forehead against her temple. '*Dio*, that image…you touching yourself… But right now I'm the one in control.' He continued to move his fingers in slow circles as he spoke softly in her ear. 'You're going to relax and come for me…right here. I won't stop until you do.'

Dani felt a breathless laugh in her throat at the thought that this arrogant man believed he could simply will her to orgasm. But, God, she loved it. This artful combination of being commanded and cared for so thoroughly…it was almost too much for her to take. Her body seemed to relax just with his sensual presence.

She shook wildly at the lazy thrust and curl of his touch, feeling the pressure within her rise once again. This time she didn't fight it, and she listened helplessly as he whispered all the things he planned to do to her, letting his words add fuel to the fire that was already burning in her, wildly out of control.

When the wave of pleasure finally reached an earth-shattering climax, she could do nothing but hold on to him as the waves took her again and again. The intensity of the orgasm was too much, and she buried her face against his shoulder, his name falling from her lips like a prayer. Still he kept it going, only slowing down as she shook and fell slowly back to earth.

'I think I've proved your theory incorrect.'

Valerio bit his lower lip as he took in the rosy flush of Dani's cheeks and the delicious pout of her lips.

'I can't even think straight.' She smiled, half hiding her face against his shoulder.

'I don't plan to stop until you've lost the ability to speak.'

He fought the edge of his control as he took her by the hand and guided her back inside the villa, stopping to light two of the lamps on the bedroom wall. Letting go of her hand, he sat on the edge of the bed, looking up to take in the beautiful silhouette of the woman in front of him.

This was a bad idea—she had said it herself. But he no longer remembered any of the reasons why. Nothing mattered any more other than having her body under his and taking the entire night to explore every inch of her silky caramel skin.

She stepped towards him, dropping the towel from the tight clutch of her hands, baring her body to him.

Dio, he had never seen anything as erotic as the sight of her blushing. Her hands flexed as though she wanted to cover her breasts, then dropped slowly down to her sides.

He remembered her words from before—her belief that she was somehow less feminine because of her size and her competitive streak. Less desirable because she was so unlike most of the women in her social circles. She had no idea how much she had tortured him with this delectable body for years… sitting across a boardroom table in her smart skirts, commanding the room with her brilliance.

This powerful woman actually doubted her beauty. Doubted herself in the bedroom because of some unqualified idiot in her past.

He bit his lower lip, anger and desire making his pulse pound in his veins. He would make it his personal mission to ensure she never doubted a single thing about herself again.

'Come here,' he rasped, gripping her hips and guiding her to straddle his lap.

Her breasts were the perfect size for his hands. He took his time, trailing his lips and tongue across one delicate dusky nipple before moving to pay equal attention to its twin. The soft moans that escaped her throat made him so hard it took all his willpower not to just do away with the idea of going slowly. The thought of burying himself inside her made him feel primal…on the verge of losing his mind completely.

But if this kind of sensual control and skill was all he had to offer her, then he was damn sure that he would prove his worth. He thrust out his hips, his erection straining against the front of his towel. Dani gasped, her eyes darkening as she followed his rhythm, grinding against him. She moved like a dancer, her hips rolling effortlessly in time with his. *Dio*, it felt so right, having her against him.

Then she stopped her movements, bracing one hand against his chest. 'Lie back.'

'I was wondering when you would start fighting me,' he breathed, following her command without question.

He lay back on the bed, raising both arms over his head in a display of submission. He watched as she positioned herself at his knees, untying his towel and pulling it away inch by agonising inch. She worked slowly, deliberately drawing out her movements as she bared him. Her hair brushed over the skin of his thighs and abdomen as she ran one finger down past his navel. His manhood pulsed, straining towards her touch.

'I've never done this before, either,' she admitted huskily, meeting his gaze with no embarrassment, just trust. 'Tell me if I'm doing it wrong.'

'*Tesoro*, I don't think you realise how effortlessly sensual you are…'

He breathed the words as she freed him and ran her fingers over his hard length. He closed his eyes for a moment as the tip of her tongue moved against him in slow exploration as she figured it out for herself. Opening his eyes against a wave of pleasure, he looked down to see her taking him all the way past her full lips, his girth disappearing into the molten heat of her mouth.

There was no way he would withstand this kind of pleasure for very long without bringing things to a very abrupt ending.

He thought about it as he watched her take him, and he imagined letting her bring him to release right here. The image sent an electric pulse up his spine, but he sat up, cupping her cheek with one hand and drawing her up along his body until she lay flush against him.

'I wasn't finished.' She smiled that slightly awkward smile he had come to recognise as a sign of nerves.

'I promise to have you in that exact position again before tonight is over, but right now it's taking all my control not to end this before we've even begun.'

Her eyes widened with understanding, a smug smile spreading across her lips as she lowered herself down to kiss him. Valerio took advantage of her position, pulling her close before rolling them over on the soft pillows so that she lay in the cage of his arms.

'My turn.'

He moved down the sun-darkened valley of her breasts, following the path of her ribcage until he reached the gentle curve of her stomach. She writhed with every touch against her skin, her honest reaction to his kisses sending him back to the brink of release once again.

'Tell me what you're thinking about,' he growled against the silky skin of her upper thigh. And then with both hands he spread her legs wide, settling his shoulders between them.

'I've…fantasised about you doing this…'

Her words came quietly from above him, spurring him on as he dropped featherlight kisses against the neatly trimmed downy curls that covered her. God, but she was perfect here too. She writhed, moving her hips against his mouth, begging him to stop his sensual torture.

He barely touched her for a few moments more, then surprised her by spreading her wide and moving his tongue directly against her in one slow stroke. She went wild, a sharp curse escaping her lips.

'Are you going to come for me again?' he murmured huskily against her skin.

'I can't…' she breathed, her head moving against the pillow with each stroke. 'Oh, God, stop—it's too much.'

He paused, only to have her hands grip his hair, as if begging him to keep going. Valerio smiled against her as he continued to stroke, again and again, keeping a smooth, firm rhythm. But the power he felt in bringing her to this point of madness was too much— he needed to have her soon.

She gasped in shock, beginning to approach another climax under his tongue, and he wasted no time in moving over her, spreading her legs wide and looking into her eyes as he entered her in one hard, urgent thrust.

He needed to be inside her as she came apart more than he needed to breathe. The time for taking it slow had passed, and he had burned out every last scrap of his control. He felt her inner muscles continue to tighten around him, heard her breaths coming in short gasps as she met the strength of his thrusts. She pulled his face down to her own, crushing her mouth against his so sweetly as her climax hit. And Valerio felt his own pleasure reach an unbearable peak, felt fire spreading up his spine and consuming him. He closed his eyes, pressing his forehead to hers as he came apart, joining her in mindless oblivion.

Dani stared out at the hazy darkness of the moon-lit night spilling in through the open terrace doors. Valerio's gentle snores sounded in the bed behind her. He had fallen asleep after another round of intense, earth-shattering sex. But she lay awake, wondering what would happen once he woke up and properly talked about what they'd just done.

She was afraid to move, as his arm was draped over her, pulling her tight to his chest. And something within her ached at the wonderful feeling of being in the cradle of his strong arms, even knowing it was only temporary.

She sighed. If she could just stay in this bed for ever she might imagine that things had deepened be-tween them. If they never had to leave this magical island they wouldn't have to confront the reality that they shared a company together. That this was an arrangement, not a love match. That, while he was apparently attracted to her on a physical level, he would probably never feel even a fraction of what she felt for him.

She paused. What exactly *was* it that she felt for him?

Frowning, Dani slipped gently free of his embrace. Sitting on the side of the bed, she looked down at the strong profile of the man who was soon to be her husband. The engagement ring on her finger felt heavier than ever, its cool metal shining in the light of the moon.

She had agreed to live with him, share her life with him and trust him to keep her safe from the unseen danger that was closing in. But what were they to one another without this arrangement? Would he ever have fallen into bed with her if he hadn't been facing possible years of celibacy as her convenient husband?

Cradling her face in her hands, she breathed deep and tried to calm the anxiety within her. She was about to *marry* him—she couldn't have this many complicated feelings warring within her. She was falling into dangerous waters and it was clear she would be the only one hurt when it eventually came to an end.

She needed to keep her feet firmly on land—starting right now. Sleeping together in one bed seemed a step beyond sharing the occasional romp in the sheets, so surely leaving now would be a firm message to show she wasn't getting the wrong idea from what they'd done?

She stood up, pulling the comforter from the edge of the bed, and walked to the door, turning back just once more to look down at Valerio's sleeping form.

She could do this—she could have what she wanted of him and still keep herself above water.

She went into her room and stepped straight into a hot shower, feeling the spray hit muscles that she hadn't used in years. She lathered soap across her skin, feeling her body tighten at the sensation, imagining it was Valerio's hands touching her, caressing her…

God, she'd had him three times and already she was fantasising about the next time.

Resting her forehead against the cool tiles, she breathed in deeply, calming her racing heartbeat. She sent up a silent prayer that she wasn't in completely over her head. They could mix a little pleasure into their arrangement and not risk ruining everything, couldn't they?

Before she could finish that thought, the shower door slid open and Valerio's broad naked form appeared through the steam as if in slow motion. The man was built like a prize fighter, and the shadow on his jawline made him look rough and dangerous. He didn't speak—just pulled her into his arms and kissed her as though he were a drowning man and she was his first gasp of air.

His hands tangled in her wet hair as the spray of hot water cascaded over them both. Framing her face in his hands, he looked down into her eyes, a wicked smile on his sinfully full lips. 'You left before I was done with you.'

'I'm just… I have no idea what this means. Us being together. I needed some space to think.' She met his eyes, feeling her heart still beating so hard she thought it might explode from her chest. 'What are we doing?'

'I have no idea, but I can't seem to stop.'

Dani felt her mind go blank as Valerio moved closer, kissing her worries away. There was comfort in knowing that he was just as powerless against this insane lust. She would worry about the consequences tomorrow. Tonight she would just live in the moment. In this perfect moment with him, with the steam of the water surrounding them, slickening their skin as the heat rose even higher.

He stopped for a moment, his eyes serious as he looked deeply into hers. 'How on earth did you ever think you were bad at this?'

Dani felt a blush creep up her cheeks. 'Um…let's just say when it comes to sex, it's the one area where I've never been an overachiever.'

He pressed the length of his erection against her, leaning down to nip gently at the sensitive skin of her collarbone. 'I strongly disagree, Miss Avelar. You're a natural.'

'Well, you're the first guy to ever get me to…to finish the race.'

He bit his lip, and something deep and dark glittered in his eyes. 'Look at me. And if some idiot in your past told you it was a race, then he was playing the wrong sport.'

He dropped down onto his knees before her, framing her thighs with his strong hands. She shivered as his lips touched her upper thigh and began to kiss inwards.

'You should have been given more than a thousand orgasms by now. You've been robbed of years of plea-sure,' he growled. 'I plan to set that right.'

Dani closed her eyes, trying to remain upright as he kept his promise again and again.

CHAPTER NINE

DANI AWOKE TO the sun streaming through the terrace doors and the glorious scent of coffee teasing her nostrils from somewhere in the distance. She sat up, momentarily disorientated as she looked around at her unfamiliar surroundings. It felt like a dream that she'd spent half the night experiencing the kind of orgasms and intense sexual chemistry she'd only ever read about in the books she'd devoured in her college dormitory. She'd never believed it could ever be for her.

Every encounter with Kitt, her ex, had been pre-arranged—no surprises. Even down to the type of underwear she had worn. Comparing her ex to Valerio now, after last night, was like looking at discount price wine after drinking a vintage reserve Chianti. It left a sour taste in her mouth and she knew she was worth more. But of course Valerio wasn't truly hers. He was just acting the part.

She quickly shut off her ridiculous thoughts with a bracing shower, throwing on her silk robe while she applied various beauty products and let her curls air-dry. She'd promised not to do any work, but nabbed her phone from the nightstand, telling herself she would just take five minutes to check the most important emails.

Twenty minutes later she was engrossed in a text conversation with an insanely curious Hermione when Valerio appeared beside her and snatched the device from her fingers.

'I was in the middle of reading something,' she squeaked, jumping up to grab the phone back—only to have him hold it further out of reach.

'You are technically on vacation, Miss Avelar.' He tilted his head to one side, lazily looking down over her scantily clad body. 'I'm demanding that you actually take the day off.'

'I can't just switch off like that. There are things I need to check on with the new plans…things that need my attention even while I'm relaxing.'

'So you don't trust the relevant teams to perform their jobs?'

She huffed out a breath, knowing he was right. She was checking on them for the simple reason that she wanted to. She couldn't let go of the relentless force telling her to keep on top of everything, to make sure nothing was missed.

'Well, since you can't control yourself, I'm cutting you off.' He smirked, tucking her phone into his back pocket. 'If you want this back, you're gonna have to work for it.'

She felt heat creep up her spine at his words, her

nipples instantly peaking at the suggestion he'd created in her mind.

He raised a brow at her, evidently noticing her physical reaction. Suddenly shy, she closed her robe a little tighter and turned around in a pretence of opening up her small case and organising her clothes. When she looked back, a shadow had crossed his features, but he quickly disguised it with an easy smile.

'Get dressed quickly. We leave in fifteen minutes.'

'Leave…for where?'

She froze in the middle of selecting a T-shirt. His eyes twinkled with the kind of mischief she hadn't seen on his face in years. He was up to something, and it made her both nervous and strangely excited.

'We're going on an adventure. I plan to make a pirate of you yet.'

Valerio was stubbornly silent as he waited for her at the end of the wooden deck, and only gestured for her to follow him down the rocky steps in the cliff face towards the tiny bay below. He carried a small bag over his shoulder and stopped occasionally to help her down as the steps began to grow steep.

He tried and failed not to be distracted by how carefree she looked in simple knee-length capris and a tank top. She hadn't got a scrap of make-up on and her curls were tied back from her face with a colourful silk scarf she'd found in one of the kitchen drawers.

He'd been unsure of what she was thinking from the moment they'd spoken that morning, so he was glad he'd arranged today's trip before the events of last night.

It sounded so simple…calling it 'the events'. As if it was a small blip they could just forget about and move on from. But maybe that was what she wanted?

The thought caught him unaware, making him almost miss his footing on the steps.

She'd been skittish around him all morning—maybe she was having second thoughts? Surely if that was the case he should be relieved. And yet the thought of her drawing a line under whatever this was before he was ready made something tighten in his gut.

It was simply pride, he assured himself. No man wanted to feel rejected—especially not by the woman they were about to marry.

They emerged through the foliage onto the most beautiful little pebbled beach. The gentle curve of the land had created a perfect shallow pool where they could see tiny fish swimming.

Valerio gestured towards the end of the inlet, where a small wooden dock had been erected. The dock housed a single sleek black speedboat. 'I had this skippered over from the marina—figured I'd take a chance while we're here to get up to speed on our latest toys.'

'Oh, I see how this is. You get to do some work but I'm not allowed to?' she jibed, accepting his hand as she stepped down into the boat.

'This has never been work to me.' Valerio inhaled deeply as he fired up the engine and set his hands firmly on the wheel. '*Dio*, I forgot how good this feels.'

She sat back, watching the waves while he focused on pulling out from the small dock and gathering speed as they moved out onto open water. The boat was effortlessly smooth, and Valerio knew he was an expert at the helm. The familiar feeling that he had every time he was out on the water washed over him. It was as though he had finally come home.

He'd always had this affinity with the sea, this soul-deep connection. It was the thing that had bonded him and Duarte—their passion for sailing and exploring the world without fear.

Something within him stilled as he realised he had barely given his best friend a thought since the night before. Perhaps it was just the natural evolution of grief—the intensity of the pain wasn't any less but the frequency was bound to change and lessen. Guilt threatened, but he pushed it away, refusing to sully what he'd shared with Dani. He refused to mark it as wrong, somehow, when it was possibly the most right he had felt in a long time.

'Where are we going?' Dani moved to sit beside him, speaking loudly above the noise of the speedboat crashing its way through the waves.

'You'll find out soon enough.' He smiled, his hands moving to take hers and place them on the helm. 'But for now it's time to ease you into your new life as an explorer. Step one: you will now captain this boat.'

She shook her head. 'No! I've never had the first idea how to drive one of these things. Take it back.'

She squeaked as he took a step away, leaving her alone and holding on for dear life.

'Just relax and feel the power in your hands. Feel the hull slice through each well.' He spoke next to her ear. 'Keep your eyes straight ahead. Brace your body and move with the water. Don't fight the current… Ease against it.'

Impulsively, he gently kneaded the tension in her shoulders. 'You're fighting it, Daniela. Breathe in deep and exhale… Lean into it.'

She rolled her eyes, doing as she was told, loosening her grip and easing forward. Her resulting smile was dazzling as she moved the boat over the swell without any tensing at all.

'Careful, now—I might start to think you're enjoying yourself,' he teased.

'I'm just very eager to earn that phone back.'

She pursed her lips against another smile as his hands covered hers on the wheel, joining her as they navigated over the water together.

Valerio had congratulated himself on his innovative idea of getting Dani to drive the speedboat to their surprise diving lesson excursion in Rodney Bay. But once he'd achieved the task of getting her out in the open water with their instructor, she had asked a million questions. The man had explained that this kind of diving was called Snuba—a cross between snorkelling and scuba diving—and that they would be connected to a small raft by air lines and safety lanyards the entire time.

Valerio tried not to laugh as Dani finally finished wrestling with the large diving mask on her face and took a long look at the depth of the water before them.

There was no certification required, because it was quite safe, but Dani still looked terrified now, as she stared down over the side of the boat.

Valerio advanced on her, his own mask making his voice sound muffled. 'We can just go back to the marina if you want?'

As he'd expected, she narrowed her eyes on him in challenge and turned to the instructor as he finished securing her weight belt, regulator and air line to the small safety raft. But as she moved to ease down the metal ladder on the side of the boat, her foot slid and she tumbled rather ungracefully sideways into the sea.

Valerio felt a shout leave his throat, moving to dive in after her, but the diving instructor stopped him with a hand on his chest, showing him he had a firm grip on her safety harness.

Sure enough, Dani emerged instantly and grabbed on to the large blue-and-white water tank floating beside the boat, pulling the regulator from her mouth and letting out a strangled cough that Valerio felt deep in his chest. He watched with awe as she gasped, holding on to the safety lanyard as she tried to adjust the mask on her face and remove the water.

'See, I'm a natural!' she shouted nervously. 'Well, Marchesi, are you coming in, or are you having second thoughts?'

Valerio finished his own set-up and eased down the ladder. They followed the guide's instructions, paddling out a specific distance from the boat before preparing to dive down. It had been a long time since his own deep-water scuba diving days, but he still felt the thrill of being out in the depths, with nothing below them but glittering blue adventure, pass through him.

He had only dived down about a metre when he looked to his side and realised Dani hadn't come with him. Using his own natural buoyancy, he kicked his way back up to where she still clutched tightly to the safety lanyard on the raft.

'Okay, so I was bluffing. You go ahead. I'll just watch from here!' She spoke over the noise of the waves.

'What about adventure?' He popped his own regulator out and pushed his mask up on his forehead, looking into her eyes. 'What about trusting me?'

'I do trust you. We both know that *you* can do this. You've always been brave and fearless. So don't let me hold you back. Go…please.'

'While you just wait around up here in the safe zone? Is that it?' He hardened his gaze. 'And how much happiness has *that* got you so far, Dani? All that fear and tiptoeing around…not taking any risks.'

'It's kept me alive, hasn't it?' she retorted, then gasped at the realisation of what she'd said, shaking her head. 'I'm going back to the boat. I'm sorry.'

'Look at me.'

He pulled her towards him, the water lapping at them on a light current. He could see the instructor watching from a short distance away. He didn't care—he wasn't letting her go without saying what he needed to say.

'There's a difference between actually feeling alive and just going through the motions of life. This, right here, being so far out of your comfort zone, is where you'll find the former.'

'What would you know? You've practically been a ghost for six months. Are you telling me that *you* feel alive?'

He took the hit of her words, knowing they were the truth. 'I deserve that. But the truth is I forgot how this felt—how healing it is to let yourself just be free. These past few days you've brought a part of me back to life that I'd thought lost for ever. I just want the chance to push you to do the same. The way I should have done the first time you asked for my help.'

She frowned, her bottom lip quivering slightly. For a moment he worried that he'd gone too far and opened too many old wounds. A part of him hoped that she would just swim away from him—that was what he deserved. Maybe it was just too little, too late, as the old saying went.

But, as usual, this woman had far more strength than anyone gave her credit for. She steeled her shoulders, taking one hand off the raft and extending it to him. 'I'll need your help. I'm shaking too hard to let go.'

For a moment Valerio stared down at her hand, shocked at such an open show of vulnerability and trust. Then, once she had the regulator in her mouth, he grabbed hold of her, feeling the tremors in her fingers vibrating against his own. He grasped her tightly, embracing her for a long moment as he pulled her bodily from the raft.

She stiffened, then moved with him, following his guidance as they trod water together in an easy rhythm. Valerio locked his eyes with hers, gesturing with the fingers on his free hand as he silently counted down from five and they slowly dropped below the surface together, hand in hand.

Daniela remembered, as a child, running after her brother through the gardens of their country home and always stopping the moment she got as far as the black gate that led into what Duarte had christened 'the haunted forest'. It had been just a normal country wood, but the trees had been so dense it was almost pitch-dark once you were a few steps in.

Her brother would assure her it was okay, but her fear would always stop her from stepping nearer the shadows and into the unknown beyond. She'd needed to see safety ahead—not jump in and think later, the way he had.

Now, even as an adult, she trod softly and kept to her plans. She was fearless in the boardroom, and fearless in what she wanted for her career, but deep down she sometimes felt that she was still that child, staring at the line between safety and the unknown and keeping herself stubbornly behind that line.

But once she'd emerged from the water with Valerio's hand still in hers, she'd finally had a taste of what it was that pushed him to test his boundaries the way he did.

Pushing past her own fear had been terrifying, but that fear had got less and less as she'd dropped down into the ocean and seen the wonders that lay below the surface. Schools of tiny, vibrant coloured fish had danced through the current, and as Valerio had guided her deeper, she'd been entranced by the play of light on the seabed. She'd watched tiny creatures as they scuttled in between rocks and coral, and had spotted a couple of spiny lobsters locking claws with one another. The highlight of the dive had been the moment a sea turtle had swum nearby, its graceful body turning in the water and reflecting glorious beams of turquoise and blue light.

Dani had been utterly charmed by the world below the surface, filled with such simple quiet wonders. Wonders that she would never have seen from her spot on that life raft. She was grateful that Valerio had pushed her. Clearly he had seen something missing in her life—something she had never known she needed. And he was right. This feeling of adrenaline and triumph was healing.

She felt free. She felt as if she could take on the whole world.

The feeling carried on for the rest of the afternoon as, back on the speedboat, Valerio unveiled a small picnic lunch which he'd had delivered from a local restaurant. She knew he was still worried about her safety, and was thankful for the time he was giving them alone together, without their security detail.

Valerio took them out to a remote spot along the coast of Rodney Bay, from where they could view the impressive length of Pigeon Island in the distance. The food was from one of the finest chefs on the island: a delicious spread of green figs and fresh lobster, followed by a dessert of banana cake—a special St Lucian recipe that was deliciously spiced and sweet.

They talked for what felt like hours and she remembered exactly why she had always liked talking to him. He didn't just listen and nod; he gave his full focus to her—just like with everything he did.

She found herself telling him how she'd been relieved to cancel her plans for her own firm and how fear had always held her back. He seemed surprised at first, then quietly pensive as he listened to her ramble.

For the first time ever, she admitted out loud that it had been a need for comfort and closeness and safety that had driven her to work at Velamar after her parents had died. Then, when success had come upon her, she'd found excuses to not run on ahead into the unknown. She had held on tight to her position at Velamar, holding herself back by only taking on short-term outside contracts.

In turn, he told her of his decision to drop out of college and how disappointed his parents had been—how he had almost gone back just to please them. But he had known he would never have been happy in the perfect corporate tower with his perfect brother, as much as he wished he could have been. There had always been something wild in him—something that needed the open sea and the pull of adventure.

Sailing had always been his first love, so he'd

bought his first yacht, and the tabloids' 'Playboy Pirate' had been born—a result of uncertainty and youthful pride.

A companionable silence fell between them and Dani realised that she'd always known there must be a lot more to Valerio Marchesi than anyone saw. He wasn't just the party-mad reprobate the media painted him as. Perhaps on some level he had purposely harnessed that image as a means to control his fall from the supposed grace of the Marchesi dynasty—to defend himself from the possibility of failure. It was strangely comforting to think that perhaps she wasn't completely alone in her fears.

Dani watched as Valerio began to pack away the remains of their food and tried not to focus on the swirl of emotions warring inside her. She was grateful to him for giving her this perfect day, but it wasn't gratitude that had her skin heating as he lay back on the blanket and let out a deep sigh of satisfaction.

They hadn't really talked about the night before and what it meant. Suddenly she found herself wondering if maybe he wanted to draw a line and leave it as a one-night stand. It would be understandable, considering the complications that carrying on would mean. But seriously…how was she ever going to look at him again without remembering all the things they'd done?

His body was an impossible distraction. He already looked more tanned and vital after only a few hours in the strong afternoon sunshine, and the pale blue linen shirt he wore only served to draw more attention to the impressive power of his shoulders and biceps. A memory of having those arms around her the night before rose up, her skin tingling with an electric current as she forced herself to look away.

'You have the most expressive features—did you know that?' He spoke softly, with a smile in his voice. 'What were you thinking just now?'

Dani looked back to see his sunglasses were off and the sun and sea were reflected in his cobalt-blue eyes. She cleared her throat, finding her mind blank and all her snappy retorts having deserted her. This man made her brain malfunction. She should be furious— should use that anger to stop herself from diving into this crazy fire that felt as if it was just waiting to explode between them again at any moment.

They were going to be married, for goodness' sake. This inconvenient attraction was fast turning into something deeper. The man was a drug—one taste and she couldn't think of anything but her next hit. But she couldn't torture herself like this. That way lay only danger and pain.

She bit her bottom lip, standing up and climbing down to the cockpit to grab a bottle of water in a vain effort to cool herself down. She heard him approach from behind.

'I told myself I'd let you lead the way—but, *Dio*, Daniela… I want to kiss you again.' He spoke softly. 'I haven't been able to think of anything else all day. Have you forgotten so easily?'

Her breath was shaky as she braced her hands on the smooth surface in front of her. 'I don't think I'll ever forget…but we both know this is a bad idea, Valerio.'

Warmth pressed against her from behind…the barest touch of strong, calloused fingers on her hips through the fabric of her dress. She closed her eyes, preparing herself to turn round and tell him that they had to be sensible. Then his lips traced featherlight kisses along her nape and she felt her traitorous body leap to attention. She pressed back against him, feeling him hard and aching, exactly the same way she felt deep inside.

She turned in his arms, her mouth finding his like a homing beacon, needing to taste him, needing all of him.

After a minute they were both frantic with need and tearing at one another's clothing. Her brief, momentary panic at being out in the open, where anyone could sail past and see them, was quickly overcome by his wicked whispers to enjoy the risk. So she did.

She leaned back against the side of the boat, spreading herself wide for him, letting him know that she was his for the taking. She was *all* his.

His guttural groan was almost enough to push her over the edge as he grasped both her thighs, his fingers like a brand on her skin as he forced her even wider to accept his length. His lovemaking was primal, and frantic with longing, as though he too felt as if at any moment one of them would come to their senses and bring things to a halt.

She felt the swaying movement of the boat underneath them as he thrust hard and fast, taking her closer and closer to heaven. As she came, she looked up at the sky and let out a sound of pure abandon, not caring who heard her.

After a second, slower exploration of one another, Valerio helped her back into her clothes and insisted she sail them back to the small dock at the villa. His powerful body behind her guided her the whole way. And as she helped him gather their things and finish docking, she felt laughter bubbling in her throat at the fact that not only had she sailed a boat and deep-dived off one in a single day, she had also had two very public orgasms on it too.

'Something funny?' He raised a brow, offering her his hand as she stepped off the wooden pier onto the soft pebbles of the beach.

She smiled. 'I can't remember the last time I just felt…happy.'

'I'll never look at that boat again without remembering you, spread out against the mahogany deck with the glow of another orgasm on your skin.' He pulled her close. 'How many is that now? Not nearly enough yet.'

His use of the word 'yet' seemed to break a spell of sorts. It seemed that both of them had remembered there was a time limit on whatever it was that they were doing. She bit back the words on her tongue— the urge to ask him when it would be enough. When it would be over.

They both knew that there was no room for casual sex in their arrangement, that they had to get a handle on this. Besides, she wasn't sure 'casual' even began to describe the need she felt when he touched her.

She had agreed to share a home with him when they got back to Europe—but to sleep in a bed alone, knowing he was separated from her by only a thin wall. She shut her eyes against that unwelcome reminder of reality.

'I'm not ready for today to be over yet,' she whispered against his chest as she listened to the sound of the waves crashing against the pebbles on the shoreline.

'Who said it was over?' Valerio smiled. 'You may have tackled your fear of open water, but you have far from learned your lesson about pleasure.'

'I'm pretty sure I have bite marks on my neck that contradict that statement.' She laughed as they began the tortuous climb back up the cliff steps to the villa.

'Not all pleasure is sex, Daniela,' he scolded, his eyes wicked and full of mischief.

He smiled down at her as they reached the top step, then turned to look up at the house—and his entire body suddenly froze.

Dani bumped straight into his muscular back, clinging to the material of his shirt to stop herself from toppling backwards, down the way they'd come. 'Valerio, what on earth—?'

She gasped out the breath she'd sucked in, and then followed his narrowed gaze to see a small gathering of people on the upper deck, peering down at them with interest.

'Is that your brother up there?' Dani spotted Rigo

Marchesi, smiling down at them, and by his side she was pretty sure were Valerio's mother and father.

Valerio cursed something in fierce Italian under his breath, gripping her hand tighter and hauling her up by his side. 'We might have to hold off on the pleasure. It appears that my family have invited themselves to our wedding.'

CHAPTER TEN

IT TRANSPIRED THAT his family, namely his mother, had arrived to perform an intervention of sorts.

Valerio held his annoyance in check by a thin thread, his gaze anxiously seeking out his fiancée throughout dinner as she was practically interrogated over their sudden alliance and why they'd selfishly kept it hidden for so long. He felt the tension building between his brows as he watched his mother and sister-in-law fawn over Dani's engagement ring at the opposite end of the table. The three women had barely stopped talking—and his mother was asking question after question about what exactly they'd planned for the wedding. He had been a fool to think that Renata Marchesi would pass up the chance to be mother of the groom a second time.

His father had been his usual reserved self throughout dinner so far, but Valerio's brother, Rigo, had more than made up for it with his subtle ribbing about how relaxed and well-rested Valerio looked.

'I hope we haven't interrupted anything here between you and your fiancée?' Rigo said now, raising one dark brow as he took a sip of red wine.

'Should your wife be flying all this way at this stage in her pregnancy?' Valerio changed the subject swiftly.

'She's still in her second trimester. We decided to have the older girls minded and treat ourselves to a romantic weekend before the baby arrives.' Rigo raised his glass to his wife, meeting her eyes across the table for one heated moment.

Valerio cleared his throat pointedly. 'A pity you couldn't have taken your romantic weekend somewhere else, rather than ruining my private elopement,' Valerio said, feeling a strange mixture of discomfort and awe at the fact his family had taken the time to fly all this way.

Nicole Marchesi stood up and moved to take the seat beside her husband. 'Dani's friend Hermione has already told us the truth about your trip here.'

Dani froze at the end of the table. 'Hermione has spoken to you?'

'She styled our wedding years ago, and we've kept in touch. She's horrified about the whole thing. Really, Valerio, I can't believe you.'

Valerio felt heat creep up the back of his neck. 'You don't understand the whole situation, and I didn't want to worry you.'

'I understand very well.' His mother stood up, censure in her tone. 'Romantic elopement? You didn't even book a proper venue to say your vows, for goodness' sake. It's a disgrace!'

'Papà thinks you've got your fiancée pregnant.' Rigo's eyes twinkled.

Valerio exhaled slowly and saw Dani's shoulders drop with relief. Her friend clearly hadn't told his family the whole story—just enough to ensure this intervention of sorts.

'I know my son.' Renata turned to Dani, shaking her head. 'He's an impulsive fool, which might seem romantic right now, but he doesn't think things through. *Per l'amore di Dio*, I don't care if she's pregnant or not. You're on one of the most romantic islands in the world and you were going to get married in a courthouse?'

Valerio had tensed at the word 'impulsive', hating it that his family fully expected him to be running off for a shotgun wedding. Clearly they still painted him as a wild fool. But they knew nothing of his life— only what he allowed them to see.

'Daniela is not pregnant. We were just trying to keep things small and intimate.'

He groaned inwardly, knowing that calculating look in his mother's eyes all too well. She wasn't deliberately trying to be unkind. She was big on creating memories, ensuring beautiful moments were made at important events. To Renata Marchesi, very little would seem more important than ensuring her second son got married in a way that befitted their family name.

'Small and intimate?' She nodded. 'I can do that. Just give me twenty-four hours.'

As his brother let out a bark of laughter, Valerio

pinched the bridge of his nose between his fingers. He should have expected this. His parents' wedding was still talked about and they had been married for thirty-five years. They had stood together to watch their oldest son say his vows in a spectacular ceremony at a French chateau, and were now feeling the joy of welcoming grandchildren into their growing family.

How could he tell them that he didn't want an audience for what was only going to be a short-lived venture—another perceived failure to add to his ever-growing list? He couldn't tell them about the nature of his marriage to Dani without revealing the danger she was in. Maybe some day he would tell them the truth, but right now he had no choice but to go along with the charade.

The evening wound down in companionable conversation, with Rigo taking a moment apart from the others to quietly update him on the plans he'd put in place to tie up Daniela's inheritance and ask what progress had been made on the investigation.

After a while they joined the women on the terrace, and Valerio was once again drawn back into the charade of normal family life. He rested his arm across Dani's shoulders, feeling her settle her weight against him.

Across the table, Nicole announced that the baby had started kicking that week. Dani's eyes lit up with wonder as she asked if it hurt, at which Renata laughed and said that some day soon she might find out for herself.

He felt her tense against him, moving away ever so subtly. Dani's withdrawal got under his skin for some reason. As did the way his brother interacted so easily with his family, making jokes and talking about plans to build a tree house during the summer.

He had never before been jealous of the pressure Rigo had been put under as heir to the Marchesi fortune. But right now, seeing his brother rest his hand possessively across his wife's stomach, he felt an uncomfortable tightening in his chest. Needing to excuse himself, he stood and moved inside the house.

In the master bathroom, he splashed cold water on his face and glowered into the mirror. *Get it together, Marchesi.*

Dani appeared in the doorway behind him, her eyes filled with concern. God, she was so beautiful. It almost hurt to look at her without touching her. He wanted to take her, to consume her until the emptiness inside him was full of her laughter and her brilliance.

It was hard not to feel as if he was using her like a drug when the effect of just being in her company was so addictive. And it wasn't just the sex, either. He enjoyed being with her…found himself looking for ways to make her smile. What was happening to him? They had agreed on a time limit for whatever this thing was between them. And neither of them was interested in risking their business partnership over a fling. And it *was* just a fling.

A fling that was about to escalate into a marriage.

Valerio turned around and leaned back against the

vanity unit. She didn't move closer and he told himself he was relieved. If his face showed anything of the chaos of emotions warring inside him, she would probably turn around and call off the whole wedding.

She *should* call it off. She deserved so much better than this. She deserved more than a brief few days of hot sex with a man who didn't come close to deserving her. She deserved the wedding of her dreams with a good man who was reliable and logical and safe—everything he could never be for her. And this fictional perfect husband would make her happy—he would be with her as she carried their perfect children and lived her life in blissful happiness.

Valerio was shocked at the swift kick of jealousy in his gut.

'You left the table so suddenly I was worried.' She stepped forward, reaching out to touch his arm in a soft caress. 'What's wrong?'

Her gentle touch was more than he could process. The pressure in his forehead was close to the breaking point and he couldn't seem to gather his thoughts.

'You shouldn't have followed me.'

Even as he said the words, he knew he didn't mean them. He knew he wanted nothing more than for her to keep looking at him that way, caring about him.

A look of uncertainty flashed in her beautiful eyes and she quickly removed her hand. 'I'll get back to the others, then.'

'I'm fine.'

He turned away from her, splashing water over his face again and avoiding her burning gaze.

* * *

'Before I go, I want to talk to you about this whole ceremony thing.' Dani cleared her throat to try to stop the sudden shake in her voice. 'The flowers... the violin players...'

'My mother enjoys making an occasion of things, and I can't deny her after the year she's had. I hope that's okay?'

He was watching her reflection in the mirror, clearly waiting until she nodded.

'They're all expecting to see a happy couple saying their vows, so that is what we will give them. We have no other choice.'

Dani felt his words hit her somewhere in the chest with all the subtlety of a sledgehammer on porcelain. She had followed him expecting him to have been set a little off balance by this sudden seismic shift in their plans. But this... It was as if shutters had come down over his eyes, blocking her out.

Confusion mixed with hurt, and anger rose briefly, before she shut them down tight and stretched her lips into a smile.

'If anything, it will add to the authenticity of the whole thing,' she said, and a breathless ghost of a laugh escaped her lips, seeming to bounce off the bathroom walls, mocking her. 'I'm a little jealous that I didn't think of it, to be honest.'

He turned around and stared at her, a muscle in his jaw beginning to tic rather menacingly. She waited for him to speak, in her own foolish mind still clinging on to a thread of hope that he might have something good to say. Something that wasn't about the coldness in his eyes, the detachment.

'We have no other choice,' he'd said. As if he'd already been forcing himself to do this and now it was becoming an unbearable spectacle.

The fact that she had felt so connected to him for a moment just now only served to cheapen things further, making her feel weak and used even though he'd made it quite clear where he stood when it came to any feelings between them.

She felt the shameful threat of tears building in her eyes and turned quickly towards the door.

'Dani, wait.'

She turned back, swallowing hard past the lump in her throat and pasting on another bright smile. 'Yes?'

'I...I just wanted to say that I don't regret this weekend,' he said stiffly, his expression hard and intense. 'I don't regret whatever this was between us.'

'Neither do I.' She smiled—as though her heart *wasn't* breaking into a thousand tiny pieces at his use of the past tense. 'It was...exactly what I needed. Thank you.'

She turned away again before she completely lost her composure and moved to close the door softly behind her. She wasn't prepared for him to barge through it, bearing down on her in the hallway.

'"Thank you"?' he growled quietly, eyes glinting like sapphires in the evening light.

'What do you *want* me to say?' She felt her head shaking, her insides trembling dangerously. She needed to get away from him—get some breathing room before she totally embarrassed herself.

'I didn't do this as some sort of *service*, if that's what you're telling yourself.' His voice was low and gravelly, his eyes refusing to leave hers. 'The marriage is one thing, but let there be no misunderstanding that this…whatever this energy is between you and I…was just for us.'

'Valerio…' She bit her lip as he moved towards her and flattened his hands against the wall on either side of her head.

'Tell me you don't want me,' he whispered. 'Even just one more time.'

'Why don't you tell me what it is that *you* want, Valerio?'

She heard the longing in her voice. Felt the choking fear of this coming to an end and the foolish desire for him to offer her everything she dreamed of. She didn't just want one more time. She couldn't bear the idea of accepting whatever little offering he wanted to give to get her out of his system and move on to someone else. She wanted it all and it terrified her.

'Right now? I just want you to kiss me,' he murmured huskily.

She reached up, her lips seeking his. Her hands dug into his hair and pulled him close. The growl he let out in his throat sent heat flooding straight to her groin. God, would he ever stop setting her off like this?

But he had never given any indication that he thought of this as anything more. He remained rooted firmly in the present, refusing to think ahead, to see the risks. She couldn't ignore the red flags any longer—she couldn't place all her faith in blind hope. She was no longer just falling into dangerous territory with this powerful, fierce warrior of a man. She had plummeted right into the unknown.

She was in love with him.

She broke the kiss, closing her eyes tight against the realisation, her throat convulsing wildly as his breath fanned her cheek. His delicious scent was everywhere, his warm body so close, and she could feel his eyes on her. But she had a feeling that even if he wasn't right there she would still feel him. He had climbed his way into her chest, folding himself around her heart.

What had she got herself into?

'Are you crying?' He held her chin, tilting up her face with a deep frown.

She swiped the tears from her face, forcing herself to meet his eyes even as she felt her heart break. 'Valerio…let's not make this harder than it needs to be. I don't think either of us are ready for the fallout. I think…this needs to end now. While we can still go back to being friends and partners in this arrangement.'

Footsteps sounded in the hallway, and without warning, Valerio's mother advanced on them, a phone hooked in between her ear and her shoulder. Dani scrambled to rub the moisture from her eyes and regain some composure.

'Daniela, I just wanted to check if you prefer white

roses or…' Renata paused, taking in the sight of the two of them standing stiffly side by side.

Dani groaned inwardly, knowing her nose was likely bright pink and her feelings completely obvious. She prayed that the smile she forced would be convincing and mumbled something about adoring white roses before quickly excusing herself and going back into the bathroom.

She slid the lock closed before moving to the mirror and grabbing a wet flannel to scrub at the slightly smeared mascara under her eyes. Mortification crept up her chest and heated her cheeks.

Closing her eyes, she scrambled for her phone and hit the button to call Hermione, but was greeted by her friend's voicemail. She compensated by sending a single text, all in capital letters, asking what on earth she'd been thinking to tell Nicole about their elopement. No reply came.

Eventually she was going to have to leave this bathroom and face her fiancé. It was no big deal, she told herself, and straightened her shoulders and took a few deep breaths. She was in the business of presenting an image of what people wanted to see. She could do this—she could pretend to be his adoring fiancée for the rest of this trip. She could stand by Valerio's side and vow to love and cherish him as his wife without falling to pieces, couldn't she?

She sucked in a sharp breath. No big deal… No big deal at all.

CHAPTER ELEVEN

THERE WAS NO opportunity for Valerio to continue their conversation, as they weren't given any more time alone together. At the insistence of Renata, the men were hurried away to stay in one of the new yachts on the marina for the night, while the women stayed at the villa.

Valerio had explained the heightened security presence as his own need for protection, which his family had accepted with a slight look of worry. In the short time since Dani had come crashing back into his life, he had almost forgotten that the world still presumed him mad with paranoia.

Now Valerio stood alone on the bow of Velamar's brand-new luxury mega-yacht and tried to ignore the sense of restlessness that had hounded him since leaving Dani at the villa. His father and his brother had gone ahead to create an impromptu bachelor party, promising that it wouldn't involve anything inappropriate but that he would need his wits about him.

Valerio looked at his watch. He had another five minutes before they expected him to follow. He guessed it would involve gambling of some sort. His father was an avid poker player and was known for his skill. He sighed. Even the thought of a night of mindless gambling wasn't enough to calm the irritation brought by how badly he had handled things earlier.

She had *thanked* him for bedding her, as if he had been doing her a service. As though he had been trying to assuage his guilt by giving her orgasms as penance? His jaw tightened with anger at how little she must think of herself if she believed such utter nonsense. There was nothing charitable about his behaviour towards her.

If he'd been a better man, he would have kept his attraction under control. He wouldn't have complicated their arrangement and risked the fragile friendship they had formed. He had played with fire and ignited a full-blown blaze. He should be thankful that she'd seen sense and ended things.

But even now being away from her felt wrong, somehow, even though he knew she wasn't any safer with him by her side. He had left his two best security men with strict instructions to ensure she was completely secure. He had finalised all the necessary arrangements for the surprise he'd planned for her tomorrow. He'd wanted to see her face when she saw it, but it was probably better if he kept his distance until the ceremony. He wished they hadn't had that argument…that his family hadn't arrived and set off all alarm bells in his mind.

But above all, he realised a part of him missed her,

needed her company, as if they had spent years of this fragile new intimacy together—not just a few days.

He frowned at the thought. He *didn't* need her— he had always made sure he didn't need anyone. He was Mr No Strings. They had just both been celibate for a long time, so it was only natural that it would add to the kind of explosive sexual chemistry they had… It was a recipe for this addictive feeling. But he was not going to become hooked. They'd had one amazing weekend of blowing off some steam and that was over.

Gritting his teeth, he closed his eyes and focused on the sound of the sea lapping against the stern to try to unwind the tension in his gut. Maybe having his family here planning this wedding had got under his skin? There was no other explanation for the crazy thoughts he had been entertaining since he'd left the villa.

He knew that someone like him could never have the kind of stable, normal lifestyle his father and brother enjoyed. It was utterly ridiculous. Did he actually think he could give a woman like Dani the life she deserved?

He had already resigned himself to being alone until he found out who was behind Duarte's murder. He hadn't thought further beyond that. It was hard enough just getting through each day with his rigid handle on his PTSD intact. He was broken. His body and mind had been damaged and scarred and, no matter how hard he tried, he would always have to bear the reminders of what had happened in Brazil—a catastrophic event that he had caused by being his usual impulsive, reckless self.

His head security guard appeared, snapping him out of his thoughts. 'Mr Marchesi, there's a man here to see you. Says it's urgent.'

It was his private investigator from Rio, Juan, his face looking entirely the worse for wear and his clothes dishevelled.

'You didn't answer my calls, so I put a flight on your tab.' He stepped forward, placing a tablet computer in his hands. 'You can thank me later.'

The man sank down onto a nearby lounger as Valerio's eyes scanned the file, seeing Angelus Fiero's name. He felt anger begin to surge within him, expecting the worst. But the contents of the report were so far from what he'd expected that he found himself needing to sit down.

'Get me Fiero on the phone—now.' His voice was a dry rasp.

'He's currently in an operating theatre after sustaining a gunshot wound.' Juan sat forward. 'He'll survive. He went after them himself, it seems. The politician who ordered the kidnapping is dead and all evidence of the blackmail material he'd been keeping about Duarte has been destroyed, thanks to Fiero's clever manoeuvrings over the past few weeks. I believe the threat to Miss Avelar has been neutralised.'

Valerio felt the air leave his lungs. Angelus Fiero had been on their side all along. 'How do we know there aren't still others who are waiting to take over? How do I know she isn't still in danger?'

'Fiero has used his intel to turn the tables on a few other corrupt individuals linked to the Brazilian government. He's had the Avelar land and properties in Brazil made untouchable. They can only be used for charity, so they're worthless to any other money-grabbing corrupt developers now. As is every other piece of her inheritance. She's safe. I'm sure of it.'

Valerio nodded slowly, wondering why he didn't feel a sense of elation at the news.

He thanked Juan, and instructed his security guard to ensure that the PI was paid handsomely for his efforts. Alone again, he debated heading straight over to the villa and telling Dani the news. Telling her everything. But it was late…and he didn't want his mother to overhear their conversation.

Renata Marchesi was going to be upset enough at the cancellation of her dream island wedding ceremony. Because if there was no longer a threat, there was no longer any need for a wedding. He could tell his family what had happened—why he had been so secretive. Maybe one day they would all look back on this and laugh.

They would have made one another miserable anyway…he and Dani. But, then again, maybe they might have found some way to be happy in their arrangement…

He stood still for a long time in the dark, staring out at the inky black waves as he imagined what his life might have looked like if things had been different.

* * *

After a fitful night of sleep, alone in the bed that still smelled like Valerio, Dani barely registered the conversation at the breakfast table. It was dawn, and the whole house was buzzing with activity in preparation for the wedding. Renata and Nicole were talking about the details of the ceremony planned for that evening—a sunset wedding, followed by an intimate family dinner prepared by a world-famous chef who lived on the island.

The moment she was able to, she slipped away and wandered out onto the deck, staring at the glorious sunrise as it kissed pink and orange along the waves and wondering how on earth she had managed to get herself into such a mess. It was her wedding day and she was utterly miserable. If she'd been the brave, fearless type, she would have just run away. She almost smiled, imagining herself commandeering Valerio's boat and sailing towards the horizon.

Heels tapped across the deck towards her and she inhaled, turning and preparing herself to tell even more lies to this wonderful family who had made her feel so accepted.

But it wasn't Renata or Nicole who stood in front of her.

'Jeez, this place is locked up tighter than a prison.' Hermione smirked. 'I had to show my ID and videocall your fiancé just to get his goons to let me past the gates.'

Dani's mind had barely recognised her best friend's smiling face before she launched herself full force into

Hermione's arms. It was as though all the pressures of the day had been released, and she did nothing but hold her tight for a long time.

When they finally separated, she took a step back and lightly punched Hermione in the bicep.

'Hey, is that how you thank me for blowing off a job with royalty to come and be your maid of honour?'

'I wasn't planning to have an elaborate wedding at all until *you* intervened!' Dani said under her breath. 'His family aren't supposed to know anything about what's really going on here.'

'By that you mean the fact that you're having hot sex with your soon-to-be husband?' Hermione said dryly. 'That's utterly scandalous, Dani. How will they ever recover?'

Dani suddenly regretted the instant messages she'd been firing back and forth with her best friend. 'Be serious. It's not a real marriage—none of this is real—and it's only going to hurt them once they find out it's all lies.'

'*Is* it all lies, though?' Hermione asked softly. 'Because the look on your face in that picture you sent me of you two out on the boat… It's the first time I've seen you look happy in a long time. Does he make you happy?'

Dani swallowed hard, turning around to hide the sudden flood of wetness to her eyes. Yes, he made her happy. He made her feel stronger than she'd thought she was capable of being. He made her feel beautiful and powerful and utterly devastated all in the space

of one day. He made her feel far too much for it not
to be utterly catastrophic to her soul once he eventually walked away. Because he didn't feel anything
for her other than a fleeting physical attraction and a
responsibility to keep her safe.

'Dani…' Hermione spoke softly, laying a hand on
her shoulder. 'Did I mess up here? I just thought of
the wedding you lost out on before, and the awful-
ness of the past few years, and I wanted something
beautiful for you.'

Silence fell between them. Then Dani exhaled a
slow, shaking breath and turned to press her face into
her friend's shoulder. 'Thank you. I'm really glad
you're here now.'

They were interrupted by the arrival of Renata
and Nicole, holding champagne glasses. Sharing a
pointed look with Hermione, she joined their toast to
a beautiful wedding and a happy marriage to follow.

'I'm sorry now that I didn't buy a proper dress.'
Dani frowned, realising for the first time that the
simple beige linen dress she'd packed was really not
going to be appropriate any longer. She watched as
the three women exchanged a look of pure mischief,
and then Hermione leaned towards Dani's future
mother-in-law and whispered in her ear.

'I asked these ladies to wait until I got here to surprise you,' Hermione said, and smiled, pulling her by
the hand towards the house.

Dani followed Hermione upstairs to the master
bedroom—Valerio's bedroom. At some point it had
been filled with boxes of flowers and small bags bear-

ing designer labels. Hanging on the frame of the four-poster bed was a large white garment bag.

Dani felt time stop as Hermione slid the zip downwards and revealed the most spectacular blush-coloured gown she had ever set eyes on. It was the dress Dani had pointed out to her friend at a fashion week over a year ago, when she had confessed that her ex had influenced the choice of her first traditional white wedding gown, which she'd had to embarrassingly return when he jilted her.

Hermione had been outraged, but had never brought up the conversation again. Clearly she had not forgotten.

In a blur, Dani was undressed and zipped into the gown, awed at how it fitted perfectly to her body like a second skin and flowed in all the right places.

'You remembered... How did you get this?' she breathed slowly, her hands stroking the material with awe. It was the same one. There was no doubting it. Even down to the hand-sewn rose-shaped gathering on the bodice.

'Your fiancé called my office yesterday, the moment he realised the wedding was going to be more than a simple affair. He asked me to choose the perfect dress as a wedding gift—and to bring myself, of course.' Hermione moved beside her, tipping her face up and wiping away a small errant tear that had slipped out. 'This is a *real* wedding, Dani. You both just haven't realised it yet.'

Dani thought of Valerio's thoughtfulness in helping her tackle her fear of the ocean. The way he'd held her as he told her how beautiful she was. The way he'd looked into her eyes as they made love. The sense of overwhelming rightness between them.

Now she was being told that he had gone so far as to make sure she had her best friend here, to obtain her dream dress… It was more than anyone had ever done for her before… It was too much.

She was overcome with the need to know what it all meant. What they meant to one another.

'I need to go to him.' She turned to Hermione and saw her friend's eyes light up with glee. 'There's no way I can marry him without laying everything out on the table, consequences be damned. I'm done with being afraid.'

'I like this change in you.' Hermione hugged her close. 'And I hope that man knows how lucky he is.'

They both knew there was no way Renata would allow Dani to leave without asking a million questions and worrying, so Hermione offered to spin a story and cause a distraction while Dani slipped away.

She briefly considered the speedboat, and a dramatic exit, but she wasn't quite that adventurous yet. So she walked up the driveway to the small hut that housed the two security guards and turned on her best smile, matched with her most authoritative tone. She didn't have time for any of their safety protocol nonsense.

'I need to see your boss. Right now.'

Valerio had just stepped out of the shower when he heard the door to the master cabin burst open. Like something from a dream, Dani walked into the bath-room, her eyes filled with blazing emotion.

'You're wearing the dress...' His voice was some-where between disbelief and wonder, and a part of him was cursing fate for throwing this vision at him when he had been preparing to go to her and call off their entire wedding. 'Why are you here?'

'I had a whole speech planned on the drive over...' Her voice shook as she looked down and realised he only wore a towel. 'Oh, God... I should go.'

Valerio gripped her wrist and pulled her back to-wards him. 'Don't.'

She moved closer to him, her eyes filled with a look that both terrified and delighted him. A look he had no right to see. She needed to know all the facts. She needed to know that she didn't have to trust him or rely on him any longer. That she didn't need him.

'I need to talk to you before...' She paused, one hand reaching out to lay against his bare chest. 'Be-fore we go ahead with this.'

'I need to talk to you too.' He inhaled deeply, glad that they were alone for this moment. That he could give her privacy, away from prying eyes and ears.

'I lied,' she said suddenly. 'I don't want things to end. The thought of not being with you again is un-bearable.'

With disbelief and shock, he pulled her closer until they stood chest to chest. 'I've hardly been able to stop thinking of this...of what you do to me. It's like I have no control when it comes to you.'

'Me too.'

Her voice was a husky whisper as she pressed herself to him, her eyes widening as she brushed against the hard ridge of his erection. The look of instant heat she gave him was enough to bring him close to the edge as his lips lowered to hers in a fury of urgent need and frustration.

The sound she made against his mouth was half surprise and half seductive whimper as she slowly melted against him. His hands cupped the delicious curve of her behind, grinding her against the unbearable hardness that ached to be inside her.

Dani felt the urgency in him like a rising tide as he walked her backwards until she was pressed against the cool tiled walls. His eyes glimmered with intent as he slowly raised the full skirt of her wedding dress up her thighs. The material was light, and easily folded around her waist. She worried for a split second about crushing the fabric, but then decided it would be fine.

He moved to touch her, to feel how slick and hot and ready she was for him. His eyes darkened to the colour of a raging storm.

Her white lace underwear refused to stay to one side, and he let out a low growl, tearing at one side and throwing the scrap of lace to the floor. She bit her lower lip, feeling a thrill go through her at such a primal display. His lips nuzzled against her neck, biting softly.

'*Dio*... I need to be inside you right now.'

'Yes...' she breathed, feeling his hands grip the

curve of one thigh and lift it so she was spread wide
for him.

He dropped his towel and slid into her easily, her
body singing out in sweet relief at being filled with
such perfect hard heat. His thrusts were demanding,
but his rhythm was just what she needed—she needed
to feel that warm tension building deep inside her.

Every hard stroke brought her higher, and she
clamped a hand over her mouth as she fought not to
moan. They were far enough away from anyone else
on the yacht not to truly risk being caught, but the
thrill of it only added to her arousal.

Without warning, he gripped her other thigh and
lifted her against the wall for even deeper access. She
stiffened and tried to stop him. He shut off her pro-
tests with his mouth, the urgency in his body telling
her he was far from burdened by her size. He pulled
at one strap of her dress with his teeth, freeing one
dark nipple above the fabric and taking it greedily
into his mouth.

With his head bent low she could clearly see the
reflection of him taking her in the mirror on the opposite wall. He followed her gaze, his eyes wicked
as sin as he quickened his pace, giving no mercy as
he took her over and over until she cried out against
her hand.

'Just look at you,' he growled, his eyes almost reverent. 'Do you see how beautiful you are?'

She looked at the flush on her cheeks as she felt
pleasure mounting, at the plump swollen flesh of her
lips. She looked like a stranger.

She felt utterly weightless in his arms as she rode out her climax, feeling it crest and take her like a rush of electricity until her entire body shook. He was right there with her. A few hard thrusts and he came hard inside her, his head tilted back and eyes closed tight as though he were in pain.

After a moment he stepped back and grabbed a towel from the rack, wetting it and kneeling down to cleanse her. The movement was so caring she felt her throat clench. He didn't meet her eyes, however, as he stood up and put himself to rights. Then he reached down to grab her torn underwear from the floor and stared at it with such ferocity that she inhaled a sharp breath.

'I didn't mean for that to happen.'

He spoke with his jaw tight, and there was a sudden tension in him that made Dani feel the need to reassure him.

'Well… That's not exactly what I came here for, either.' She forced a small laugh, still slightly out of breath as she pulled her dress down.

'What *did* you come here for, then?' he asked roughly. 'Because I was just on my way to see you.'

She tried not to read into his words, into his implication that sex was all they had. Even though he had told her that was all he was capable of giving her. They'd agreed to end things, but here they were after ten seconds alone together, panting in the aftermath of what had possibly been the most intense lovemaking she'd experienced with him. That had to mean something, didn't it?

'I came here to say that I'm not going to marry you today without telling you how I really feel.' She inhaled once more, fighting the twist of anxiety in her stomach at the leap of faith she was about to take. 'I can't pretend to be your wife, Valerio. Because I'm in love with you, and the only way I'm marrying you today is if it's real.'

Silence stretched between them for a moment, and she felt her heartbeat racing wildly in her chest. She forced herself to stand tall and meet his eyes, knowing she owed herself this moment of risk. She knew she would never regret giving him her heart, even if he handed it right back and walked away.

'I don't want to be your wife in name only. I want it all. I want everything that you said you can never give me.'

'What if I told you there was no need for us to get married any more?' He spoke quietly, his eyes stubbornly refusing to meet hers.

'What do you mean?'

'The threat to you has been neutralised.'

'You should have come straight to tell me. How long were you planning to keep this to yourself?'

'My private investigator informed me late last night. I waited to confirm the details myself and it's true.'

He told her of Angelus Fiero's involvement, about the blackmail and the corrupt politician. He went on laying everything out on the table until his head hurt and she sagged back against the wall, her face filled with disbelief.

'You said you were coming to see me this morning,' she said. "Were you planning to call off the wedding?'

'Yes, of course,' he said quickly, then caught her sharp wince. 'I mean...I was going to tell you everything. We both agreed that this marriage was just for your protection, but now...there is no more danger. Does that not change things?'

She nodded once, her lips pressed into a thin line. 'Of course... It changes everything. I just wish you'd told me before I came here.'

'Dani, wait.' He placed his arm on the wall to stop her leaving. 'I've told you who I am... I've told you that I'm not the right kind of guy for you. You need to go and find out who you are and what you want without the threat of danger influencing you.'

'Valerio. I just laid my entire heart on the line.' She flashed him a deep look of disdain. 'My feelings for you never depended on you being wrong or right for me. I accepted you for the man you are—not the one you think you should be.'

'I don't want to leave things like this.' He frowned, hating it that he was hurting her but knowing he had to let her go.

'If you don't have anything else to say, then I'm going to leave, before anyone sees me in this dress.'

She waited another moment, refusing to look up at him, before disappearing quickly through the doorway and out into the hall beyond.

He let her go, telling himself that it was better this way even as everything in him fought to follow her.

As though distance might help, he launched himself into the first speedboat he could find in the yacht's docking bay, pushing the vessel to its limits, needing to feel the lightness that always came with being on the water.

The lightness didn't come.

After a while he gave up punishing the boat and cut the engine, bobbing in the open water as he watched the sun rise higher in the sky. He could be selfish, he thought. He could follow her and take all that precious love she'd offered for himself. He could pretend she wouldn't grow to hate him, even though everything in him knew she would. He wasn't built for the kind of love she needed.

She would move on from this and start anew…find someone better. As for him… He wasn't so changed that he would pine over a woman, was he? He cursed aloud, slamming his fist against the wheel. He couldn't feel any pain, but the awful emptiness in his chest was a different matter entirely.

CHAPTER TWELVE

THE AIR IN Rio de Janeiro was warm and heavy as Dani walked out of the airport and into a waiting car. Blissfully, the chauffeur was not eager for conversation, so she had plenty of time to rest her eyes and prepare herself for whatever lay ahead.

Heartbreak was just another inconvenience right now—along with Angelus Fiero, who had refused to stop calling her every day for the past week until she'd reluctantly agreed to book a flight to Rio and hear him out.

It wasn't that she didn't feel gratitude for the part the older man had played in bringing justice against those who had been responsible for so much pain and loss. But something about coming back to Brazil felt wrong, somehow.

It was as if she was adrift amongst the old shadows of a life and had no idea how to navigate. The last time she'd set foot in Rio, she'd had her parents and her brother by her side, her family unit intact. Memories of her childhood were just as foggy as the cloudy sky above, which threatened to spill with rain at any moment.

Dani frowned as her car came to a stop outside wrought-iron gates and looked up at the concrete façade of the Avelar family villa for the first time in over two decades. It seemed like a lifetime ago that her ten-year-old self had said goodbye to the palatial mansion just outside the city, as she was torn away from the only home she'd ever known and forced to start over in England.

Was it any wonder that she had clung to her twin amidst all the constant change in their lives over the past two decades?

As she stepped out into the warm afternoon and told the driver to wait, Valerio's words rang in her ears. *'You need to figure out who you are and what you really want.'* The trouble was, she *had* figured it out. She had told him exactly what she wanted and who she wanted.

The memory of Valerio's eyes before she'd walked away from him seemed like a dream. She shook her head. Had it really been a week since she'd seen him? It seemed as if only hours had passed since St Lucia. Since he'd held her hand as they dived into the depths of the ocean together…since he had looked into her eyes in Monte Carlo after he had kissed her for the first time in front of all those people…since she'd felt the heat and power of his body as he'd turned the tables on her that first night and tied her to her own bed.

Anger fuelled her as she dug through her bag in search of the old brass key. She rubbed roughly at the space in the centre of her chest, refusing to give in to another bout of tears and self-pity. She had done enough of that in the days after she'd returned to London.

She'd left St Lucia a week ago, returning to her tidy white apartment in Kensington and immediately sending a formal letter announcing that she was completely removing herself as an active partner of Velamar. Valerio had not attempted to contact her, but she'd told herself she didn't care that he was glad she wouldn't be working alongside him. It was irrelevant, and it wouldn't change her own course of action in finally taking the plunge and launching her firm. She should have done it years ago.

It stung like a fresh wound, entering what had once been her family home now completely alone. The air was dry and utterly still inside, where white dust sheets covered furniture like old-movie-style ghosts. A shiver ran from the base of her neck down her spine. But she surprised herself with how boldly she stepped over the threshold and laid her bags on the floor.

A quick scan of the barren downstairs space had her chest tight with emotion, so she distracted herself by opening shutters and windows, bringing light and much-needed fresh air into the stagnant dark rooms.

When she next looked at her watch, she was shocked to see that almost an hour had passed. She was covered in dust, sweat glistening on her brow, but something warm and precious hummed within her that felt suspiciously like relief.

It had never sat well with her to leave this beautiful

house closed up and vacant. Her parents would have been happy to see it being taken care of, to see their daughter reconnecting with her roots in the home that held such precious memories.

She cleaned herself up as best she could and then set out for the hospital, to find out what exactly it was that Angelus Fiero simply had to tell her in person.

Two hours later she finally emerged from Angelus Fiero's hospital bedside onto the street, her legs feeling as if they might give out at any moment. It turned out the man had a very pressing reason for bringing her here. One that involved a web of secrets and strategies that her brother himself had created. Once she was safely alone in the dark interior of the car, she fought the urge to give in to the hysteria and tears threatening to burst free from her chest as she processed everything the old man had revealed. But one fact shone out high above the others.

Her brother had survived.

Duarte was alive. He'd been recovering from severe brain trauma and was being kept in a secret location, but he was alive.

A thousand thoughts flew through her mind at once, but one drowned out all the others. She wished Valerio had been there with her for this. She wished she hadn't been alone to take the hit of a bombshell of this magnitude.

She was hardly aware of the drive back to Casa Avelar. Her brain was stuck somewhere between numb shock and trying to analyse what the logical next step might be. But there was nothing logical about any of this. Nothing at all.

Stepping out of the car, she paused as she noticed that the lights in the villa were all blazing bright and a sleek black car was parked at the top of the driveway. She paused on the stone steps, her senses on high alert. The front door opened and she felt the tightness in her chest released on a heavy exhalation of breath.

Valerio.

His shoulders filled the doorway, the light grey material of his silk shirt making him seem ethereal, as if she could reach out to touch him and he might not even be there.

'You didn't answer my calls.' His voice was low and effortlessly seductive, with just a little hesitance thrown in.

'So you flew to Rio? You could have just left a message with my PA.'

She fought the shiver that ran down her spine as he held her in place with that intense gaze. The look in his eyes startled her. It was how she imagined she must have looked every day for the past week.

Miserable.

She needed to tell him what she'd just found out—that her brother was still alive and had been kept hidden somewhere in Brazil. But a part of her wanted to know why he was here, how he felt about her, before he knew about Duarte.

Had he missed her?

The look in his eyes was almost enough to tip her over the edge of control and send her melting into a puddle at his feet. Was it simply regret at the loss of the precious friendship he'd spoken of? She held back, schooling her features as much as possible. Once burned, twice shy might not apply to every situation, but that didn't mean she should dive headfirst into this particular fire without thinking it through.

She crossed her arms and allowed the silence of the evening air to fall heavily between them. He moved first, taking a few steps down the gravel driveway with ease, showcasing long, powerful legs encased in worn designer denim. Of course he *would* look more delicious than ever, she groaned inwardly, imagining how awful she must look in comparison.

'I spoke to Angelus Fiero.' She tried to control the wavering of her voice, determined not to break down in front of him but desperately needing to unburden herself. 'He told me that Duarte is alive.'

Valerio froze. 'That's impossible. I saw him die.'

Dani opened her bag and handed him the folded hospital document as she relayed the information she'd been given of Duarte's injuries and rehabilitation in a facility deep in the rainforest.

For a long time Valerio just stared at the piece of paper in his hand.

'I thought about what I would say for the entire flight here...' He spoke softly, his hand moving for a moment as though he wanted to touch her but decided against it. 'I didn't plan on you telling me any of this. I'll come with you. We will find him together.'

Dani nodded thankfully, letting the silence pulse

between them before she spoke. 'Valerio…why did you come if it wasn't to hear what Fiero had to say?'

Valerio hesitated, then seemed to make a snap decision. 'I came for you, Dani. I should have come sooner. I should have followed you the minute you left my yacht. I told myself I should be relieved that everything had changed, that you were free of needing me, but…' He shook his head, looking away from her.

Dani felt something in her heart stretch—something that felt foolishly like hope blossoming. 'You were scared,' she said softly, a thrill of electricity shooting through her when he looked up and met her eyes.

'I'm known for taking risks and following my instincts, even if it leads to trouble.' He shook his head. 'But the things I've done in the past…risking my safety and my wealth on crazy ventures… None of that scared me. I never truly valued my own life. I always saw myself as dispensable.'

She shook her head, ready to launch into a vehement protest, but he reached out a hand, stopping her.

'I thought that risking our friendship and disrespecting the promise I'd made to Duarte was what terrified me. But seeing this paper now…knowing he's alive out there somewhere… It doesn't change anything for me. We will deal with that as it comes.' He took a deep breath, laying the document down on the step behind him. 'Dani…look at me. I now know I was just afraid of what I felt—not the consequences or the risks. I don't need anyone's permission. Letting you move on without ever telling you how I feel is no longer an option.'

He laid his hand over hers, turning it to find she still wore the diamond engagement ring on her finger. She hadn't been able to part with it just yet. He looked down at her, meeting her eyes with such reverence that it took her breath away all over again.

'I think I've been slowly falling in love with you since we were teenagers and I didn't have a clue. So I ignored you—I ran away or I provoked you. I'm far from perfect, and I'll probably make mistakes, but I'm asking you for a second chance.'

She felt emotion clog her throat as she fought to formulate the words rushing through her head. In the end she just threw her arms around his neck, burying her face in his shoulder.

Eventually she leaned back, looking into his eyes and seeing the relief and emotion there. 'You put far too much effort into playing a part and worrying about what others think...but I see a man who is so much more than a playboy pirate. You put me first every single time, and I...' She felt her throat catch. 'You told me that if you want something you just have to take a deep breath and dive... So I knew that I couldn't walk away without telling you how I felt. Without telling you what you could have if you were only brave enough to take a risk of your own.'

He closed the small distance between them with lightning speed and pulled her up into a kiss that made her entire body shake with emotion. His hands entwined with hers, coming up to press against his thundering heartbeat.

Dani smiled against his lips as he devoured her.

He kissed her until she was kissing him back with every ounce of love she had…until she felt the breath sigh from her and her entire body melt into his arms. Only then did he pause for breath, burying his face in her neck and exhaling on a deep, primal growl.

'Sorry, I'm not good with pretty words or speeches,' he said softly into her hair, his hands still clutching her tightly against him, as though he feared she might run away if he loosened his grip.

'That was pretty eloquent, I think.' She bit her bottom lip, feeling as if there was a hint of magic in the air—as if this couldn't be real, this perfect moment. But the smile that spread across his full lips mixed with a look of fierce possession told her everything she needed to know.

She gasped, looking down as he slid her engagement ring off her finger with one smooth movement. Silencing her with a finger on her lips, he took a step back and slowly lowered himself down to one knee.

'I know I've technically proposed already, but I feel the situation requires a do-over.' His eyes met hers with intense heat and emotion. '*Tesoro*... I want to be your husband and your partner. I want us to create a family and a life together. I swear I will spend the rest of my life giving you every single thing you desire if you'll have me.'

'I've never wanted anything as much as I want to be your wife for real. I love you. I want us to live together, work our crazy schedules around each other. I want to have your babies, Valerio Marchesi. I want all of it.'

She took a deep breath, fearing her heart might actually burst out of her chest with the effort of getting the words out. She felt shivers run down her spine as he slid the ring back onto her finger and stood up, pulling her into a tight embrace.

She felt a calm settle over her like nothing she'd ever experienced before. Despite the unknown of what might lie ahead of them, she knew he would be by her side. Together they would dive headfirst into whatever adventures lay ahead, and as long as she had her hand in his, she knew things would be okay.

EPILOGUE

THE NOVEMBER RAIN poured down on his face as Valerio raced across the busy rush hour streets, narrowly missing a black cab as he finally reached the door of the hospital. He barely stopped to announce himself at the desk, his breath crashing in and out of his lungs as he took the stairs two by two.

The prestigious London hospital was a maze of corridors as he passed by door after door, finally finding the one he was looking for. The one he'd been inside every day for the past week. He came to a stop inside the brightly lit room—only to see an empty bed, perfectly made up with white linen. Fear closed off his air supply for a long, panic-ridden moment, before a woman entered the room behind him, wearing bright blue scrubs and a white mask.

'Mr Marchesi, you're just in time. Your wife is in Theatre.'

He was rushed down to the emergency operating theatre and handed a bundle of scrubs to change into. His hands shook as he pushed open the door to the bright surgical space and saw Dani's beautiful face, white with fear, as she lay surrounded by doctors and nurses and the rhythmic beeping of medical equipment.

'Valerio!' Her shout of relief was palpable as she reached out to clutch at his sleeve and pull him close to her face. 'I can't believe this is happening. It's too early!'

Valerio steeled himself at the anguish in her voice and murmured words of encouragement in her ear, his hand gripping hers tightly as the surgeons performed their work on the other side of a blue screen.

It seemed as if hours passed before the doctors announced that the baby was out, then spent a while bending over Dani with furrowed brows. Moments later a loud, healthy infant's cry erupted in the room and he felt his shoulders sag with relief as he pressed his forehead to Dani's and let emotion take over.

After a flurry of movement and various checks, the doctor assured them that their daughter was perfectly healthy and didn't need any care other than her mother's skin.

A nurse placed the tiny form on Dani's chest and Valerio felt his heart swell with love and gratitude as they both cradled and stroked their child's glorious head of jet-black curls.

'What do you think Leandro will say when he finds out he got a baby sister instead of a brother?' Dani asked softly, her eyes filled with laughter.

Valerio winced, thinking of the serious-faced three-year-old at home in their town house, being spoiled by Nonna and Nonno Marchesi. Leandro had been quite clear that a baby brother was the only thing he would tolerate.

'I'm sure we'll figure out a way to bring him around,' he said, and smiled, leaning in to brush a kiss on his wife's forehead.

Once the surgical team had finished the aftercare for her emergency caesarean procedure, Dani was returned to her comfortable private room, where she promptly fell asleep. She awoke a short while later, to the sight of her husband cradling their infant daughter in his strong arms.

She was quiet for a while as she watched them, her heart threatening to burst with joy and relief that they had been blessed with a healthy child for the second time.

Their firstborn son had been born exactly on his due date almost two years previously, on the day of their second wedding anniversary. Valerio had joked that he was just like his mother: shockingly efficient and punctual.

The comment had turned out to be quite accurate. Leandro *was* just like her and Duarte had been as children, in spirit and in looks—apart from the brilliant Marchesi blue eyes that accompanied his rather serious gaze. She thought of her twin brother, feeling an echo of that old sadness mixed with relief. Her relationship with her twin had been strained for a time once they'd found him and discovered the depths of his ordeal and the web of deception behind it. But now…now she could hardly believe her luck at having so much family around her.

'I'll have to tell Duarte he won our bet,' Valerio murmured, looking at their daughter. 'I thought we'd have all boys. This girl is definitely going to steal my heart.'

Dani laughed. 'What are we going to call her?'

'I was thinking…Lucia.' He turned brilliant cobalt eyes on her.

Instantly Dani's thoughts travelled back to the island where they had fallen in love, said their vows, and where they'd returned every single year since, to the villa they'd now bought together.

'Valerio…' She felt her throat close with emotion. 'That's perfect.'

'*She's* perfect. Just like her mother.'

He placed their daughter in her small crib, his movements careful and confident. She had almost forgotten how natural he was with babies. He had been the one to show her tricks to get Leandro to sleep for longer and to bring his wind up, while she had been a shivering mess of nerves for months.

She sighed and leaned back on the pillows. He moved to sit alongside her, being careful of her tender abdomen and the tubes still attached to her arms.

'I have never been more afraid than when I walked into that room today and saw an empty bed.' A frown marred his handsome brow as he looked down at her, stroking one hand across her cheek.

'I was terrified too, once I realised something was wrong and they wanted to get her out so suddenly. I was so worried that you wouldn't get here in time. But I swear I could hear my mother's voice in my head, telling me to breathe. And I knew that we would all get through it okay.'

'You were amazing. You are a goddess of a woman—have I told you that?' He leaned forward, his lips brushing across hers softly, one hand cradling her neck. 'Your strength never ceases to amaze me. How on earth did I get so lucky?'

'I love you so much,' she whispered against his lips. 'But all this sweet talk isn't going to make me want more babies.'

'You said the same after the first one.' He smiled, nuzzling her ear. 'But two is perfect for me. I think your staff will kill me if I keep getting you pregnant—that company of yours is skyrocketing and they need their fearless leader.'

'Motherhood only adds to my superpowers.'

Dani smiled, thinking of the perfect top-floor London offices of Avelar Inc.

She had done it all—her own company, her perfect home in the English countryside and her wonderful family. Valerio had promised he would give her everything and he'd stood by her every step of the way, giving her his full support as they juggled their work and home lives together as a team.

'Lucia Marchesi…' Dani smiled down at her sleeping daughter. 'I don't think the world could handle another Riviera pirate—especially if she looks anything like you.'

'If she's like me she'll need to find the right person

to balance out her wild spirit.' He leaned back, draping an arm carefully over her shoulders and dropping a kiss on her collarbone.

Dani leaned back into the power of his embrace, letting out a soul-deep sigh of contentment and happiness. 'This is quite an adventure you've taken me on.'

'We've only just started, *tesoro*.'

* * * * *

Keep reading for an excerpt of a new title
from the Modern series,
UNDOING HIS INNOCENT ENEMY by Heidi Rice

CHAPTER ONE

CARA DOYLE EXHALED SLOWLY, allowing her breath to plume in the icy air. She lifted the camera she'd spent a small fortune on and watched the lynx in the viewfinder as it prowled across the powdery snow.

She had been trailing the female huntress for over a week—in between shifts as a barista at a resort hotel in Saariselkä—but today she'd got so many exceptional shots excitement made her heart rate soar. Which was good because, with the temperature plummeting to minus thirty degrees this morning, she couldn't spend much longer out here before she froze.

A shiver ran through her body as the camera's shutter purred through its twenty frames per second. Even with six layers of thermal clothing she could feel the cold embalming her. She ignored the discomfort. This moment was the culmination of six months' work doing crummy jobs in a succession of Lapland hotels and resorts, all through the summer and autumn, to pay for her trip studying the behaviour of the famously elusive wildcats for her breakout portfolio as a wildlife photographer.

The lynx's head lifted, her silvery gaze locking on Cara's.

Hello, there, girl, you're grand, aren't you? Just a few more shots, I promise. Then I'll be leaving you in peace.

Cara's heart rose into her throat. The picture in her viewfinder was so stunning she could hardly breathe—the lynx's graceful feline form stood stock-still, almost as if posing for the shot. Her tawny white fur blended into the glittering landscape before she ducked beneath the snow-laden branches of the frozen spruce trees and disappeared into the monochromatic beauty of the boreal forest.

Cara waited a few more minutes. But the lynx was gone.

She rolled onto her back, stared up at the pearly sky through the trees. It was almost three o'clock—darkness would be falling soon, with only four hours of daylight at this time of year in Finnish Lapland. She had to get back to the skimobile she'd left on the edge of the forest so she didn't disturb the wildcat's habitat.

But she took a few precious moments, her lips

lifting beneath the layers protecting her face from the freezing air.

It only took a few heartbeats though to realise her body temperature was dropping from lack of movement. It would be no good getting the shots she'd been working on for six months through summer, autumn and finally into the short crisp winter days, if she froze to death before she could sell them.

She levered herself onto her feet and began the trek back to the snowmobile, picking up her pace as twilight edged in around her.

Feck, exactly how long had she been out here?

It had only seemed like minutes but, when she was totally focussed on her work, time tended to dissolve as she hunted for that single perfect shot.

At last, she saw the small skimobile where she'd left it, parked near the hide she'd been using for weeks.

She packed the camera away in its insulated box in the saddlebag, aware that her hands were getting clumsy, the piercing cold turning to a numb pain.

Not good.

The delight and excitement at finally capturing the creature she'd been trailing for months began to turn to dismay though as she switched on the ignition, and nothing happened. Annoyed, she went for option two. Grabbing the start cord, she tugged hard. Again, nothing, not even the clunking sound of the engine turning over.

Don't panic...you're grand...you know the protocol.

But even as she tried to calm herself and continued yanking the cord, all the reasons why she shouldn't have followed the lynx so far into the national forest, why she shouldn't have stayed out so long, bombarded her tired mind.

Eventually, she was forced to give up on starting the snowmobile. Her arms hurt and she was losing what was left of her strength, plus sweating under the layers of clothing only made her colder. Maybe the engine had frozen—it had been inactive here too long. She should have left it running, but she hadn't expected to stay out so long and fuel cost a fortune. She fished the satellite phone out of her pack.

There was no phone signal this far north, and no communities nearby. She knew there were rumours of some reclusive US-Finnish billionaire, who lived in the uninhabited frozen wilderness on the far side of the national forest in a stunning glass house few people had ever seen or located... The resort workers whispered about him because apparently there was some tragic story involving the murder of his parents, and the fortune he had inherited as a kid before he disappeared from the public eye. But whatever the details were, they hadn't reached Ireland, and she couldn't rely on stumbling across some mythical Fortress of Solitude in the middle of nowhere—which could be hundreds of miles away. If it even existed at all.

She tuned into the last signal she'd used.

'Mayday, Mayday. I'm in the n-national forest about f-forty miles north-east of Saariselkä. My vehicle won't start. Please respond.'

Her eyelids drooped, the strange numbness wrapping around her ribs and slowing her breathing, as the last of the sunlight disappeared. She continued to broadcast as her energy drained.

If she could just sleep for a minute, she'd be fine.

No, don't sleep, Cara.

Just when it seemed the situation couldn't possibly get any worse, she felt the first swirl of wind, the prickle of ice on her face.

What the...?

There had been no suggestion of a snowstorm today in the weather forecast or on the radar. Because she'd checked.

But as the swirl lifted and twisted, and a whistling howl picked up through the canyon of trees, turning the winter silence into a wall of terrifying sound, she could barely hear her own voice, still shouting out the Mayday.

She burrowed into the gathering drift beside the broken snowmobile, to shelter from the wind. No one had responded. No one was coming. The battery light on the phone started to wink, the only thing she could see in the white-out.

Her mother's voice, practical, and tired, hissed through her consciousness. Bringing back their last frustrating conversation two days ago.

'You're a fine one...why would you want to go all the way there when we have more than enough creatures here to photograph on the farm?'

'Because a wildlife photographer photographs creatures in the wild, Mammy, not cows and sheep.'

'Shouldn't you be settling already? You're twenty-one and have barely had a boyfriend. All your brothers are having babies already.'

Because my brothers have no desire to get out of County Wexford, just like you, Mammy.

The answer she'd wanted to say swirled in her head, the icy cold making her eyes water.

Don't you dare cry, Cara Doyle, or your eyelids will stick to your eyeballs and then where will you be?

Everywhere was starting to hurt now. The six layers of expensive thermal clothing she'd maxed out one of her many credit cards to buy felt like a layer of tissue paper against the frigid wind.

The dying phone, forgotten in her hand, crackled and then barked.

'Yes… Yes?' she croaked out on a barely audible sob.

Please let that be someone coming to rescue me.

'The cat's lights. Turn them on.' The furious voice seemed to shoot through the wind and burrow into her brain.

Relief swept through her. She nodded, her throat too raw to reply. She pushed herself into the wind with the last of her strength. Her bones felt so brittle now she was sure they were frozen too. She flicked the switch, then collapsed over the seat.

The single yellow beam shone out into the storm—and made her think of all those stories she'd heard as a child, in Bible study as she prepped for her first holy communion, about the white light of Jesus beckoning you, which you saw before death.

Sister Mary Clodagh had always scared the hell out of them with that tale.

But Cara didn't feel scared now, she just felt exhausted.

Her sore eyelids drooped.

'Keep talking.' The gruff voice on the phone reverberated in her skull.

She pressed the mouthpiece to her lips, mumbled what she could through the layers of her balaclavas.

'Louder,' the shout barked back.

'I'm trying…' she managed. Her fingers and face didn't hurt any more, because the embalming warmth pressed against her chest like a hot blanket.

Whoever Mr Angry is, he'd better be getting a move on.

A dark shape appeared in the pearly beam, the outline making her think of the majestic brown bears she'd spent the summer in Lapland observing and photographing… The hum of an engine cut through the howling wind as the bear got closer. It detached from its base, the dark shape looming over her.

Piercing silvery blue eyes locked on hers through the thin strip of skin visible under his helmet and above his face coverings and reminded her of the lynx—who she'd photographed what felt like several lifetimes ago.

Hard hands clasped her arms, lifting her. She tried to struggle free, scared her bones would snap.

'Don't fight me,' the bear shouted. 'Stay awake, don't sleep.'

Why was the bear shaking her? Was he attacking her? Shouldn't he be hibernating?

She tried to reply, but the words got stuck in her throat as his big body shielded her from the ice storm. The slaps were firm, but not painful, glancing off her cheek.

'Your name, tell me your name. Don't sleep.'

Why did a bear want to know her name? And how come it could talk?

She couldn't say anything, it hurt to speak. It hurt to even think.

She just wanted to sleep.

She heard cursing, angry, upset, reminding her of her father when he came home from the pub... So long ago now. Good riddance.

Don't sleep or he will come back and call you names again...

But as she found herself bundled onto a raft and being whisked through the storm, the icy wind shifting into a magical dance of blue and green light, the twinkle of stars like fairy lights in the canopy of darkness over her head, a comforting rumble seeped into her soul and chased away the old fear of her da.

Then the brutal, beautiful exhaustion claimed her at last.

Logan Arto Coltan III rode the utility snowmobile into the underground garage of his home and slammed the heavy machine into park.

He swore viciously as he jumped from the

saddle and raced to the flatbed he'd hooked up to load supplies.

'Wake up,' he shouted at the body lying on top of the boxes of canned goods and frozen meat he'd been transporting when he'd picked up the Mayday. Accidentally.

He never monitored the emergency frequencies, but the dial must have slipped after he had called his supply pilot.

Why had he answered the call? He should have ignored it. Why hadn't he?

The person's eyelids—the long lashes white with frost—fluttered open. Revealing bright young eyes, coloured a deep emerald green.

He felt the odd jolt of something… And ignored it.

Not unconscious. Yet.

'Stay with me,' he said, then repeated it in Finnish—just in case English wasn't their first language—as he assessed the person's size under their bulky outdoor wear. Around five six. Probably a woman, he decided, as he stripped off the outer layers of his own clothing. The garage was kept at nineteen degrees, so he didn't overheat before removing his snowsuit to enter the house. But right now, he needed to be able to move, so he could get this fool inside.

Once he'd got down to his undershirt and track-pants, he headed to the garage's small utility room and grabbed the first-aid box. Dragging off his last pair of gloves, he found the thermometer, shoved it into his pants' pocket and returned to the trailer.

If this idiot had managed to give themselves hypothermia, he'd have to call an air ambulance.

He frowned, struggling to focus around the anger—and panic—that had been roiling in his gut ever since he'd answered the call.

Lifting the woman, he placed her as gently as he could over his shoulder. If she was hypothermic sudden movements could trigger a fatal heart arrhythmia. He toted her across the concrete space to climb the steps into the house. His home, ever since his grandfather had died ten years ago. A space no one else had ever entered while he was in residence.

'Avata,' he shouted to the house's integrated smart system, ignoring the roll and pitch in his gut as the locks clicked and he kicked the heavy metal door open with his boot.

'Tuli päälle,' he added to instruct the fire to come on, as he walked into the vast living area. He set the girl on one of the sunken sofas that surrounded a stone fire pit.

The orange flames leapt up and reflected off the panoramic window that opened the luxury space into the winter landscape beyond, obscuring the night-time view of the forest gorge lit by the eerie glow of moonlight.

Safe.

He'd always been safe here, alone. But as he peeled off the woman's layers of headwear, a tumble of wavy reddish-blonde hair was revealed and the strange jolt returned, making him not feel safe any more.

Focus, Logan. You had no choice. It was bring her here or let her die.

She was still staring at him, her eyes glazed but somehow alert, in a way that immediately made him suspicious.

What the hell had she been doing on his land? So far from the nearest centre of civilisation, alone, as night fell?

'How do you feel?' he asked as he reached into his back pocket to grab the thermometer.

'C-c-cold,' she said, starting to shiver violently.

He nodded. Shivering was good.

He shook the thermometer, snapping off its protective covering. Then he pressed his thumb to her chapped bottom lip and placed it under her tongue.

He clicked the timer on his watch, to count down four minutes.

'Wh-wh…?'

'Don't talk.' He glared at the girl, who was

staring at him now with a dazed, confused expression in those bright eyes as she continued to shudder.

Not so good.

The timer dinged.

He tugged out the thermometer. Ninety-four point nine degrees.

He cursed softly.

Anything below ninety-five was mild hypothermia.

Great.

'Come on.' He dumped the thermometer on the coffee table, stood, and scooped her carefully into his arms. 'We must get you warm,' he said as he strode towards the wooden staircase that led to the guest bedroom that had never been used on the ground level.

As he marched through the house, with her still shivering, he considered his options.

Perhaps he should call the EMT station in Saariselkä. But she was young, still lucid, looked healthy enough. And he'd located her fairly quickly. Plus she was conscious and her temperature was on the cusp. If he could get it back past ninety-five quickly, there would be no need for hospital treatment and hopefully no ill effects. It would take over an hour for the EMTs to get here even in a chopper and the storm still stood between them.

And he'd be damned if he'd give up the location of his home to help out a stranger before he absolutely had to… And before he knew who this person was, and what she had been doing on his land—getting herself lost in a snowstorm.

That said, he thought grimly as he began stripping off the wet outer layers of her clothing, while she stood shivering and docile… This promised to be a very long night.